Wedding Countdown

It's a race to the altar!

By
Request™

Praise for three best-selling authors –
Helen Bianchin, Kim Lawrence and Liz Fielding

About THE BRIDAL BED

'Helen Bianchin offers lush scenery and
passionate characters in THE BRIDAL BED.'
—*Romantic Times*

About Kim Lawrence

'Ms Lawrence [has] great character rapport,
charming scenes and strong chemistry.'
—*Romantic Times*

About ELOPING WITH EMMY

'Liz Fielding creates non-stop action with
dynamic scenes and vivid characterisation.'
—*Romantic Times*

Wedding Countdown

THE BRIDAL BED
by
Helen Bianchin

WIFE BY AGREEMENT
by
Kim Lawrence

ELOPING WITH EMMY
by
Liz Fielding

MILLS & BOON®

DID YOU PURCHASE THIS BOOK WITHOUT A COVER?

If you did, you should be aware it is **stolen property** as it was reported *unsold and destroyed* by a retailer. Neither the author nor the publisher has received any payment for this book.

All the characters in this book have no existence outside the imagination of the author, and have no relation whatsoever to anyone bearing the same name or names. They are not even distantly inspired by any individual known or unknown to the author, and all the incidents are pure invention.

All Rights Reserved including the right of reproduction in whole or in part in any form. This edition is published by arrangement with Harlequin Enterprises II B.V. The text of this publication or any part thereof may not be reproduced or transmitted in any form or by any means, electronic or mechanical, including photocopying, recording, storage in an information retrieval system, or otherwise, without the written permission of the publisher.

This book is sold subject to the condition that it shall not, by way of trade or otherwise, be lent, resold, hired out or otherwise circulated without the prior consent of the publisher in any form of binding or cover other than that in which it is published and without a similar condition including this condition being imposed on the subsequent purchaser.

MILLS & BOON and MILLS & BOON with the Rose Device are registered trademarks of the publisher.
Harlequin Mills & Boon Limited,
Eton House, 18-24 Paradise Road, Richmond, Surrey, TW9 1SR

WEDDING COUNTDOWN
© by Harlequin Enterprises II B.V., 2002

The Bridal Bed, Wife by Agreement and *Eloping with Emmy*
were first published in Great Britain by Harlequin Mills & Boon Limited
in separate, single volumes.

The Bridal Bed © Helen Bianchin 1998
Wife by Agreement © Kim Lawrence 1998
Eloping with Emmy © Liz Fielding 1998

ISBN 0 263 83157 4

05-0602

Printed and bound in Spain
by Litografía Rosés S.A., Barcelona

Helen Bianchin was born in New Zealand and travelled to Australia before marrying her Italian-born husband. After three years they moved, returned to New Zealand with their daughter, had two sons then resettled in Australia. Encouraged by friends to recount anecdotes of her years as a tobacco sharefarmer's wife living in an Italian community, Helen began setting words on paper and her first novel was published in 1975. An animal lover, she says her terrier and Persian cat regard her study as much theirs as hers.

Australian author Helen Bianchin's books are
laced with glamour and sophistication, and she's
become a star of Modern Romance™.

*Look out for Helen's next book, the first in a duet
of linked stories:*

A PASSIONATE SURRENDER

Ana had secretly hoped her marriage of convenience
to Luc Dimitriades would turn into the real thing.
Yet one year after exchanging their vows, Ana knew
she had to leave – but Luc wasn't prepared to let her
go. Could she resist his passionate persuasion?

on-sale September, in Modern Romance™

THE BRIDAL BED
by
Helen Bianchin

CHAPTER ONE

IT SHOULD be Friday the thirteenth, Suzanne determined as she perused the perfectly printed legal document on her desk and noted yet another clause she knew wasn't worded to her client's best interest.

Midwinter had delivered metropolitan Sydney with a shocking day, and she'd woken to howling winds and heavy rain. Consequently she'd got wet traversing the external stairs leading from her tiny Manly flat down to the garage beneath.

Her car, which had up until now behaved impeccably, had decided not to start. A telephone call to the automobile association had elicited there was a backlog of calls, and it would be at least an hour before someone could come to her rescue. Two hours later the diagnosis had been a dead battery, and it had taken a further hour to organise a replacement and drive into the city.

Consequently she'd been late, very late arriving at the inner-city legal office where she worked as one of several junior solicitors. A fact that hadn't sat well with two waiting clients who had been virtuously punctual. Nor had the senior partner been very happy that she'd missed an important staff meeting.

There had been files piled up on her desk, messages that required attention, and three rescheduled appointments lined up one after the other. Lunch hadn't even been an option.

Mid-afternoon came and went as she struggled to catch up on a workload that threatened to spill over into work she would have to take home.

'Suzanne, urgent call on line three.' The receptionist's voice sounded hesitant, diffident, and vaguely apologetic for breaching a 'hold all calls' instruction. 'It's your mother.'

Her mother *never* rang her at work. An icy hand clutched Suzanne's heart as she snatched up the receiver. 'Georgia? Is something wrong?'

A light, husky laugh echoed down the line. 'Darling, everything's fine. It's just that I wanted you to be the first to hear my news.'

'*News*, Mama?' She kept her voice deliberately light. 'You've won a fabulous prize? Bought a new car? Booked an overseas trip?'

There was a breathless pause. 'Right on two counts.'

'Which two?'

'Well, sweetheart,' Georgia began with a delicious chuckle, 'the overseas trip is booked…*Paris*, would you believe? And I *have* won a fabulous prize.'

'That's wonderful.' Really wonderful. Suzanne shook her head in silent amazement. Georgia was always taking lottery and raffle tickets, but had never won anything other than the most minor of prizes until now.

'It's not exactly a *prize* prize.'

The faintly cautious tone had Suzanne sinking back

in her chair. 'You're talking in riddles, Mama. Is there a catch to any of this?'

'No catch. At least, not the kind you mean.'

What had her cautious mother got herself into? 'I'm listening.'

'Bear with me, darling.' Georgia's voice hitched, then raced on in an excited rush. 'It's all so new, I still have a hard time believing it. And I wouldn't have rung you at work, except I really couldn't wait a minute longer.'

'Tell me.'

There was silence for a few seconds. 'I'm getting married.'

Initial joy was quickly followed by concern, and it was a frightening mix. Her mother didn't *date*. There was a collection of friends, but no *one* man. 'I didn't know you were seeing anyone,' Suzanne said slowly, and heard her mother's light laughter in response. 'Who is he, and where did you meet him?'

'We met at your engagement party, darling.'

Three months. They'd only known each other three months. 'Who, Mama?'

'Trenton Wilson-Willoughby. Sloane's father.'

Oh, my God. Heat rushed through her veins, then chilled to ice. 'You're not serious?' Tell me you're not serious, she pleaded silently.

'You sound—shocked,' Georgia responded slowly, and Suzanne quickly gathered her wits.

Recoup, regroup, *fast*. 'Surprised,' she amended. 'It seems so sudden.'

'Sometimes love happens that way. Sloane swept you off your feet in a matter of weeks.'

Like father, like son. 'Yes,' she agreed cautiously. Sloane had gifted her a sparkling diamond, whisked her down to Sydney from Brisbane, and moved her into his Rose Bay penthouse apartment before she'd had time to think, let alone catch her breath. Blinded by a riveting attraction and primitive alchemy.

'When is the wedding taking place?' A few months from now would give her plenty of time to—what? Explain that she was no longer living with Sloane?

'This weekend, darling.' Georgia sounded vaguely breathless and tremendously excited.

This weekend. Today was *Wednesday*, for heaven's sake. 'Don't you think—?'

'It's a bit sudden?' her mother finished. 'Yes, darling, I do. But Trenton is a very convincing man.'

Suzanne took a deep breath, then released it slowly. 'You're quite sure about this?'

'As sure as I can be.' There was a funny catch in her voice. 'Aren't you going to congratulate me?'

Oh, *hell*. She had to collect her thoughts together. 'Of course I am. And give you my blessing. I'm just so happy *you* are happy.' She was babbling, she knew, but she couldn't stop. 'Where is the wedding taking place? Have you chosen what you'll wear?'

Georgia began to laugh, and, Suzanne suspected, to cry. 'Bedarra Island, Saturday afternoon. Would you believe Trenton has booked all the accommodation on the island to ensure total privacy? I'm wearing a cream silk suit, with matching shoes and hat. We want you and Sloane to be witnesses.'

Bedarra Island was a privately owned resort situated high in North Queensland's Whitsunday group of tropical islands. A minimum three-hour flight, followed by a launch trip to Bedarra.

'Trenton has organised for you both to fly up on Friday morning and stay until Monday.'

Oh, my. Trenton's organisation would include the family jet, the charter of a private launch.

Sloane.

It was three weeks since she'd walked out of his apartment, leaving a penned note briefly spelling out her need for some time alone. It attributed nothing to the reality of an anonymous threat if she didn't end the engagement.

A threat she hadn't taken seriously until the young socialite who'd initiated it had almost run Suzanne's car off the road to emphasise her intent, then identified herself and promised grievous bodily harm if Suzanne failed to comply.

The sequence of events had been very carefully planned, she reflected, to coincide with Sloane's absence overseas. Bitter, vitriolic invective had merely added doubt as to the socialite's mental stability, and extreme caution had motivated Suzanne to leave Sloane's apartment and move all her clothes into a flat on the other side of the city.

However, she had underestimated Sloane. When she'd refused to take his calls on his return, he'd pulled rank and walked unannounced into her office.

His icy anger when she had refused to elaborate on the contents of her note had been so chilling, it had been all she could do not to fall in a heap the second the door had closed behind him.

Now it appeared she had little option but to see him again.

Suzanne slowly replaced the receiver, then stared sightlessly at the wall in front of her. Georgia and Trenton. Could her mother possibly guess at the complications she'd created?

Allowing no time for hesitation, Suzanne punched in the digit to access an outside line, then completed the set of numbers that would connect with Sloane's law chambers.

Not that the call did much good. All she received was a relayed message stating that Sloane Wilson-Willoughby was in court and wasn't expected back until late afternoon. Suzanne logged in her name and phone number on his message bank.

Damn. The silent curse did little to ease her frustration as she turned her attention to the documents requiring her perusal. She made a note of two clauses she felt were not entirely to her client's advantage, pencilled in a notation to delete one, and re phrase another. Then she had her secretary lodge the necessary call in order to apprise the client of her suggested alterations.

The afternoon was hectic, and the nerves inside her stomach became increasingly tense as the minutes ticked by. Each time the phone rang, she mentally prepared herself for it to be Sloane, only to have her secretary announce someone else.

Was he deliberately delaying the call? Just to make her sweat a little? Whatever, it was playing havoc with her nervous system.

At five her phone buzzed just as she ushered a client from her office, and she crossed to her desk and picked up the receiver.

'Sloane Wilson-Willoughby on line two.' The information was imparted in a faintly breathless voice, and Suzanne momentarily raised her eyes towards the ceiling.

Sloane tended to have that effect on people. Women, especially, responded to something in his deep, smoky voice. Once they sighted him in the flesh, the response went into overdrive and tended to make vamps and vixens out of the most sensible of females.

She should know. She'd been there herself. Part of her ached for the promise, the dream of what they might have had together.

Then she drew in a deep breath, released it, and picked up the receiver. 'Sloane.' To ask 'how are you?' seemed incredibly banal.

'Suzanne.' The polite acknowledgement seared something deep inside, and she resolutely kept her voice even as she sank back in her chair. 'Georgia rang me. I believe Trenton has relayed their news?'

'Yes.' Brief, succinct, and unforthcoming.

He wasn't making it easy for her. There was no

way out of this, and it was best if she just got on with it.

'We need to talk.'

'I agree,' Sloane indicated silkily. 'Make it dinner tonight.' He named a restaurant in a city hotel. 'Seven.'

She needed to put in another hour in order to appease her employer. 'I don't think—'

'It's the restaurant or your flat.' His voice acquired the sound of silk being razed by steel. 'Choose.'

She didn't hesitate. 'Seven-thirty.' A public place where there were people was the lesser of two evils. The thought of Sloane appearing at her flat, demanding entry…

'Wise.'

No, it was most *un*wise, but she didn't appear to have much option.

Suzanne replaced the receiver and attempted to concentrate on notations she needed to finalise.

Consequently it was well after six when she left the office, and almost seven before she reached home.

Within half an hour she'd showered, dressed, swept her damp hair into a sleek twist, applied make-up with practised precision, and she was on her way out of the door, retracing a familiar route into the city.

Except this time the traffic was more civilised. And there was the advantage of valet parking. Even so, she was fifteen minutes late.

Suzanne pushed open the heavy glass door and entered the hotel lobby. It took only seconds to locate a familiar dark-suited figure standing several metres distant.

Her pulse tripped its beat and accelerated to a faster pace as she watched him unfold his lengthy frame from a deep-cushioned lounge chair.

Sloane Wilson-Willoughby stood four inches over six feet, with the broad shoulders and muscled frame of a superbly trained athlete. Inherited genes had bestowed ruggedly attractive facial features, piercing brown eyes, and thick dark brown hair. Evident was an aura of power, and the ease of a man well versed in the strengths and weaknesses of his fellow men.

He watched as she moved towards him, his appraisal swift, taking in the red power suit adorning her petite frame, the upswept hairstyle and the stiletto heels she invariably wore to add inches to her height. She possessed an innate femininity that was at variance with the professional image she tried so hard to maintain. Slight but very feminine curves, slender, shapely legs, silken-smooth honey-gold skin, deep blue eyes, and a mouth to die for.

He'd tasted its delights, savoured the pleasures of her body, and put an engagement ring on her finger. It had stayed there precisely ten weeks before she'd taken it off with an excuse he'd no more believed then than he did now.

'Sloane.' She moved forward and accepted the touch of his hand at her elbow. And told herself she was impervious to the clean male smell of him mingling with the faint aroma of his exclusive brand of cologne. Immune to the latent sensuality that seemed to emanate from every pore.

He searched her pale features, and noted the faint smudges beneath eyes that seemed too large for her face. 'Working hard?'

The deceptive mildness of his voice didn't fool her in the slightest. She effected a light shrug and opted for flippancy. 'Next you'll tell me I've dropped weight.'

He lifted a hand and traced her jawline with his thumb. And saw her eyes dilate. 'Two or three essential kilos, at a guess.'

His touch was like fire, and a muscle flickered in involuntary reaction. 'Judge, advocate and jury rolled into one?'

'Lover,' Sloane amended.

'Ex-lover,' she corrected him, and saw the sensual curve of his lower lip.

'Your choice, not mine.'

She deliberately moved back a pace, and met his gaze squarely. 'Shall we go in to dinner?'

'You wouldn't prefer a drink first?'

She really wanted to keep this as short as possible. 'No.' She sought to qualify her decision. 'I really can't stay long.'

There was a tinge of wry humour evident in his voice as they walked towards the bank of lifts. 'Dedication to duty, Suzanne?'

The humour stung. 'Suffice it to say it's been one of those days, and I have work to catch up on.'

A set of doors slid open and she preceded him into

the lift. They were the only occupants, and he leaned forward to depress the button for the appropriate floor.

His suit sleeve brushed against her arm, and she tried to ignore the shivery sensation feathering over her skin. Her fine body hairs rose in protective self-defence, and she felt her pulse trip and surge to a faster beat.

Did he realise he still had this effect on her? Probably not, she reassured herself silently, for she strove very hard to project detached disinterest.

The restaurant was well patronised, and the *maître d'* led them to a reserved table, saw them seated, and summoned the drinks waiter.

Suzanne viewed the menu with interest, and she ordered soup *du jour*, a seafood starter, and grilled fish as a main course.

'Do we attempt to engage in polite conversation,' Sloane drawled as soon as the waiter disappeared, 'or shall we cut straight to the chase?'

Suzanne forced herself to hold his gaze. 'Dinner was your idea.'

Evident was the leashed anger beneath his control. 'What did you expect? A curt directive to meet me at the airport Friday morning?'

'Yes.'

His smile was totally without humour. 'Ah, *honesty.*'

'It's one of my more admirable traits.'

Their drinks were delivered, and Suzanne sipped the iced water, almost wishing it were something stronger. Alcohol might soothe her fractured nerves.

She watched as Sloane took an appreciative swallow of his customary spritzer before setting the glass onto the table, then leaning back in his chair.

'You haven't responded to any of my messages.'

It was difficult to retain his gaze, but she managed. 'There didn't seem much point.'

'I beg to differ.'

He was a skilled wordsmith and a brilliant strategist. He was also icy calm. When all he wanted to do was reach forward and *shake* her.

'We're here to discuss our respective parents' marriage to each other,' she managed civilly. 'Not conduct a post-mortem on our affair.'

'Post-mortem?' His voice was a sibilant threat. *'Affair?'*

He was playing with her, much as a predatory animal played with its prey. Waiting, watching, assessing each and every move, in no doubt of the kill. It was just a matter of *when*.

Suzanne rose to her feet and reached for her bag. 'I've had one hell of a day. I have work to get through when I get home.' Her eyes flashed angrily. 'I don't need you playing cat-and-mouse with me.'

A hand closed over her arm, and it took all her control not to shake it free.

'Sit down.'

She would have liked nothing better than to turn and walk out of the door. But there was Georgia to consider. No matter how difficult the weekend might prove to be, she *had* to be present at her mother's wedding. Anything else was unthinkable.

'Please,' Sloane added, and without a word she sank down into her chair.

Almost on cue the waiter delivered their soup, and she spooned it slowly, grateful for the ensuing silence. When their plates were removed she picked up her glass and sipped the contents.

'Tell me about your day,' Sloane commanded with studied ease.

Suzanne looked at him carefully. 'Genuine interest, or an adept attempt to keep our conversation on an even keel?'

'Both.'

His faint, mocking smile was almost her undoing, and she felt like screaming with vexation. 'I'd prefer to discuss the weekend.'

'Indulge me. We have yet to begin the main course.'

At this rate she'd suffer indigestion. As it was, her stomach seemed to be tied in numerous knots.

'The car refused to start, the automobile club took ages to send someone out, I was late in to work, and I got soaked in the rain.' She effected a light shrug. 'That about encapsulates it.'

'I'll organise for you to have the use of one of my cars while yours is being checked out.'

A surge of anger rose to the surface. 'No. You won't.'

'Now you're being stubborn,' he drawled hatefully.

'Practical.' And wary of being seen driving his Porsche or Jaguar.

'Stubborn,' Sloane reiterated.

'You sound like my mother,' Suzanne responded with a deliberately slow, sweet smile.

'Heaven forbid.'

Anger rose once more, and her eyes assumed a fiery sparkle. 'You disapprove of Georgia?'

'Of being compared to anything vaguely *parental* where you're concerned,' Sloane corrected her with ill-concealed mockery.

Suzanne looked at him carefully, then honed a verbal dart. 'I doubt you've ever lacked a solitary thing in your privileged life.'

One eyebrow rose, and there was a certain wryness apparent. 'Except for the love of a good woman?'

'Most women fall over themselves to get to you,' she stated with marked cynicism.

'To the social prestige the Wilson-Willoughby name carries,' Sloane amended drily. 'And let's not forget the family wealth.'

The multi-million-dollar family home with its incredible views over Sydney harbour, the fleet of luxurious cars, servants. Not to mention Sloane's penthouse apartment, *his* cars. Homes, apartments in major European cities. The family cruiser, the family jet.

And then there was Wilson-Willoughby, headed by Trenton and notably one of Sydney's leading law firms. One had only to enter its exclusive portals, see the expensive antique furniture gracing every office, the original artwork on the walls, to appreciate the elegance of limitless wealth.

'You're a cynic.'

His expression didn't change. 'A realist.'

Their starter arrived, and Suzanne took her time savouring the delicate texture of the prawns in a superb sauce many a chef would kill to reproduce.

'Now that you've had some food, perhaps you'd like a glass of wine?'

And have it go straight to her head? 'Half a glass,' she qualified, and determined to sip it slowly during the main course.

'I hear you've taken on a very challenging brief,' she said.

Sloane pressed the napkin to the edge of his mouth, then discarded it down onto the damask-covered table. 'News travels fast.'

As did anything attached to Sloane Wilson-Willoughby. In or out of the courtroom.

He part-filled her glass with wine, then set it back in the ice bucket, dismissing the wine steward who appeared with apologetic deference.

Their main course arrived, and Suzanne admired the superbly presented fish and artistically displayed vegetable portions. It seemed almost a sacrilege to disturb the arrangement, and she forked delicate mouthfuls with enjoyment.

'Am I to understand Georgia meets with your approval as a prospective stepmother?'

Sloane viewed her with studied ease. She looked more relaxed, and her cheeks bore a slight colour. 'Georgia is a charming woman. I'm sure she and my father will be very happy together.'

The deceptive mildness of his tone brought forth a

musing smile. 'I would have to say the same about Trenton.'

Sloane lifted his glass and took a sip of wine, then regarded her thoughtfully over the rim. 'The question remains… What do you want to do about us?'

Her stomach executed a painful backflip. 'What do you mean, what do I want to do about *us*?'

The waiter arrived to remove their plates, then delivered a platter of fresh fruit, added a bowl of freshly whipped cream, and withdrew.

'Unless you've told Georgia differently, our respective parents believe we're living in pre-nuptial bliss,' Sloane relayed with deliberate patience. 'Do we spend the weekend pretending we're still together? Or do you want to spoil their day by telling them we're living apart?'

She didn't want to think about *together*. It merely heightened memories she longed to forget. Fat chance, a tiny voice taunted.

Fine clothes did little to tame a body honed to the height of physical fitness, or lessen his brooding sensuality. Too many nights she'd lain awake remembering just how it felt to be held in those arms, kissed in places she'd never thought to grant a licence to, and taught to scale unbelievable heights with a man who knew every path, every journey.

'Your choice, Suzanne.'

She looked at him and glimpsed the implacability beneath the charming façade, the velvet-encased steel.

As a barrister in a court of law he was skilled with the command of words and their delivery. She'd seen him in action, and been enthralled. Mes merised. And had known, even then, that she'd have reason to quake if ever he became her enemy.

A game of pretence, and she wondered why she was even considering it. Yet would it be so bad?

There wasn't much choice if she didn't want to spoil her mother's happiness. The truth was something she intended to keep to herself.

'I imagine it isn't possible to fly in and out of Bedarra on the same day?'

'No.'

It was a slim hope, given the distance and the time of the wedding. 'There are no strings you can pull?'

'Afraid to spend time with me, Suzanne?' Sloane queried smoothly.

'I'd prefer to keep it to a minimum,' she said with innate honesty. 'And you didn't answer the question.'

'What strings would you have me pull?'

'It would be more suitable to arrive on Bedarra Saturday morning, and return Sunday.'

'And disappoint Trenton and Georgia?' He lifted his glass and took an appreciative swallow of excellent vintage wine. 'Did it occur to you that perhaps Georgia might need your help and moral support *before* the wedding?'

It made sense, Suzanne conceded. 'Surely we could return on Sunday?'

'I think not.'

'*Why?*'

He set the glass down onto the table with the utmost care. 'Because *I* won't be returning until Monday.'

She looked at him with a feeling of helpless anger. 'You're deliberately making this as difficult as possible, aren't you?'

'Trenton has organised to leave Sydney on Friday and return on Monday. I see no reason to disrupt those arrangements.'

A tiny shiver feathered its way down her spine.

Three days. Well, four if you wanted to be precise. Could she go through with it?

'Do you want to renege, Suzanne?'

The silkily voiced query strengthened her resolve, and her eyes speared his. 'No.'

'Can I interest you in the dessert trolley?'

The waiter's appearance was timely, and Suzanne turned her attention to the collection of delicious confections presented, and selected an utterly sinful slice of chocolate cake decorated with fresh cream and strawberries.

'Decadent,' she commented for the waiter's benefit. 'I'll need to run an extra kilometre and do twenty more sit-ups in the morning to combat the extra kilojoules.'

Even when she'd lived with Sloane, she'd preferred the suburban footpaths and fresh air to the professional gym housed in his apartment.

'I can think of something infinitely more enjoyable by way of exercise.'

'Sex?' Was it the wine that had made her suddenly brave? With ladylike delicacy, she indicated his selection of *crème caramel.* 'You should live a little, walk on the wild side.'

'Wild, Suzanne?' His voice was pure silk with the honeyed intonation he used to great effect in the courtroom.

Knowing she would probably lose didn't prevent her from enjoying a verbal sparring. 'Figuratively speaking.'

'Perhaps you'd care to elaborate?'

Her eyes were wide, luminous, and tinged with wicked humour. 'Do the unexpected.'

Very few women sought to challenge him on any level, and none had in quite the same manner this petite, independent blonde employed. 'Define unexpected.'

Her head tilted to one side. 'Be less—conventional.'

'You think I should play more?' The subtle emphasis was intended, and he watched the slight flicker of her lashes, the faint pink that coloured her cheeks. Glimpsed the way her throat moved as she swallowed. And felt a sense of satisfaction. With innate skill, he honed the blade and pierced her vulnerable heart. 'I have a vivid memory of just how well we *played* together.'

So did she, damn him. Very carefully she replaced her spoon on the plate. 'Perhaps you'd care to tell me what arrangements you've made for Friday morning.'

'I've instructed the pilot we'll be leaving at eight.'

'I'll meet you at the airport.'

'Isn't that carrying independence a little too far?'

'Why should you drive to the North Shore, only to have to double back again?' Suzanne countered.

Something shifted in his eyes, then it was successfully masked. 'It isn't a problem.'

Of course it wasn't. *She* was making a problem out of sheer perversity. 'I'll drive to your apartment and garage my car there for the weekend,' she conceded.

Sloane inclined his head in mocking acquiescence. 'If you insist.'

It was a minor victory, one she had the instinctive feeling wasn't a victory at all.

Sloane ordered coffee, then settled the bill. She didn't linger, and he escorted her to the lobby, instructed the concierge to organise her car, and waited until it was brought to the main entrance.

'Goodnight, Suzanne.'

His features appeared extraordinarily dark in the angled shadows, his tone vaguely cynical. An image of sight and sound that remained with her long after she slid wearily into bed.

CHAPTER TWO

THURSDAY proved to be a fraught day as Suzanne applied for and was granted two days' leave, then she rescheduled appointments and consultations, attended to the most pressing work, delegated the remainder, *and* donated her entire lunch hour to selecting something suitable to wear to Georgia's wedding.

Dedication to duty ensured she stayed back an extra few hours, and she arrived home shortly after eight, hungry and not a little disgruntled at having to eat on the run while she sorted through clothes and packed.

Elegant, casual, and beachwear, she determined as she riffled through her wardrobe, grateful she had sufficient knowledge of the Wilson-Willoughby lifestyle to know she need select the best of her best.

Comfortable baggy shorts and sweat-tops were out. *In* were tailored trousers, smart shirts, silk dresses, tennis gear. And the obligatory swimwear essential in the tropical north's Midwinter temperatures.

Some of Trenton Wilson-Willoughby's guests would arrive with large Louis Vuitton travelling cases containing what they considered the minimum essentials for a weekend sojourn.

Suzanne managed to confine all she needed into one cabin bag, which she stored on the floor at the foot of her bed in readiness for last-minute essentials in the morning, then she returned to the kitchen and took a can of Diet Coke from the refrigerator.

She crossed into the lounge, switched on the television and flicked through the channels in the hope of finding something that might hold her interest. A legal drama, a medical ditto, sport, a foreign movie, and something dire relating to the occult. She switched off the set, collected a magazine and sank into a nearby chair to leaf through the pages.

She felt too restless to settle for long, and after ten minutes she tossed the magazine aside, carried the empty can into the kitchen, then undressed and took a shower.

It wasn't late *late*, but she felt tired and edgy, and knew she should go to bed given the early hour she'd need to rise in the morning.

Except when she did she was unable to sleep, and she tossed and turned, then lay staring at the ceiling for an age.

With a low growl of frustration she slid out of bed and padded into the lounge. If she was going to stare at something, she might as well curl up in a chair and stare at the television.

It was there that she woke, with a stiff neck and the television screen fizzing from a closed channel.

Suzanne peered at her watch in the semi-darkness, saw that it was almost dawn, and groaned. There was no point in crawling back to bed for such a short time. Instead she stretched her legs and wandered into the kitchen to make coffee.

Casual elegance denoted her apparel for the day,

and after a quick shower and something to eat she stepped into linen trousers and a matching silk sleeveless top. Make-up was minimal, a little colour to her cheeks, mascara to give emphasis to her eyes, and a touch of rose-pink to her lips. An upswept hairstyle was likely to come adrift, so she left her hair loose.

At seven she added a trendy black jacket, checked the flat, then she fastened her cabin bag, took it downstairs and secured it in the boot. Then she slid in behind the wheel and reversed her car out onto the road.

At this relatively early hour the traffic flowed freely, and she enjoyed a smooth run through the northern suburbs.

The city skyline was visible as she drew close to the harbour bridge, the tall buildings bathed in a faint post-dawn mist that merged with the greyness of a midwinter morning and hinted at rain.

Even the harbour waters appeared dull and grey, and the ferries traversing its depths seemed to move heavily towards their respective berths.

Once clear of the bridge, it took minimum time to reach the attractive eastern suburb of Rose Bay. Sloane's penthouse apartment was housed in a modern structure only metres from the edge of the wide, curving bay.

A number of large, beautiful old homes graced the tree-lined street and Suzanne admired the elegant two- and three-storeyd structures in brick and paint-washed stucco, situated in attractive landscaped grounds, as she turned into the brick-tiled apron adjoining Sloane's apartment building.

He was waiting for her, his tall frame propped against the driver's side of his sleek, top-of-the-range Jaguar. Casual trousers, an open-necked shirt and jacket had replaced his usual three-piece business suit, and he looked the epitome of the wealthy professional.

The trousers, shirt and jacket were beautifully cut, the shoes hand-stitched Italian. He didn't favour male jewellery, and the only accessory he chose to wear was a thin gold watch whose make was undoubtedly exorbitantly expensive. His wardrobe contained a superb collection, yet none had been acquired as a status symbol.

Suzanne shifted the gear lever into neutral, then she slid out from behind the wheel and turned to greet him. 'Good morning. I'm not late, am I?' She knew she wasn't, but she couldn't resist the query.

Independence was a fine thing in a woman, but Suzanne's strict adherence to it was something Sloane found mildly irritating. His eyes were cool as they swept her slim form. Cream tailored trousers, cream top and black jacket emphasised her slender curves, and lent a heightened sense of fragility to her features. Clever make-up had almost dealt with the shadows beneath her eyes. He derived a certain satisfaction from the knowledge. She obviously hadn't slept any better than he had.

'I'll take your car down into the car park,' Sloane indicated as he removed the cabin bag from her grasp and stowed it in the open boot of his car.

Within minutes he'd transferred her vehicle, then

returned to slide in behind the wheel of his own car. The engine fired, and he eased the Jaguar out onto the road.

'The jet will touch down in Brisbane to collect Trenton and Georgia,' Sloane drawled as the car picked up speed.

Suzanne endeavoured not to show her surprise. 'I thought Trenton would travel with us from Sydney.'

'My father has been in Brisbane for the past week.' He paused to spare her a quick glance, then added with perfect timing, 'Ensuring, so he said, that Georgia didn't have the opportunity to get cold feet.'

Georgia had rarely, if ever, dated. There had been no male friends visiting the house, no succession of temporary 'uncles'. Georgia had been a devoted mother first and foremost, and a dedicated dressmaker who worked from the privacy of her own home.

For as long as Suzanne could remember they'd shared a close bond that was based on affectionate friendship. Genuine equals, rather than simply mother and daughter.

At forty-seven, Georgia was an attractive woman with a slim, petite frame, carefully tended blonde hair, blue eyes, and a wonderfully caring nature. She *deserved* happiness with an equally caring partner.

'From Brisbane we'll fly direct to Dunk Island, then take the launch to Bedarra,' said Sloane.

Suzanne turned her head and took in the moving scenery, the houses where everyone inside them was stirring to begin a new day. Mothers cooking breakfast, sleepy-eyed children preparing to wash and dress before eating and taking public transport to school.

The traffic was beginning to build up, and it was almost eight when Sloane took the turn-off to the airport, then bypassed the main terminal and headed for the area where private aircraft were housed. He gained clearance, and drove onto the apron of bitumen.

Suzanne undid her seat belt and reached for the door-handle, only to pause as he leaned towards her.

'You forgot something.'

Her breath caught as Sloane took hold of her left hand and slid her engagement ring onto her finger.

She looked at the sparkling solitaire diamond, then lifted her head to meet his gaze.

'Trenton and Georgia will think it a little strange if you're not wearing it,' he drawled with hateful cynicism.

The charade was about to begin. A slightly hysterical laugh rose and died in her throat. Who was she kidding? 'This is going to be some weekend.'

'Indeed.'

'Sloane—' She paused, hesitant to say the words, but needing quite desperately to set a few ground rules. 'You won't—'

Dammit, his eyes were too dark, too discerning.

'Won't *what*, Suzanne?'

'Overact.'

His expression remained unchanged. 'Define overacting.'

She should have kept her mouth shut. Parrying words with him was a futile battle, for he always won.

'I'd prefer it if you kept any body contact to a mini-mum.'

His eyes gleamed with latent humour. 'Afraid, Suzanne?'

'Of you? No, of course not.'

His gaze didn't falter, and she felt the breath hitch in her chest. 'Perhaps you should be,' he intimated softly.

A chill settled over the surface of her skin, and she controlled a desire to shiver. She should call this off *now*. Insist on using his mobile phone so she could ring Georgia and explain.

'No,' Sloane said quietly. 'We'll see it through.'

'You read minds?'

'Yours is particularly transparent.'

It irked her unbearably that he was able to deter-mine her thoughts. With anyone else it was possible to present an impenetrable façade. Sloane dispensed with each and every barrier she erected as if it didn't exist.

Suzanne fervently wished it were Monday, and they were making the return trip. Then the weekend would be over.

A sleek Lear jet bearing the W-W insignia stood waiting for them, its baggage hold open. Sloane trans-ferred their bags, then spoke to the pilot before they boarded.

The interior portrayed the ultimate in luxury. Plush carpets, superior fittings—the jet was a wealthy man's expensive possession.

A slim, attractive stewardess greeted them inside

the cabin. 'If you'd each care to be seated and fasten your seat belts, we'll be ready for immediate take-off.' She moved to close the door and secure it, checked her two passengers were comfortable, then she acknowledged internal clearance via intercom with the pilot.

The jet's engines increased their whining pitch, then the sleek silver plane eased off the bitumen apron and cruised a path to the runway.

Within minutes they were in the air, climbing high in a northerly flight pattern that hugged the coastline.

'Juice, tea or coffee?'

Suzanne opted for juice while Sloane settled for coffee, and when it was served the stewardess retreated into the rear section.

'No laptop?' Suzanne queried as Sloane made no attempt to take optimum advantage of the ensuing few hours. 'No documents to peruse?'

He regarded her thoughtfully. 'The laptop and my briefcase are stowed in the baggage compartment. However, I thought I'd take a break,' he revealed with indolent amusement.

'I have no objection if you want to work.'

'Thereby negating the need for conversation, Suzanne?'

She aimed a slow, sweet smile at him. 'How did you guess?'

Sloane's eyes narrowed fractionally. 'We should, don't you think, ensure our stories match on events during the past three weeks?' He leant back in his chair. 'Minor details like movies we might have seen, the theatre, dinner with friends.'

Separate residences, separate lives. Hectic work-filled days, empty lonely nights.

A particularly lacklustre social calendar, Suzanne conceded on reflection, and was unable to prevent a comparison to the halcyon days when she'd shared Sloane's apartment and his life. Then there had been a succession of dinners, parties, and few evenings together alone at home. Long nights of loving, a wonderfully warm male body to curl into, and being awakened each morning by the stroke of his fingers, his lips.

Something clenched deep inside her, and she closed her eyes, then opened them again in an effort to clear the image.

'Suzanne?'

Clarity of mind was essential, and she met his gaze, acknowledged the enigmatic expression, and managed a slight smile. 'Of course.' Her attendance at the cinema had been her only social excursion. She named the movie, and provided him with a brief plot line. 'And you? I imagine you maintained a fairly hectic social schedule?'

'Reasonably quiet,' Sloane relayed. 'I declined a dinner invitation with the Parkinsons.' His level gaze held hers. 'You supposedly had a migraine.'

'And the rest of the time?'

His expression held a degree of cynical humour. 'We dined *à deux*, or stayed home.'

Suzanne remembered too well what had inevitably

transpired during the evenings they'd stayed in. The long, slow foreplay that had begun when they'd entered the apartment. Sipping from each other's glass, offering morsels of food as they'd eaten a leisurely meal. A liqueur coffee, and the deliberate choice of viewing cable television or a video. The drift of fingers over sensitised skin, the soft touch of lips savouring delicate hollows, a sensual awakening that had held the promise of continued arousal and the ultimate coupling of two people who had delighted in each other on every plane.

Sometimes there had been no foreplay at all. Just compelling passion, the melding of mouths as urgent fingers had freed buttons and dispensed with clothes. Occasionally they hadn't even made it to the bedroom.

Suzanne met his gaze and held it, fought against a compulsive movement in her throat as she contained the lump lodged there, and chose not to comment.

A hollow laugh died before it was born. Who was she kidding? There was no choice at all. If she opened her mouth, only the most strangled of sounds would emerge.

She saw the darkness reflected in his eyes, glimpsed the flare of passion and his banking of it, then wanted to die as his lips curved into a slow, sensual smile.

'Memories, Suzanne?'

Try for lightness, a touch of humour. Then he'd never know just how much she ached inside. 'Some of them were good, very good.' He deserved that, if nothing else. Others were particularly forgettable. Such as the bitchiness of some of his social equals.

Oh, damn. She was treading into deeper water with every step she took. And she'd only been in his company an hour. What state would she be in at the end of the weekend, for heaven's sake?

She fished a magazine from a strategically placed pocket, and began flipping through the glossy pages until she discovered an article that held her interest. Or at least she could feign that it did for the duration of the short flight to Brisbane.

It was a relief when the jet landed and cruised to a halt on the far side of the terminal. Suzanne glimpsed a limousine parked close to the hangar, and Sloane's father boarded as soon as the jet's door opened and the steps were unfolded.

'Good morning.'

Trenton moved lithely down the aisle and closed the distance to greet them.

The family resemblance between father and son was clearly evident, the frame almost identical, although Trenton was a little heavier through the chest, slightly thicker in the waist, and his hair was streaked with grey.

He was a kind man, possessed of a gentle wit, beneath which was a shrewd and knowledgeable business mind.

Suzanne rose to her feet and allowed herself to be enveloped in a bear-hug.

'Suzanne. Lovely to see you, my dear.' He released her, and acknowledged his son with a warm smile.

'Sloane.' He indicated the limousine. 'Georgia is making a call from the car.' The smile broadened, and his eyes twinkled with humour as he placed a hand on Suzanne's shoulder. 'A last-minute confirmation of floral arrangements for the wedding. Go down and talk to her while I check the luggage being loaded on board.'

Georgia was fixing her lipstick, a slight pink colouring her cheeks as Suzanne slid into the rear seat, and she leaned forward and brushed her mother's cheek with her own. 'Nervous?'

'No,' her mother denied. 'Just needing someone to tell me I'm not being foolish.'

Georgia had been widowed at a young age, left to rear a child who retained little memory of the father who had been killed on a dark road in the depth of night by a joyriding, unlicensed lout high on drugs and alcohol. Life thereafter hadn't exactly been a struggle, as circumspect saving and a relatively strict budget had ensured there were holidays and a few of life's pleasures.

'You're not being foolish,' Suzanne said gently.

Georgia appeared anxious as she lifted a hand and pressed fingers to Suzanne's cheek. 'I would have preferred to put my plans on hold until after your wedding to Sloane. You don't mind, do you?'

It was difficult to maintain her existing expression beneath the degree of guilt and remorse she experienced for embarking on a deliberately deceitful course.

'Don't be silly, Mama,' she said gently. 'Sloane has

briefs stacked back to back. We can't plan anything until he's free to take a few weeks' break.' She tried for levity, and won. 'Besides, I doubt Trenton would hear of any delay.'

'No,' a deep voice drawled. 'He wouldn't.'

Trenton held out his hand and Suzanne took it, then stepped out of the car, watching as he gave Georgia a teasing look. 'Time to fly, sweetheart.'

Suzanne boarded the jet, closely followed by her mother and Trenton, and within minutes the jet cruised a path to a distant runway, paused for clearance, then accelerated for take-off.

An intimate cabin, intimate company, with the emphasis on *intimacy*. It took only one look to see that Trenton was equally enamoured of Georgia as she was of him.

Any doubts Suzanne might have had were soon dispensed with, for there was a magical chemistry existent that tore the breath from her throat.

You shared a similar alchemy with Sloane, an inner voice taunted.

Almost as soon as the 'fasten seat belts' sign flashed off Trenton rose to his feet and extracted a bottle of champagne and four flutes from the bar fridge.

'A toast is fitting, don't you agree?' He removed the cork and proceeded to fill each flute with vintage Dom Perignon, handed them round, then raised his own. 'To health, happiness—' his eyes met and held Georgia's, then he turned to spare Sloane and Suzanne a carefree smile '—and love.'

Sloane touched the rim of his flute to that of Suzanne's, and his gaze held a warmth that almost stole her breath away.

Careful, she cautioned. It's only an act. And, because of it, she was able to direct him a stunning smile before turning towards her mother and Trenton. 'To you both.'

Alcohol before lunch was something she usually chose to avoid, and champagne on a near-empty stomach wasn't the wisest way to proceed with the day.

Thankfully there was a selection of wafer-thin sandwiches set out on a platter, and she ate one before sipping more champagne.

Sloane lifted a hand and tucked a stray tendril of hair back behind her ear in a deliberately evocative gesture. It pleased him to see her eyelashes sweep wide, feel the faint quiver beneath his touch, and glimpse the increased pulse-beat at the base of her throat.

It would prove to be an interesting four days. And three nights, he perceived with a degree of cynical amusement.

Suzanne felt the breath hitch in her throat. *Was she out of her mind?* What had seemed a logical, common-sense option now loomed as an emotional minefield.

CHAPTER THREE

BEDARRA ISLAND resembled a lush green jewel in a sapphire sea. Secluded, reclusive, a haven of natural beauty, and reached only by launch from nearby Dunk Island.

Bedarra Island at first sight appeared covered entirely by rainforest. It wasn't until the launch drew closer that Suzanne glimpsed a high-domed terracotta-tiled villa roof peeping through dense foliage, then another and another.

There were sixteen private villas, walking was the only form of transport, and children under fifteen were not catered for, she mused idly, having studied the brochure she'd collected the day after she'd become aware of their destination.

She stood admiring the translucent sea as the launch cleaved through the water. It looked such a peaceful haven, the ideal place to get away from the rush and bustle of city life.

Acute sensory perception alerted her to Sloane's presence, and she contained a faint shivery sensation as he moved in close behind her, successfully forming a casual cage as he placed a hand at either side of her on the railing.

No part of his body touched hers, but she was intensely aware of the few inches separating them and how easy it would be to lean back into that hard-muscled frame.

She closed her eyes against the painful image of memory of when they had stood together just like this. Looking out over a sleeping city from any one of several floor-to-ceiling windows in his penthouse; in the kitchen, where she'd adored taking the domestic role; the large *en suite*. On any one of many occasions when he'd enfolded her close and nuzzled the sensitive slope of her neck, her nape, the hollow behind each earlobe.

Times when she had exulted in his touch and turned into the circle of his arms to lift her face to his for a kiss that was alternately slow and gentle, or hard and hungry. Inevitably, it had led them to the bedroom and long hours of passion.

Suzanne's fingers tightened on the railing as the launch decreased speed and began to ease in against the small jetty. Was Sloane's memory as vivid as her own? Or was he unmoved, and merely playing an expected role?

Damn. She'd have to get a grip on such wayward emotions, or she'd become a nervous wreck!

'Time to disembark.'

She felt rather than heard him move, and the spell was broken as Georgia's voice intruded, mingling with that of Trenton.

'It's beautiful,' Georgia remarked simply as they trod the path through to the main complex and reception.

'Secluded,' Trenton concurred. 'With guaranteed privacy, and no unwanted intrusion by the media.'

For which he was prepared to pay any price, Suzanne concluded, knowing only too well how difficult it was at times to enjoy a private dinner out without being interrupted by some society photographer bent on capturing a scoop for the tabloid social pages.

Exotic native timbers provided a background for the merging colour and tone of furnishings adorning the reception area.

The reception manager greeted them warmly, processed their check-in with practised speed, indicated their luggage would be taken to their individual villas and placed two keys on the counter.

Suzanne felt as if she'd been hit in the solar plexus by a sledgehammer. *Fool.* Of course she and Sloane were to share a villa. Why on earth not, given they were supposedly still engaged and living together?

'We'll meet in the dinin groom for lunch.' Trenton collected one key and spared his watch a glance. 'Say—half an hour?'

Together they traversed a curving path and reached Trenton and Georgia's villa first, leaving Sloane and Suzanne to continue to their own.

Suzanne could hear the faint screech of birds high in the trees, and she wondered at their breed, whether they were red-crested parrots with their brilliant blue and green plumage, or perhaps the white cockatoo, or pink-breasted galah.

Sloane unlocked the door and she preceded him

inside, waiting only until he closed the door behind him before turning towards him.

'You knew, didn't you?' she demanded with suppressed anger.

'That we'd share? Yes.' He regarded her steadily. 'You surely didn't imagine we'd have separate accommodation?'

She watched as he moved into the room, and wanted to throw something—preferably at him. 'And, of course, as Trenton has booked out the entire island there are no free villas.'

He turned and directed her a level look. 'That's true. Although even if there were we'd still share.'

'The projected image of togetherness,' Suzanne said with heavy cynicism, and glimpsed one eyebrow slant in silent query.

'Something we agreed as being the favoured option, I believe?'

A temporary moment of insanity when she'd put her mother's feelings to the forefront with very little thought for her own, she decided disparagingly. Then felt bad, for she'd do anything rather than upset Georgia.

The villa was spacious, open-plan living on two levels. And it was remarkably easy to determine via an open staircase that the upper level was given over to one bedroom, albeit that it was large and housed a queen and single bed, as well as an adjoining *en suite* bathroom.

Suzanne followed him upstairs, and discovered the bedroom was larger than she'd expected, with glossy timber floors and a high ceiling. A central fan stirred recycled air-conditioned air, and dense external foliage provided an almost jungle-like atmosphere that heightened the sensation of secluded tra nquillity.

Her eyes skimmed over both beds, and quickly skittered towards the functional *en suite*. Four days of enforced sharing. It had hardly begun, and already she could feel several nerve-ends curling in protective self-defence.

'Which bed would you prefer?' she asked in civil tones, wanting, needing to set down a few ground rules. Rules were good, they imposed boundaries, and if they adhered to them they should be able to get through the weekend with minimum conflict.

He regarded her thoughtfully. 'You don't want to share?'

'No.' She didn't want to think about it, didn't *dare*. It was bad enough having to share the same villa, the same bedroom.

To share the same bed was definitely impossible. Unless she was into casual sex, for the sake of sex. And she wasn't. To her, sex meant intimacy, sensuality, *love*. Not a physical exercise to be indulged in simply to satisfy a basic urge.

Sloane watched her expressive features, perceived each deliberation and recognised every one of them. 'Pity.'

Suzanne's lashes swept upwards, and her eyes sparked with anger. 'You surely didn't expect me to agree?'

'No.' His smile held wry humour, and there was a

musing gleam evident in the depth of his appraisal. He reached out an idle finger and touched its tip to the end of her nose. The smile broadened. 'But you rise so beautifully to the bait.'

Of all the... She drew in a deep breath, and expelled it slowly in an effort to defuse the simmering heat of her rage. 'I think,' she vouchsafed with the utmost care, 'we had better agree not to ruffle each other's feathers. Or we're likely to come to blows.'

'Verbal, of course.'

His faint mockery further incensed her. '*Physical*, if you don't watch your step!'

'Now there's an interesting image.' He gave a silent laugh, and his eyes were as dark as she imagined the devil's own to be. 'A word of warning, Suzanne,' he said softly. 'Don't expect me to behave like a gentleman.'

This conversation had veered way off course, and she attempted to get back on it. With deliberate calm she turned her attention to one bed, then the other, entertained a brief image of Sloane attempting to fold his lengthy frame into the single one, and made a decision. 'You can have the larger bed.'

'Generous of you.'

'Half the wardrobe is mine,' she managed firmly. 'With equal time and space in the bathroom.'

A lazy smile curved the edges of his mouth. 'Done.'

She looked at him warily. His calm acceptance of her suggested sleeping arrangement was...unexpected.

There was a loud knock on the door, and Sloane moved indolently downstairs to allow the porter to deposit their bags, then, taking hold of one in each hand, he ascended the short flight of stairs.

'I'll unpack.' A prosaic task that would take only minutes.

She was all too aware of Sloane's matching actions as she hung a few changes of clothes on hangers in the wardrobe, lay underclothes into a drawer, and set out toiletries and make-up on one half of the vanity unit.

'Anything for valet pressing?'

'No.' She watched as he extracted the appropriate bag, added two shirts, then filled in the slip and slung it down onto the bed.

'When you're ready, we'll go join Georgia and Trenton in the dining room.'

She needed to run a quick brush through her hair and retouch her lipstick. 'Give me a few minutes.'

In the *en suite* she regarded her mirror image with critical appraisal. Her eyes were too darkly pensive, her features too pale.

A few swift strokes of eyeshadow, blusher and lipstick added essential colour, and she made a split-second decision to twist the length of her hair into a careless knot atop her head.

Her hand automatically reached for the light *parfum* spray Sloane had gifted her. Her fingers hesitated, then retreated.

Oh, to hell with it. She wore perfume because she liked the fragrance, not because of any attempt to tantalise a man. If Sloane chose to think the fresh application was attributed to *him*, he was mistaken.

A quick spray to the delicate veins crossing each wrist, the valley between each breast. Better, much better, she determined as she emerged into the bedroom.

Sloane regarded her with one swift encompassing glance, then caught up his sunglasses and held out her own before standing to one side to allow her to precede him down onto the lower level.

Suzanne was supremely conscious of the intense maleness emanating from his broad frame as they stepped outside their villa. It was like a magnet, pulling at something deep inside her, heightening emotions to a level she didn't want to acknowledge.

'Hungry?'

The sun's warmth caressed her skin, the slight breeze teasing free a few tendrils of her hair as she offered him a brilliant smile. 'Yes.'

A gleam lit his expressive eyes, and he gave a soft laugh as he caught hold of her hand and lifted it to his lips.

Her stomach curled at the implied intimacy, and she silently damned the way each and every one of her nerve-ends sprang into acutely sensitised life.

She attempted to pull her hand free without success. 'The act is a little premature, don't you think?'

'Not really, given we're in a public place and unsure who can see and hear us.'

The tinge of humour in his voice brought forth a rueful smile. 'You're enjoying this, aren't you?'

One eyebrow slanted upwards. 'It's a rare opportunity for me to gain an upper hand.'

'Don't overdo it, Sloane,' she warned in a low voice, and glimpsed his mocking smile.

'What a vivid imagination you have.'

Much too vivid. That was the problem.

The restaurant was spacious, with tables set wide apart indoors and beneath the covered terrace. It was a peaceful setting overlooking the wide sweep of the bay as it curved out into the ocean, the bush-clad undulations of the island providing a tranquil remoteness.

'Would you prefer to sit indoors or out on the terrace?'

'The terrace,' Suzanne said without hesitation.

Georgia and Trenton had yet to arrive, and she selected a table protected from the sun's warm rays.

She watched as Sloane folded his length into an adjoining seat, and was grateful for the tinted lenses shading her eyes. They provided a barrier that made it a fraction more comfortable to deal with him.

A silent laugh stuck in her throat. Who was she kidding? No one *dealt* with Sloane. That was his prerogative. Control, which some would call manipulative strategy, was a skill he'd honed to an enviable degree in the business arena. In his private life, he added charm and seductive warmth with dangerous effect.

'Mineral water?'

She met his gaze, partly masked by tinted lenses, and offered a slight smile. 'Orange juice.'

The generous curve of his mouth relaxed and humour tugged its edge. 'Preference, Suzanne? Or a determined effort to thwart me?'

'Why would I want to do that, Sloane,' she queried evenly, 'when the next three days are supposed to project peace, harmony and celebration?'

'Why, indeed?'

His tone was pure silk, with the merest hint of caution should she attempt to try his patience too far in this game they'd each agreed to play.

A young waitress crossed to the table to take their order, her smile bright, her expression faintly envious as her eyes lingered fractionally longer than necessary on Sloane's attractive features.

Suzanne felt a slight stab of something she refused to accept as jealousy. Dammit, *why* was her body so attuned to this man, when she'd determinedly dismissed him from her mind?

It was one thing to uphold when she had the distance and protection of a telephone conversation. It was something else entirely when confronted with his presence, for then the barriers she'd erected seemed in danger of disintegrating into a heap at her feet.

Conversation seemed safer than silence. 'Tell me about the case you're currently involved in.'

'Genuine interest, Suzanne?'

His amused drawl touched a raw nerve. 'What would you prefer? A polite dissertation about the weather?'

'You could try for an unexpurgated version of what motivated you to walk out on me.'

Straight for the jugular. She aimed for levity. Anything else was impossible. 'And risk the possibility of having Georgia and Trenton appear in the middle of a heated discussion?'

He sank back in the chair and folded his hands together behind his head. 'My dear Suzanne, I rarely have the need to raise my voice.'

Why should he resort to anger when he could employ a wealth of words with such innate skill, their delivery sliced with the deadliness of an expertly wielded scalpel? Anger had been *her* emotional defence.

'This isn't the time, or the place.'

The waitress's reappearance bearing a tray containing two tall glasses filled with orange juice and chinking ice cubes brought a halt to the conversation, and Suzanne watched as the young girl made a production of placing decorative coasters down onto the table, followed by each individual glass.

'If there's anything else you need, just call.' The smile was pure female and aimed at Sloane before she turned and retreated to the bar.

'Oh, my,' Suzanne said with saccharine sweetness. 'You don't even have to try.'

His smile held wry cynicism. 'I suppose I should be grateful you noticed it was entirely one-sided.'

I notice, she silently assured him. Everything about you. She reached for her glass, lifted it, and took an appreciative sip of the iced liquid. 'She looks—available.'

His eyes narrowed. 'You forget,' he remarked in a

silky drawl. 'I'm with you.' The words alone were simple. His delivery of them was not.

It cost her to lift one eyebrow in a gesture of ill-concealed mockery. 'It's only day one, and already we're into verbal sparring. What will we both be like at the end of day four?'

There was warm humour evident in his smile, and she felt her stomach clench with something she refused to acknowledge as pain.

'Oh, I don't know,' he replied indolently. 'I'm rather looking forward to the progression.' He lifted his glass and touched its rim to her own. 'Here's to us.'

'There is no *us*,' Suzanne declared adamantly.

'Isn't there?'

She shot him a baleful glare. 'Get too close, Sloane, and you'll discover I bite.'

'Be warned I'll retaliate.'

Yes, he'd do that, and ensure that, while he might permit her to win a battle, he had every intention of winning the war.

It was a chilling thought, and one which had her poised for a stinging response.

'Georgia and Trenton have just entered the restaurant,' he warned, and she changed a glare to a slow, sweet smile, glad of the tinted shield shading her eyes as he leaned forward and brushed his fingers against her cheek.

A blatant action if ever there was one, signalling his intention to take advantage of each and every situation during their island sojourn. If he was intent on playing a game, then it shouldn't be uneven, she decided with a touch of vengeance.

With deliberate calm she captured his hand with her own and brought it to her lips, then used her teeth to nip the soft pad of one finger...*hard*.

Triumph, albeit temporary, was very sweet. Despite the faint warning flare that promised retribution.

'Isn't this an idyllic place?' Georgia enthused as she sank into the chair Trenton held out for her.

'Wonderful,' Suzanne agreed lightly. Almost anything was worth it to see her mother so blissfully happy. Even wielding emotional and verbal swords with Sloane.

'I've checked arrangements with the hotel staff,' Trenton disclosed as he settled into the remaining chair.

The waitress appeared at his side, took an order, then retreated to the bar to fill it.

'Everything's under control.'

Why wouldn't it be? Suzanne questioned silently. The Wilson-Willoughby name was sufficient to ensure assistants scrambled over one another in the need to please.

Success wasn't born of those who were faint-hearted, insecure, or inept. And no one in their right mind could accuse Trenton or Sloane of possessing any one of those character flaws.

Power was the keynote, and with it came a certain ruthlessness Suzanne found difficult to condone. A paradox, for it was a quality she could also admire.

'When do the guests arrive?'

'Tomorrow morning. The launch will make an unscheduled run from Dunk Island.'

Lunch comprised a superb seafood starter, followed by freshly caught grilled fish and salad, and they each chose a selection of succulent fresh fruit for dessert.

'Have I met each of the invited guests?' Suzanne voiced the query with what she hoped was casual interest, and tried to ignore the faint knot twisting in her stomach as she waited for Trenton's response.

Sloane's eyes sharpened, although his expression remained unchanged.

'I'm almost certain of it,' Trenton concurred with a relaxed smile. He named them, and Suzanne endeavoured to breathe normally as she waited for one specific name, and felt the easing of tension when it wasn't mentioned.

Sloane was aware of every nuance, every gesture, no matter how slight. His suspicions, laser-sharp, moved up a notch.

'Shall we leave?' Georgia broached with a sunny smile. 'I haven't finished unpacking, and there are a few things I want to check on.'

Sloane rose to his feet, and held Suzanne's chair as she followed his actions. His hand brushed her arm, and she felt warmth flood her veins in an instantaneous reaction to his touch. There was little she could do to prevent the casual arm he placed around her waist as he led her from the restaurant. Nor could she give in to temptation and shrug it off as they lingered outside.

With a hint of desperation she turned towards her

mother. 'Do you need help with anything this afternoon?' Say *yes*. *Please*, she begged silently, doubtful anyone, least of all her radiant mother, would take heed. Murphy's law had prevailed from the moment she'd picked up the phone the day before yesterday to take Georgia's call.

'Oh, darling, thank you. But no, there's nothing.'

Of course not. Anything that needed to be done had been taken care of before Georgia had boarded the plane in Brisbane. And here on this idyllic island there were ample staff to cater to a guest's slightest whim.

'The past few days have been so hectic,' Georgia continued, sparing Trenton a warm glance. 'Now that we're here, I just want to relax.' The warmth heated, and was diffused with a generous, faintly humorous smile. 'You and Sloane take time out to explore. We'll join you for a drink before dinner. Shall we say six?'

There was little to do except agree, and Suzanne suffered Sloane's loose hold as he led the way back to their villa, pulling free as soon as they were safely inside with the door closed behind them.

Suzanne glanced around the elegant tropical-designed furnishings, the four spacious walls, and felt the need to escape.

'I think I'll go for a walk.' She moved towards the stairs leading to the bedroom. She'd change into cotton shorts and sleeveless top, and exchange her shoes for light trainers.

'I'll come with you.'

His drawling tone halted her steps and she turned to face him. 'What if I don't want you to?'

'Tough.'

Anger rose to the surface, tingeing her cheeks with colour, and adding a dangerous sparkle to her eyes. 'You're determined to make this as difficult as possible, aren't you?'

He closed the distance between them. 'Everything we do this weekend, we do together. Understood?'

'*Everything*, Sloane?' Her chin tilted. 'Isn't that a bit too *literal*?'

Those dark eyes above her own hardened fractionally, and she forced herself not to blink as he lifted a hand and cupped her cheek. 'We agreed to a temporary truce. Let's try to keep it, shall we?'

She'd never seen him lose his temper, only witnessed a chilled expression turn his eyes almost black, detected the ice in his voice more than once in the courtroom, and on a few occasions when dealing with an adversary over the phone. But never with her.

A faint shiver shimmied across the surface of her skin, and she fought to diffuse the intense, potentially dangerous air that swirled between them.

'I hope you packed trainers,' she said lightly. 'Those hand-stitched Italian shoes you wear weren't made for trekking through sand and bush.'

The edges of his mouth quirked, then relaxed into a musing smile. 'A temporary escape, Suzanne?'

'Got it in one.'

His thumb brushed across her lower lip, then he let

his hand fall to his side. 'Give me a few minutes to change, then let's go try to enjoy it.'

She ascended the stairs and quickly changed, deciding on the spur of the moment to don a bikini beneath shorts and top. With a deft movement she pulled on a peaked cap, slid her sunglasses into place, caught up a towel and turned to face him.

'Ready?'

Shorts had replaced tailored trousers, and the hand-stitched shoes had been exchanged for trainers. He looked, Suzanne decided, relaxed and at ease. A projected persona that could be infinitely deceiving.

She followed in his wake, aware of the broad set of his shoulders, the powerful back beneath the cotton polo shirt. The exclusive tones of his cologne teased her senses, heightening them to a degree that made her want to scream.

Elusive scents, the movement of honed muscle and sinew, *knowing* their power, the sensual magic this one man could create within her—it was torture.

It had taken her every hour of every day since she'd left him to build up invisible walls from within which she could protect and defend herself against his powerful alchemy. Night after night she'd lain awake rationalising her motives for leaving him; applied logic, indulged in amateur psychology, and resolved that she'd reached a satisfactory and sane decision.

Yet somehow instinct continued to war with rationale, and she disliked the contrariness of her ambivalence.

'OK, where shall we begin?' Determination was the key. 'The beach?'

'Why not?'

Sloane's voice held a tinge of amusement, and she spared him a searching glance for evidence of cynical humour. However, it was impossible to detect anything behind the dark lenses of his sunglasses.

CHAPTER FOUR

THE sand resembled light honey, marked high by a thin line of shells, most broken, some whole, and scraps of seaweed: the flotsam of an outgoing tide.

Suzanne paused every now and then to select a few, only to send them skimming out into the translucent blue-green water.

It was quiet, so quiet as to imagine there was no one else on the island. The sun was pleasantly warm in a tropical climate known as the winterless north, and tempered only by a slight breeze drifting in from the sea.

She was supremely conscious of the man at her side; how, now she was in casual trainers, her height seemed diminished in comparison to his. It made her feel fragile and vaguely vulnerable, which was crazy.

'Do you want to clamber over those rocks and discover what's on the other side?'

They had followed the beach's gentle curve to a wide outcrop of boulders that separated land and sea.

Anything was better than going back to their villa. 'OK.'

They came to a small cove, the shallows bounded by an irregular scatter of huge boulders, and patches of soft crunchy sand above the shoreline. Isolated, and quite breathtakingly beautiful.

'Want to continue on?'

'Swim,' Suzanne said without hesitation, and she spared him a quick glance.

His warm smile caused the breath to catch in her throat. 'I'll join you.'

Was he wearing briefs? This was a sufficiently isolated spot for it not to matter. So why should it bother her? Except it did, of course. Badly.

'You object?' His soft drawl made her stomach dip and execute a series of slow somersaults.

'No, of course not.' How come a decision to swim suddenly seemed dangerous? *Fool*, she silently castigated herself as she quickly stripped down to her bikini.

Suzanne was conscious of Sloane matching her actions, and a surreptitious glance beneath her lashes was sufficient to determine that thin black silk provided an adequate covering.

Although *adequate* hardly equated with a hard-muscled masculine frame at the peak of physical fitness. A visual attestation of powerful male destined to cause the female heart to leap into a quickened beat.

Yet it was more than that, much more.

Sloane possessed a primitive magnetism, an animalistic sense of power which, combined with an intimate knowledge of the human psyche, set him apart from other men. It was evident in his eyes, an essential hardness that alluded to an old soul, one that had seen much, dealt with it and triumphed. Equally, those dark, almost black depths could soften and warm for a woman, give hint to sensual delight, the promise of devastating sexual pleasure.

Remembering just how devastating had kept her awake nights, tossing and turning in an attempt to forget.

In the daylight hours she could convince herself she was fine, really fine.

Now, she was faced with his constant company for three, almost four days. Mistake; big mistake. Seven hours into this farcical misadventure, and she was already a bundle of nerves, almost jumping out of her skin whenever he came within touching distance.

Why, why, *why* had she put herself in such jeopardy?

For Georgia. Dear sweet Georgia, who *deserved* happiness during her wedding celebration unclouded by an edge of anxiety for her only beloved daughter.

It wasn't so much to ask, was it?

'Do you want to swim, or simply gaze at the ocean?'

Sloane's drawling voice snapped Suzanne's introspection, and she summoned a faint smile.

'Race you in.'

She sprinted into the cool blue-green water until it reached waist-level, then she broke into long, strong strokes that took her a few metres out from the shore.

Seconds later a sleek dark head broke the surface beside her, and she regarded him a trifle warily as she trod water.

'You look,' Sloane said softly, 'as if you're waiting for me to pounce.'

She should never play poker, he decided silently. Her eyes were too expressive. He knew every nuance in her voice, could read each movement of that wide, mobile mouth.

'Why would you do that?' Suzanne queried evenly. 'There's not a soul in sight.'

'No need for you to be under any illusion, hmm?'

He moved close, much too close, and his legs curled around hers before she could attempt to put some distance between them. A hand curved round her waist, while the other held fast her nape, and she didn't have a chance to utter a sound before his mouth closed over hers in a kiss that was incredibly gentle in its possessiveness.

She felt as if she was drowning, sinking, and entirely at his mercy as he took her down beneath the water's surface. He held her so close she was aware of the pressure of his body, the strength of his arousal, the absorption of his mouth on hers, then the power of his thighs as he kicked to bring them up for air.

The breath tore at her throat, and she gasped deeply as he released her mouth and slowly eased his hold. Her eyes were wide with a mixture of shocked surprise and anger, and her lips moved soundlessly for an instant before she broke into spluttering speech, only to lapse into an inaudible murmur as he pressed a forefinger over her mouth.

'Just so you're not in any doubt,' Sloane murmured in a husky undertone, and covered her mouth with his own.

This time there was nothing gentle about his possession, and her head whirled as his tongue mated with hers, sweeping deeply and in total control. She whimpered as he took his fill, his jaw powerful in its demanding onslaught until compliance was her only option.

She had no idea how long it lasted, only that it seemed an age before the pressure began to ease. She felt the light brush of his lips as he explored the bruised softness of her mouth before he lifted his head.

His eyes were incredibly dark, almost black as he regarded her pale features, and for one infinitesimal second he experienced a tinge of regret.

She wanted to hit him. Would have, if she thought she could connect and physically *hurt* him. Instead, she resorted to words.

'If you've quite finished playing the masterful macho *male*, I'd like to go ashore and dry out.' Nothing would allow her to admit how *shaken* she felt. Or how ravaged.

His soft laughter almost unleashed her control, and she kicked out at him, then swore when she failed to connect.

'Most unladylike,' Sloane chided with an indolence that set her teeth on edge.

'I don't *feel* ladylike,' she assured him, hating him for tearing her emotions to shreds. Claim-staking. A reminder of how it had been between them; a promise of how it could be again.

Without another word she turned and swam back to shore, uncaring whether he followed her or not.

The sun's rays warmed her body as she emerged onto the sand, and she lifted her hands to squeeze excess water from her hair, then combed her fingers through its length so that it would dry more quickly, before tending to the moisture beading her body with a towel.

She possessed naturally fair skin which she took care to protect with sunscreen, and she applied coverage from the slim tube she'd brought with her.

By the time she finished the Lycra bikini was almost dry, and she pulled on shorts and top, slid her feet into trainers, then made her way towards the rocky outcrop to explore…in solitude.

Breathing space, she qualified, uncaring how Sloane chose to occupy himself. As long as it wasn't with her.

There were pools of water trapped in several natural rock hollows, tiny lizards the length of her finger which scattered out of sight, and the occasional shell of a dead crustacean.

She could hear the faint lap of water against the rocks, and every now and then there came the screeching call from parrots disturbed in their natural habitat.

Suzanne rounded the corner, and paused to admire the long curve of clean golden sand stretching to the northern point of the island. Beautiful, she thought, stepping from one rock to another.

Was it some form of sensory perception that made her pause and glance to her rear? Or simply an elusive connection she shared with the one man from whom she'd sought a temporary escape?

Sloane stood highlighted against the sky as he closed the distance between them, and she turned back, quickening her steps.

Foolishly, for she misjudged, slipped, and cushioned her fall with an outstretched hand.

Nothing, she determined within seconds, was twisted or broken. Tomorrow she might have a bruised hip, but she could bear with it. There wasn't even a graze on either leg, and her ankles were both fine.

'What in sweet *hell* were you thinking of?'

Sloane's anger was palpable as he crouched down beside her, and she directed him a dark look as she aimed for brutal honesty.

'Aiming to get down onto the sand before you caught up with me.'

His hands skimmed her arms, her legs with professional ease. 'Are you hurt?'

Now there was a question. If she said her emotions were, what good would it do?

He caught hold of her hands, examined the fine bones, then extended his attention to each palm.

Blood seeped from a deep graze on the fleshy mound beneath her left thumb, and she regarded it with a degree of fascination, wondering why it should sting quite badly when at the time she hadn't been conscious of it at all.

'I'll go wash it in the sea.'

'It needs antiseptic.'

She gave a slight shrug. 'So I'll put some on when I get back to the villa.'

Sloane gave her a penetrating look. 'Are your tetanus shots up to date?'

'Oh, for heaven's sake. *Yes.*' She tried to wrench her hand from his grasp. Unsuccessfully, which only served to increase her exasperation.

His eyes were steady, their depths too intensely dark for her to mistake the implacability evident, then without a further word he lifted her hand to his lips, took the fleshy mound into his mouth, and began cleansing the wound with his tongue.

The provocative action caused sensation to feather the length of her spine, and she suppressed a faint shiver at the sheer power of her emotions.

Everything faded beyond the periphery of her vision. There was only the man as she became caught up in the spell of him. Acute sensuality, so potent it robbed the strength from her limbs.

She was aware of the soft body hair that curled darkly, visible in the deep V of his polo shirt, and the faint musky aroma of cologne and salt emanating from his skin.

Her heart began to race, and she became supremely conscious of the need to regulate her breathing in an effort to portray a dispassionate calmness.

Fire coursed through her veins, heating pleasure that pooled in each erogenous zone and became evident with every pulsing beat.

This close, it was possible to detect the dark shadow of almost a day's growth of beard he deemed necessary to dispense with night and morning. It was an intensely masculine feature, and one she found attractive.

Dear heaven, she had to get a grip, otherwise she'd never survive the next few days with any semblance of emotional sanity.

'Don't.' The single negation sounded vaguely husky, and she swallowed compulsively as he raised his head.

'Don't—what?' His eyes pierced hers. 'Take care of you?' His voice dropped a tone. '*Love* you?'

It felt as if a fist slammed into her chest at the last two words, and she held her breath in silent pain. 'Sloane—'

'Another *don't*, Suzanne?' His voice was too quiet, too controlled as he released her hand. 'You think ignoring what we share together will make it go away?'

Her eyes were remarkably clear as they met and held his. 'No. But I plan to work on it.'

'Why?'

The silky tone aroused a dormant rage that coloured her fine-textured skin and turned her eyes to pure crystalline sapphire.

'You don't get it, do you?' The heat emanated from the pores of her skin. '*Love*—' she paused, drew in a deep breath, then expelled it '—doesn't provide a security blanket against reality.' She rose to her feet in one fluid movement, and immediately lost the momentary advantage as he followed her actions.

'You demean my intelligence.'

'Really?' Her chin tilted in open contempt. 'Then perhaps you should consider re-evaluating it.'

She turned away and traversed the few remaining rocks to the sandy stretch below, aware that he followed close behind.

'Suzanne.'

She swung round to face him. *Fine.* If a confrontation was what he wanted, then so be it!

'What do you want, Sloane? A pound of my flesh because I dared assess a situation, and decided retreat was the wisest course of action?' She was defiant, determined to hide the utter defencelessness she hadn't been able to deal with then, any more than she could now.

His eyes darkened into a deep flaming brilliance. 'Dammit, were you so emotionally unsure of yourself—of *me*, that you felt the only option you had was to throw in the towel?'

Anger flashed in her clear blue eyes. 'I didn't throw in the towel!'

A slight smile curved his mouth, lending it a cynical edge. 'Yes, you did.'

'No, I didn't!'

One eyebrow rose slightly. 'What would you call it?'

'A tactical withdrawal.'

He was silent for several long minutes, his regard unwavering. 'You possess a high degree of common sense.' His gaze intensified, and his eyes became incredibly dark. 'Sufficient, I would have thought, to judge me for the man I am beneath the superficiality of material possessions.'

It hurt to enunciate the words without allowing a slight catch to affect her voice. 'Oh, I did, Sloane. I fell in love with the man.' Her expression became pensive, her eyes incredibly sad. 'Then I discovered it was impossible to separate the man from everything that comes with the Wilson-Willoughby tag.'

'On that basis, you took the easy route and threw what we had together away?'

She felt like a laboratory specimen being examined beneath a microscope, and at that precise moment she hated him. 'Damn you, Sloane! What was I supposed to do?'

'Stay.'

One word. Yet it conveyed so much. 'I'm not into masochism.'

His eyes narrowed. 'What in hell are you talking about?'

'*You* are regarded as the ultimate prize in a field of wealthy, well-connected men.' A tight smile momentarily widened her mouth. 'And I, heaven forgive me, am merely a nonentity who dared to usurp each and every one of the women aspiring to share your life.'

The hurt, some of the pain clouded her eyes, and her lashes lowered to form a protective veil. 'I chose not to compete.' There was more, much more she could have said. Repeated the bitchy comments, relayed one very real threat.

'Unnecessary, when there was no contest.' Sloane enunciated the words with quiet emphasis, and felt a wrench of pain at the momentary sadness reflected in her expression.

'No?'

'You hold me responsible for other women's aspirations?'

Her hands clenched until the knuckles showed white, although she managed to keep her voice remarkably calm. 'No more than I hold you responsible for being who you are.'

He wanted to shake her. 'And, being *who I am*, I should select any one of several society princesses from the requisite gene pool, have her grace my arm, my bed, and produce the expected two children?'

The image hurt. So much, it was all she could do not to close her eyes in an attempt to shut it out.

'Be content with a marriage devoid of passion?' Sloane persisted ruthlessly. 'Based on duty and a degree of affection?' His voice lowered and became almost brutally merciless. 'Is that what you're saying?'

Her eyes flashed with latent anger at his analytical and persistent questioning. 'Damn you! I'm not on the witness stand.'

He didn't touch her, but she felt as if he had. 'Humour me. Pretend that you are.'

'And play the truth deal, entirely for your benefit? Sorry, Sloane. I'm not in favour of game-playing.'

His eyes held hers, and she was unable to look away. 'Neither am I.'

'Yet you do it every day in the courtroom,' Suzanne retaliated, and saw his mouth form a cynical twist.

'I don't allow my profession to intrude into my personal life.'

His compelling scrutiny was unsettling, and her eyes gleamed with hidden anger. 'You're so skilled with word play, I doubt it's possible to separate one from the other.'

'You think so?' He moved forward, and she had to forcibly refrain from taking a step backwards. His action wasn't intimidating, but nevertheless she felt threatened.

'Sloane—'

He lifted a hand and brushed a thumb along her jawline. 'Tell me the love changed.'

Oh, God. She closed her eyes, then opened them again, stricken by the tearing pain deep inside. She was powerless to move as he lowered his mouth to capture hers in a kiss that made her ache for more.

She physically had to prevent her body from leaning into his as she tried to stem the hunger that activated every nerve-ending. It would be so easy to wind her arms up around his neck and hold on as he took her on an emotional ride, the equal of which she'd never experienced with anyone else. Yet eventually the ride would be over, and she'd be left with only battered pride.

The sensual magic that was his alone tore at the very foundation of her being, tugging her free until she had no concept of anything but the heat of his mouth and the wild, sweet promise of heavy, satiated senses as they merged as one entity, meshing mind and soul.

A hollow groan rose and died in her throat at the need for *more*, much more than this. She wanted to dispense with the restriction of their clothes, to feel the texture of his skin, the flex of muscle beneath her hands, and have his lips, his mouth savour every inch of her body as they urged each other from one sensual plane to another.

What are you doing? The insidious query rose silently to taunt her. For a few long seconds she ignored it, then reality intervened as the magnitude of what she was inciting doused the heat and began cooling the warm blood in her veins.

Sloane sensed the moment it happened and mentally cursed the swing of her emotions. For the space of a few seconds he considered conquering the subtle change, then discarded the urge, aware that she would hold it against him.

Instead, he lightened the depth of emotion. Slowly easing the pressure of his mouth as he withdrew his possession, he allowed his lips to linger against her own as he pressed a number of light kisses over the full, slightly swollen contours.

At the same time his hands soothed her body, sliding gently over her slim curves, subtly massaging her nape, the delicate bones at the base of her scalp, the fine slope of her back, the firm waist.

Then his mouth left hers and trailed down the edge of her neck to savour the faint hollows at the base of her throat.

He wanted to lift her into his arms and take her here, *now*, remove what remained of her clothes, his, and make love until there could be no vestige of doubt in her mind as to how he felt.

Except she would equate that with sexual satisfaction. And while it would certainly ease the ache it wasn't enough while there were doubts to appease. He wanted her mind, her soul. *Everything.*

Who had poisoned the verbal darts and aimed them with careful precision, sufficient to undermine her confidence to such a level that she felt the only option she had was to leave?

Any one of many, came the cynical knowledge as he ran a mental gamut of numerous female acquaintances capable of sowing the seeds of doubt…and revelling in the byplay.

Sloane trailed his lips to her mouth, pressed a warm kiss to its edge, then withdrew to within touching distance, his smile tinged with a certain wry humour as he surveyed her bemused expression.

'There's a path leading off from the beach. Shall we see if it leads back to the villa?'

He was letting her off the hook…for now. She told herself she was relieved, and made a valiant effort to ignore the vague stirrings of disappointment.

'Let's go,' Suzanne declared decisively. 'Maybe we can fit in a set of tennis before dinner.'

His gaze was far too discerning. 'With the intention of wearing yourself out?'

How could she say she wanted to collapse into bed, too tired to do anything but sleep, instead of lying awake for most of the night cautioning herself not to toss or turn in case the movement disturbed the man occupying the large bed a short distance from her own?

'I might even permit you to win,' she said lightly. Some chance. He had the height, the strength, the experience to trounce her off the court!

Sloane's husky chuckle set the nerves in her stomach into action, and he slid on his sunglasses, then extended his hand.

Suzanne hesitated fractionally, then threaded slender fingers through his own.

They crossed to a sandy path that curved through increasingly dense rainforest, and initiated a leisurely pace. Sunlight filtered between wide-branched trees, lowering the warm temperature by several degrees.

There had to be a variety of tropical insects, but none was immediately evident. It was so quiet. Peaceful. Almost idyllic. A wonderful place to get away from it all.

If only... She stopped the traitorous thought right there. Life was crowded with 'if only's and 'what if?'s. And in the weeks since she'd moved out of Sloane's apartment she'd covered a plethora of each.

Silence allowed for too much introspection, and she sought a temporary distraction.

'Word has it you'll win a large settlement in the Allenberg trial.'

Sloane had a reputation for scrupulous research and meticulous attention to detail. He enjoyed pitting his skill in the court arena, and was known to accept difficult and complex cases for the mental challenge rather than his barrister's fee.

'Interesting.'

Now there was an ambiguous statement if ever there was one. Interesting that she'd mentioned the brief? Or interesting that she'd opted to veer away from anything personal by way of conversation?

She looked at him carefully. 'You have doubts?'

The path levelled out and began following the shoreline. Leading, she suspected, in a meandering fashion back to the main complex.

'I never discount the element of surprise.'

Suzanne had the strangest feeling he wasn't referring to the brief. 'I imagine you've covered all the angles.' Impossible that he hadn't.

He spared her a penetrating glance, then lightened it with a faint smile. 'It's to be hoped so.'

There was a sense of isolation in the stillness surrounding them. Possible almost to believe they were the only inhabitants on the island.

It was comforting to know that staff and civilisation lay within a short distance. Trenton and Georgia were also in residence, and tomorrow the guests would arrive.

People, in this resort deliberately designed for solitude, would be a welcome advantage, Suzanne determined. It meant there would be plenty of opportunity to socialise, and less time spent alone with Sloane.

CHAPTER FIVE

THE path was clear, but not well trodden, and Suzanne suspected it was deliberately kept that way by the resort management to provide the ambience of lush rainforest.

Sloane walked at her side, matching his stride to her own. How long would it take them to reach the main complex? Ten minutes? Longer? A lot depended on how the path was structured. The trip would be leisurely, she imagined, if the upward slant and winding curves were anything to go by.

'It probably would have been quicker to go back via the beach,' Suzanne offered, and he projected an indolent smile.

'At least this way we don't have to traverse a collection of boulders and rocks.'

She met his gaze with equanimity. 'They were relatively easy to navigate.'

He tipped his head and allowed his sunglasses to slip fractionally down the slope of his nose. One eyebrow lifted as he regarded her with a degree of quizzical humour. 'Yet you slipped and injured yourself.'

'It's the effect you have on people,' she declared with wicked mockery.

'People?'

'They either covet your company or choose to avoid it.'

'That's a particularly basic observation,' he said lazily. 'Would you care to elaborate?'

Her response was a succinct negative, and a husky chuckle emerged from his throat as she quickened her pace to step ahead of him.

The trees provided excellent shade, and did much to reduce the sun's heat. It was a lovely day, a beautiful island, and given different circumstances she would have considered herself in seventh heaven to be here alone with Sloane.

'Suppose you enlighten me as to precisely which verbal exchange, if not by whom, caused you so much grief?'

She drew in a deep breath and released it slowly. 'You don't give up, do you?'

'No.'

Whatever had made her think that he would? 'There's no point.'

'I beg to differ.'

She was mercilessly vengeful. 'I wasn't born into the social hierarchy.' She held up one hand, fingers extended, ready to provide a graphic example by ticking off each one as she cited the given reasons. 'No private schooling. At least, not at one of the few élite establishments. My mother still *works*, would you believe?' She was on a roll. 'How could someone like me dare to think she could compete with the *crème de la crème* of Sydney's society? For you to have a fling with me was quite acceptable, but marriage? *Never.*'

It was impossible to gauge anything from his expression. Dammit, didn't he care how each criticism had been like a finely honed barb that had speared through her heart? *Why* didn't he say anything?

'Your response was no doubt interesting.'

His drawled amusement set her teeth on edge, and she glared at him balefully when he brushed his knuckles across one cheekbone.

'I took the line of least resistance, smiled sweetly and assured her you kept me because I was incredibly good in bed.'

It was *he* who possessed incredible skill, *she* who became a willing wanton at his slightest touch.

'And the rest of it?'

'What makes you think there's more?'

'I can't imagine you taking notice of a few bitchy remarks.'

Verbal threats hadn't worried her. Written missives were something else entirely.

'I received an anonymous note in the mail.'

His eyes sharpened, and there was a still quality about him she found disquieting. 'What type of note?'

'Plain paper with an assemblage of cut-out letters from various news publications.'

'Pasted together and worded to say?'

'I had two days to get out of your life.' Even now she could recall it so vividly.

'Or?'

'I would be sorry.'

A muscle bunched at the edge of his jaw, and a string of pithy oaths escaped in husky condemnation. 'Why in hell didn't you tell me?'

'Because I didn't take it seriously.'

He barely restrained himself from shaking her. 'Something obviously occurred to persuade you otherwise?'

A few isolated incidents which had at first seemed coincidental. Except for one. And her mistake had been an attempt to deal with it herself.

'Suzanne.' Sloane's voice was too quiet. Ominous.

She suppressed a shiver, and held his gaze. 'I was driving home after work, and someone tried to run me off the road, then demonstrated very graphically that the next time I wouldn't be so fortunate.' She paused, and drew in a deep breath. 'It was followed by a personal confrontation demanding I get out of your life.'

'Why in *hell* didn't you tell me?'

She didn't flinch at the icy viciousness of his tone. 'You were away at the time.'

He was hard-pressed not to shake her within an inch of her life. 'That shouldn't have stopped you.'

Her eyes assumed an angry sparkle. 'And what could you have done?'

'Taken the next flight back.'

Knowing the importance of his London-based client and the seriousness of the case...

'Believe it,' Sloane assured her inflexibly.

'I dealt with it myself.'

'How, precisely?'

'Assuring her a full report would be lodged with

the police and followed by legal action if I ever heard from her again.' Her eyes were dark crystalline sapphire, her features pale. 'Or if another suspicious accident should eventuate.'

And removing herself from his apartment, and to all intents and purposes from his life. Choosing not to confide in him, or seek external help. The silent rage deep within him intensified. Putting him through hell, not to mention herself.

Now, there was only one question.

'Who?' His tone hadn't altered, but she recognised the anger beneath the surface. And his immense effort to control it.

'It's my decision not to name her.'

His eyes held a ruthlessness that was frightening. Merciless, almost brutal with intent. 'It isn't your decision to make.'

He was a formidable force, but she refused to back down. 'Yes, it is.'

'You're aware I can override you? Initiate enquiries, and eventually obtain the answer I need?'

Her gaze didn't falter. 'To what end? What charges can you lay? I wasn't molested, or hurt.' Just very badly shaken by a vindictive woman who should have been seeking professional help for a sick obsession.

'Harassment constitutes a threat that, proven, is punishable by law.' His eyes were so dark they resembled obsidian shards.

'I'm as much aware of that as you are.' Her resolve was determined. 'Her father has a very high profile which would be irreparably damaged should this come out. It's out of my respect for him that I've chosen to keep quiet.'

He held onto control by a bare thread, and wondered if she knew just how close he was to full-blown anger. Twelve inches less in height and half his weight didn't diminish her stance in comparison to his own. Nor did she reflect any fear. Just steadfast intent that would be difficult to bend. But not impossible.

'You disappoint me.'

She was already ahead of him, for she'd had weeks to prepare for this moment. 'A psychological shift into skilled tactician mode, Sloane?' Her chin tilted fractionally. 'Don't waste your time. Or attempt to persuade me that *love conquers all*. We're heavily into reality, not fantasy. That combination is immiscible.'

'You want *reality*, Suzanne?'

His head lowered down to hers, his breath warm as it fanned her lips before his mouth settled over hers in a kiss that tore at the foundations of her being.

In an imitation of the sexual act itself, his tongue teased hers in a mating dance so evocatively persuasive that her bones seemed to liquefy, and she lifted her arms and held on as her body instinctively arched into his.

One arm curved across her back, while a hand tangled in her hair, holding her head fast as he deepened the kiss into something so incredibly erotic she lost track of time and place.

Her skin felt alive, each sensory nerve-ending so acutely attuned to this one man's touch that she groaned out loud as one hand cupped her bottom and he lifted her up against his body so that his mouth could pay homage to the slope of her neck, the soft hollows at the base of her throat, before tracing a path to the delicate curve of her breast.

She was incapable of offering any protest as he pulled up her top and undid the clip fastening of her bikini bra, nor when he pushed the thin Lycra aside and sought one rosy peak, taking it into his mouth and suckling it until she cried out at the wealth of sensation that swept through her body.

It wasn't enough, not nearly enough. And her hands clung to his deeply muscled shoulders, then slid down his chest in a tactile exploration of the dark whorls of hair stretching from one male nipple to the other.

She felt the flex of sinew beneath the pads of her fingers as she slid her hands over his ribcage to the back of his waist, slipped beneath the elasticated band of his shorts, then curved low over tensely muscled buttocks to hold him close.

His arousal was a potent entity, a powerfully male shaft pressing against the softness of her belly.

An anguished moan escaped her lips as his hand slid beneath her shorts and bikini briefs and teased the soft curling hair at the apex of her thighs, and she cried out as he sought and found the damp folds guarding entrance to her feminine core.

A touch was all it took. *His* touch. And she climbed a mental wall as he stroked the highly sensitised folds, sending her mindless with a desire so strong it was almost too much to bear.

Her whole body seemed to throb as acute sensation took possession of every nerve-ending, and the blood pulsed through her veins to a quickened beat as awareness transcended onto a higher plane.

Sloane knew he could take her now, here, and she wouldn't stop him. It would be so easy, the act so primal, so intensely satisfying, it took all his strength not to take the final step that would make it happen.

He felt the damp heat of her climax, exulted in her soft, throaty cries, the warm savagery of her mouth on his as she lost herself to him with stunning completeness.

Slowly, gradually, Suzanne became aware of where she was and with whom. And what had almost transpired.

Warmth coloured her cheeks, and he watched as her eyes darkened, then became shadowed as long lashes swept down to form a protective veil.

She didn't struggle as he allowed her to slip down to her feet, and he saw a lump form and rise in her throat, only to fall as her mouth worked silently in an effort to form a few words.

'Don't,' Sloane cautioned gently, and pressed a forefinger to her lips. 'What we share is more powerful than mere sexual gratification.' His eyes darkened, and became almost black. '*That* is the reality I have no intention of abandoning.' His finger slid to the corner of her mouth, then traced the curve of her jaw.

He smiled, a soft, slightly humorous, warm curve of his mouth that melted every bone in her body. 'Until the day you can look at me and say the love isn't there any more. Then…' he paused, and depressed her lower lip with one forefinger '…I might listen to you.'

Suzanne felt as ambivalent as a feather floating in a fragile breeze. Surely he didn't—couldn't be implying what she thought he meant?

'Shall we head back?'

Her lips parted, then closed again. 'Sloane, I don't think—'

'You want to stay here?'

Oh, God, no. She didn't dare. To risk a repeat of the past—how long? Ten, twenty minutes? A slight shiver shook her slim shoulders as she remembered with vivid clarity just how deep her involvement had been.

Total wipe-out, she accorded silently. If she allowed him to kiss, *touch* her again, she would be reduced to begging for the wildness of total consummation. And that was a divine madness she could ill afford if she was to walk away from this weekend with her dignity intact.

Sloane watched the fleeting emotions chase across her expressive features, and interpreted each and every one of them.

He extended his hand, and she took it, all too aware of the way he curled her fingers within the enveloping warmth of his own.

They followed the path along its winding curve through the rainforest until it took a steady downward slant to the beach adjacent to the main complex. Their conversation was, as if by tacit consent, confined to inconsequential subjects unrelated to family or any-thing personal.

It was, Suzanne determined from a quick glance at her watch, almost five. Allowing thirty minutes to shower and wash her hair, then dress for dinner, she had half an hour to spare.

'Want to try out the pool?'

Had he guessed she was hesitant to return to their villa? Determined the reason why?

Tension created knots inside her stomach, and a tiny bubble of faintly hysterical laughter rose in her throat. She was fast becoming an emotional mess. A wicked irony considering she was almost entirely to blame.

It was the *almost* part that bothered her most. Sloane's participation couldn't be ignored, and she could only wonder why. The convenience of casual sex for old times' sake? An attempt to show her what she was missing?

Somehow neither reason seemed to fit the man, and introspection didn't help at all.

Suzanne turned towards Sloane with a brilliant smile. 'Why not?' Suiting words to action, she moved towards the tiled surround area bordering the pool, shrugged off her shirt and shorts, and executed a neat dive.

The water was deliciously cool, and she stroked several lengths with leisurely ease before turning onto her back and allowing her body to float at will.

She could close her eyes and shut out the world. It was so quiet, it was almost possible to believe that everything was right, and here on this idyllic island they were inviolate from the pressures of business and social obligations. No one could get to them, unless they chose to allow it. Paradise, she mused.

A splash sounded loud in the stillness, and seconds later a dark head surfaced a short distance from her own.

'Sleeping in water isn't a good idea,' Sloane drawled, flicking cool, salty droplets onto her midriff.

'I wasn't asleep.'

'First one out gets exclusive use of the shower.' He lifted a hand and trailed idle fingers across her cheek. 'Unless you feel inclined to share?'

Heat suffused her body and pooled deep within, a sensual flaring over which she had no control.

Suzanne caught his dark, gleaming gaze, glimpsed the faint curl of humour tilt the edge of his mouth. Dammit, he was enjoying this.

She offered him a languid smile. 'Do I get a head start?'

His mouth widened and showed his even white teeth. 'I'm feeling generous.'

She jackknifed into racing position. 'First one out, huh?'

She was a strong swimmer, but Sloane had the superior advantage of height and male power. They reached the pool's tiled edge together, and in one synchronised movement levered themselves up onto its perimeter.

'A perfect finish,' Sloane accorded with indolent amusement as he rose to his feet, watching as she smoothed back the streaming length of her hair while matching her movements with his own.

Suzanne bent to collect her clothes. 'Now why doesn't that surprise me?'

'No shared shower, I take it?'

Her fingers stilled at the sudden graphic image, then shook slightly as she thrust first one arm into a sleeve of her shirt, then the other. 'In your dreams, Sloane.'

'That's the problem—they're remarkably vivid.' His voice was silk-soft and dangerous. 'What about yours?'

Glorious Technicolor complete with sound and emotional effects.

Without a further word she turned and stepped quickly towards the path leading to their villa, uncaring whether he followed her or not, grateful that she'd had the foresight to pick up the duplicate key on their way out.

Inside she made straight for the upper level, collected fresh underwear and a silk robe, then entered the *en suite*.

She set the temperature dial to warm, stripped off her clothes, then stepped beneath the cascade of water.

Ten minutes later she emerged into the bedroom, a towel wound turban-fashion around her hair, to discover Sloane in the process of selecting casual trousers and shirt.

'Finished?'

He'd discarded his shirt, if in fact he'd opted to put it on when leaving the pool area, and the cotton-knit shorts moulded firm-muscled buttocks, gave credence to the power of his manhood, and accentuated long, heavily muscled thighs. To say nothing of the exposed breadth of chest and shoulder.

Suzanne dragged her eyes away from him. 'I need to use the hair-drier when you're done.' She crossed to the wardrobe and extracted an elegant trouser suit in deep aqua, added matching heeled sandals, and slowly expelled the breath she'd unconsciously held as she heard the *en suite* door close behind him.

Just when she thought she had a handle on which way he would move and when, he did the opposite. If she was of a suspicious mind, she could almost swear he was being deliberately unpredictable.

Suzanne discarded her robe, stepped into the trouser suit, then slid her feet into the sandals, and reached for her make-up bag, only to realise she'd left it in the bathroom earlier.

Damn. What would be Sloane's reaction if she invaded his privacy? After all, it wouldn't be anything new. They'd shared a lot more than a bathroom in the past. Except then the game had been love and they'd been unable to keep their hands off each other.

Whereas now... Now, it was an entirely different ball game. The rules had shifted, and both players had regrouped.

Almost ten minutes later Sloane emerged, showered and freshly shaven, a towel hitched low on his hips.

One eyebrow rose in silent query as he examined her bare complexion. 'Too shy to share the bathroom with me, Suzanne?'

She wanted to hit him. 'You allowed me sole use.'

His husky laughter brought a soft tinge of colour to her cheeks. 'Only because you'd have fought me tooth and nail if I hadn't.' He reached for briefs, loosened the towel, and stepped into them. Trousers followed, and his eyes met hers as he slid home the zip fastener. 'And there isn't enough time to enjoy the fight.' He reached for his shirt and shrugged into it. 'Or its aftermath. If we're to make dinner.'

Anger flared, deepening her colour to a rosy hue, and her eyes assumed the brilliance of dark sapphire. 'There wouldn't *be* an aftermath,' she vouched with unaccustomed vehemence.

His gaze didn't waver for endless seconds, then he conducted a slow, sweeping appraisal of her body.

Suzanne felt as if he touched her. Her skin tingled beneath his probing assessment, and her pulse leapt to a faster beat she was sure had to be visible at the base of her throat. Even her breath seemed to catch, and she had to make a conscious effort to prevent her chest from heaving in tell-tale evidence of his effect on her.

His eyes when they met hers again were dark, faintly mocking and held vague cynicism. 'No?'

Sloane wondered if she knew just how appealing she looked with her hair all damply tousled, her cheeks flushed with an intriguing mix of temper and desire.

It made him want to tumble her down onto the bed and show her, *prove* that what they had together was good. Too good to allow anything or anyone to come between them.

Except afterwards she wouldn't thank him for it, and only hate herself.

He wanted her. Dear heaven, *how* he wanted her. His body ached, painfully, with need. But he was after the long haul, not a short transitory ride.

Suzanne drew herself up to her full height and glared at him balefully. 'If you think that sharing this villa, this *bedroom*, means I'll agree to sex, then you can go to hell!'

Did she imagine he hadn't been there? Ever since the evening he'd entered his apartment and discovered she had gone.

'Go dry your hair, Suzanne. Then I'll take a look at your hand.'

His voice was deceptively quiet, and didn't fool her in the slightest. What she'd perceived as being a dangerous situation had just moved up a notch or two.

Five minutes with the hair-drier was sufficient, a further five took care of her make-up, then she emerged into the bedroom.

Sloane was waiting, standing at the full-length window, and he turned as she crossed the room.

'I have some antiseptic in my wet-pack.'

'It's fine.' She dismissed his offer, and her breath caught as he reached her side. 'Really. There's no need to play nurse.'

'Humour me.'

'This is ridiculous!' Exasperation was a mild word for describing how she felt at being shepherded back into the bathroom, and having her hand examined and dabbed with anti-bacterial solution.

'There. All done,' Sloane said with satisfaction.

'I could easily have done that myself!' She wanted to *hit* him.

'Don't,' he warned with dangerous softness, reading her mind.

'Or you'll do *what*?' she flung, incensed.

'Take all your fine anger,' he threatened in a voice that was pure silk, 'and ensure you expend it in a way you won't forget.'

Her stomach executed a torturous somersault, and for a few endless seconds she forgot to breathe. 'By displaying masculine strength and sexual superiority?' She managed to keep her voice even. 'I don't find caveman tactics a turn-on.'

His eyes were dark, so impossibly dark she found them unfathomable. 'Make no mistake, Suzanne,' Sloane drawled with hateful cynicism. 'There would be no need for coercion of any kind.'

Tension filled the room, an explosive, dangerous entity just waiting for the trigger to let a certain hell break loose.

With considerable effort she banked down her anger, then she turned towards him and marshalled her voice to an incredibly polite level. 'Shall we leave?'

'Wise, Suzanne,' he taunted silkily.

How long would such wisdom last? she wondered with a sense of desperation. Sooner or later she was going to lose control of her temper. With every hour that passed she could feel the pressure of it building, and she hated him for deliberately stoking the fire.

They walked in silence to the main complex and

joined Georgia and Trenton for a drink in the lounge before entering the restaurant.

Dinner was a casual meal eaten alfresco on the terrace, their choice a selection of varied seafood with delicate accompanying sauces. They enjoyed salads, fresh bread brought daily onto the island, and they settled on fresh fruit from a selection of succulent pineapple, cantaloupe, sweet melon, and strawberries, served with a delightful lemon and lime sorbet, for dessert.

They declined coffee, and lingered over tall glasses containing deliciously cool piña colada.

'We thought we might take a walk along the beach,' Trenton declared. 'Care to join us?'

And play gooseberry? 'I've challenged Sloane to a game of tennis,' Suzanne indicated, casting the source of that challenge a singularly sweet smile. 'Haven't I, darling?'

Sloane reached forward and brushed gentle fingers down the length of her bare arm. And smiled as he glimpsed the way her eyes dilated in damnable reaction. 'Indeed. I'll even grant a handicap in your favour.'

'How…' she hesitated fractionally '…kind.' She touched a hand to his, and summoned a doting look. 'Especially when we both know you could run me off the court.'

He didn't miss an opportunity, and his eyes were openly daring as he lifted her hand to his lips and kissed each finger in turn.

'We need to go change first.'

There was hardly any point in saying she'd changed her mind. 'We should wait half an hour.' Her eyes took on a wicked gleam. 'Exercise so soon after a meal isn't advisable.' Her mouth curved into a winsome smile. 'I don't want you to collapse with a heart attack.'

Trenton laughed, and Georgia's eyes twinkled as she rose to her feet. 'I don't think that's likely, darling. Come for a walk with us. That'll fill in some time.'

'Sloane?' Suzanne deferred to him, sparing him a level glance.

'An excellent suggestion, Georgia.' He stood and together they strolled along the path leading down to the beach.

Suzanne slipped off her sandals and held them in one hand, watching as Sloane followed her actions with his shoes, aware that Georgia and Trenton did the same.

It was a beautiful evening, the sky a deep indigo with a clear moon and a sprinkle of stars. The sort of night for lovers, Suzanne perceived as she stepped onto the sand and felt its firm crunch beneath her feet.

There wasn't much she could do about the hard, masculine arm that curved along the back of her waist as they formed a foursome and began following the gentle curve of the bay.

'Do you have everything ready for tomorrow, Mama?' Suzanne queried, conscious of the man who walked at her side. The arm that bound her to him would tighten if she attempted to put some distance between them. For a moment she almost considered it, simply for the sake of enforcing her position, only to discard it as she thought of the consequences.

'Yes.' Georgia cast her a warm glance in the semi-darkness. 'Although I probably won't sleep tonight as I go through everything again and again in my mind.'

'I have a remedy for that,' Trenton declared, and Georgia laughed.

'Perhaps we'll join you later for a game of tennis. How long do you intend to play?'

'I'll leave it up to Suzanne,' Sloane drawled, and she turned towards him with a sweet smile that was lost in the fading light.

'Passing the buck, darling? What if I'm feeling particularly energetic?' As soon as the words left her mouth she wanted to curse herself for uttering them.

'I think I can match you.'

In more ways than one. Silence, she decided, was golden. Something she intended to observe unless anyone asked her a specific question.

The ocean resembled a dark mass that merged with the sky. There were no visible lights, no silvery path reflected from a low-set moon. Tonight it rose high, a clear milk-white orb in the galaxy.

Suzanne felt the increased pressure of Sloane's fingers at the edge of her waist, and a tiny spiral of sensation unfurled inside her stomach.

'I think we'll turn back,' Sloane declared, drawing to a halt. 'If we don't see you on the court, we'll meet for breakfast. Eight, or earlier?'

'Eight,' Trenton agreed. 'Enjoy.'

As soon as they had progressed out of earshot Suzanne broke free from Sloane's grasp. Lights were visible through the trees, and as they drew close the main complex came into view.

Within minutes they reached their villa, and indoors she quickly changed into shorts and a top, added socks and trainers, aware that Sloane was doing likewise.

Securing the court wasn't a problem, because there were no other guests to compete with. The hiring of racquets and balls was achieved in minutes, and Suzanne preceded Sloane into the enclosure.

CHAPTER SIX

'ONE set, or two?'

'Two,' Suzanne declared as she crossed the court and took up her position at its furthest end.

'A practice rally first,' Sloane called. 'Best of three gets to serve. OK?'

'Sure.'

He had the height, the strength and the expertise to defeat her with minimum effort. It was the measure of the man that he chose not to do so in the following hour as she returned one shot after another, won some, lost most, and while it was an uneven match she managed to finish with two games to her credit in the first set and three in the second. A concession, she was sure, that was as deliberate as it was diplomatic.

'Your backhand has improved.'

Suzanne caught the towel he tossed her, and patted the faint film of sweat from her face and neck. He, damn him, didn't show any visible sign of exertion. Not a drop of sweat, and he was breathing as evenly as if he'd just taken a leisurely walk in the park.

'I expected your serve to singe the ball.'

Sloane's eyes gleamed with latent humour. 'Were you disappointed that it didn't?'

Expending physical energy had been a good idea.

The heat was there, but banked down to a level she could deal with.

'You played as I expected you to,' she responded sweetly, and waited a beat. 'Like a gentleman.'

He rubbed the towel over the back of his neck, and sent her a musing smile. 'Ah, a mark in my favour.'

'Are we keeping score?'

'Believe it.'

Why did she get the instinctive feeling he had his own hidden agenda?

Her agenda was to survive the weekend with her emotions intact. *His* she could only guess at.

'Let's get a drink from the bar, shall we?' Sloane suggested smoothly.

A diversionary tactic which Suzanne let pass only because she was thirsty.

It was an unexpected surprise, and a welcome one, to see Georgia and Trenton seated comfortably at a table adjacent to the well-stocked bar. Surprise, because she'd thought not to see them again before breakfast, and the welcome part was a definite plus, for it meant she wasn't alone with Sloane.

'We thought we'd join you for a game of doubles,' Georgia said as Suzanne slid into a seat at her mother's side.

'Georgia's idea,' Trenton drawled with amused resignation. 'I had another form of exercise in mind.'

'Don't tease, darling. You'll embarrass the children.'

Children? Suzanne looked at Georgia in keen surprise. Those beautiful eyes the colour of her own bore a faintly wicked gleam that promised much to the man seated at her side. Loving sex without artifice, a joyous sharing and caring.

Suzanne felt a lump rise in her throat at the latent emotion evident, and she took a generous sip from the tall glass of iced water a waiter had placed in front of her only moments before.

She risked a glance at Sloane and glimpsed his wry amusement. 'The *children*, of course,' she ventured conversationally, 'are less likely to score a handsome win after expending their energy on court.'

Trenton sent her a devilish smile. 'Georgia and I need any advantage we can get.'

'So sharing a drink is seen as a five-minute break for refreshment?'

'Definitely.'

'Of course, we're playing two sets?'

'One,' Trenton decreed.

'In that case,' Sloane drawled, collecting his racquet as he rose to his feet, 'let's get started.'

Father and son chose not to play competitively, and Georgia and Suzanne were fairly evenly matched. It was a lot of fun. Suzanne couldn't remember ever seeing her mother appear so brilliantly alive, or so happy.

After an hour and a narrow win in Suzanne and Sloane's favour, they exited the floodlit court and crossed to the lounge bar.

Trenton led the way, his arm curved round Georgia's shoulders, and there was little Suzanne could do about the casual arm Sloane placed at her waist.

'A cool drink?' Trenton suggested as they selected a table and sank down into individual chairs. 'Or would you prefer an Irish coffee?'

It was after ten when Trenton and Georgia got to their feet.

'We'll see you at breakfast. Eight o'clock,' Trenton said. He clasped Georgia's hand in his and brought it up to his lips with a warm intimacy. Suzanne felt her heart flip with something she refused to acknowledge as envy.

'Want to follow them, or stay here for a while?'

Suzanne spared Sloane a considering glance from beneath her long-fringed lashes. 'We could take a walk in the moonlight.'

'A delaying tactic, Suzanne?'

Her lashes swept upwards, and she regarded him with ill-concealed mockery. 'How did you guess?'

'Afraid?' His voice was so quiet it sent shivers down her spine.

That was an understatement. But it was fear of herself that made her reluctant to be alone with him. 'Yes.'

'Such simple honesty,' Sloane said with unmistakable indolence. He rose to his feet and extended his hand. It had been a long day. An even longer night lay ahead.

A swift retort rose to her lips, and remained unuttered. 'It's one of my more admirable traits.' She wanted to take hold of his hand, feel it enclose her own, and bask in the warmth of his intimate smile. Yet to do so would amount to a fine madness of a kind she dared not afford.

'One of many.'

She rose, ignored his outstretched hand, and skirted the table *en route* to the entrance. 'Flattery will get you nowhere.'

He drew level with her. 'Try sincerity.'

She spared him a sideways glance, and chose not to comment. She quickened her step, and felt mildly irritated at the ease with which he lengthened his to match it.

They reached their villa, and inside she crossed the lounge and quickly trod the stairs to the bedroom. She paused only long enough to collect her nightshirt before entering the *en suite*, and carefully closed the door behind her.

A foolish, childish action that nevertheless afforded her a measure of satisfaction. Until it was time to emerge some ten minutes later, when all of the former fire had died and wary apprehension reposed in its place.

Sloane was standing at the window, looking out into the darkness.

'Bathroom's all yours.'

He turned to face her, aware of the moment she'd entered the bedroom via the darkened glass reflection.

She looked about sixteen, her skin scrubbed clean, her hair tied back in a pony-tail. Did she have any idea how sexy she looked in that mid-thigh-length tee shirt? As a cover-up the soft cotton merely moulded

her firm breasts and was more provocative than designer silk and lace.

'How's the hand?'

Oh, hell, she'd almost forgotten. 'Fine.'

'And your hip?'

Painful, and showing the promise of a nasty bruise.
'OK.' She moved towards the bed she'd nominated
as her own, turned back the cover, and slid between
the sheets. 'Goodnight.'

'Sweet dreams, Suzanne.'

She didn't care for the mocking humour in his
voice, and as soon as the bathroom door closed behind
him she propped herself up on one hand and plumped
the pillow vigorously with the other, then she shifted
onto her left side and almost groaned out loud as her
bruised hip came into contact with the mattress.

She was tired, and, if she closed her eyes and willed
herself to believe she was comfortable, surely she
should sleep.

Suzanne heard the shower run, then stop minutes
later. The bathroom door opened, a shaft of light illuminated the room, then there was darkness, the soft
pad of Sloane's feet on the polished floorboards as he
crossed to the bed, the faint slither of cotton percale,
and the almost inaudible depression of mattress
springs settling beneath a solid male frame.

Despite counting imaginary sheep and practising
various relaxing techniques, Suzanne found sleep remained elusive.

Her hip ached. Throbbed, she corrected, deep into

specific analysis in the darkness of night. Pain-killers would dull the pain's keen edge and help her sleep.

If only she had some. Maybe there was a foil strip in her vanity bag, or, failing that, it was possible Sloane had some in his wet-pack.

Damn, damn, *damn*. If she lay wide awake for much longer, she'd be in a fine state by the end of Georgia and Trenton's wedding festivities.

You would think, she ruefully decided as she slid carefully from the bed, that an over-abundance of emotional and nervous tension together with long walks, rock-clambering, and three sets of tennis, would fell the fittest of the physically fit.

Instead, she felt as if she'd trebled a daily dose of caffeine.

Suzanne crept to the bathroom, closed the door, then switched on the light and rummaged through her vanity bag to no avail. Her fingers delved into Sloane's wet-pack, hesitated, then, driven more by need than courtesy, she separated compartments and almost cried out with relief when she discovered a slim pack of paracetamol.

She broke off two, part-filled a glass with water and swallowed them, then she replaced the glass and switched off the light. She'd allow a few seconds for her eyes to adjust, then she'd open the door and tiptoe back to bed.

It was a remarkably simple plan. Except in attempting to give Sloane's bed a wide berth she veered too far and brushed against a chair.

A soft curse fell from her lips at the same time Sloane activated the bed-lamp.

'What in sweet hell are you doing?'

Suzanne threw him a dark glance, and resorted to flippancy. 'Rearranging the furniture.'

He slid into a sitting position and leaned against the headboard. His dark hair was slightly tousled and he was bare to the waist.

Probably bare beneath the waist as well, she reflected a trifle ruefully, all too aware of his penchant for sleeping nude.

It was too much. *He* was too much.

'You should have turned on the light.'

Oh, sure. The last thing she'd wanted to do was to wake him. Coping with a darkly brooding male wasn't a favoured option.

Suzanne pushed in the chair and took the few steps necessary to reach her bed, then slid carefully between the sheets.

'Headache?'

She should have known he wouldn't leave it alone. The look she cast him held such fulsome anger it was a wonder he didn't *burn*. *'Yes.'* In this instance she had no compunction in resorting to fabrication.

'Want me to give you a neck and scalp massage?'

Oh, God. 'No.' Would he detect the faint desperation in her voice? She hoped not. 'Thank you.'

'Seduction isn't part of the deal,' he drawled with musing cynicism, and she closed her eyes, then opened them again.

He read her far too easily, and it rankled unbearably. 'Well, now, that's a relief,' she said with pseudo-sweetness.

'Unless you want it to be,' Sloane added with killing softness.

The thought of that hard male body curved over her own in a tasting, teasing supplication of each and every pleasure spot filled her with such intense longing it was all she could do to respond, let alone keep her voice even.

'If you come anywhere near me,' she warned in a tense whisper, 'I'll render you serious bodily harm.'

His husky chuckle further enraged her. 'It might almost be worth it.'

Without thought Suzanne picked up the spare pillow and threw it at him, watching in seemingly slow motion as he fielded it and unhurriedly tossed the bedcovers aside.

'Dammit—don't.' She turned and scrambled to the furthest side of the bed, only to give a sharp cry as her hip dragged painfully against the mattress.

It was no contest. She simply didn't have a chance as Sloane's hands caught hold of her shoulders and turned her back to face him.

For a long moment she gazed at him in open defiance, aware that the slightest move, the faintest word would invite crushing retribution.

His eyes were impossibly dark, their depths unfathomable as he reached for the edge of the bedcovers and wrenched them off with one powerful pull of his hand, then drew her down onto the mattress.

His head lowered and she felt one hand grasp hold of her thigh, then slide to her hip.

Her gasp of pain was very real, and he paused, his mouth only inches from her own. She saw his eyes narrow, glimpsed the tiny lines fanning out from each outer edge, and felt him tense for a few long seconds before he slid the hem of her nightshirt to her waist.

It was a long bruise, red, purpling, and growing more ugly with every hour.

He swore, words she'd never heard him use before, and she flinched as he traced the line of her hip-bone, then probed the surrounding flesh.

'You walked through the rainforest,' Sloane said with deadly softness, 'played three sets of tennis, nursing *this*?'

'It didn't hurt much then.'

His eyes appeared as dark obsidian shards, infinitely forbidding. 'It does now.' He levered himself off the bed and descended the stairs to the lower floor.

She heard the chink of glass, the bar-fridge door close, then he was back with a chilled half-bottle in his hand.

'What are you doing?'

'Applying the equivalent of an ice-pack.'

'A magnum of champagne?' Suzanne queried in disbelief, and shivered as the cold frosted glass touched her skin.

'It'll serve the purpose. Now, lie still.'

She didn't plan on moving. Besides, fighting him would prove a futile exercise.

'What did you find to take in the bathroom?'

'Paracetamol,' she said huskily as he adjusted the bottle. 'Two. In your wet-pack,' she added. An icy numbness settled in, minimising the pain, and she closed her eyes so she didn't have to look at him.

The proximity of his male body was a heady entity, despite the skimpy black silk briefs providing a modicum of decency. As a concession to her?

She could smell the clean scent of expensive soap and male deodorant on skin only inches away from her own. All her senses were acutely attuned, almost in recognition of a rare and special alchemy existent in two separate halves that were meant to make a perfect whole.

It didn't make sense. Nothing made sense.

The pain slowly ebbed, and her eyelids grew heavy. Gentle fingers soothed, kneaded, and dispensed with the tight knots in the muscles of her shoulders, back and thighs.

Heaven, she acknowledged as she relaxed and let him work his magic. She made only a token protest when he lifted her into his arms and transferred her to the other bed.

His bed. Her eyes sprang open, and she made to scramble to the edge as he climbed in beside her.

'I don't think this is a good idea,' she said helplessly as he curved an arm beneath her shoulders and drew her close.

'Just shut up and let it be.' He pillowed her head against his chest, then curled an arm round her waist.

He was deliciously warm, and she cautiously moved one arm so that it rested across his midriff.

It was like coming home. *Déjà vu*, she reflected. With one exception. Lacking was the satiation of lovemaking.

The temptation to begin a tactile exploration was strong. Just the slight movement of her fingers and she could trace the outline of his ribcage, tease one brown nipple, then trail a path to his navel.

He possessed a strong-boned frame, with symmetrical muscle structure, textured skin that emanated its own musky male aroma. Clean and slick with sweat at the height of sexual possession, it became an aphrodisiac that drove her wild. Sensual heat, raw and primal. As primitive as the man himself.

Don't even think about it, an inner voice cautioned. Unless you want to dice with dynamite.

Soon he'd fall asleep, then she'd gradually ease free and slip into her own bed.

It was the last coherent thought she had, and she woke to find warm sunshine filtering through the curtains, the smell of fresh coffee teasing her nostrils. One quick glance was all it took to determine she was alone in the bed. Another to see Sloane's broad back curved over a newspaper spread out on the buffet bar.

At that precise moment he turned towards her, almost as if he was acutely attuned to her every move, and his warm smile melted her bones.

'Good morning.'

Suzanne felt awkward, sleep-rumpled, and she dragged a hand over her tousled hair. 'Hi.'

He had the advantage, dressed and freshly shaven,

and she watched him step from the stool and cross to the edge of the bed. 'How is the bruise?'

She caught hold of the sheet in a compulsive movement, almost as if she expected him to insist on a personal inspection. She flexed her leg. 'It doesn't seem to hurt as much.'

'Want to try another makeshift ice-pack?'

In the clear light of day, she didn't want to be beholden to him in any way. *Too late.* You slept with him, remember? *Sleep* being the operative word...but how much more *beholden* could you get?

'I doubt it's necessary,' Suzanne said quickly. Thinking on her feet seemed a vast improvement to staying in bed, and she managed it in one dignified movement. *Dignity* was the key, she assured herself, and being dressed would be better than wandering around in an over-large tee shirt.

She collected underwear, tailored cream linen trousers and a light cotton top *en route* to the *en suite*, emerging ten minutes later feeling refreshed after a quick shower. And in control. Well, she corrected wryly, as much in control as she could hope for in the circumstances!

Sloane checked his watch. 'It's almost eight. If you're ready, we'll go down to the restaurant.'

Lipstick was all it would take, and perhaps a light touch of blusher. 'Give me a minute.'

Georgia and Trenton were already seated beneath the large airy veranda when Suzanne and Sloane arrived.

'We went for a walk along the beach. It was so

quiet and peaceful. Heaven,' Georgia enthused warmly.

Suzanne caught the sparkle in her mother's eyes, glimpsed the soft curve of her mouth as she smiled, and deduced that while the island possessed a magic all its own, *heaven* to Georgia was the man at her side.

'No pre-wedding nerves?' she queried teasingly as she accepted the waitress's offer to fill her cup with coffee.

'A few,' her mother conceded. 'Last-minute doubts about what I've chosen to wear for the ceremony. Whether my heels are too high, and hoping I'll remember to tread carefully so as not to trip. And whether I should wear the hat the salesgirl insisted was just perfect.' Her mouth shook slightly, then widened into a helpless smile. 'I can't decide whether to wear a bright lipstick or go for something pale.'

Suzanne looked at Trenton and grinned. 'Ah, serious stuff, huh?'

He spread his hands wide and responded with an easy smile. 'My assurance that I don't give a damn what she wears doesn't appear to hold much weight.'

'The mysterious vagaries of the female mind,' Sloane remarked, and met Suzanne's mocking glare with gleaming humour.

'Men,' Suzanne denounced him, 'simply have no idea.' She shot her mother a stunning smile. 'After we finish here, I'll come and give you my considered opinion, shall I?'

'Oh, darling. Please. I'd be so grateful.'

'You can safely say goodbye to a few hours,' Sloane inferred aloud to his father, and Suzanne couldn't suppress the bubble of laughter that emerged from her throat.

'At least.' And was totally unprepared for the brush of his fingers across one cheek, and the warm intimacy of his smile.

'Then I suggest we go eat, so you can get started.'

Why, when she lapsed into a comfort zone, did he do something to jolt her out of it? Her eyes clouded. It's an act, just an act. For Georgia and Trenton's benefit.

The breakfast smorgasbord was a delight, comprising several varieties of cereal, fresh fruit, yoghurt, as well as croissants and toast. Sausages, steak, eggs, hashbrowns, mushrooms. A veritable feast.

It was almost nine when they emerged into the sunshine, and the two men opted to retire to the lounge on the pretext of discussing business, while Suzanne and Georgia made their way to the villa Georgia shared with Trenton.

The design was identical to that of their own villa, although the soft furnishings were different, Suzanne noticed as they entered the air-conditioned interior.

Georgia crossed the lounge. 'Come upstairs, darling.'

Suzanne followed and stood to one side as her mother opened the wardrobe, the drawers, and reverently draped each item of apparel over the bed.

'Let's do the fashion parade thing,' Suzanne suggested, shaking her head as Georgia wrinkled her nose. 'It's the only way I can get the complete picture.'

Fifteen minutes later Suzanne stood back and expressed her admiration. 'Perfect. Everything.'

'Even the hat?'

'Especially the hat,' she assured her mother. 'It's stunning.'

Georgia's eyes moistened with gratitude. 'Do you really think so?'

'Really.'

Suzanne stood still, her head tilted to one side as she regarded the slim, beautiful woman in front of her. 'Now, let's take off the hat, get rid of the shoes, and we'll try each lipstick and decide which one suits best.'

The deep rose, definitely. Pale was too pale, and the coral too bright.

'OK,' Suzanne declared as Georgia carefully divested herself of her wedding suit, and hung it back on padded hangers beneath its protective bag. 'All done.' She grinned, and caught hold of her mother's hands. 'You're going to knock 'em dead.'

A warm smile tugged the edges of Georgia's mouth. 'How nice of you to say so, darling.' She drew a deep breath. 'Now, shall we have a cold drink, and talk girl-talk?' A light laugh spilled out, and her eyes danced. 'Isn't that what the prospective bride and her maid of honour are supposed to do?'

Suzanne fetched a bottle of mineral water from the bar-fridge, poured the contents into two glasses and handed one to her mother.

'Here's to health and happiness. A wonderful day. A wonderful life,' she added gently.

Georgia touched the rim of Suzanne's glass in silent acknowledgement. 'You, too, sweetheart.'

They each took an appreciative sip. 'It'll be nice that we'll be living in the same city,' Georgia said a trifle wistfully. 'I can meet you for lunch. We'll attend a lot of the same functions, too, I imagine. And we'll be able to shop together.'

An arrow of pain pierced Suzanne's stomach. The lunch and the shopping part were fine, but attending the same social functions wouldn't be a good idea. In all probability Sloane would be there, and she would rather die than have to watch him with another woman at his side.

'Tell me where you're staying in Paris.' The honeymoon was a safe topic. 'The shops there are supposed to be marvellous. The Eiffel Tower,' she enthused. 'Make sure you take plenty of photos, and write up a diary. I want to hear everything.'

Georgia laughed. 'Not quite everything, darling.'

Suzanne's eyes danced with impish humour. 'Well, no, I guess not.'

Her mother possessed a rare integrity. And charm. Something that came from the heart. Trenton Wilson-Willoughby was a very fortunate man. But then, she guessed he knew that. It explained why he wanted his ring on Georgia's finger without delay.

'Do you remember when we lived in St Lucia in Brisbane?' Georgia reminisced. 'That adorable little terrace house?'

'And the cat who called both adjoining houses *home*?' Suzanne queried, laughing. 'We fed him mince for breakfast, the man next door gave him fresh fish for lunch, and dear old Mrs Simmons dished out tinned salmon for his tea. He was such a gorgeous bundle of grey fluff.'

The school years, carefree for the most part, with increasing study as she decided on the legal fraternity as her profession. University, law school. Dating. Friends.

Hers had been a happy childhood, despite the lack of a father-figure, and there were many memories to cherish. She and Georgia were so close, *friends* and equals rather than mother and daughter. They had shared so much.

And now it was going to change. Don't go down that path, Suzanne mentally chided herself. Today was meant to be happy, joyous.

CHAPTER SEVEN

THE launch deposited the wedding guests, together with the photographer and celebrant, each of whom had undergone a security check at Dunk Island before boarding the chartered launch to ensure no unwanted media were able to intrude.

Suzanne could only admire Trenton's determination that their weekend sojourn, and particularly the wedding itself, remain a strictly private affair.

There would be time for the guests to check into their respective villas, enjoy a leisurely lunch, and explore Bedarra's facilities before assembling next to the main complex for an outdoor marriage ceremony.

Trenton and Sloane joined the guests in the restaurant for lunch, while Georgia and Suzanne ate a light salad together in Georgia's villa.

It ensured there was plenty of time for them to style their hair, complete their make-up, then dress.

Georgia was ready ahead of time, looking lovely, if slightly nervous. Suzanne gave her mother's hand a reassuring squeeze, then quickly stepped into the elegant pale blue silk slip-dress she'd chosen to wear.

There was a matching jacket and shoes, and she opted to leave her hair loose. Make-up was kept to a minimum, except for skilful application of eyeshadow and mascara, and she selected a clear rose lipstick to add colour.

Then she spared her watch a quick glance. 'This is it.' She cast her mother an impish grin. 'Are you OK?' There was no need to ask if there were any last-minute doubts.

Georgia smiled a trifle shakily. 'In half an hour, I'll be fine.'

Suzanne crossed to tuck a hand beneath her mother's elbow. 'Then let's get this show on the road, shall we?'

The short walk to the main complex was achieved in minutes. Georgia didn't falter as she crossed the lawn to where Sloane stood waiting at the head of a stretch of red carpet dividing three small rows of seated guests and leading to an artistically decorated archway, where Trenton waited with the celebrant.

Suzanne felt her breath catch as Sloane turned towards her with a slow, warm smile, then he took Georgia's hand in his and walked her down the carpeted aisle.

Suzanne followed, and when they reached the archway she moved to Sloane's side as Trenton took hold of Georgia's hand.

Glorious sunshine, the merest hint of a soft breeze, and a small gathering of immediate family and close friends assembled on an idyllic island resort. What more could a bride ask for?

Nothing, if Georgia's radiant expression was anything to go by, Suzanne decided, unable to still a faint stirring of wistful envy.

Her mother looked beautiful, and much younger than her forty-seven years as she stood at Trenton's side while the celebrant intoned the words of the marriage ceremony.

Georgia's response was clear, Trenton's deep and meaningful, and his incredibly gentle kiss at the close of the ceremony tugged Suzanne's heartstrings.

She moved forward to congratulate and hug them both, and the faint shimmer of tears in Georgia's eyes was reflected in her own.

Sloane did the unexpected and kissed Suzanne briefly, but hard, and the pressure of his mouth on hers sent her lashes sweeping wide in silent disapproval.

His answering smile didn't come close in explanation, and she stood at his side, almost *anchored* there as they greeted guests, made social small talk, and accepted the occasional gushing compliment about the happiness of the bride and groom.

The encroaching dusk meant everyone moved indoors, and it was essentially *smile* time. In fact, Suzanne smiled so much and so often, her facial muscles began to ache from sheer effort.

'You're doing well,' Sloane drawled as she took a further sip from her flute of champagne.

'Why, thank you, darling. *Wonderfully* well is what I'm aiming for.'

'And a hair's breadth from overkill.'

She cast him a stunning glance. 'No more than anyone else. Even as we speak, deals are being implemented by two of the country's top business moguls.'

Her eyes sparkled wickedly. 'Their respective second wives are at daggers drawn beneath the soph isticated façade as they size up *who* is wearing the more expensive designer outfit.'

'Second and third wife,' Sloane corrected, and she inclined her head in mocking acceptance.

'Sandrine Lanier and Bettina—?' She arched her eyebrows speculatively. 'Just *who* in Sydney's social élite tied the knot with Bettina?'

He lowered his head and brushed his lips against her temple. 'Cynicism doesn't suit you.'

'Ah, but given the right context it can be fun,' she declared solemnly.

'Sandrine works very hard at being the successful wife.'

It was true. The former actress was delightful, and devoted herself tirelessly to charitable causes. She was also an excellent hostess who enjoyed entertaining her husband's business associates. Michel Lanier was a very fortunate man.

Bettina, however, fell into an entirely different category. The glamorous blonde had frequented every social event Suzanne had attended with Sloane. And had taken great pleasure in flirting with him outrageously at every opportunity. As well as with every wealthy eligible man on the social circuit in a bid to cover her options.

'Just who did Bettina choose?' There could be no doubt on that issue!

'Frank Kahler. They married two weeks ago.'

She didn't need to ask. 'You attended the wedding.'

'Yes.' Sloane's acquiescence held a certain wryness for the occasion that had been far too over the top to be described as being in good taste.

What excuse had he given for her absence?

'You were visiting your mother in Brisbane for the weekend.'

Suzanne looked at him, and glimpsed the fine lines fanning out from the corners of his eyes, then her gaze travelled to the vertical crease slashing each cheek, the wide, sensual mouth, and the strong set of his jaw.

'Feasible, in the circumstances, wouldn't you say?'

Very feasible, she silently agreed. 'You could easily have admitted our relationship was over.'

'Now why would I do that?'

'Because it was. *Is.*'

'No.'

'What do you mean, *no*?'

He leaned forward and brushed his lips against her own, and then he raised his head fractionally. His eyes were dark, and appeared so incredibly deep she became momentarily lost.

Her heart thudded in her chest, and for a split second she forgot to breathe. Then reality kicked in, and she took in a deep, ragged breath, then shakily released it.

'Did you honestly think I'd let it rest on the basis of the explanation you presented to me?' Sloane queried, and saw her eyes dilate with something akin to apprehension, then be replaced with an attempt at humour.

'Impossible, of course, that I might have had a

hissy fit about the number of women who fawn over you, and acted on impulse?'

His lips parted to show even white teeth behind an amused smile. 'A hissy fit?' The edge of his mouth curved. 'Now that's an expression which conjures up an interesting image.'

'Doesn't it just?'

His eyes became even darker, and something moved deep within. Something she dared not define. 'Not your style, Suzanne.'

No, it wasn't. Nor did she act on impulse.

'Nor was your note,' Sloane continued in a dangerously mild voice.

'You *know* why I left,' she said fiercely.

'*Whatever* the motivation, the action was all wrong.'

'Sloane. Suzanne. We need you for photographs.' Trenton's voice intruded, and Suzanne drew a deep breath and collected her scattered thoughts as they moved across the room to the position the photographer indicated.

The man was a hired professional, and aware of the scoop his work would create. He wanted the best shots.

It took a while. The eye of the camera was very perceptive, and Suzanne should, she felt, have earned an award for her performance in playing the loving fiancée of the bride's stepson. Not to mention the groom's son.

Afterwards trays of exquisitely presented hors d'oeuvre were proffered and the champagne flowed like water. Background music from a selection of CDs filtered from strategically placed speakers as the guests mixed and mingled.

'Sloane, so *nice* to see you again.'

Suzanne turned at the sound of a breathy feminine voice, and summoned a stunning smile for the second—no, *third* wife of one of Trenton's friends.

'Bettina,' Sloane acknowledged her. 'You've met Suzanne?'

Bettina's laugh was the closest thing to a tinkling bell that Suzanne had ever heard. 'Of course, darling.'

Kittenish, Suzanne decided. Definitely cultivated kitten. The short, tight shell-pink skirt, the almost-too-tight matching camisole top covered by a designer jacket one size too small. Her hair and make-up were perfection, her lacquered nails a work of art, and the jewellery she wore just had to be worth a small fortune. Bored, and with an inclination to flirt.

'Such a cute idea to have an island wedding.' She touched careless fingers to Sloane's sleeve and deliberately fluttered her lashes. 'You will save a dance for me, won't you?' The *moue* was contrived. 'Frank isn't the partying type.'

Frank Kahler was a substantial catch, Suzanne mused, and felt a pang of sympathy for the much older entrepreneur whose fame and fortune were Bettina's main attraction.

'I doubt Suzanne would be willing to share,' Sloane responded with a musing smile.

'Oh, *darling*, of course you must dance with Bettina,' she said in mild reproach, and her eyes shimmered with simmering sensuality. 'After all, I'm the one who gets to take you home.'

He caught hold of her hand and lifted it to his lips, then kissed each finger in turn. 'Indeed,' he intoned softly.

Oh, my, he was good. She could almost believe he meant it. Then she came to her senses, and she smiled, aware that *her* acting ability was on a par with his own.

'I think I'll have some more champagne.' Bettina cast Sloane an arch look from beneath artificially curled lashes. 'You'll fetch another for me, won't you?'

Interesting, Suzanne decided, that Bettina should use such a well-used ploy. Sloane's eyes gleamed in silent recognition, and Suzanne derived a certain pleasure from handing him her flute. 'I think I'll join Bettina. Thank you, *darling*.' The emphasis was very slight, but there nonetheless.

'He's a hunk, isn't he?' Bettina sighed as Sloane turned and began threading his way to the bar.

And then some. 'Yes,' Suzanne agreed, waiting for the moment Bettina would slip in the knife.

'Sloane came alone to my wedding. Were you sick, or something, darling?' A dimple appeared in one cheek, although there was no humour apparent in Bettina's expression. 'For a moment there, I thought you were no longer an item.'

Suzanne hated fabrication, but she refused to give Bettina any satisfaction by differing her story from the one Sloane had provided. 'I was in Brisbane visiting Georgia.'

'Quite a coup.' The almost-green eyes hardened and her expression became brittle. 'Mother and daughter snaring both father and son.'

'Yes, isn't it?' Suzanne's smile was in place, and she appeared perfectly at ease.

'You must have worked very hard.'

'Impossible, of course,' Suzanne said with the utmost charm, 'that Trenton and Georgia could have fallen genuinely in love?'

'Oh, really, Suzanne. No one falls *in love* with a wealthy man. Steering them into marriage involves an extremely delicate strategy.'

'Of the manipulative kind?' There were no rules in this game, and, as loath as she was to play it, she was damned if she'd allow Bettina a victory. 'Is that how you snared Frank?'

'I cater to his needs.'

Suzanne deserved an award for her performance as she touched a finger to the diamond-encrusted watch fastened on Bettina's wrist. 'Catering obviously pays well. Perhaps I should try it.'

'What,' a familiar deep voice drawled, 'should you try?'

Suzanne turned slightly and met Sloane's indolent gaze. She accepted a flute of champagne and watched as he handed another to Bettina.

'Bettina and I were discussing catering to our men's needs.' Her eyes sparkled with deliberate guile. 'My car has been playing up lately, darling. I rather fancy a Porsche Carrera. Black.' Her mouth widened into a beautiful pout as she lifted a finger to her lips, licked it suggestively, then placed it against the centre of his lower lip. 'Perhaps we could negotiate—later?'

Sensation spiralled from her central core as he nipped her finger, then drew it into his mouth and swirled the tip with his tongue before releasing it.

His eyes were dark, gleaming depths reflecting desire and thinly disguised passion. 'I'm sure we can reach an agreeable compromise.'

Are you mad? a tiny voice taunted. Don't you know you're playing with *fire*?

'One imagines you intend tying the knot *soon*?'

'Trenton and Georgia's arrangements have taken precedence over our own,' Sloane informed Bettina smoothly, and incurred her tinkling laugh.

'Don't wait *too* long, darling. There's quite a few who would be happy to push Suzanne out of the way.'

Suzanne saw Sloane's eyes narrow slightly, sensed the predatory stillness, and felt all her muscles tense.

'Should that happen, they'd have me to deal with.' His voice was ominously soft, and intensely dangerous.

Bettina's light laugh held a slight note of incredulity. '*Figuratively* speaking. Not literally, for heaven's sake.'

Sloane's expression didn't change. 'I'm relieved to hear it.' His eyes hardened measurably. 'Any threat, impulsive or premeditated, is something I'd take very seriously.'

His meaning was unmistakable, and Bettina blinked rather rapidly.

'Well, of *course*.' She sipped her champagne, then offered a brilliant smile. 'If you'll excuse me, I really should get back to Frank.'

'Wasn't that just a bit too menacing?'

His eyes were still hard when they swept over Suzanne's features. 'No.'

She opened her mouth, only to have it pressed closed by his in a brief, hard kiss.

'Don't argue.'

Mixing and mingling was a social art form, and Sloane did it extremely well, slowly circulating between guests as he enquired about various family members, listened to an amusing anecdote or two, and shared a few reminiscences.

Dinner was served at seven. Tables in the restaurant had been assembled to ensure the bridal party of four were easily visible to the guests, and the food, comprising several courses, was superb.

There were two speeches: one which Sloane delivered welcoming Georgia into the family, and the other a response from Trenton.

The wedding cake was an exquisite work of art, with intricately iced orchids so incredibly lifelike that one almost wanted to touch a petal to see if it was authentic.

When it was cut, sliced and handed to each guest, Sloane bit into his before feeding some of it to Suzanne in a sensual display she opted to return, for the benefit of their audience. Or so she told herself, for there was a part of her that wished it were real.

The kiss was something else. Evocative and incredibly thorough; there was absolutely nothing she could do about it without causing a stir.

When he lifted his head she could only look at him with a measure of reflected hurt, and just for a second she thought she glimpsed regret beneath the gleaming purpose, then it was gone.

The music changed and Trenton led Georgia onto the floor to dance.

'We'll follow suit,' Sloane indicated, rising to his feet and catching her hand in his.

Now *this*…this was dangerous, she mused as she moved into his arms. It was like coming home. Heaven. Her body fitted his with intimate familiarity, and she felt it quiver in recognition of something beyond which she had little control.

Sexuality. Heightened sensuality. Potent alchemy. If love was like a river, then theirs ran deep. And fast.

She was acutely aware of her own response and, held close like this, she found it impossible to ignore the evidence of desire in his.

It was all she could do not to link her hands together at his nape, and her eyes held bemusement as his lips trailed to one temple.

Suzanne heard her mother's soft laugh, and Sloane's hold loosened as each couple came to a brief halt in order to switch partners.

'It's a beautiful wedding,' Suzanne commented as

Trenton led her into another waltz. Other guests began to join them on the floor.

'Georgia is a beautiful woman. On the inside, where it counts,' he said gently. 'As you are.'

It was a lovely compliment. 'Thank you.'

'I can promise to take good care of her.'

'I know.' It was nothing less than the truth. 'Just as I know you'll both be very happy together.'

They circled the floor again, then Sloane effected the change. Five minutes later another guest cut in, and during the ensuing hour Suzanne danced with almost every man in the room.

Bettina manoeuvred things very skilfully so that she got to dance with Sloane. Suzanne saw each move the glamorous blonde made, and had to commend her tactics.

To anyone else in the room Bettina looked a vivacious guest, and their fleeting attention would have admired the practised smile, the faint flutter of perfectly manicured lacquered nails.

Suzanne, whose examination was much more precise, saw the subtle promise in Bettina's almost-green eyes, the apparent accidental brush of her generous and silicone-enhanced breasts, the inviting part of those perfectly painted lips, and had to still the desire to tear Bettina's eyes out.

Three minutes, four? They each seemed to acquire a tremendous magnitude before Sloane executed a change in partners and drew Suzanne close.

She held herself stiffly within the circle of his arms,

and she moved her head slightly so that his lips brushed her ear and not her cheek as he intended.

'Bettina,' Sloane drawled with stunning accuracy.

'You're *so* perceptive.'

'It's an inherent trait,' he declared musingly. 'Do you know you quiver when you're angry?'

Quiver? 'Really?' She wanted to hit him.

'Which one of us did you want to tear limb from limb?'

'Bettina,' she declared with soft vehemence, and heard his husky chuckle.

'Claws, when there's absolutely no need?'

'Careful,' Suzanne warned. 'I haven't sheathed them yet.'

She leaned into him a little, and heard the strong beat of his heart, felt the strength of his body, and enjoyed the moment for as long as the slow music lasted. Then she joined Georgia and Trenton for a few minutes before slipping to the powder-room to freshen up.

When she returned most of the couples had drifted off the floor to sit in groups at various tables. Sloane was deep in conversation with Bettina's husband, Frank, and Suzanne made her way out onto the terrace where a breeze teased its way in from the ocean.

At this time of year the tropical far north was close to perfection. Lovely sunny days, cool clear nights, and little or no rain. Ideal for those who lived in southern states where winter tended to be cold and wet with winds that gusted round corners and buffeted buildings.

In two days Georgia would fly to Paris. The city for lovers, with its historic buildings and magnificent art collections. Haute couture, food, the total ambience. She'd read about it, viewed the travel documentaries on film, and felt vaguely envious.

No, that wasn't strictly true. There were always goals in life, some achievable, others merely dreams. The aim was to strive for the dream, but not lose sight of the reality.

There was also avarice and greed, which she deplored, along with artificial superficiality. And those who sought and fought for it. Love had been destroyed, lives wrecked, even lost, in pursuit of an abundance of wealth and all it could provide.

A slight shiver shook her slim frame. She'd tasted it, felt the fear and opted to remove herself from its orbit. Had she been right to handle it herself? The doubts, ever present, rose to the surface.

'Voluntary solitude, or an escape?'

Suzanne straightened at the sound of Sloane's drawled query, and she didn't move as he slid his arms round her waist and drew her back against him.

'A little of both,' she answered honestly.

'Want to share?'

Her eyes sprang open at that quietly voiced query. Share her innermost thoughts? That would give the *danger* a new dimension.

'I'll take a rain check.'

She felt his chin rest down on top of her head. 'You realise I'll call it in?'

Yes, he would. But not now. 'Perhaps we should go inside.'

'I came out to find you,' Sloane said. 'Trenton and Georgia intend to retire soon.'

'Leaving the guests to party on?' Was it that late?

'It's almost midnight.'

Where had the evening gone? 'Time flies when you're having fun,' she said lightly, and felt her stomach curl as Sloane moved one hand towards her breast while the other splayed across her hip.

They were, she knew, visible to the guests inside. 'Don't. Please,' she added quietly.

'Then come indoors, and bid our respective parents goodnight.'

Out of the way of temptation. But not for long. Sooner or later they'd return to their villa. What then? She couldn't afford the ecstasy of one long night of loving, or the resulting agony when she had to leave him.

Without a word she slipped free of his hold and led the way indoors.

'Oh, there you are, darling,' Georgia said warmly. 'Trenton and I are about to leave.' She leant forward and gave her daughter a fond hug. 'It's been a splendid party, hasn't it?'

'Really lovely,' Suzanne agreed as she caught hold of her mother's hands.

'Most of the guests are meeting around nine for a champagne breakfast. You'll join us, of course.'

'Of course, Mama.'

'Now we're going to get out of here,' Trenton declared as he bestowed upon his new wife a look of passionate warmth.

Georgia's eyes held a delightful sparkle, and her cheeks bore the faintest tinge of colour.

Trenton took care of their escape by simply declaring, 'Goodnight,' and led Georgia from the restaurant.

'Would you like me to get you some coffee?' Sloane queried.

'Please,' Suzanne replied, and within seconds of his return they were joined by Bettina, which, Suzanne decided, was stretching coincidence a bit far.

'Frank doesn't want to stay and party on. We thought we might go for a walk along the beach. Maybe go for a swim. Want to join us?'

And watch Bettina strip down to nothing and display those voluptuous curves, cavort in the moonlight and attempt to capture more than one man's attention?

'Thanks, but no.' Sloane tempered the refusal with a quizzical smile, then cast Suzanne a dark, gleaming look. 'We have other plans.'

'A party?'

'For two,' he responded evenly. He took Suzanne's cup and saucer and deposited them down onto a nearby table, then he caught hold of her hand. 'If you'll excuse us?'

'We should,' Suzanne admonished mildly, 'say goodnight to the guests.'

'We shall. Very briefly.'

'And have them speculate why we're in such a hurry to leave?'

'Do you want to stay?'

Not really. But she wasn't sure she wanted to go back to the villa, either. Nor did she want to walk along the beach and encounter Bettina.

'No.'

Ten minutes later Sloane unlocked their door, then closed it behind them. Suzanne watched as he shrugged off his suit jacket and draped it over a nearby chair, tugged free his tie and loosened the top two buttons of his shirt.

Then he crossed to the bar-fridge, extracted a magnum of champagne, opened it, filled two flutes, then handed her one. He touched the rim of her flute with his own, then lifted it in silent salute before sipping the contents.

Suzanne was acutely aware of him, and the raw, primitive chemistry that was his alone. There was a brooding sensuality apparent that fired a deep answering need inside her.

She could almost *feel* the blood move more quickly through her veins, the fine hairs on her skin rise as sensitised nerve-ends came alive, and slow heat radiated throughout her whole body.

Imagining how it would be with him almost brought her to a state of climax. Three weeks seemed an eternity, each night apart so long and lonely she'd lain awake aching in solitary pain.

CHAPTER EIGHT

SLOANE glimpsed the faint fleeting shadows, determined their cause, and fought the urge to sweep Suzanne into his arms. The sex would be a wonderful release…for both of them. Wild, wanton, and uninhibited. He could almost smell the bloom of sensual heat on her skin, taste her exotic scent. The thought of sinking into her, hearing the soft purr in her voice change to something deep and driven, the cries of ecstasy as he took her with him…

'It was a lovely wedding.' She had the feeling she'd already said those words, and fought to keep the wistfulness out of her voice, the awkward hesitancy. Dammit, it must be the champagne's eroding effect on her self confidence. Warm and fuzzy wasn't a feeling she wanted to cultivate. 'Georgia looked radiant.'

'Yes, she did.'

'And Trenton—'

'Wouldn't allow anything or anyone to interfere with their plans,' Sloane interceded. He was silent for a few long seconds, and when he spoke his voice held an inflexible edge. 'Any more than I will.'

There was something in his eyes, the powerful set of his features that triggered alarm bells in her brain.

She regarded him carefully, apprehension upper-

130

most as it merged with sickening knowledge. 'You've discovered who she is, haven't you?'

His expression hardened, muscles sculpting broad facial bones into a daunting mask. 'Yes. I had the answer I needed this morning.'

Suzanne didn't have to ask *how*. He had the power and the contacts to elicit any information he wanted. It was impossible to believe that he wouldn't take action. 'What are you going to do?'

'It's already done. Zoe's father is now aware of the facts. And extremely grateful we've chosen not to prosecute. He will personally ensure she seeks professional help.'

Her eyes searched his, and she almost died at the ruthlessness apparent. There was something else she couldn't define, and it frightened her.

'No one,' Sloane intoned with brutal mercilessness, 'threatens me. Directly, or indirectly.' He kept his anger under tight rein. The e-mail report had listed extensive repairs to her car. He could only imagine the verbal assault.

Suzanne saw his clenched fists, evidenced the cold fury in those dark eyes, and placed her partly empty flute onto a nearby pedestal.

She needed to get out of this room, away from him, even if it was only briefly. 'I'm going for a walk.'

'Not alone.'

She tilted her head to look at him, uncaring that the conversation had taken a dangerous shift. 'Don't play the heavy, Sloane.' She walked across the room to the door, her anger so intense she knew she'd *hit* him if he tried to stop her.

Outside the darkness seemed like a shroud, and she followed the lit path down to the beach. When she reached the sand she stepped out of her heeled shoes and bent to collect them in one hand.

Sloane was a short distance behind her, and it was all she could do not to throw something at him. If he wanted to follow her, he could. But she was damned if she'd allow him to dictate her actions, or when she'd return to the villa. *If* she returned, she decided darkly. There were plenty of beach loungers that would make an adequate place to rest for what remained of the night.

The moonlight bathed the beach with an eerie glow, and she trod the crunchy sand to the water's edge, then followed its curve towards the outcrop of rocks.

The tide eddied and flowed at her feet, and on impulse she paused, shed her clothes and dropped them onto dry sand, then turned and walked into the sea.

The water felt silky and wonderfully cool against her skin, and when it reached her waist she eased into a lazy breast-stroke parallel to the shore. Then she turned onto her back and floated, idly counting the sprinkle of stars.

A faint splash alerted her bare seconds before Sloane's dark head appeared less than a metre away.

He didn't say a word, didn't need to, and she moved away from him and rose to her feet. If he was intent on invading her space, then she'd simply shift it somewhere else!

She had only taken two steps towards the shore when hard hands grasped hold of her shoulders and turned her back to face him. 'Let me—'

Anything else she might have said remained locked in her throat as his mouth closed over hers in a kiss that *possessed*...mind, body and soul.

She tried to struggle, and got nowhere. Dear Lord, he was strong. If she could only bite him...but his jaw had possession of her own, dictating its movements as he ravaged the inner tissues with his tongue, his teeth, in a deliberate assault on her senses.

One hand curved down to cup her bottom, while the other held fast her head. She pummelled his back with her fists, and attempted to kick his shin...with totally ineffectual results.

Just when she thought she couldn't bear any more, he loosened his hold, only to change it as he hefted her over one shoulder and walked out of the sea onto the sand.

'What in *hell* do you think you're doing?'

He bent down and she automatically clutched the back of his waist. And found no purchase.

'Collecting our clothes.'

'Put me down!'

He stood upright, adjusted his hold of her, then calmly strode towards the path. 'No.'

'For heaven's sake,' Suzanne hissed. 'Someone might see us.'

'I don't give a damn.'

'At least give me your shirt.' The request came out as a hollow groan.

'I happen to be holding it in front of a vulnerable part of my anatomy,' he responded drily.

'You'd better pray we make it undetected,' she threatened direly. 'Or I'll never forgive you.'

The path to their villa was reasonably short, but Suzanne was conscious of every step Sloane took until they were safely indoors.

'You fiend! How *dare* you?' She pummelled his back with her fists, and attempted to kick him. 'Put me *down*.'

He kept walking, ascended the steps to the bedroom, paused long enough to toss their clothes onto the bed, then he crossed into the *en suite* and turned on the shower.

'What in sweet hell do you think you're doing?'

'Precisely what it looks like.' He stepped into the shower stall and closed the glass sliding door. Then he pulled her down to stand in front of him.

Without thought she lifted a hand and slapped his jaw. Anger, sheer helpless rage, exuded from every pore, and when she lifted her hand a second time he caught it mid-air in a punishing grip.

'You want to fight, Suzanne?'

'*Yes*, damn you!'

'Then go ahead.' He released her hand and stood still, his arms folded across his chest.

His eyes gleamed darkly, silently daring her to thwart him, and she lashed out, both fists flailing as she connected with his chest, his shoulders, anywhere she could land a punch.

He took each and every one, and only grunted once.

Hot, angry tears filled her eyes, then spilled to run in twin rivulets down to her chin. Her knuckles hurt from where she'd struck strong muscle and sinew. And bone. He didn't move, and her arms slowed, then dropped to her sides.

'Are you done?'

The water lashed his shoulders and coursed down his back, and she turned blindly towards the glass door, only to halt as he prevented her escape.

Without a word he pulled her into his arms, effectively stilling any further struggle.

'Let me go.' To stay like this was madness.

Fingers splayed across the base of her spine began a subtle movement, sufficient to make her breath catch, and she tried to pull away from him without success.

The hand that held her nape slid to capture her head, tilting it so she had no defence against his descending mouth.

She expected a devastating invasion, and was unprepared for the soft slide of his tongue against her own. Teasing, tantalising, he made it a sensual assault as he explored and caressed, encouraging her response in a manner that soon left her weak-willed and malleable.

Uncaring of the consequences, she lifted her arms and twined them round his neck, melting into him as she kissed him back. Slowly, tentatively, then with an increasing urgency that left both of them labouring for breath.

'Please.' *Now.* She didn't think she could wait a

second longer, and an exultant laugh broke free from her throat as he parted her thighs and lifted her high to straddle his waist.

With one supple action he buried himself inside her, and she gloried in the hard, deep thrust that stretched silken tissues to a level where she gasped at his degree of penetration.

For several seconds he remained still, then he began to move, slowly at first, each thrust deeper than the last as he increased the pace until their actions became a synchronised match leading to an explosive climax.

Suzanne had thought she'd experienced every facet of his lovemaking, but this had held a wild quality, almost unbridled, as if he was barely retaining a hold on his emotions.

She could only bury her head against his neck as he cradled her close, his lips warm and evocative as they traced a path across one exposed cheek.

How long they stood like that, she had no idea. Long seconds, *minutes* maybe. Eventually her breathing steadied, and with infinite care he set her down onto her feet.

Then he reached for the soap and slowly lathered every inch of her body before turning his attention to his own.

Suzanne felt as if she wasn't capable of moving, much less uttering a single word, and when he switched off the water she stepped out from the shower stall and caught up a towel, only to have him take it from her to blot their skin free of moisture.

Not once did his eyes leave hers, and she became

lost in the darkness, every cell flaring brilliantly *alive* in the knowledge of what would follow.

She wanted him. Dear heaven, so much. But what about afterwards? How could she board the launch on Monday and return to Sydney, her own apartment, and attempt to get on with her life as if this weekend had never happened?

It would be a living nightmare of unfulfilled needing, wanting…*empty*. She doubted if she could survive.

'Sloane—' She couldn't say the words, and she lifted a hand then let it fall helplessly down to her side.

He brushed gentle fingers against her cheek, then let them drift to trace the pulsing cord at her neck.

She was melting inside, subsiding into a state of sensual inertia where all she wanted was for him to continue until the slow warmth heated to white-hot fire.

He knew. She could see it in his eyes, feel it in his touch as his hand slid to her breast and caressed the soft contours before wreaking havoc with the sensitive peak.

His head lowered and his mouth closed over hers in a deep evocative kiss that tore what little defences she had left to shreds. His mouth left hers and followed a sensual path to her breast, savouring, suckling on the tender nub as she arched her neck in silent invitation.

One night, she groaned silently. Just one night.

Her hands reached for him, the movement compulsive as she began exploring tight muscle and sinew, touching, tasting, and wanting more. So much more.

The blood flowed through her veins like quicksilver, feeding every nerve-cell until her whole body ached with need. Sensual heat at its zenith.

Sloane carried her into the bedroom and sank down with her onto the bed. She looked magnificent, her eyes deep blue crystalline, her soft mouth slightly swollen and parted from his kiss. There was a faint sheen on her skin, and her hair hung in tousled disarray.

She leaned forward and initiated a deep kiss, enjoying the feeling of power as he allowed her free rein. Then in one smooth movement she arched her body and took him deep inside, gasping faintly as she felt inner tissues stretch to accommodate him.

Dear God, he felt good. *This* was so good, the feeling of completeness, the joining of two bodies in perfect accord. Sensation spiralled, and she began to move, creating a deep penetrating rhythm as old as time.

His hands reached for her waist, and he joined in the ride, taking her higher and higher until she cried out her release.

Slowly she raised her head and looked down at him, met the dark, slumberous depths and defined the degree of passion evident.

Extending a hand, she touched a gentle finger to his lower lip and traced its outline, then slid it down his chin to his throat, trailing a central line past his chest, his stomach, to where they were still joined, before travelling a similar path to her own mouth.

Slow, sweet warmth swirled deep within, heating her body, and she gave a soft laugh as his hands reached up to bring her head down to his.

This time there was no gentleness in his kiss. It became a foray that was claim-staking, possession at its most damnable as she met and matched the dramatic primitiveness that lay deep within him.

It transcended mere sexual gratification. It was much more than sensual satiation.

A faint groan emerged from her throat as he shifted position and rolled so that she lay on her back.

The control was his, and she wrapped her legs round his hips and pulled him down to her, glorying in his strength.

Afterwards she could only lie still, unable to move as he let his fingers drift idly over the softness of her skin.

She must have slept, for she came awake to the touch of his lips exploring the delicate contours of her body, tasting the spent bloom on her skin as he trailed lower to savour the intimate heart of her.

A banked flame flared into pulsating life, licking through her veins, igniting nerve-ends as she came achingly alive. Consummate skill took her high and tipped her over the edge, and she cried out as she fell.

Afterwards she pleasured him, exulting in the faint sheen of sweat that heated his skin, the quivering muscles of his stomach, the way his breath caught in his throat.

For much of what remained of the night, they indulged in lovemaking, creating a sensual ecstasy that was alternately wild and untamed and slow and evocative.

Suzanne didn't want the magic to end. With the dawn came sleep, and afterwards a long, lingering loving that was so incredibly gentle it made her want to weep.

'We should shower and go down to breakfast,' she said reluctantly as she swept a glance to the digital radio clock.

Sloane's eyes held a mocking gleam that didn't fool her in the slightest. 'Should we?'

'I think so.'

He touched her mouth with his own, savoured its inner sweetness, then trailed soft kisses along the softly swollen contours of her lower lip. 'Why is that?'

Assertiveness was the key. Definitely. For to stay here any longer would be a madness she could ill afford. 'Because I'm hungry.' His eyes became dark and slumberous. 'For food. Sustenance,' she elaborated with an impish grin. 'And I'd almost kill for a cup of strong coffee.' She slid to her feet, stretched her arms high…and felt the pull of muscles. 'I'll hit the shower first.' She directed him a faintly wry glance. 'Alone. Otherwise we'll never get out of here.'

He reached out a hand and pulled her back down to him for a brief, hard kiss, then he let her go. 'Five minutes, then I join you.'

It was almost nine when they entered the restaurant, and Suzanne chose a table on the terrace, ordered coffee, then helped herself to a selection of fresh fruit and cereal from the smorgasbord.

'You're looking rather fragile this morning, darling. Had a hard night?'

She turned and met Bettina's deliberately guileless smile, and proffered one of her own. 'Surely that's rather a personal question?'

'Why pretend? I have my eye on a magnificent emerald and diamond ring.' Her eyes glittered acquisitively. 'Frank needs a little persuasion to buy it for me.'

'Which you have every intention of providing.'

'Why, of course. Women have traded sexual favours for gifts since—*forever*.' Bettina's lashes swept wide. 'Aren't you working hard to persuade Sloane to buy you a Porsche Carrera?'

'*Repaying* me will become a lifetime commitment.'

Suzanne turned at the sound of Sloane's drawling voice, caught his faintly wry, musing smile, glimpsed the dark gleam in his eyes, and opted to respond in kind.

'Not necessarily. My tastes are simple.'

'So are mine,' he said solemnly. '*You.*'

Her pulse tripped and raced to a faster beat. He saw the evidence of it in the hollow at the base of her throat, the dilation of those sapphire depths, the soft parting of her lips.

'The Porsche was meant to be a joke,' she said as she carried her plate back to their table.

'I know.'

'If you gave me one,' she declared fiercely, 'I'd hand it straight back.'

Sloane sank into his chair and ordered fresh coffee. 'I do believe you would.'

'Sloane—'

'You think I don't know Bettina enjoys making mischief?' His dry, mocking tone was matched by a hardness in his eyes.

She was all too aware of the tensile steel beneath the sophisticated veneer. Only a fool would believe he wasn't aware of every angle, and adept in determining the foibles of human nature.

'She has her eye on you.'

His soft laughter brought a fiery sparkle to her eyes. 'Bettina needs confirmation of her attraction to the opposite sex. Her choice of clothes, make-up, jewellery is a blatant attempt at attention-seeking.' His expression assumed a degree of cynicism. 'Any man will do.'

'I disagree,' Suzanne declared as she reached for her coffee. 'That should amend to any well-connected, wealthy man.' She lifted her cup, took an appreciative sip, then replaced it back on its saucer and cast him a wry look. 'And you're more sought after than most.'

'But spoken for,' Sloane asserted tolerantly.

'"A hunk" were her exact words,' she continued as if he hadn't spoken.

'Really?'

He was amused, damn him. 'Definitely *mistress* material.'

'Now why,' he drawled lazily, 'would I covet a mistress, when I have you?'

Suzanne took the time to spear a segment of fresh fruit, which she savoured, then slowly chewed and swallowed, before voicing a response. She chose her words with care, and tempered them with a faint smile. 'You don't *have* me.'

He placed his fork down carefully on his plate, then leant back in his chair, looking, she decided, indolently relaxed and not poised to deliver a verbal sally. 'I retain a particularly vivid memory of how we spent the night.' His dark brown eyes held gleaming humour. 'And the early dawn hours.'

So did she. So much so that it was all she could do to contain the stain of colour spreading high on each cheek. 'I don't think that's entirely relevant.'

She saw one eyebrow lift to form a mocking arch. 'No? I beg to disagree.'

'It was just sex.' Albeit very good sex, she acknowledged silently. And knew she lied. *Sex* didn't even begin to describe what they'd shared.

'I think I should take you back to bed,' Sloane drawled with musing mockery. 'It's the one place where we're in perfect accord.'

She captured another portion of fruit with her fork. 'Our absence would be noticed.'

His regard was warm and infinitely sensual. 'I fail to see that as a problem.'

'You possess a one-track mind,' she admonished him, and reached for her coffee once more.

'Three weeks' abstinence tends to have that effect on a man.'

Not only a man. Even thinking about what they'd shared through much of the night was enough to flood her veins with telling warmth.

The damnable thing was that he knew. The knowledge was apparent in the way his eyes lingered on her mouth, then slid slowly to the heavily beating pulse at the edge of her neck, the slight thrust of each breast.

'I think,' she began, hating the faint raggedness in her voice, 'I've had enough to eat.'

'Georgia and Trenton have just arrived,' Sloane advised quietly, 'and indicated they'll join us.'

The meal became a leisurely affair with the connotation of a champagne brunch as the champagne flowed and staff provided a selection of finger food.

'Tennis this afternoon, definitely,' Georgia declared as she sipped a second cup of black coffee. 'And I think I'll just have fruit for lunch, or forgo it altogether.'

'Likewise.' Followed by a swim, and a nap on the beach, Suzanne decided. A lazily spent afternoon was just what she needed. After last night.

An arrow of pain pierced her body. What of tonight? Would Sloane…? Yes, a silent voice taunted. Of course he will. How would she survive another night of loving without breaking into a thousand pieces? Perhaps if she explained, maybe pleaded with him…

She spared him a quick glance, and then wished she hadn't. His gaze was focused on her features, reading each and every fleeting expression…with damning accuracy, unless she was mistaken.

Did anyone else guess she was a mass of nervous tension beneath the composed exterior? After last night the boundaries she'd imposed had been moved, and she was unsure of their position.

What would happen when she returned to Sydney? *No*, don't think about it, she told herself. *Thinking* wasn't a good idea, for there were just two scenarios. Neither of which she wanted to explore right now.

Her stomach executed a series of painful somersaults, and she forcibly controlled her breathing into a steady, regulated rise and fall. Her heart felt heavy in her chest, and she was sure her contribution to the conversation sounded terribly inane.

In a way it was a relief to circulate among the guests, to lose herself, even briefly, in a social exchange with women whose main topics of conversation seemed to be whose hairdresser was the best, which fashion designer would take out the annual award, and whose parties on the social circuit were *de rigueur* for the remainder of the winter season.

Sloane seemed similarly immersed with Trenton's, and doubtless his own, associates. Twice she glanced in his direction only to have him meet her gaze.

'No hint of a date yet, Suzanne?' one woman asked, while another ventured,

'Paul and I have a very tight schedule until Christmas. Get those invitations out early, darling.'

'You *must* visit Stefano; he'll do wonders with your

hair,' an elegant brunette assured Suzanne, and a glossy dark-haired sylph advised,

'Marie-Louise is without equal for the nails.'

'Gianfranco,' the stylish redhead insisted. 'You must see him about your dress, darling. Tell him Claudia sent you.'

'Of course, there is only O'Neil for the flowers.'

'Frank spent almost a million on my reception,' Bettina offered, and didn't notice the electric silence that followed her announcement.

Suzanne sensed their momentary withdrawal, and their disapproval. Any mention of actual amounts of money among the upper social echelon was *de trop*. One could mention the yacht, the villa in France, the apartment in Venice, Rome or Milan. The Swiss chalet, the New York Fifth Avenue apartment, the London Knightsbridge town house or the mansion in Surrey. *Anything*, except how much it cost. Unless it was an outrageous bargain. Delusions of grandeur were not entertained among society's élite.

It was almost eleven when the guests departed to board the launch that would transfer them to Dunk Island to connect with their flight south.

Suzanne and Sloane joined Georgia and Trenton on the jetty to see them off.

CHAPTER NINE

'Now I can relax.' Georgia wound an arm round Trenton's waist and leaned in against him. 'It's been a wonderful weekend. Thank you, darling.'

The look he directed at her mother brought a lump to Suzanne's throat. So much love, so clearly visible. It made her heart ache. 'I don't think I could eat or drink a thing,' she declared lightly. 'I'm going to take a book down onto the beach, then go for a dip in the ocean.'

'We'll meet for tennis,' Trenton indicated. 'Four o'clock, OK?'

'You could,' Sloane drawled minutes later as they entered their villa, 'relax here.'

Suzanne twisted her head to look at him. 'Uh-uh. I don't think our ideas of *relaxation* match.' She ran quickly up the steps to the bedroom and extracted a black bikini.

'Afraid to be alone with me?'

He posed a tremendous threat to her equilibrium, but *fear* had no part in it. 'No.'

Sloane crossed to her side and placed his hands at the base of her nape, initiating a soothing massage that felt so good…too damned good. 'Tired?'

She wanted to close her eyes and sink back against him, have him hold her, kiss her. Slow, oh, so slowly.

If she gave in to such feelings, they'd never get out of the villa before nightfall.

'A little.'

'Let me indulge you,' he commanded quietly.

Need curled deep inside her, then twisted into a spiral that radiated through her body. Her smile was incredibly sad, and tinged with regret. 'I don't think that's such a good idea.'

His breath feathered her temple. 'No?'

His fingers skimmed beneath the hair at her nape, lifting it aside as he traced his lips down to the sensitive spot behind one ear, savoured it, then trailed the pulsing cord to the edge of her neck.

'Sloane.' The protest fell from her lips in scarcely more than an agonised whisper as his fingers loosened tight shoulder muscles.

'Shh,' he bade her gently. 'Just relax.'

Dared she? Maybe just for a few minutes. There was no harm in just a few minutes, surely?

Suzanne closed her eyes and let all her muscles relax as he began weaving a subtle magic that seemed to seep into her very bones.

She was hardly aware of him sliding the zip free at the back of her dress, or the faint slither as it slipped to the floor. Her bra clasp undid with ease, and his hands smoothed her slip down over her hips.

'I don't think—'

'Don't *think*,' Sloane said huskily. 'Just feel.'

His lips tasted her skin, embraced it, and roamed at will over her neck, her shoulders, then trailed down one arm to the sensitive hollow at her elbow, before tracing the delicate veins down to the inside of her wrist.

A despairing groan escaped her throat as he rendered a similar treatment to the other arm, and when he turned her into his arms she had no will of her own to prevent him laying her gently down on the bed.

What followed was a long, slow supplication of every pleasure point, each pulse. The curve of her hip, the inside of one thigh, the hollow behind each knee. The sensitive slope of her calf, the tender hollows at her ankle, the acutely vulnerable arch of her foot.

She felt as if she was slowly dying as pleasure radiated from every pore, each nerve-cell, as his hands, his lips roved at will. Her breasts, their sensitised peaks, the soft concave of her stomach. The rapidly discolouring bruise at her hip. Nothing escaped his attention.

Her blood leapt as he brushed the most intimate crevice of all, and her limbs slid against the sheet in agitation, then her whole body jerked as he began effecting a simulation of the sexual act itself.

His hands cupped her hips and held them as he wreaked a havoc that was so incredibly tender, so intensely evocative, her body seemed to sing as one vibration after another shook her central core and radiated in all-consuming waves.

He felt her shudder in release, and gifted her an open-mouthed kiss before travelling a slow path to her waist, then the soft contour of one breast.

It was a torturous journey until his mouth reached hers, and the kiss was so gentle she felt the prick of tears and their warm spill as they trickled slowly across each cheekbone and disappeared into her hair.

Sloane felt the faint tremor as her body shook, and he lifted his head fractionally, glimpsed the drenched sapphire pools and removed the trail of moisture with his tongue.

Then he stretched out close and gathered her in against him. 'Better?'

Dear Lord, did he have any conception of how she felt? 'There's only one problem,' she murmured shakily.

His fingers brushed against her cheek. 'What's that?'

Her mouth trembled as she reached for him. 'You're wearing too many clothes.'

His smile was infinitely warm and sensual. 'You could have fun taking them off.'

'Is that an invitation?'

Lips traced the clean line of her jaw. 'Do you need one?'

This was special. Something so precious, the memory would last her for the rest of her life. Through all the lonely, empty nights, an inner voice sighed in sorrow.

His shoes came first, then she took time with the buckle of his trousers, the zip fastening, silently encouraging his help as she slid the garment free. Undoing each shirt button became a tantalising exercise as her fingers tangled with the springy hair curling in a sparse pattern across his tightly muscled chest.

All that remained was a pair of silk briefs, and she

traced the waistband as it stretched across his hip-bone, the firm plane of his stomach, and allowed her fingers to brush fleetingly over his arousal.

Control. He had it. Part of her wanted to see what it would take to break it as she tucked her fingers into the waistband and eased the briefs free.

With incredible slowness she copied his example, teasing, tasting, glorying in the soft tremor of his stomach, each flexed muscle as she traversed every inch of his body.

The most vulnerable, the most erotic part of his anatomy she left until last, laving it with such delicate artistry, he groaned in the effort to maintain control.

Minutes later his breath rasped in one husky exhalation, and hard hands grasped her shoulders as he rolled her onto her back and drove into her in one deep thrust.

Suzanne gave an exultant laugh and met his mouth as it came down in possession of her own, and together they climbed to each crest as raw, primitive sensation took them high in a mutual climax so devastatingly flagrant there were no words to define it.

Afterwards he cradled her against him as his fingers trailed a soothing pattern up and down her back, tracing each indentation of her spine.

She slept, drifting into blissful somnolence, secure in the knowledge that she was safe. *His.* Undoubtedly his.

Suzanne came awake at the soft pressure of lips brushing against her own, and she opened her eyes slowly, allowing the lashes to drift wide as she focused on the man who was intent on disturbing a dreamy ambience she was loath to leave.

'It's almost four,' Sloane informed her huskily, and she offered him a slow, sweet smile.

'Time to shower, dress, and meet Trenton and Georgia for tennis.'

'I could ring through to their villa and cancel.'

'We shouldn't disappoint them,' she opined solemnly, and he uttered a faint laugh. 'Should we?'

'Witch.' He levered himself off the bed, and extended a hand. 'Come on, then, or we'll be late.'

They were, but only by ten minutes, and Georgia and Trenton were already on the court, quite happily enjoying a relaxing rally.

Together, they agreed on one set, and although both men were evenly matched the pace was laid-back rather than competitive, ending an hour later with a seven-five win in favour of Sloane and Suzanne.

'A drink in the bar?' Sloane suggested as they exited the court, and Trenton clapped a hand to his son's shoulder in silent agreement.

'I must be feeling my age,' Georgia declared with a sparkling laugh as they entered the main complex and sank into comfortable chairs.

Trenton signalled to the waiter and within minutes they were each sipping something long and cool.

'Dinner at six-thirty?' Trenton proposed. 'I'll have someone alert the dining room.'

That would give them time to shower and change.

Their final night on the island, Suzanne reflected, unsure whether to feel relieved or regretful that the extended weekend sojourn was almost at an end.

What had begun as something she'd have given anything to avoid had become quite different in many respects from anything she'd envisaged.

The anger, the resentment was gone. Yet what was in its place? The sex was great. Better than great...magnificent. But was that *all* it was?

She wanted to ask, but she was afraid of the answer. *Knew* that if she was to survive emotionally she had to cull some form of self-preservation.

'It'll be the last night we spend with Georgia and Trenton for a while,' Sloane reflected with indolent ease. 'Shall we view a video, play cards, or just take a leisurely stroll along the beach for a while after dinner?'

Trenton looked from his wife to his stepdaughter for confirmation. 'Georgia? Suzanne?'

Georgia's smile was infectious. 'Cards. Suzanne and I are rather good, aren't we, darling?'

It was, Suzanne decided gratefully, the more mentally stimulating choice. 'Yes,' she conceded with droll humour. 'Let's pit our combined skills and see if we can beat them.'

Sloane arched an eyebrow and spared his father a wry look. 'Men against the women?'

Trenton indulged in a husky chuckle. 'You do play, Sloane? Otherwise we're in deep trouble.'

'Your villa or ours?'

'Yours,' Trenton drawled, and shot Georgia a wicked glance. 'Then we can leave when we want to.'

'Bring matchsticks,' Suzanne bade them solemnly. 'Georgia and I never play for money.'

They finished their drinks and wandered out into the cool evening air. Darkness was falling, and already the garden lights illuminated the complex and grounds.

Trenton and Georgia paused at a fork in the path leading to their villa. 'We'll meet in the restaurant in half an hour.'

Once indoors, Suzanne made straight for the *en suite*, stripped off her clothes, and stepped beneath the warm pulsing water. Then gasped in surprise when Sloane followed close behind her.

His presence triggered a spiral of electric energy, and she reached for the soap only to have it removed from her hand.

What followed became an incredibly sensual assault that heightened every nerve-ending until her entire body seemed to pulse with sensory awareness.

When he finished he silently handed her the soap, and she returned his ministrations, then stood still as he rinsed the lather from his skin.

He reached for the water dial and closed it, then he cupped her face and kissed her hard and all too briefly before reaching out for a towel.

'I don't think we need dress up. Something casual will do.'

Nevertheless she did, selecting black silk evening trousers and a matching silk singlet top. She kept make-up to a minimum, and added a slim gold chain Georgia had gifted her on her twenty-first birthday. Medium-heeled strappy sandals completed the outfit.

Wearing immaculate ivory linen trousers and a deep blue cotton shirt, Sloane exuded a vibrant energy that was intensely male, and her senses leapt when he enfolded her hand in his as they made their way to the restaurant.

Dinner was a convivial meal, and they each chose locally caught seafood, garnished with a variety of fresh salad greens. They opted out of dessert and selected the cheeseboard instead, with fresh grapes and cantaloupe, followed by a sinfully rich liqueur coffee.

A leisurely walk among the lamp-lit grounds and gardens extended the time it took to reach the villa, and once inside they seated themselves comfortably at the table while Trenton extracted and shuffled a pack of cards.

It wasn't so much the game, or winning, Suzanne mused as she collected the cards she'd been dealt. She found the pitting of mental skills honed by chance to be an enjoyable challenge. Predicting how the suits and the numbers would run, and the odds. She didn't believe in tricks, or sleight of hand, and abhorred players who utilised any system.

As a pair, she and Georgia won the first game, then the second. When the third meant another loss for the men, there was keen speculation about the fourth game.

'I think we're about to go down,' Trenton declared, meeting Sloane's musing smile with one of his own.

'If we win, we'll split up and change partners,' Georgia offered generously.

'Now that could make things interesting,' Sloane drawled, and Suzanne spared him a wicked grin.

'Must we, Mama? This might be the only advantage we'll ever gain over them.'

Sloane lifted a hand and brushed his knuckles across her cheek. 'Oh, I don't know,' he intoned tolerantly. 'I can think of other advantages.' His eyes were dark with lambent warmth, his meaning unmistakable, and there was absolutely nothing she could do about the soft tinge of colour that flared high across her cheekbones.

'You'll embarrass my mother,' she chided, and Trenton laughed.

'Doubtful, darling,' Georgia assured her.

Suzanne looked from one gleaming gaze to another, and conceded defeat. 'I think we should play on.' Afterwards, when they were alone, she'd pay Sloane back. And relish every second of it. She shot him a silently threatening glance from beneath her lashes, and glimpsed the teasing gleam in those dark depths.

It gave her a degree of satisfaction to win, and she chose to be paired with Trenton against Georgia and Sloane in a series of games that brought a finish so close, the margin was minuscule in Georgia and Sloane's favour.

Being seated opposite him provided the opportunity to watch every move, glimpse each facial expression, the faint narrowing of his eyes as he considered which card to play, which one to discard.

He was a superb tactician, a supreme strategist. And he learned really fast. Too fast. It made her wonder if he hadn't deliberately played to lose earlier.

'Anyone for coffee?'

'No, thank you, darling.' Georgia spared a glance at her watch, then rose to her feet. 'We'll see you at breakfast. Around eight?'

Sloane walked at Suzanne's side to the door. 'We'll be there.'

Georgia leaned forward and brushed her daughter's cheek with her own. 'Sleep well.'

As soon as the door had closed behind them, Suzanne crossed to the table and gathered up the pile of matchsticks, then collected the cards.

'Leave them.'

His smile was warm with implied intimacy, and she almost melted at its mesmerising quality. 'It'll only take a minute. Then I'll pack.'

His expression didn't change. 'There's plenty of time to do that in the morning.'

She looked at him helplessly. 'Sloane—' How could she say she was a mass of nerves, relieved in one way the weekend was almost over, yet deep inside fighting off a feeling of inconsolable grief? Wanting him, but reluctant to add another night of loving that would only add to the heartache? She shook her head in silent remonstrance, then drew on inner strength. 'It won't take long.'

He was close, much too close. Her breathing seemed to hang suspended as her pulse raced into overdrive.

'Look at me.'

Her stomach executed a painful flip. 'Sloane—'

'Look at me, Suzanne,' he commanded in a voice that was deceptively mild—too mild.

She turned from her task of clearing the table, and hugged her arms together in an involuntary defensive gesture.

'You're as skittish as a newborn foal.' And consumed by a confusing mix of contrary emotions, he added silently, aware of almost every one of them. 'Want to talk about *why*?'

How did she begin, and *where*? Or should she even begin at all? *Words* seemed superfluous and contradictory, yet there were things that needed to be said.

She looked at his strongly etched features, and felt as if she was teetering on the edge of a bottomless pit.

'I'd like to go to bed. It's late, and I'm tired.'

He reached out a hand and took hold of her chin, then tilted it. 'You're avoiding the issue.'

Her eyes darkened, and she felt them begin to ache with suppressed emotion. 'Tomorrow we go back to Sydney and lead separate lives.'

'If you believe I'm going to let that happen, then you're sadly mistaken.'

He lowered his head and angled his mouth over hers in a gentle possession that soon hardened into something deep and incredibly erotic.

It was all she could do not to respond, and she fought against the dictates of her own traitorous body, almost hating herself for being so mindless, so incredibly vulnerable where he was concerned.

Want; need. The two were entwined, yet separate. With differing meanings, depending on the gender.

A man could want, and use seducing skills to achieve sexual satisfaction. Was that what Sloane was doing? Making the most of the weekend?

Yet it was two-sided. She hadn't exactly displayed too much reluctance.

When he lifted his head she could only stand in silence, her eyes wide and hiding her pain.

His arm slid down her back, and she tried to put some distance between them. Without success. 'Please, don't.'

'Don't *what*, Suzanne? Take you to bed? Is that what this is all about?' His eyes searched hers, and glimpsed the slight flaring evident in her own.

'Sex isn't the answer to everything.'

He noted the faint wariness in the set of her beautiful mouth, the bruised softness in those crystalline blue eyes, and wanted to wipe away all the indecision, the doubt, and replace it with the uninhibited emotion she'd gifted him in the beginning.

'I don't call what we share *sex*,' Sloane opined gently.

No, it was never just sex. Shared intimacy, lovemaking, a sensual exploration and satiation of the senses with *love* the ultimate goal.

'Last night—'

'Last night was a mistake.'

His eyes hardened to dark obsidian shards, and his expression became a bleak, angry mask.

CHAPTER TEN

'THE hell it was.'

'Sloane—'

'What excuse are you going to try for, Suzanne? Too much champagne, when you barely touched a second glass? It seemed like a good idea at the time?' His dark eyes bored into her with relentless and deadly anger. 'What?'

Oh, God. She closed her eyes, then opened them again. 'It wasn't like that.'

'Then explain how it was.'

Magical, euphoric. Devastating in more ways than one. She tried for an ineffectual shrug and almost got it right. 'I let the pretence become reality.' The burning need to experience heaven one last time.

'You expect me to believe that?' His voice was dangerously quiet.

'Dammit, Sloane. What do you want? A blow-by-blow analysis of my emotions?'

'The truth might help.'

'What truth?'

'There were two people in that bed. And you were with me every inch of the way.'

'So what does that prove, other than you're a skilled lover?'

'Are you saying you'd respond to any man the way you respond to me?'

No. Never. So deep was her certainty, it robbed the power from her voice.

'Suzanne?'

His eyes sharpened, homing in on the thinly disguised bleakness. 'You didn't answer the question.'

Her eyes blazed, and she lifted her chin to a defiant angle. 'What would you do if I said *yes*?'

His expression frightened her. 'Be tempted to beat you within an inch of your life.'

'You're not a violent man,' she said with certainty, only to have that conviction waver at the brilliant flare of intense emotion evident in his eyes, the deep set of his features projecting a mask that made her feel suddenly afraid. Which was ridiculous.

'Try me.' The silky softness of his voice sent a chill chasing the length of her spine.

Gone was the cool, implacable control of the courtroom barrister. Absent, too, was the veneer of sophistication. In its place was a man intent on fighting—if not physically then verbally—to the bitter end to effect a resolution. Here, now. No matter what the outcome.

Suzanne moved her shoulders in an infinitely weary gesture. 'Can't this wait until morning?' It had been a long night, and an even longer day.

He folded both arms across his chest. 'No.'

'Sloane—'

'No,' he reiterated with dangerous softness.

She was almost at the end of her tether, tired in

spirit, physically, emotionally. All she wanted to do was undress, curl into bed and sleep.

Then, when she woke in the morning, the long weekend would be over. She'd board the launch, take the flight back to Sydney, and attempt to take up with her life again. Without Sloane.

'What do you *want* from me?' It was a tortured cry straight from the heart.

A muscle bunched at the edge of his jaw. 'You. Just you.'

Her throat ached with emotion, and she was willing to swear her heart stopped beating.

'As my wife, my partner, the twin half of my soul. For the rest of my life.'

She could only look at him in silence as she tried to assemble a few words that made sense.

He didn't give her the chance. 'I have a Notice of Intention to Marry in my possession.' He let his arms fall to his sides. 'All you have to do is attach your signature prior to the service tomorrow morning.' Her voice emerged from her throat with difficulty. 'To-morrow?' The single query was little more than a soundless gasp. 'Are you mad?'

'Remarkably sane.'

Suzanne felt as if she needed to sit down. 'We can't possibly—'

'We can,' Sloane insisted. 'You're as aware of the legalities as I am.' He paused fractionally, then touched a gentle finger to the corner of her mouth, traced its outline, then let his hand fall. 'Georgia and Trenton will act as witnesses.'

'You expect me to agree to all this?' she questioned weakly.

He looked at her for long, timeless minutes, examining the fall of clean blonde hair, the fine-textured skin with minimum make-up coverage, the beautiful crystalline blue eyes. And played his last card.

'We can go back to Sydney tomorrow and begin organising the *social event of the year*. Plan the date, the venue, the marquee, the guest list, your designer gown, the media. If that's what you want, I'll go along with it. Happily.' He paused, his voice softening. 'As long as it means I get *you*.' He lifted a hand and brushed gentle fingers down her cheek, then cupped her jaw. 'Or we can marry quietly here, tomorrow.' His smile held incredible warmth. 'The choice is yours.'

Life with Sloane. Life without Sloane. There really wasn't any choice at all. Never had been.

'Tomorrow?' she reiterated in stunned disbelief.

'Tomorrow,' Sloane insisted.

Suzanne's brain whirled with numerous implications. 'You planned it like this,' she said unsteadily. 'Didn't you?'

He touched a forefinger to her lips. 'I planned to marry you. The time, the place were irrelevant.'

She searched his features and glimpsed the strength of purpose evident. 'Georgia and Trenton's wedding, this remote island resort—' She faltered, absently lifting a hand to push a lock of hair behind her ear. 'Their plans made it easy for you to—'

'Discover the truth,' he finished.

'But what if—'

There was a faint edge of tension beneath the surface of his control that he fought hard to subdue. Losing her temporarily had nearly cost him his sanity.

'You said you needed time and space,' Sloane declared quietly. 'Something I vowed to give you... within reason.'

Suzanne digested his words, and perceived the meaning behind them. 'You had that much faith in me?'

A slight tremor in her voice brought a faint smile, and he lifted a hand and tucked another loose tendril of hair behind her ear. 'Yes.'

She saw the passion visible in those dark, arresting features, and her bones began to melt. 'Thank you,' she said simply.

His mouth curved with sensual warmth, deepening the darkness of his eyes as he leaned forward and trailed his lips along her cheekbone, then traced her jaw and settled near the edge of her mouth.

Without hesitation she shifted slightly and parted her lips to meet his in a kiss that merged from warmth to flaring heat in the space of a heartbeat.

It seemed an age before he lifted his head. 'We have a wedding to organise.'

Suzanne's eyes gleamed as she sought to tease him a little. 'I don't have anything suitable to wear.'

'Yes, you do.'

In her mind's eye she skimmed the clothes she'd brought with her. 'I do?' The pale blue silk slip dress she'd worn the day before would suffice...providing the resort staff could work a cleaning miracle in time.

'Trust me.'

She opened her mouth, then closed it again.

He smiled, and it sent lines fanning out from the corners of each eye. 'Do I take that to mean a *yes*?'

Suzanne tried for solemnity, and failed. 'It depends what I'm saying *yes* to.'

He leaned forward and brushed his lips to the curve of her neck. His mouth moved lower, trailed a path up her throat and hovered above her lips. He angled his mouth down to hers and took his fill, plundering, possessing, until she could be in no doubt of his feelings, *hers*.

'Marrying me.'

His mouth was intent on wreaking such delicious havoc with her senses, savouring the delicate flavour of her skin, while his hands sought and found the acutely sensitised pleasure spots that drove her wild.

'Tomorrow.'

Yes, she cried silently. There were words she wanted to say, assurances she felt the need to give.

'Sloane.'

His hands stilled at the way her voice caught in saying his name, and his mouth paused in its downward path. He lifted his head and took in the soft fullness of her lips, the dilated depths of her eyes.

'I love you.' Words, just three of them. Yet in saying them she gifted more than her body. Her heart, her soul. Everything.

His hands shook slightly as they slid up to cup her face, and his expression was devoid of any artifice.

Joy, *love*, slow-burning deep emotion. Passion. Just for her.

'Thank you,' he said gently.

The anger, the frustration, the sheer helplessness that had coloured the past few weeks disappeared. He knew he never wanted to experience them again.

No one would ever be permitted to diminish what they shared, or seek to damage it in any way. There would be no more doubts, no room for any insecurity. He would personally see to it. Every day of his life.

Suzanne watched the changing emotions and successfully read every one of them. The resolution, the caring. And love.

His thumb moved across the fullness of her lower lip with a reverence that made her want to cry. 'I'm yours,' he said softly. 'Always.' His lips curved into a slow smile that melted her bones. 'For ever.'

She had to blink rapidly to dispel the suspicious moistness behind her eyes. 'Then I guess we get married tomorrow.' Her mouth moved to form a shaky smile. 'What on earth will Georgia and Trenton think?'

Sloane kissed the tip of her nose. 'Be delighted, I imagine.'

She leaned into him, overwhelmed by the sheer feel and power of him. 'Let's—' She paused slightly as Sloane's hand slid beneath the hem of her top and worked an evocative path towards one hip.

'Make love?' His husky chuckle was low and infinitely sensual.

'Go for a walk along the beach afterwards?' In the moonlight, in the stillness of night, with the sound of water lapping softly against the sand. Enjoying the magic of an island that was removed from civilisation, where solitude and privacy were guaranteed.

'Sure,' Sloane agreed easily.

'Providing you have sufficient energy left, of course,' she said with demure amusement, and had her laugh cut short as his mouth closed over hers in a kiss that promised total ravishment.

'Planning on wearing me out, huh?' he teased as he carried her upstairs, then laid her down on the bed.

As he undressed his eyes were so dark, magnificent. And alive with a passion that made her catch her breath. Slowly, and with a sensuality that wasn't contrived, she lifted the hem of her top, pulled it over her head and dropped it onto the floor.

He eased himself down onto the bed beside her and she lowered her head and kissed his shoulder, trailing her mouth down to one hard male nipple, savoured it, then followed the dark hair arrowing down to his navel.

Beneath the fine black silk briefs his arousal was a potent force, and she caressed its outline with the tip of her tongue. It created a slight friction that made him catch his breath, and with a boldness she didn't pause to question she took the waistband between her teeth and gradually eased them down, inch by inch until the briefs were reduced to a narrow fold across the top of his thighs.

There was a tremendous beauty in the aroused male form, the knowledge of what that harnessed power could achieve in the pleasure stakes. For each of them.

Suzanne felt as if she wanted to laugh and cry, both at the same time, with the intense joy of being with this man, for she couldn't remember feeling so *alive*, so complete. It was like coming home, the knowledge of everything being *right*. She wanted to tell him, show him.

And she did. With infinite care, and a passion unfettered by uncertainty or reservation.

She wasn't sure when Sloane took control. Only that together they experienced emotions at their zenith again and again during the ensuing night hours.

Suzanne stirred as fingers trailed a light path across the flat plane of her stomach, and nuzzled the warm flesh beneath her cheek.

She didn't want to move. Didn't think she *could* move.

'I guess the moonlit walk along the beach will have to wait.'

Suzanne registered Sloane's amused drawl, felt his warm breath tease her temple, and slowly opened her eyes to discover an early dawn fingering soft light into the room.

'Well,' she murmured, 'there's always the early morning swim.'

His soft laughter reverberated beneath her ear, and she lifted her head to look at him, glimpsed the teasing warmth evident in the generous curve of his mouth, the liquid darkness of his eyes, and wrinkled her nose.

'Don't you think I'm capable?'

The corners of his eyes creased, and the darkness intensified. 'I should come along in case you drown.'

'You, of course, are a bundle of energy this fine morning?' She trailed her fingers across his midriff, felt the muscles tighten and created a playful pattern with the dark hair there.

'Go any lower, and I won't answer to the consequences,' Sloane warned huskily.

'Just checking,' she told him with impish mischievousness, then gasped as he lifted her across his chest, rolled her onto her back, and fastened his mouth on hers with devastating accuracy.

She clung to him, meeting his ardour with her own, loving the fierceness before it altered and softened into something that was incredibly gentle.

'A swim,' she said with a shaky smile. 'Definitely a swim. Otherwise we'll never get out of here.'

They rose, donned minimum swimwear, and Suzanne caught up a cotton wrap as Sloane collected a towel.

Outside it was still, and there wasn't a sound. No birdlife, not so much as a breeze to riffle the foliage as they made their way onto the sand.

A new day, she mused, watching as the colours around her gradually intensified. Crisp white sand, the sea changing hue from blue to aqua, clearly defined from an azure sky. The air was warm and devoid of the sun's heat.

As she watched, the golden orb's outer rim crept above the horizon, bringing with it the clarity of light, and she heard the first twitter as birds awoke.

Sloane watched her expressive features, the way her mouth curved slightly open, the softness in those vivid blue eyes as she stood there.

'Want to walk along the shoreline?'

She turned slowly towards him, and her eyes teased his. 'Dip our toes in the water, skim a few shells out over the surface?'

'Commune with Nature, and maybe sacrifice a swim for a long warm shower?'

Suzanne gave a throaty laugh as she caught hold of his hand. 'Chicken,' she teased. 'A bracing cold swim, a hearty breakfast…' She trailed off with a grin. 'Just what we need to kick-start the day.' Her eyes sparkled with humour. 'Last one in—' She didn't get to finish as she was swept off her feet and carried into the water. 'Sloane. Don't you *dare*.'

Cool, not cold, and definitely bracing. The hearty breakfast came way after the long warm shower.

Then things seemed to move very swiftly into action.

The celebrant didn't turn a hair when asked to perform another ceremony. Georgia and Trenton were thrilled with the news. The restaurant management appeared completely unfazed at the request to prepare a small but sumptuous midday wedding feast.

Suzanne gasped out loud when Georgia removed a

pale ivory creation of silk and lace from its protective covering, added shoes, and a fingertip veil.

Sloane's contingency plan.

She reached out a hand and touched the exquisite lace overlay. 'It's beautiful.' The correct size, the right length, perfect.

'Did you—?'

'Help?' Georgia queried. 'No, I swear.'

'You're not going to ask if I have doubts?'

'I don't need to,' her mother said gently. 'You wouldn't be about to do this if you had them.'

No, Suzanne agreed in contemplative silence as she crossed to the mirror and began tending to her make-up.

It was almost eleven-thirty when she made the final adjustment to her veil and stood back from the mirror.

'You take my breath away,' Georgia said with a tremulous smile.

'Don't you dare cry,' Suzanne admonished her with a shaky grin. 'Or I will too, then we'll have to redo our make-up, which will make us late, and Sloane will send Trenton on a rescue mission, only to follow closely on his heels with the celebrant in tow.' Her eyes danced with expressive mischief. 'Not exactly a scene I would choose. Besides, we can't have this hastily arranged service misconstrued as a kidnap attempt of the bride by the groom, can we? Think what a field day the gossip columns would have with that!'

Georgia's mouth quivered as she caught hold of her daughter's outstretched hand. 'Unthinkable,' she agreed solemnly.

Tables had been cleared at one end of the restaurant to make room for an elegant archway threaded with hibiscus and frangipani in brilliant shades of pink. Soft music filtered from a stereo system, and red carpet formed a temporary aisle.

Suzanne took a deep breath, accepted the reassuring squeeze from her mother's fingers, then began walking slowly towards the archway where Sloane and Trenton waited with the celebrant.

Father and son were similar in height and stature, their breadth of shoulder outlined by superb tailoring, and almost in unison both men turned to watch the two women in their lives walk towards them.

Suzanne felt as if time stood still. Her eyes met Sloane's, and clung. Everything else faded to the periphery of her vision as she drew close, and there was him, only him.

The expression in those liquid brown eyes held a warmth that threatened to melt her bones. There was a wealth of emotion apparent as he smiled, and her step almost faltered as she reached his side.

Sloane caught hold of her hand and lifted it to his lips, then he kissed each finger in turn, slowly, as her heart went into overdrive.

She was barely aware that Georgia moved to one side, and she endeavoured to focus on the celebrant's voice as he intoned the words, elicited their individual responses, then solemnly accorded them man and wife after the exchanging of rings.

'You may now kiss the bride.'

Sloane lifted the fine veil with infinite care, then

his hands slid to cup her face, and his head descended as he took possession of her mouth in a kiss that claimed and pleasured with such thoroughness, her skin tinged a delicate pink at the blatant promise apparent.

Afterwards they sipped Cristal champagne from slim crystal flutes, posed for the essential few photographs, then took their seats at an elegantly decorated table where they were served the finest seafood in delicate sauces, fresh salads, an incredible pavlova decorated with fresh cream and fruit for dessert, followed by the pièce de résistance, an iced wedding cake. Which necessitated more champagne, a toast, followed by coffee.

As weddings went, it had to be one of the smallest, most intimate affairs on record, Suzanne mused as they stood and thanked Georgia and Trenton, the staff, the celebrant, then led the way from the restaurant.

Sadly, the romantic idyll was almost over, for in half an hour the launch would leave for Dunk Island, where the family jet was on standby to fly them to Sydney.

Inside the villa Sloane caught hold of her hands and drew her close.

'I don't think we have time for this,' Suzanne said a trifle breathlessly as his head descended to hers.

'Depends on your definition of *this*,' Sloane teased, touching his lips to the corner of her mouth as he trailed a tantalising path along the contours of her lower lip.

A groan escaped her throat, and she angled her

mouth so that it fitted his, encouraging a possession he didn't hesitate to give.

It seemed an age before he lifted his head, and she could only look at him in total bemusement. 'I think,' she managed huskily, 'we should change and pack.'

His lips brushed across her forehead. 'Change, but not pack.' He lingered at her temple, then traced the edge of her jaw. 'We're staying here.'

'How can we stay? I'm due back at work tomorrow.' Her eyes widened. 'You must have court appearances.' Her voice husked down to a mere whisper. 'It's not possible.'

He lifted his head and surveyed her features with musing indulgence. 'Yes, it is.' He placed a forefinger beneath her chin and lifted it. 'All it took was a few phone calls.'

'But you can't—'

'I just have.'

'My job—'

'Secure,' Sloane assured her. 'For as long as you want it.'

She drew in a shaky breath, then released it. 'What did you tell them?'

His thumb traced the column of her throat, felt the convulsive movement as she swallowed, and soothed it with the gentle brush of his fingers. 'The truth.' He explored the hollow at the edge of her neck, and felt her quivering response. 'You have a week's leave with their blessing.'

It was feasible her work could be shared around.

Sloane, however, was in a vastly different position. 'But what about you?'

'Forward planning,' he declared, and effected a slight shrug. 'I did a bit of shuffling, called in a few favours.'

'How long?' It couldn't possibly be more than a day or two.

'I'm not due in court until Friday.'

She wanted to kiss and hug him, both at the same time. 'I love you,' she said reverently. 'Later, I intend to show you just how much.'

'Promises?'

She offered him a brilliant smile. 'Oh, yes. Definitely. But now,' she declared, 'we change, then we'll go see Georgia and Trenton onto the launch.'

His mouth quirked with humour, playing her game. 'And after?'

'A girl's wedding day is special.' Her smile was infinitely wicked. 'Something of which memories are made and reminisced over down the years.' She lifted both hands and ticked off her fingers, one by one. 'There's the champagne, the bridal waltz, and the throwing of the bridal bouquet.' Irrepressible humour intensified the blue of her eyes. 'You planned the first half of the day. Are you willing to leave the second half to me?'

Sloane caught hold of her hands, and kissed the inside of each wrist before releasing them. 'I guess I can do that.'

CHAPTER ELEVEN

THEY reached the jetty a few minutes before Georgia and Trenton, together with the celebrant, were due to board the launch. Goodbyes were affectionate, but brief.

'I want postcards from Paris,' Suzanne insisted gently as she kissed Georgia.

'Done.'

Suzanne stood within the circle of Sloane's arms as the launch moved out of sight, then she turned and curved an arm around his waist.

'Let's walk along the beach.'

He looked down at her expressive features, caught the faint shadows beneath her eyes and experienced a faint pang of regret that he was the cause. She needed to catch up on sleep. Dammit, they both did.

'No rock-climbing,' he warned, and she laughed, a light, infectious sound that curled round his heart.

'Intent on preserving the energy levels?'

The smile he slanted her held warm humour. 'Yours, as well as my own.'

They trod the soft sand to the first promontory, then turned and slowly retraced their steps. The pool looked inviting, and they stroked a few lengths in lazy rhythm before emerging to lie supine side by side on two loungers, allowing the soft warm breeze to dry the brief, thin pieces of silk they each wore.

Suzanne must have slept, for she dreamt of isolated incidents that had no common linkage, and woke to the drift of fingers tracing a soft pattern down her forearm.

The sun was low in the sky, and there were long shadows deepening the colour of the sand.

'It's late.'

'Does it matter?' Sloane queried, propping himself up on one arm.

She rose to her feet in one fluid movement. 'We have a dinner reservation in half an hour.' She stretched a hand towards him. 'Time to rise and shine and shower and dress.'

They made it with barely a minute to spare, and were seated out on the terrace overlooking the bay.

Suzanne requested champagne, conferred with Sloane over the menu choices, and they opted for a light meal, preferring entrée servings with salads and fresh fruit.

The scallops mornay were superb, the oysters kilpatrick divine, and the prawns delectable.

They delighted in feeding each other morsels of food in a feast that equally fed their palates and their senses.

Anticipation was a powerful aphrodisiac, and they deliberately lingered, delaying the return to their villa by tacit consent.

There was background music, and Suzanne smiled as Sloane stood and held out his hand.

'You mentioned something about dancing.'

Heaven didn't get any better than this, she decided dreamily as she slipped into his arms. His hold was hardly conventional, and his lips grazed her temple, creating an evocative pattern that heated her blood to fever pitch.

It would be all too easy to whisper, Let's get out of here.

He sensed the moment she almost wavered, and brushed a kiss down the slope of her nose. There were other nights, a whole lifetime of them. He closed his eyes, then opened them again. *Thank God*, he thought in silent reverence.

Did she realise how much she meant to him? How the prospect of a life without her was akin to slowly dying?

He had known from the first moment they met that she was special. Courting her should have been easy. Never once had he even had to *try* with a woman. They were there for the taking, the selection entirely his. Suzanne had been different. There was no façade, no games, no emotional baggage. Just honesty, and a beautiful soul.

In retrospect, he acknowledged he'd moved too fast. The *image* of Wilson-Willoughby had proved to be a deterrent, for instead of enticing it had earned unaccustomed caution.

The night he'd walked into an empty penthouse and discovered she'd gone had been the worst night of his life. In the space of mere minutes he'd experienced very real fear, devastating loss, and a slow-mounting rage, the like of which he'd never known before. The note had left no phone number, no address, and no way of contacting her until eight-thirty the next morning when she arrived at the office.

'It's time to throw the bridal bouquet.'

He relaxed his hold and let her slip out from his arms, watching as she scooped up a display of frangipani and hibiscus from a nearby table centrepiece.

'To whom do you intend to throw it?'

'Ah, now there's a thing,' she said solemnly. 'The waiter? The waitress at the bar?'

All he had to do was raise his hand, murmur his request, and within minutes there were five staff members forming a line.

'It's not really a bouquet.'

'I don't think they'll care.'

They didn't, not at all, and she gave an infectious laugh as the flowers sailed a few metres and then separated easily between two pairs of hands.

Suzanne turned towards Sloane, and her eyes shone with mischief. 'Now we get to leave.'

There was a moon, bathing everything with a dim light, and halfway along the path she reached up and kissed him, only to gasp when he pulled her close and turned the impulsive gesture into something infinitely sensual.

They had almost an entire week of lazily spent days and long nights of lovemaking ahead of them, Suzanne reflected dreamily as they reached their villa. Time out for romance, before the return to reality in a cosmopolitan southern city and a faster pace of life.

Somehow their inevitable social obligations no longer seemed daunting.

Sloane unlocked the door, then switched on the light. Suzanne stepped inside, then came to an abrupt halt.

Inside, both downstairs and visible in the bedroom, grouped in vases, were masses of deep red roses, filling the villa with their delicate perfume.

She felt her eyes widen with sheer pleasure, then mist with the threat of tears. Slowly she turned to face him, her mouth shaky with emotion as she looked at him in silent query.

'While you were planning,' Sloane declared gently, 'I did a little planning of my own.'

'So many,' she said breathlessly, as she moved forward and touched a gentle finger to one velvet bud.

He crossed to stand behind her, curving her close into his body. His warm breath teased the hair at her temple as she sank back against him.

'A dozen to represent every year for the rest of our lives.'

Her heart seemed to turn over in her chest. She turned in his arms and reached up to link her hands together at his nape. His eyes were dark, so darkly gleaming she could almost see herself in their reflection.

'I love you. So much,' Suzanne whispered. 'I always have.'

His lips grazed hers, then lifted fractionally. 'I know,' he said gently. Her lips parted, and he pressed them closed. 'It was the only thing that kept me sane.'

His mouth closed over hers, seeking, finding everything she had to give and more, as he gave in return.

It wasn't enough, not nearly enough. Suzanne groaned as her fingers sought the hard flesh beneath his clothes, and she gasped as he swung an arm beneath her knees and lifted her high against his chest.

Her lips were slightly swollen, and her eyes deep and slumberous, as he strode towards the steps leading up to the bedroom.

'I am capable of walking,' she teased, and nearly died at the depth of passion evident in his gaze.

'Isn't the groom supposed to carry the bride over the threshold?'

'Something like that,' she said with mock seriousness. She lifted a hand and trailed her fingers down the edge of his cheek. 'What other traditions do you have in mind?'

He reached the upper level, crossed to the large bed, and lowered her down to stand within the circle of his arms. 'One or two.'

His fingers freed the loops attaching two tiny buttons at her nape, then he slid the zip fastening down the length of her back. The pale silk whispered to the floor to pool at her feet.

Soft opaque lining had negated the need to wear a bra, and she quivered beneath the intensity of his gaze, all too aware of her body's reaction. Only lace bikini briefs remained, and her eyes widened as he reached out a hand and extracted a single rose from a nearby vase.

With exquisite care he touched the velvet-petalled

bud to her cheek, then trailed it gently to the edge of her mouth.

The delicate scent teased her nostrils, and she felt all her fine body hairs rise in acute sensual expectation as he traced an evocative pattern to the valley between each breast.

Slowly, with infinite care, he gently outlined one breast, then the other, before trailing down to rest at her navel.

Suzanne's breath caught as desire arrowed through her body, igniting each erogenous zone in a conflagrant path and sending fire coursing through her veins.

With one deliberate movement he reached forward and pulled the covers from the bed, and she watched in mesmerised fascination as he lifted the rosebud to his lips.

Her eyes widened, dilating into huge pools of dark blue sapphire as he carefully peeled one petal free and let it flutter down on the bedsheets. Then another, and another, slowly, until only the rose stem and its stamen remained.

Suzanne thought her bones would melt, and a slow, sweet smile curved her generous mouth as she stepped out of her shoes.

She reached for the buttons on his shirt and undid them one by one, then discarded it. Her fingers moved to the buckle at his waist, dispensed with it, then she freed the zip fastening his trousers. Shoes and socks slid off easily.

Without a word she collected a rose, then, giving

his chest a gentle push, she tumbled him down onto the bed.

His husky laughter brought forth a wickedly teasing gleam and her eyes danced at the thought of what she had in store for him.

Mirroring his actions, she slowly peeled one petal and let it drift down onto his torso. Then another, and another, with infinite care, until there was none.

With a witching smile she reached forward and plucked another rose from a nearby vase, and gently placed it against his mouth.

Sloane doubted he would ever be able to look at a rose again without experiencing a damning and very intimate reaction. Petals softer than a woman's touch, their brush against sensitive skin incredibly evocative, the eroticism so intense it took all his will-power to lie supine while she conducted the sensual stroking. Much more of this…

Suzanne saw the instant his eyes darkened, and she gave a soft, throaty laugh as he pulled her down on top of him.

The rose slipped from her fingers and fell to the floor as he surged into her, and she reached for his forearms as he caught hold of her hips, commanding a ride that had no equal in her experience.

Moisture filmed her skin, his, as he took her to a place where control had no meaning and the senses exploded in a starburst of heat so intense she thought she might *burn* with it.

Afterwards she collapsed against his chest in a state of emotional exhaustion. She could feel the drift of his fingers against her skin as he caressed the indentations of her spine.

Gradually her breathing steadied, and her heart slowed to an even beat.

She wanted to stay close to him like this for ever. To feel, to know that their loving would always be so intense, so emotive. A true meshing of the emotions, physical, mental and spiritual.

Suzanne lifted her head and looked down into those dark, passion-filled eyes, and felt her body turn to jelly.

'I love you,' Sloane said with heartfelt simplicity. 'I know I couldn't survive a life without you in it. You're everything there is, and more. So much more.'

Tears filmed her eyes, and she lifted a hand to brush gentle fingers across his mouth. 'Same goes.'

He parted his teeth and nipped one finger, then drew it into his mouth and laved it with his tongue.

Awareness swirled into active life, spiralling through her body with damning ease, and she shifted slightly, exulting in the quickening power of his arousal as it swelled inside her.

In one smooth movement he rolled over and pinned her against the mattress.

The scent of crushed rose petals was strong, and she curved her legs around his hips, drawing him in close as she linked her hands together and pulled his head down to hers.

'Thank you.' She brushed his mouth with her own.

'For today. The roses. Everything. *You*, especially you.'

'My pleasure,' Sloane murmured against her lips, aware the pleasure was mutual. As it always would be.

Kim Lawrence lives on a farm in rural Anglesey. She runs two miles daily and finds this an excellent opportunity to unwind and seek inspiration for her writing! It also helps her keep up with her husband, two active sons, and the various stray animals which have adopted them. Always a fanatical consumer of fiction, she is now equally enthusiastic about writing. She loves a happy ending!

Kim Lawrence is a rising star in Modern Romance™. Her fast-paced, exciting stories are packed full of sizzling attraction and laugh out loud moments – they'll whisk you away!

Don't miss Kim's latest book

THE BLACKMAILED BRIDE

Kate was determined to protect her sister from scandal – and Javier Montero is the only man who can help. But Javier wants something in return: he needs a wife and Kate's perfect! Negotiating with Javier isn't easy, and Kate knows she's about to become a blackmailed bride!

on-sale next month in Modern Romance™

WIFE BY AGREEMENT

by

Kim Lawrence

CHAPTER ONE

HANNAH slid the key very carefully into the lock. Inside the only sound was the ticking of the clock. Nobody was up, thank goodness. She leant back against the door and gave a slow sigh of relief—at last!

She didn't bother switching on the light, but slipped thankfully out of the remains of her patent leather court shoes. Tucking them under her arm, she felt her way carefully past the big scrubbed table that had centre stage in the room. She thought with longing of a hot, cleansing shower. The sudden illumination made her freeze and blink like a startled animal.

'Is all this subterfuge really necessary? There isn't a curfew.' Ethan had moved to sit at the table, a half-empty glass of brandy in front of him. The vaguely bored irony faded dramatically from his voice as he took in her bedraggled state. 'What the hell has happened?'

The last thing Hannah felt like was reliving the past hour, and the last person she wanted to explain to was Ethan. Her hand went self-consciously to the torn material of her shirt lapel, but her attempts to hold the fabric together only drew his attention to the pale skin the rent exposed. What was he doing sitting in the dark anyway? She grimaced as she risked a swift glance down.

The unkind electric lights revealed it was even worse than she had thought. Her legs were covered with mud and her fine denier tights were in shreds; her velvet skirt was torn in several places and the pale skin of her shoulders and midriff showed through the gaping tears in her silk shirt.

'It looks a lot worse than it is,' she said soothingly. It didn't feel it, though. The scratches on her cheek were beginning to sting as the warmth of the room thawed her cold body. There was a promise of winter in the autumn air tonight.

With an impatient gesture Ethan dismissed her weak attempt to pacify him. 'Have you been in a car crash?'

'Not exactly.' You couldn't call jumping out of a car moving at thirty miles an hour a crash, exactly. She had a pretty good idea what Ethan would call it—insanity, probably. He hadn't been there, though. It had been— A deep shudder rippled through her body and she swayed as the whole room pitched.

Ethan reached out and touched her arm. 'My God, you're like ice.' He took off his robe and wrapped it around her. 'Sit down before you fall down.' He pressed her into a chair.

The nausea passed and Hannah opened her eyes. 'You'll get cold,' she protested. Under the robe Ethan was wearing a pair of dark blue pyjama trousers and nothing else. They'd taken the children to the South of France in June, and she noticed irrelevantly that his olive-toned skin was still tanned a deep golden brown.

'Drink this.' She tried to turn her head away as her nostrils flared against the scent of raw alcohol. 'Do as I say.'

It was only under duress that she obeyed; brandy wasn't a taste she'd ever acquired.

'Now tell me exactly what happened.'

'I want a shower,' she fretted. A hand on her shoulders prevented her from rising.

'After I've had my explanation. I was under the impression that you were going out for a meal with your fellow night-class members.' His sceptical tone made it sound as though this was an elaborate lie.

Why would she need to lie to him? Did he think she led a double life or something? 'I was…I did.' She raised her eyes to his face and read implacability there. Best just get it over with. 'Debbie and Alan took me.' Ethan had met the young couple who were learning French with her and he nodded briefly. 'Craig Finch, he only joined the class last month, offered to bring me home. He said it wasn't out of his way and it would save Alan a detour.' She swallowed hard. 'Only Craig took a detour, and when I mentioned it he…he…'

'What did he do?' He spoke quietly, but Ethan Kemp's grey eyes had narrowed to slits and a nerve throbbed erratically in his lean cheek.

'He laughed.' She felt sick just thinking about the expression in Craig's eyes. She'd already been tense—some of the things he'd been saying had been particularly personal, and slimily coarse—but it had been that smile that had really set the alarm bells ringing.

'Laughed?' Ethan echoed incredulously. It wasn't what he'd expected to hear.

'You weren't there!' she shot back angrily. 'He'd been…saying *things*.' In a large group, Craig's behaviour had been unexceptionable, but once he'd got Hannah alone his entire attitude had changed. Everything he'd said had been laced with grubby innuendo. Her frigid silence hadn't put him off at all.

'He hurt you?' Looming over her, Ethan looked a lot more threatening than Craig had been. She felt guilty for making the comparison: Ethan had his faults, but he was a decent man, and no bully, despite the way he was interrogating her right now. Normally he didn't interfere with her life at all.

'No, this happened when I jumped out of the car.'

Some of the repressed violence that had been implicit in his tense stance faded as he stared at her, to be replaced by astonishment. Ethan Kemp wasn't a man easily astonished. His big hands unfurled from the fists they had instinctively formed.

'I don't suppose it was stationary at the time?'

She shook her head and gave him an exasperated look. Ethan wasn't usually so slow. 'I was lucky he hadn't thought to lock the door,' she reflected soberly.

'I can see why you might be thanking your lucky stars,' he agreed drily.

'I landed in brambles and my clothes got a bit ripped getting out,' she explained in a matter-of-fact way. 'I hid in a ditch for a while, just in case he'd followed me, then I walked home over the fields.'

'Where did all this happen?'

'The junction near the Tinkersdale Road.'

'That has to be six miles away.'

'It felt like more, but you're probably right. Her smile was limp at best. 'Don't worry, nobody saw me. Her wide, smooth brow creased as she sought to reassure him. Ethan Kemp's wife strolling through the market town where they lived in this state wouldn't create the sort of image he would approve of, and Ethan cared about the image they presented to the world. Didn't it occur to you to ring me—or the police for that matter?'

'I didn't think to grab my bag; I had no money—nothing. The police aren't interested in crimes that didn't happen. He didn't actually touch me.'

'You're sure he was going to?'

This was an insinuation too far! Anger enabled her to nudge aside the incipient exhaustion that made her eyelids heavy.

'It was one of those occasions when prevention seemed better than cure,' she snapped crisply. The snap seemed to surprise him. Tough, she thought with uncharacteristic venom. Under the circumstances she thought she was being quite restrained. What did he expect her to do? Sit back and wait to be a crime statistic? 'I don't let my imagination run away with me, Ethan.'

This was unarguable: Hannah Smith was the most placid, practical female that he had, in his thirty-six years, ever met. He frowned—after a year's marriage he still thought of her as Hannah Smith, not Kemp. If anyone had suggested to him this morning that she was capable of throwing herself from a moving vehicle he'd have laughed at the absurdity of such an idea.

Hannah was not exactly timid, although her reserved manner made people initially assume she was, but she was not the sort of woman calmly to wade through muddy fields and brambles after extricating herself from a dangerous situation. At least he hadn't thought she was. Would she have told him about it at all if he hadn't witnessed her return? Had she intended appearing at breakfast just as if nothing had happened?

'We should contact the police.'

'Why? Nothing happened. I expect they'd write me off as a neurotic female.' If Ethan could think it, why not total strangers? 'I would like to get my bag back, though—my wallet's in it.'

'Wouldn't you like to see that swine get his just deserts?' he growled incredulously. He found it hard to identify with a turn-the-other-cheek philosophy.

'Like?' she said quietly. She raised her head and at first he didn't realise the tears glistening in her hazel eyes were tears of rage. This only became obvious when she spoke and her voice shook with suppressed fury. 'What I'd *like* to do is make him endure, just for five minutes, the sort of helplessness and terror I...' She bit down hard on her lower lip to stop it trembling. 'We rarely get what we *like*, Ethan.'

'That's a depressing philosophy.' The depth of her

passion shocked him; that she had any passion at all
shocked him! More than shocked him—it made him uneasy. What other surprises lurked beneath the placid exterior?

'It's just an observation. Now, if you don't mind I'd
like to go to bed.'

He kept a hold on her elbow, as though he expected
her to collapse at any moment. At the door of her bedroom she slipped the robe off her shoulders.

'Thank you. Sorry if I got it grubby. Goodnight,
Ethan.' This polite, but firm, dismissal appeared to make
him change his mind about what he was going to say.
She smiled vaguely at him as she disappeared into her
bedroom. A few seconds later she heard the sound of
Ethan's bedroom door slamming.

Her lip curled with distaste as she stripped. Even if
she could have salvaged the clothes, she'd have put them
out with the rubbish. As it was they hung off her like
rags.

A glance in the full-length cheval-mirror shocked her.
Her glossy brown hair had pulled loose of its neat French
braid and was liberally anointed with mud. The long
scratches along the right side of her face showed through
the dirt. The streaks of mascara that gave her the look
of a startled panda blended in with the general grime.
The amount of flesh exposed through the gaping holes
in her shirt was nothing short of indecent. No wonder
Ethan had been shocked—she looked appalling!

It was a relief to stand under the hot spray of the
shower and let the steamy water wash away some of her
tension along with the dirt. It didn't matter how hard she
scrubbed, thinking about Craig made her feel grubby.
How could a man who seemed so—well, *normal* act like
that? Had she given the impression she would welcome

such advances? She dismissed this horrifying notion swiftly. No, this hadn't been her fault.

In her *naïveté* she had imagined that a ring on her finger gave a girl automatic protection from unwanted advances. She automatically glanced down at her finger—it looked oddly bare without the slim gold band. On her knees, she searched the floor of the shower cubicle. It wasn't there. Panic out of proportion with the loss flooded through her.

She stepped out of the shower and hastily wrapped a towel sarong-wise about her body. She left a minor flood in the bathroom as she searched the floor there before retracing her footsteps into the bedroom. It was nowhere to be found.

'I knocked,' Ethan said as he appeared through the interconnecting door. It was the first time he'd used the door, and he knew it was ridiculous but he felt like an intruder in his own home. He didn't see Hannah at first, and then he spotted her small figure crouched beside the dressing table, silent tears pouring down her cheeks. The obvious conclusion to draw from such grief was that she hadn't told him everything that had happened. As he anticipated the worst his face darkened.

'I've lost my ring!' she wailed as she caught sight of him.

'What ring?' he asked blankly, moving to her side.

'My wedding ring.'

He felt relief. 'Is that all?' he said dismissively.

She hardly seemed to hear him. 'It might be in the kitchen, or on the stairs. I'll go and check.' She got rapidly to her feet—too rapidly, as it happened.

'You'll do nothing of the sort,' he said, catching hold of her elbows from behind and half lifting her across the room as her knees folded.

With a soft grunt he transferred her into his arms. She

was incredibly light. Was she naturally slender, or were there more surprises in store for him in the form of eating disorders? Nothing would surprise him after tonight!

'The ring doesn't matter; I can buy you a new one. You're overwrought!' The last sounded almost like an accusation.

Hannah sniffed as he placed her on her bed. Of course he could; why on earth had she reacted like that? Why should a ring that symbolised their marriage of convenience be precious to her? She must be more careful. He was probably suspecting he was married to a madwoman, she surmised, fairly accurately.

'Sorry,' she whispered huskily.

'You've had a bad night.' Her tears made him uncomfortable. It occurred to him that he hadn't seen this much of his wife before—even on the beach that summer she'd worn a baggy tee shirt over her swimming costume, and not even the children's pleas could make her enter the water.

The towel she wore cut across the high swell of her small breasts and ended... Her legs were quite long in proportion to her diminutive frame. His wandering gaze encountered a pair of solemn hazel eyes, watching him watching, and he looked away abruptly.

'I fetched this for the scratches.' He held out a tube of antiseptic cream.

'That's kind of you, Ethan.'

'Your back is badly scratched,' he observed.

'I can't see.'

'Or reach,' he pointed out practically. 'I expect you'll feel it tomorrow—there are some nasty bruises coming out. Are you covered for tetanus?'

'I think so.'

'"Think so" isn't sufficient; you must go to the surgery first thing in the morning for a booster. Turn around and I'll put some cream on your back.'

His touch was impersonal, firm, but gentle. She felt warm and relaxed, and—for the first time since she'd leapt from the moving vehicle—safe.

'You'll have to loosen this,' he said, pulling at the edge of the towel. The warm glow that had enveloped her was abruptly dispelled by a flurry of irrational anxiety.

'No, that's fine.'

'I'll probably be able to restrain myself at the sight of your flesh,' he observed drily.

'I didn't think that…' Her instinctive rejection of a more intimate touch had been no reflection on Ethan's intentions and she was mortified at the conclusion he'd drawn. She knew he didn't find her attractive. Even so, his next words did hurt.

'You're too thin.'

'I know.' In her teens she'd fantasised about waking up one morning and finding her awkward angles had been transformed into lissome curves. Now she knew better.

'Do you eat?'

'You know I do—' She stopped. In actual fact, it was rare that they ate together, only socially on the occasions they dined out together or had guests. Normally she ate with the children and Ethan ate alone later. He commuted to the City, and being a successful barrister seemed to keep him away from home a lot. He was tipped to be the next head of chambers when Sir James retired next year—the youngest in the chambers' long history.

Actually she didn't mind these absences; she was a lot more comfortable when he wasn't there—not that she found his company oppressive, exactly. She was always acutely conscious in his company of her deficiencies. When he looked at her she was always sure he was comparing her unfavourably with his first wife As always, the thought of the sainted Catherine made her wince.

'Mrs Turner will confirm the fact I could probably eat you under the table.' He wouldn't consider the children impartial witnesses—they doted on her—but the housekeeper was another matter.

'I've only ever seen you pick at your food. That's it.' He pulled up the towel. 'They're not deep; you won't scar.'

Should she tell him she was usually so nervous of making a social *faux pas* on the occasions he referred to that she couldn't stomach anything? On reflection she decided not to. Inadequacies—at least, hers—made Ethan impatient.

'I think that under the circumstances these French classes aren't such a good idea,' he mused slowly.

His words filled her with deep dismay and the first stirrings of rebellion. 'But Thursday is my night off, Ethan.'

'Night off?' he repeated coldly. 'You're not the nanny now, Hannah. You're my wife.'

'Of course I still work for you, Ethan. I just call you Ethan, not Mr Kemp.' And that had taken some getting used to! 'The contract's more permanent, and less flexible,' she added thoughtfully. 'That's all.'

He couldn't have looked more astounded if she'd popped him one on the nose. He breathed in sharply and the slab of his belly muscles became more noticeably concave. Hannah had heard girls on the beach in Nice commenting on his 'great pecs'; these too were visible, because even though he'd slipped on a blue top that matched his trousers he hadn't bothered to fasten it. She was no expert, but she didn't think their enthusiasm for his body had been misplaced.

'There is no need to think of yourself in that way,' he said, his colour heightened.

'Then as your wife I don't necessarily have to take your…advice.' Advice had a more tactful ring than order.

A combative light had entered his grey eyes. Possibly it was due to the unusual events of the evening, but Hannah found the circumstance more exhilarating than alarming.

'Perhaps you should consider your track record in the decision-making arena before throwing my advice back in my face.'

'Did you have a particular decision in mind?'

Despite the fact that she had remained meticulously polite, there was no mistaking the obstinate set of her rounded jaw. He viewed said jaw with serious misgivings.

'Getting into a car with a perfect stranger? Only a complete idiot would do anything so grossly irresponsible,' he said scornfully. 'Emma, at seven, would have more sense.'

She'd been stupid to imagine she could win an argument with Ethan. 'You wouldn't say that if I was a man,' she complained belligerently.

He blinked: she was pouting, actually pouting—Hannah! The sight of her rather full pink lips had the most unexpected effect on his body. 'Well, you're not a man,' he snapped. 'And in that outfit it's patently obvious.'

Hannah went bright pink and, after a furtive glance down at her body, began to tug the towel higher, but the material would only stretch just so far.

'I'm sorry if my skinny body offends you, but I didn't invite you into my room.' Even a fluffy bunny rabbit could get aggressive if you backed it into a corner, and she wasn't actually as weak and pliable as Ethan thought.

Early on she'd decided confrontation wasn't her style, but to survive ten years relatively unscathed after her spells in assorted foster homes, interspersed by the inevitable return to the children's home, wasn't the sign of a weak character. It wasn't an advantage in life to be brought up in care, but Hannah had never allowed herself to grow bitter, just as she'd never allowed herself to be influenced by the less savoury influences she had been surrounded by.

'I'll keep that in mind in the future,' he observed stiffly.

'I didn't mean…' She gave a sigh of frustration. 'The French classes mean a lot to me,' she admitted.

'Very obviously,' he drawled. With growing dismay she observed the pinched look around his nostrils.

It had been a waste of time appealing to his softer nature! 'I need to get away, be…I don't know—*me!*'

'Does that usually involve removing your wedding ring?'

Hannah could only stare at him in astonishment. He couldn't actually believe… 'I lost my ring.' It had always been too big; if she hadn't hated asking him for anything, she'd have told him so.

'You seem awfully passionate about a night-class.'

His faint condescending sneer really made her see red. 'Just a *class* to you!' she yelled. 'But then you have dozens of friends. You go out every day and meet people. I see the children—' And, as much as she loved Emma and Tom, the children weren't always enough. She broke off, breathing hard. Though one part of her felt appalled at her outburst, another part—a small part—felt relief.

'We have an active social life. My friends…'

'*Your* friends despise me. They only put up with me because I'm your appendage. Actually—' she smiled briefly, amazed at her daring '—I don't much like them, at least not most of them.'

The colour that suffused the pale, perfect oval of her small face was quite becoming. 'Colourless' was the adjective he most frequently associated with this girl he'd married—it sure as hell wasn't applicable now!

'Then why haven't you seen fit to mention it before?'

'I didn't think it was relevant. I'm quite prepared to take the rough with the smooth.' But I won't give up the French classes. It wasn't necessary to add this; Ethan wasn't dense.

'That's very tolerant of you. Do you consider there to have been much that is *rough* for you to endure over the past year?'

'Next you'll be saying I was in the gutter when you found me,' she cut in impatiently. She ignored his sharp inhalation of anger and continued firmly. 'You can expect my loyalty, but not my unstinting gratitude, Ethan. If you remember, I did warn you I wouldn't be the world's best hostess, but I'm a good mother.'

'Mother substitute.' She flinched, and his expression seemed to indicate he regretted his hasty response. 'The children love you.' This was meant to soften his sharp correction but only served to bring a lump of emotion to Hannah's throat. 'Do you find me such an ungenerous husband?'

It wasn't fair of him to bring affection into the discussion because affection, or rather the lack of it, had been implicit in their bargain.

'I didn't say that.'

Right from the outset he'd insisted that she spent money from the generous personal allowance that appeared in her bank account every month. Ethan Kemp's wife couldn't have a wardrobe that consisted of jeans and jumpers. When he'd discovered she couldn't overcome her reluctance to spend money, he'd sought the help of the wife of one of his colleagues.

Hannah wasn't sure whether Alice Chambers had genuinely awful taste or she just didn't like her. Whichever was the truth, the clothes Hannah came home with from their joint shopping expedition did nothing whatever for her slight figure, and the colours made her appear washed out and insipid.

Some of the annoyance faded from Ethan's expression as he took in the pale fragility of her unhappy face. With her glossy hair hanging softly about her face she looked incredibly young. She *was* incredibly young; he was apt to overlook the age gap sometimes. Usually she had the composure of someone much older.

'No, you didn't, but it is fairly obvious you're discontented. I had no idea.'

'How could you?' The retort escaped before she could censor it. Some days they barely exchanged two words. 'I'm not discontent, just tired,' she said dully. The loneliness of her position rushed in on her and it was more than she could bear tonight. Just go, please go! she thought miserably.

As if he detected her passionate wish, he turned abruptly. 'We'll talk in the morning.'

Now there's something to look forward to, she thought, torn between tears and laughter as the door closed. In the privacy of her secret dreams she'd imagined him using that door. Usually he'd just woken up to the fact that he'd been unaccountably blind to her charms. In none of those meticulously constructed scenarios had she had a runny nose, scratches over half her body or hair flopping in her eyes.

Falling in love with Ethan Kemp was the only truly spontaneous thing she could recall doing in her life. You didn't have to be a starry-eyed believer in love at first sight to have it happen to you; she was the living proof. Her prosaic soul had been set alight the instant she'd set eyes on him. He was tall, with an impressive athletic build, and one glance into those shrewd eyes had told her he had an intellect to match his muscles. Never one to respond to superficial beauty, she'd been inexplicably bowled over. None of these passionate cravings had been evident in her colourless replies as she'd sat through the interview. If they had she doubted she'd have got the job.

Worshipping him from afar had always made her particularly inarticulate in his presence, but, so long as the children were happy, Ethan's interest in their nanny had been minimal. When he'd first started to show an interest in her lukewarm friendship with Matt Carter, a local primary school teacher, she had almost allowed herself to think he might have noticed her as a person.

As it had turned out, he'd just been afraid history was about to repeat itself. Emma and Tom had had three nannies in the year before she'd arrived. Tom had been one, and he'd simply responded to anyone who'd offered him love and warmth. His sister had been a different proposition—five when Hannah had first arrived, and it had been an uphill battle for Hannah to win her trust. Her short life had taught Emma it was painful to love someone only to have them vanish. Hannah could identify with her suspicion, and slowly she'd won the child's trust, until by the end of that first year she'd become an integral part of the children's lives.

An indispensable part, as far as Ethan was concerned. They were now confident, happy children, and he'd been prepared to go to extraordinary lengths to provide them with continuing stability. He'd been shocked to recognise the possibility that Hannah might just follow the example of the previous three nannies and do something inconvenient like fall in love or get pregnant. He didn't actually *want* a wife, and, just in case Hannah had any doubts on the subject, he'd told her so.

He'd known her history when he'd offered her a home and financial security. No doubt he'd considered the bait irresistible to someone who was completely alone in the world. She'd never have to budget her meagre resources again; she'd have the family she'd always dreamed of— in short it was a fairy tale. The *but* was inescapable: he would never view her as anything other than a paid employee, no matter what her title. The pre-nuptial agreement he'd had her sign prior to the wedding had only served to reinforce this fact.

He had probably congratulated himself on his subtle, but clever presentation of the package when she'd appeared the next morning, looking unusually pale and subdued, and said the all-important 'yes'. He wouldn't have looked so happy if he'd suspected that, no matter how tempting his offer might appear to a girl who longed for roots and stability, it was love that had been the vital ingredient in the equation. Love that had made her ignore the logical part of her brain that told her that such a union could only give her pain.

CHAPTER TWO

TOM usually woke Hannah by creeping into her bed, often before six in the morning. This morning there was no solid little body against hers when she awoke. A light sleeper, she didn't normally need to set her alarm clock, but there had been nothing *normal* about the previous night! A whistle-stop, vaguely panicky tour revealed the children weren't in their rooms.

'Why didn't anyone wake me?' Hannah demanded breathlessly as she ran into the kitchen still tying the belt on her robe. 'Ouf, sorry,' she gasped as she rushed full tilt into her husband.

'I told them not to,' Ethan replied calmly.

She was conscious of the intimate contact of their bodies only for a few seconds before he solicitously steadied her and stepped away. It was enough to send her pulse-rate hammering. Although he didn't douse himself in masculine cologne, she could have recognised his presence blindfolded in any room. Her nostrils automatically flared as she got a full dose of his signature male fragrance.

'What are you doing here?' She instantly wished the words unsaid. Ethan didn't want or need her interest, and any suggestion of interrogation would be met with a sharp rebuttal. Now was the time to get their relationship back on its neatly designed unchallenging lines. Last night had been a blip in normality not a new chapter.

One dark brow quirked. 'I live here, remember.'

His dry tone brought a flush to her cheeks. 'Shouldn't you be in work?' There I go again.

As she spoke Hannah was conscious of the fact that they weren't alone; despite appearances, at least one pair of ears was undoubtedly taking in every word. The housekeeper had never made any comment on her employer's odd choice of bride, but she wouldn't have been human if the situation hadn't intrigued her.

Hannah sometimes wondered what she said about them to her husband when she returned home in the evenings. She'd been *in situ* when the first Mrs Kemp had been alive, and Hannah had half expected her to keep the sort of suspicious, unfriendly distance many of Ethan's friends did. To her relief this hadn't been the case. So long as Hannah didn't trespass on her domestic territory, she seemed perfectly at ease with the arrangement.

Ethan didn't normally participate in the usual morning chaos of dressing and feeding the children, then ferrying Emma to school. He was generally leaving the house as Hannah fetched the children downstairs. He appeared to start the day with nothing more substantial than a cup of strong black coffee, a practice Hannah privately had serious reservations about. She had never voiced her concerns, because Ethan's welfare was one of those things that were out of bounds. She had no doubt that with a few well-chosen words he could and would subdue any pretensions she had in that direction.

'Not this morning, Hannah. Dear God,' he murmured, inspecting the streak of strawberry jam he'd just discovered down the sleeve of his dark jacket with a grimace. 'How does he manage to spread it that far?' he wondered, casting a fascinated look in the direction of his

chubby-faced son, who smiled back with cherubic innocence from his highchair.

'I want down!' he announced, banging his spoon on
the plastic table-top.

'Soon, Tom,' Hannah responded automatically. She
pushed her hair behind her ears and tried to work out
what Ethan was doing here. A devoted father he might
be, but he'd never involved himself in the more mundane of parental duties. 'You should have woken me.
I'll be late getting Emma to school.'

'Daddy's taking me, Mummy.'

The 'Mummy' was a new thing, and it still gave
Hannah a glow of pleasure to hear it. Ethan had never
commented on her promotion from 'Hannah' in his
daughter's eyes, but she was sure he didn't like it. His
restraint only reminded her that from his point of view
her role within the household would always be one of
necessity rather than desire.

'You are?' she gasped, unable to hide her surprise.

'You consider the task too complex for me?'

'You just sit down, my dear, and I'll get you a nice
cup of tea. Mr Kemp has told me about the nasty accident you were in. What you need is a rest,' the housekeeper advised.

Hannah's eyes flew to Ethan's face as her hand went
automatically to her scratched cheek. So that was to be
the story, she thought philosophically. It certainly made
her appear less foolish than the truth.

'I feel fine—just a little stiff, Mrs Turner.'

'I want out, now!' Patience was uncharted territory
for a three-year-old.

Hannah unclipped his harness and heaved his sleep-
suit-clad body into her arms. His sturdy frame made her

conscious of bruises she hadn't known she had. She wasn't able totally to subdue the wince.

'Give him to me,' Ethan said, holding his arms out.

'I'm fine.'

'Martyrdom is an overrated and tedious virtue,' Ethan observed in a bored drawl.

Hannah handed over her charge with as much dignity as she could muster. Normally their parental duties were strictly, if unofficially, defined, and it was vaguely disorientating to have her role so thoroughly usurped.

Ethan might well regret his chivalry when he discovered that the wet kiss his beaming son had pressed somewhere east of his mouth had left a blob of porridge adhering to his freshly shaved cheek. A wicked impulse made her keep this information to herself.

'Will you do my hair?' Emma slid onto Hannah's knee and solemnly passed her a comb and ribbons.

'With your permission?' She shot Ethan a challenging look. She sounded cranky and didn't much care. She knew he was watching her again and it made her feel uncomfortable.

'I'd say that constitutes light duties,' he conceded. Whilst playing a tickling game, which Hannah thought might well result in his small son throwing up, he watched Hannah's expert fingers twist Emma's fluffy golden locks into the desired design. Emma was a beautiful child who looked remarkably like a miniature version of her mother. Hannah was sure Ethan didn't need the constant reminder to keep Catherine's memory fresh—several people had lost no time telling Hannah how passionately in love he'd been, how he'd worshipped her.

Hannah had been astounded the first time she'd seen Ethan with his children. Who would have guessed that behind the austere, rather daunting façade there lurked such a warm and humorous man? She'd thought his attitude towards her might bend a little over the months, but he'd never actually dropped the formality with her. She'd never been in any danger of forgetting her position in this household.

It wouldn't be long before Emma at least began to notice that her parents weren't like other people's: no hugs or teasing, no shared history of private jokes. Ethan didn't appear to have taken this aspect into account in his calculations. Children were sharp; nothing much escaped their observant eyes. It would be interesting, and probably uncomfortable, Hannah reflected, to see how he dealt with the inevitable questions.

'I'll be back shortly,' he said as he stood, the open doorway framing the sight of daughter and father hand in hand.

'Work...?' she faltered.

'I've cancelled my appointments for this morning. Cal Morgan will see you at ten. I'll take you to the surgery— for that tetanus jab,' he added as she stared at him blankly.

'Quite right, you can't be too careful,' the housekeeper observed approvingly. 'Tom will be just fine with me. I'll take him for his bath, won't I, darling? Kiss for Mummy.'

When Hannah emerged from the grubby embrace Ethan had gone. This new personal interest in her welfare obviously stemmed from his opinion that she wasn't capable of taking care of herself. It was frustrating to realise that she had nobody to blame for the situation but herself. If only he hadn't caught her last night. It had been an inconvenient time to discover the man she'd married was either an insomniac or a secret drinker, possibly both. The idea brought a whimsical smile to her lips. She couldn't imagine Ethan indulging in weaknesses of any variety!

She'd just have to reestablish herself in his eyes as being more than capable of taking care of herself. Driving herself to the doctor's surgery was step one of this process. He'd be glad to be relieved of this tedious chore.

That view took on a rapid sea change when she emerged from the surgery to find Ethan standing beside her Volvo. His long fingers were rapping an impatient tune on the bonnet. He appeared to be muttering under his breath at regular intervals. He straightened up at the sound of her feet crunching on the gravel. His dark brows met over the bridge of his nose as he recognised her.

'What the hell are you playing at?'

Whilst his attitude to her lacked warmth, she couldn't remember any occasion when his manner towards her hadn't been faultlessly polite. The flash of anger in his grey eyes and the unmistakable message his whole body language was shouting threw her totally off balance. What had she done?

'I'm not playing at anything, Ethan.'

'Don't waste that "butter wouldn't melt in your mouth" look on me, Hannah Smith... It won't wash any more.'

'Kemp, I'm Hannah Kemp.' He might like to pretend this weren't true sometimes, but it was.

He rubbed a hand through his dark hair, disrupting the sleek silhouette. 'You were less trouble as Smith,' he reflected after a thoughtful pause. 'I offered to drive you because you're very obviously not fit to sit behind a wheel. What are you trying to do—smash the parts you missed last night?'

'That's a ridiculous overstatement!' she protested. 'And don't think you're the only one regretting this marriage,' she yelled wildly.

His expression hardened into one of icy disdain as his cold glance whipped up and down her slender figure. Under the scrutiny she forced herself to straighten up, even though the ache in her ribs intensified.

'Marriage to me is one of those decisions you'd better learn to live with.' The unspoken 'or else' was clearly there in capital letters.

'Save your intimidation for the courtroom,' she told him with uncharacteristic steel.

'I'd never make that mistake—strong-arm tactics with someone who looks as vulnerable and fragile as you do right now would lose me the jury's sympathy.'

'I didn't mean to wound your professional pride.'

Her sarcastic murmur sent his dark brows towards his hairline. 'Happily we're not in the courtroom right now, so I'll continue to behave like a bully—you're obviously very at home with that image of me,' he observed tautly. 'Have you seen the way you're moving, woman? It's obvious every step hurts.'

She grimaced—that was almost exactly what Cal had said before he'd insisted on examining her. She gazed at her husband resentfully. 'My ribs are bruised, not broken, and Cal has given me a prescription for some painkillers.'

'Well, the next time you decide to get in a car with a maniac try and remember you're a mother, not a bloody stunt woman!'

Anyone would think she'd done this for the sole purpose of inconveniencing him! Ethan could be mind-bogglingly selfish at times.

'Don't worry, I don't need a nursemaid. You don't have to waste your time at home for my sake.'

'Nursemaid!' he scoffed. 'I'm beginning to think you need a minder. As for staying at home, I'm in court this afternoon. Alexa has agreed to pick Emma up from school.'

Hannah didn't have time to hide her dismay from him.

'I do think you might make a little bit more effort with Alexa—she is the children's grandmother.'

Effort, me? thought Hannah. She grated her teeth at the sheer injustice of this criticism. Alexa Harding had been horrified when she'd learnt that the nanny was to take her daughter's place. Having any woman take Catherine's place would have been hard for her to accept, but the fact that Hannah was, in her eyes, menial household help made the situation unacceptable to the older woman.

At first Hannah had thought she might come round, if she saw the children were happy, but, if anything, the closer Hannah had become to the children, the more bitter their grandmother had become. She never missed an opportunity to belittle Hannah in front of Ethan—she was about as subtle as dripping acid. Hannah longed for Ethan to side with her—*just once*. Only he never did. He remained aloof from the petty squabbles.

'It's very kind of her,' Hannah said in a expressionless voice. Anxiety crowded out the appearance of calm as she rushed on. 'You didn't tell her what actually happened, did you?' Alexa would have a field-day with that sort of information.

'Does it matter?'

Hannah grabbed his wrist, her fingers digging into his skin. 'Yes, it does,' she persisted urgently.

Ethan looked from her pale fingers to her flushed face with a quizzical expression. 'I stuck to the accident story.'

Hannah heaved a sigh of relief. 'Thank you.' Realising she was still clinging, she abruptly released her grip.

'The truth isn't the sort of story I'm likely to spread around.'

'Are you trying to imply that by getting into his car I was inviting…?'

'My God, don't be so touchy!' he exploded. 'I'm not implying anything of the sort. Hopefully you've learnt something from the experience, but that might be asking too much.'

Didn't he ever make a mistake? 'I've learnt not to expect any sympathy from you.' She flushed at the implication that she desired sympathy from him.

'Not when you act like a naïve schoolgirl,' he snapped back crisply. 'Get in the car. Not this one—mine,' he added as she reached for her car keys. 'No, don't put those away,' he said, catching her hand. 'You'd better lock it first. Do you make a habit of leaving a welcome card for car thieves?'

'I thought I had locked it. I *always* lock it.' His sceptical sneer made her want to scream.

Ethan drove a high-powered black BMW. He parked at the end of a tree-lined avenue and told her tersely he'd only be ten minutes. He didn't explain where he was going, but then he never did. Whatever his business was, he looked pretty grim.

Ethan was always punctual, and it was barely ten

minutes later that he returned. He opened the door and threw in her brown leather shoulder bag.

'I thought you'd like this back. You'd better check everything is there,' he advised, sliding into the driver's seat. 'It won't bite; you take a look.'

'Where did you get it?' she asked hoarsely.

The engine purred into life. 'Where do you think?'

'How do you know where he lives? What did you do…?'

'The college was very helpful when I explained good old Craig had left his wallet in my car last night. Shocking security,' he observed mildly.

'What did he say? Did he just hand it over?'

'He said too much,' Ethan observed curtly.

'About me?' she asked miserably. She could just imagine what sordid lies he'd wheeled out to justify his actions. She felt sick just imagining that Ethan had believed any of it. She couldn't bring herself to look at him.

'Don't worry, he admitted the truth eventually.'

'Eventually?' She looked at his grim, hard-edged profile and realised she was being pretty slow. Ethan wasn't the sort of man people intimidated, but he was more than capable of doing the intimidating if he felt the situation justified it. His next words confirmed her dawning suspicions.

'Craig is now personally acquainted with fear. That was what you wanted, wasn't it? I forget how long you had in mind, but I always think it's quality not quantity that counts.'

His thin-lipped smile made her shudder. This wasn't the indulgent father; this was a ruthless man—a dangerous man. She'd never actually appreciated before just how daunting Ethan could be.

'You didn't…didn't hit him, did you?'

His charcoal-grey suit was pristine and his silk tie lay smoothly against the white background of his shirt. He didn't look like a man who'd just been brawling. Her eyes went to his knuckles as his hands lay lightly on the steering wheel—no tell-tale marks.

'Nothing so crude. I just told him what I'd do to him if he ever touched you or any other woman again.'

'And that scared him?'

'You had to be there.' His smile was savagely silky. It made Hannah shudder. It made her realise how little she knew this man she'd married.

'Are lawyers supposed to behave like that?' she asked doubtfully.

'I didn't go in there wearing my wig, Hannah. I went in there as your husband. I didn't lay a finger on him— of course, if he'd tried…' He shook his head rather regretfully. 'I knew he'd cave in. I've seen his type often enough—inadequate bullies.' His grey eyes were filled with contempt as he flicked her a sideways glance. Happily the contempt was intended for the loathsome Craig.

She looked away and pretended to go through the contents of her bag. 'It's all here,' she said, not actually registering what was before her eyes. The words 'as your husband' kept going through her mind. The warm glow was a ludicrous response; she knew he hadn't meant anything by it. All the same…

'Aren't you stopping for lunch?' she asked, trying to sound as if it didn't matter one way or the other. She'd had a lot of experience; she could hear what sounded like authentic lack of interest in her voice.

'I'm meeting Miranda. She's assisting me this after-noon.'

Miranda, the newest recruit to Ethan's chambers, was everything Hannah would have liked to be. Not only was she beautiful, she had brains which had earned her respect in a male-dominated world.

Hannah often wondered if Miranda was the reason Ethan didn't get home until so late—suspiciously late on Friday nights. It wasn't really reasonable to suppose he remained celibate; he was a virile, attractive—*very* attractive—man. Even if he was still hopelessly in love with Catherine, he was still human. She knew he'd always be discreet; it wasn't in his nature to humiliate her by flaunting his affairs. All the same, the thought of him with the beautiful redhead tortured her.

'That's nice.'

'Is it?'

'I wouldn't know,' she said in an exasperated tone. 'I was just being polite.' She tried to slip back into their old relationship, and the only thanks she got were his snide comments. There was no pleasing some people.

'Now I know why I married you—for your lovely manners.'

What she'd done to deserve his mockery she didn't know. She'd grown accustomed to his indifference over the past year, his occasional irritation, but he actually looked as though he disliked her this morning.

'No, you married me because you wanted a low-maintenance wife who would make as little impact as possible on your life!' The resentment bubbled up and overflowed into these unwise observations before she could stop it.

He flinched as the accuracy of her husky accusation hit him. 'Well, I'd hardly call your antics over the last twenty-four hours low maintenance.' The unvarnished truth sliced uncomfortably through his rationalisations, and, not unnaturally, made him as mad as hell.

Ethan had managed to convince himself that his motives in marrying Hannah, whilst not being totally altruistic, hadn't been completely selfish. She'd had so little and he'd been offering her a standard of living that she could never have aspired to. It was a sound business arrangement. She'd always given the impression of being content. Her affection for the children was indisputable, as was theirs for her.

Until he'd been faced with the prospect of losing her, he hadn't realised how much this quiet girl had become part of the household. The part that had given it the first breath of normality and stability in a long time. It was incredible how someone so unobtrusive could make such a difference. Unobtrusive? Looking at the angry belligerence that tightened the soft contours of her face, he decided the label seemed singularly inappropriate.

'If I'd had my way you wouldn't have known at all about last night. It's your fault for being an insomniac!'

'Wouldn't have known!' He seized on the words as if they were a guilty admission. 'I thought as much—how many other *secrets* do you keep from me?'

'Secrets, *me*?' The idea was laughable. 'If I told you everything I do in a day I'd bore your socks off.' Not like the lovely Miranda, she thought. I bet he hangs on her every syllable.

The guilt he felt at the most unexpected moments came rushing in and his voice was harsh. 'So your life's drudgery, is it?'

'Luxurious drudgery,' she corrected sarcastically, her outstretched arms encompassing the elegant surroundings of the period-furnished drawing room. A room that was a tribute to the good taste of her predecessor. 'What more could a girl ask for? And you accuse me of being touchy!' she snorted.

He regarded her delicately flushed face, flashing eyes and mutinously set mouth with an odd expression. His stillness made Hannah lick her lips nervously.

Unexpectedly, he caught her chin in one hand. 'What's happened to you? You're not the same person.' Everything had been going so well. Why the hell did she have to start acting like a woman all of a sudden? And, even worse, why was he thinking of her as a woman?

'Perhaps you've confused silence with lack of feelings, Ethan. I do *feel*.'

'And what feelings arouse your passions?' he wondered out loud. His eyes dropped to the rapid rise and fall of her small, high breasts, and a look she'd never seen before slid into his eyes.

'Things,' she replied huskily.

'Like French classes.' A trace of discontent had entered his voice.

'Like French classes,' she agreed.

'Perhaps it would be safer for you to look closer to home to satisfy your passions.' His thumb moved in a circular motion over the small, rounded chin.

'Do you speak French, Ethan?'

'It wasn't the search for intellectual stimulation that made you do a dangerous thing like get in that car last night. The man turned out to be an idiot, but what if he'd had a more subtle approach? Would a furtive kiss in the dark have been so unacceptable to you, Hannah? Isn't that what you secretly wanted?'

She tore her face from his grip. 'The only person I'd like less to be touched by than Craig…is you!' The insulting picture of herself as some sexually frustrated female desperate for male attention made her blood boil. Ironically, the only male attention she craved was his. At least he couldn't taunt her with the truth.

'Brave words.'

A logical assessment later would tell her she'd backed his male ego into a corner and the outcome had been a foregone conclusion. Logic didn't come to her assistance at the time.

It was nothing like her imaginary kisses. Imagination didn't have texture and warmth and taste. 'Melting' had been a word before; now it was a reality as her body dissolved in a rush of mind-numbing sensual delight. Her lips automatically parted under the imprint of his mouth. The taste of him glutted her senses.

When it stopped her disorientation was total. She felt numb and strangely dizzy. She touched the back of her hand to her parted, slightly swollen lips. The eyes she raised to his face were still clouded with a misty languor. It afforded Hannah a tiny measure of satisfaction that Ethan looked to be equally stunned by his actions.

Over the years Hannah had formulated a vague theory that for women it was easy to stop kissing—it was only men who were driven beyond sense and reason by such an essentially innocent pastime.

Innocent! Oh, dear, it looked as if she'd have to re-evaluate her hypothesis. Limited research was obviously to blame for her inaccurate conclusions.

'That was childish of me.' He was slipping back into his cool professional persona with insulting ease. An adjustment to his gold cufflinks, a judicious twitch of the tasteful tie.

'*Childish* isn't the first word that springs to my mind,' she returned huskily. The destructive friction of his skil-

ful lips and wicked tongue had filled her with an entirely
adult ache. It began low in the pit of her belly, but spread
just about everywhere.

'I suppose you expect me to apologise.' From the
stubborn, closed expression on his face, she concluded
this was unlikely.

'Why? I liked it.'

'Dear God!' he grated, his stance growing more rigid
as he discovered she was examining his lips with dreamy
curiosity.

The sharp exclamation brought Hannah belatedly to
her senses. She bit hard on her criminally indiscreet
tongue and felt the hot colour wash up her neck until
her face was aflame.

'I mean, a kiss is just…'

'A kiss?' he suggested.

'Exactly,' she said, relief making her go a bit overboard on the enthusiasm. 'I don't think we should mention…'

'You liked it.'

Hannah frowned, not trusting his suddenly innocent
expression. 'Your loss of control.'

'That's very generous of you.' Perversely, he found
himself vaguely dissatisfied that she was suggesting
what he had wanted only seconds before.

When the doorbell rang later that afternoon Hannah
squared her shoulders and steeled herself for a dose of
Alexa. She glanced at the clock on the mantel and
frowned—she was early. Hannah was sitting cross-
legged on the carpet, playing with Tom, and she smiled
wryly as she pulled the child onto her lap, aware she
was using him almost as a shield against the battery of
criticism she knew was about to be lobbed at her head.

'Mrs Kemp, it's a Mr Dubois.'

'Jean-Paul!' Hannah exclaimed in pleasure as the figure behind Mrs Turner stepped forward.

'Hannah, forgive the intrusion.'

'It's no intrusion—come in. Would you like tea, coffee?'

'Coffee would be nice.'

'Would you mind, Mrs Turner?' She smiled at the housekeeper. 'Sit down, please.' She couldn't understand what her night-class tutor was doing here, but, having stealed herself to face the dreaded Alexa, it was marvellous to see a friendly face. You're a coward, Hannah, she told herself angrily. Show a bit more backbone!

Jean-Paul Dubois settled himself in an armchair and looked admiringly around the room. Hannah saw his glance dwell on a framed picture of Ethan with Catherine: two beautiful people, the perfect couple. He was too polite to comment.

'You have a lovely home.' He pushed his wire-framed glasses up the bridge of his nose. They were the only vaguely intellectual thing about the young Frenchman's appearance. He looked more like a male model than a university lecturer, which was his daytime job.

'Home' had an optimistically permanent ring to it. 'It's been in my husband's family for a long time.' Ethan had inherited the place years ago from his father, and though his mother had first stayed on in her marital home she had left shortly after Ethan's first marriage. Hannah had only met Faith Kemp once, at their own wedding, and the lady hadn't bothered hiding her disapproval of the match. Hannah had heard with her own ears Faith read a scalding lecture to her son on the subject.

'He is a beautiful *bébé*,' Jean-Paul, said, laughing as Tom lobbed a pink elephant at his head.

'Thank you.'

Jean-Paul nodded at the question in her eyes. 'You are wondering why I am here?'

'It's very nice to see you.'

'You are a very talented student. Some people have a natural talent for languages—you are one of them.'

Hannah flushed with pleasure. She'd certainly enjoyed the classes, but she hadn't thought she was anything special. 'I've had a good teacher.'

'That's why I wish you'd reconsider your decision to leave the class. I know there are many pressures when you have a family... The unfortunate accident—'

'Stop right there,' Hannah said, holding up her hand. Tom wriggled off her knee and went over to Jean-Paul, who took the theft of his spectacles in good part. 'What makes you think I'm leaving the class? How did you know I'd had an...accident?' She flushed a little as she said this.

'Your husband spoke to me earlier,' he explained.

Hannah drew a wrathful breath. 'He did, did he?' she said quietly, with a brilliantly false smile.

'I did tell him how sorry I would be to see you go. I know our classes are light-hearted, but I was hoping you could go further.'

'Further?' she said, startled for a moment from her contemplation of a suitable punishment for her over-bearing husband. So long as she made the children happy, he had no right to interfere so blatantly in her life. One night a week to herself wasn't too much to ask for.

'Have you ever thought of doing a degree?'

'Me?' Hannah shook her head. 'I couldn't do that— I've no formal schooling to speak of. I left school at sixteen.' That was when the State had stopped being responsible for her, and she'd woken up to the fact that taking care of herself and being in full-time education weren't compatible.

'Your family did not mind?'

'I had no family,' Hannah explained briefly. Her mouth tightened at the sympathetic light she saw in his eyes. She hated pity! 'I trained as a nursery nurse.' A job that gave her both an income and a roof over her head had seemed a practical compromise.

'I know you are very young, Hannah.'

'Twenty-three.'

'But you would still be classed as a mature candidate for university entrance. There is quite a lot of flexibility for the right candidates.'

'And you think I'm the right candidate?'

Jean-Paul smiled as he heard the hint of wistfulness creep into her voice. 'The perfect candidate. Some mature students find the finances a drain, but you…' His Gallic gesture took in the undoubted affluence of the surroundings.

'I don't know what to say.' Could she? Ethan would never agree. All the same, the idea did take hold. Over the years she'd seen people much less able than herself go to university. It had been something that had seemed always tantalisingly out of reach.

'Say yes, *chérie*.' Satisfied he'd presented his case, he didn't labour the point. 'Where, *bébé*, are my glasses? You must lead me by the hand, Hannah. I am blind.'

Laughing, Hannah reached under the sofa and retrieved the spectacles. Still on her knees at the foot of Jean-Paul's chair, she slid them obligingly back onto his nose.

At this point the door opened and the housekeeper returned, bearing a tray laden with coffee and scones. 'I put plenty on for everyone. I know how hungry Emma is when she comes home.'

'Can I have one now?' Emma skipped into the room beside the upright figure of her grandmother, whose pale blue eyes swept over the room with a look of malicious triumph. 'Can I, Mummy?'

'Get changed out of your uniform first,' Hannah said, pushing back the wing of silky hair that had flopped in her eyes. 'Hello, Alexa. It was good of you to pick Emma up.'

'Hannah, what a delightful surprise—I half expected you to be bed-bound, from the way Ethan was talking. You look glowing, my dear. Aren't you going to introduce me to your *friend*?'

Determined not to rise to the bait, Hannah simply nodded in Jean-Paul's direction. 'This is Jean-Paul Dubois, my French tutor. Jean-Paul, this is Alexa…'

Jean-Paul got to his feet and, clasping the older woman's hand lightly, raised it to his lips. '*Madame.* No, Hannah, do not get up—you are busy with your family. Will you think about what I said?'

Hannah couldn't help wincing as she got to her feet. The painkillers had improved the situation, but she was still stiff and sore. Gallant to his fingertips, Jean-Paul solicitously took her elbow.

'Thank you,' she murmured gratefully as she straightened up. 'It was good of you to call. Goodbye.'

'*Au revoir,*' he corrected.

'Does Ethan know you entertain your men whilst he is out working?' Alexa settled herself into the chair Jean-Paul had vacated. She was a handsome woman who had kept a youthful figure. The permanent lines of bitterness around her mouth robbed her of what otherwise would have been beauty.

'Man, Alexa,' Hannah corrected calmly. 'And I feel sure I can rely on you to tell Ethan.' She was well aware that it wouldn't occur to Ethan that a man like Jean-Paul would find her attractive—that was part of the reason he'd married her.

The older woman looked a little taken aback by her composure. 'I expect you've been playing up a couple of scratches for all it's worth. Catherine never let personal discomfort stop her doing what she wanted. She wasn't afraid of anything!'

Which was why she wasn't here now! Hannah repressed this unworthy observation. Tom had been barely a month old when Catherine had decided to ride in a point-to-point. When her horse had gone lame she had taken on a mount whose rider had been injured, even though the animal was renowned for an unpredictable temper. She had to have known the risk she was taking when she'd ignored advice—it was only because of her pregnancy that she'd missed out on a place in the British Olympic team. Hannah wasn't in a position to speculate about what drove someone like that; perhaps it was irrelevant. Whatever the motivation, the outcome had been tragic.

'I'm not Catherine.'

Alexa's laugh was shrill. 'And I'm sure Ethan remembers what he lost every time he looks at you,' she sneered. 'Thomas, put that down!' she cried as the little boy lifted a porcelain figure off the lower shelf of a display case.

'Give it to Mummy, Tom,' Hannah said quietly, so as not to alarm the child. 'Good boy,' she praised as he handed it over. She placed the delicate ornament on a higher shelf. Alexa's words wouldn't have hurt so much if she hadn't known they were true. She could never hope to compete with the vital, glowing creature Ethan had loved.

'That was one of Catherine's favourites.'

It would be, of course, Hannah thought philosophically. 'Well, it's safe now.'

'I don't know why you allow the children in this room. They ruin everything.'

Hannah sighed; they'd been through this before. 'This is a family home, Alexa, not a showcase. It's meant to be lived in.' The whole place was in danger of becoming a shrine. It was bad enough that almost every room was filled with photos of its late mistress; the trophies of her sporting achievements remained as a memorial to her talent and sense of adventure. Not only had she been a top-class horsewoman, she'd been an accomplished yachtswoman, and somewhere along the way she'd managed to pack in a spot of rock-climbing. She had obviously been one of those people who found danger attractive, even addictive. Her talent hadn't been limited to competing in the sporting world—she had founded and run a small manufacturing business which specialised in high-class sporting gear.

Hannah might not be able to alter the tastefully coordinated decor to suit her own taste, but she had been able to smuggle the odd toy box gradually into the drawing room and pin Emma's early attempts at art on the kitchen wall, despite Alexa's objections. A minor victory, but for Hannah a triumph. Children didn't need the stifling atmosphere of a museum.

'The place is looking positively shabby. I know Ethan doesn't like to entertain much now Catherine is gone, but…' Alexa's aristocratic nose wrinkled in disgust.

This was a patent untruth—all the main reception rooms had been redecorated a couple of months previously. The interior decorators had duplicated all the existing decor down to the smallest detail.

Emma's explosive return into the room spared Hannah Alexa's more obvious displays of dislike. She knew it went deeper than dislike. It sometimes felt as if the woman had made Hannah the focus for all her grief and anger over her daughter's death.

CHAPTER THREE

AFTER a year of marriage Ethan came knocking on Hannah's bedroom door for the second time in as many days. This time she heard him. It was Friday night and he was home late, as usual.

'This is getting to be habit-forming,' she said as he stepped into the room in response to her crisp invitation.

It was a line she'd been working on all evening, and she was quite pleased with her delivery. She might have been flustered to see him if Alexa's actions hadn't been so predictable. She'd known he'd appear at some point, demanding an explanation.

'You getting into trouble?' Elbow against the wall, he loosened his tie and looked at her in a distinctly unfriendly fashion.

In her innocence she'd imagined that with love off the menu she might settle for the closeness of a special friendship. Being ignored had been a lot easier to bear than his open dislike.

'Am I?' She didn't appear too bothered at the possibility, which she could see surprised him. She'd discovered a perverse pleasure in surprising him over the past day or so. It was satisfying, shaking him out of his iron certitude. It was only natural, she decided, to resent the person you loved when he didn't even notice you existed—at least not in *that* way.

'I suppose you've received reports of me inviting my hordes of lovers to cavort on the Aubusson carpet in the drawing room.' The mental image of bacchanalia brought a tiny smile to her lips.

'You don't seem to be taking this very seriously.' He ran a hand over the dark growth of stubble that shadowed his angular jaw.

'I'm only amazed that you are,' she fired back wearily. 'No, actually I'm not, because you don't have a very high opinion of me, do you, Ethan?'

She'd worked so damned hard to be what he wanted, but that had counted for nothing when she'd disrupted the smooth running of his life. One little slip, and he was looking at her as though she had something contagious. So her *little slip* had been spectacular—she hadn't asked him to get involved personally.

'You've always done what I've asked of you,' he observed noncommittally. Despite his words, she didn't detect any wholehearted endorsement in his slightly uncomfortable stance. He looked as though his wife's bedroom was the last place in the world he wanted to be. Anger was her best response to the pain this knowledge brought.

'You're just wondering what else I've done besides.'

'When the woman I married starts behaving like a teenager rebelling for the hell of it, I do start wondering—yes!' he agreed in a driven voice. 'You're acting completely out of character.'

'And you'd know all about my character?'

Her mockery brought an angry gleam to his narrowed eyes. 'I'm sorry if you didn't have the opportunity to get the rebellion out of your system when most of us do, but I've no desire whatever to become the focal point for your childish aggression. I don't feel even vaguely paternal towards you.' His lips twisted into a grimace of distaste.

'I wasn't looking for a father-figure when I married you!' Please, God, don't let him ask what I *was* looking for, she prayed, as she recognised the opening she'd given him. She needn't have been concerned—Ethan thought he knew all about her motivation.

'No, you were looking for security, which is understandable. Only now you're discovering that there's *more* to life than comfort. There's excitement.' Her fragile poise deserted her completely as his grey eyes raked her face. 'And sex.'

Her chest felt so tight she could hardly breathe. 'How dare you talk like that to me?'

'I *dare* because our lives here only work because we accept certain limitations,' he said brutally. 'It's a very delicate balance, and when you start flirting with French studs…'

'I expect Jean-Paul would find the stereotyping very flattering,' she breathed, furious that he could calmly taint an innocent friendship—God, it wasn't even that!—with his nasty innuendo! 'If you hadn't tried to run my life for me, Ethan, Jean-Paul wouldn't even have come here. You'll be relieved to hear it wasn't my body he was after,' she hissed sarcastically. 'But then I'm sure you didn't think that. You played safe when you picked me, didn't you?' she accused bitterly. 'You picked the plainest female you could find in the knowledge that, no matter how much you ignored me, there wasn't going to be anyone else queuing up to show me a good time!'

'If *Jean-Paul* wasn't here to show you "a good time"—' her face flamed as he quoted her heated words '—why did he come?'

'He wants me to do a degree—in French.'

He gave a short, hard laugh. 'It's more original than wanting to show you his etchings,' he conceded.

'Why do you assume it's a joke? You think I'm too stupid?' she asked from between gritted teeth.

'Well, you're not behaving like an intellectual giant right now, are you?'

'Is that a fact?' Forgetting her rather prim pose of crossed ankles and folded hands, she had deserted the chintz armchair and was pacing the room. 'How am I behaving, Ethan?'

'Over-emotionally, irrationally…'

'You, on the other hand, are the epitome of self-restraint and reason. Well, I've got news that you can file away in that rational brain of yours: not only will I *not* stop going to evening classes, I've every intention of exploring the possibility of taking it further.' If he hadn't pushed her she doubted she would have had the nerve seriously to explore the possibility. Ironically it was Ethan's scorn that had hardened her determination.

'I'm sure taking it further is exactly what Dubois had in mind,' he sneered. 'Only you're my wife!'

'My God, I hope for the sake of your clients you come up with more original arguments than that in court.'

'You can sneer, but you can't alter facts,' he countered, his face dark with anger.

He'd been inclined to dismiss Alexa's wild stories, and until he'd entered Hannah's room he'd expected to hear an adequate explanation. He'd been irritated at the necessity of confronting her after a long and tedious day, but nothing more.

Far from lulling his suspicions, her defiant attitude had made it clear she was capable of ruining their arrangement with her wilful behaviour. Her habitually calm hazel eyes had deepened to green as she glared at him before resuming her rhythmic barefooted tread of the deep-piled carpet.

He almost groaned out loud. A classic case of still waters running deep, only he didn't need, or require, deep. He needed shallow and efficient. He didn't want a glimpse of Hannah's passions; he wanted things back to normal. At the end of the day he could always come home knowing she would have coped with any household crises with quiet efficiency, his children would be happy and content and nobody would make any emotional demands on him. He hadn't realised how much he'd come to rely on this small oasis of peace until he'd been unexpectedly deprived of it.

'Some facts you can alter,' she said, coming to a dead halt with her back still to him. 'We could get a divorce— an annulment, even!' She spun around, her face alight with inspiration. 'It's not as if we have…' she shrugged '…you know.'

'Don't forget you signed the pre-nuptial—' My God, he thought, staring at her. She means it!

Her imperative gesture stopped him mid-flow. 'I don't care about that,' she said simply. All she cared about was getting out of this situation. Being married to a man she was crazy about, a man who thought of her as a sexless nonentity. She'd been mad to think she could cope; she'd been made to think it would lead down the path of her wishful thinking.

Ethan blinked, recalling the amount of money it had been agreed she would get if she stayed with him until Tom was sixteen. 'And the children?'

'That's the best part,' she told him enthusiastically, willing him to see the logic of her scheme. 'I could still look after the children. When Tom starts school I could go to university and still help with them. I wouldn't do anything to harm the children, Ethan.'

'So I'm the only part of this equation that you don't like?'

The desperate quality of her wild proposition said more about her unhappiness than anything else could have. The irony of the situation failed to amuse him. One of the reasons marriage to Hannah had been a good idea was that he'd wanted to put himself off-limits to all the women who, almost before the funeral was over, had made it obvious they were willing to offer him succour and comfort. His wife obviously found him easy to resist.

'You were a much nicer employer than husband,' she said fairly. 'And I've been an abysmal failure as a wife; admit it. I irritate you, embarrass you. I have appalling dress sense.'

'Appalling dress sense wasn't grounds for divorce the last time I looked.'

'But non-consummation is grounds for annulment.'

'So we're to annul our marriage and then you resume your job as nanny. Is that about the size of it?'

When he put it like that it didn't sound quite as feasible as it had when her feverish mind had seized on the solution. She nodded, but there was less certainty in her face now.

'Are you on some medication I don't know about?' he enquired with interest.

She sank down onto the edge of her bed with a sigh. 'Maybe I didn't think this through exactly. There's no need to be sarcastic. I was trying to help.'

'Then I hope you've put all thought of annulment out of your head. Unless both parties co-operate it's hell to prove unless you're a... Dear God,' he said slowly, staring at her averted face. 'You are, aren't you?' He sounded so profoundly shocked that in other circumstances she might have laughed.

'What if I am?' she responded belligerently. Being a virgin at the advanced age of twenty-three was certainly an embarrassment, and she was sensitive about the subject.

'It never occurred to me,' he admitted faintly. 'Why didn't you tell me?'

'It's hardly relevant, is it?' she said, trying to disguise her intense discomfort beneath a cool façade. She tucked her legs underneath her and wrapped the ends of her cotton wrap over her knees.

'Bloody time-bomb!' He didn't bang his head against the striped silk wallpaper, but as he rested his brow against it he managed to give the impression he wanted to.

'I beg your pardon?'

He turned his head away from the wall and glared at her. 'You were twenty-two,' he exploded, his voice thick with resentment. 'I naturally assumed that should you become attracted to anyone you could be relied upon to act maturely. Do you honestly think I'd have suggested this arrangement if I'd known you hadn't explored your own sexuality? It's easy to see now why you're acting so irrationally—your hormones have finally caught up with you. You'll be hanging posters of boy bands on your wall next. I can see it all!' he taunted, closing his eyes on the awful mental image this conjured.

'My hormones or lack of them have got nothing to do with this. You don't trust me!'

'Trust you! I trust you about as much as I'd trust any adolescent experimenting with sex, and we all know how reliable they are.'

'I'm not experimenting with sex!' she burst out, her

face pink with a mixture of embarrassment and frustration. 'I really resent the implication I'm not a fit person to take care of Emma and Tom.'

'I know you care about Emma and Tom—that's not the problem we're facing here. You grew up too fast, Hannah. You didn't have the opportunity to be selfish.'

'So now I'm selfish!'

'Tell me, what were you doing when other young people were being wild and irresponsible—experimenting with their freedom and lack of responsibilities? Shall I tell you?' He didn't give her the opportunity to reply. 'You were struggling to support yourself in some miserable bedsit somewhere. You were getting qualifications to earn a living and holding down part-time jobs to pay the bills. You missed out on a whole chunk of your youth. So why should I be surprised if you're trying to recapture it now?' The peculiar self-recrimination in his voice was more unsettling than his unreasonable accusations.

'How did you know…?' she began, amazed by the startling accuracy of the picture his soft words drew.

'You came into this house as an employee, remember. I followed up your references and it wasn't hard, knowing your background, to imagine what sort of life you'd had. A lot of the people I come across have had similar starts in life,' he reminded her. 'It's a road that all too frequently leads to the wrong side of the law. Not everyone is as single-minded and determined as you are.'

The immediate impression of quiet restraint and malleability had been the reason he'd missed the iron streak in her character. He suspected he was going to pay for this oversight—he already was paying!

'If you believe that, why do you doubt my ability to fulfil my obligation to the children?' His evaluation of her character came as something of a shock. Strangely, it made her feel less awkward about behaving naturally in front of him. 'I made a commitment and I won't do anything to compromise that.'

'You say that now, but what if you fall in love? Where would that leave our arrangement?'

'That's not possible,' she said hoarsely.

'A statement like that says everything about your inexperience,' he observed with the sort of lofty scorn that set her teeth on edge.

'What about you? You might fall in love.'

'I've been there and done that,' he said, his sexy mouth tightening with disapproval. 'The whole point I'm trying to make is you haven't.'

'Who says so?' she flung back recklessly.

'You mean you're not a…?'

'Just because you fall in love with someone, it doesn't necessarily follow that you sleep with them. I fell in love with someone who is unavailable.' Sometimes, she reflected, the truth—at least a cosmetic version of it, anyway—came in very handy!

'When did all this happen, or, rather, not happen?' he asked with insulting scepticism.

'Ages ago,' she said airily.

'Is he married?' he asked, frowning as he mentally reviewed all the married men who had shown any interest in his wife.

'I don't want to talk about it,' she replied with perfect honesty.

'Is it someone I know?'

'My private thoughts are one part of my life you can't control.'

'I don't try and control you!' he exclaimed in horrified denial.

'You're the one who cancelled my French classes,' she reminded him.

'We agreed—'

'*You* agreed,' she corrected him firmly. 'Like most of the decisions in this house, it was a strictly unilateral one.'

'I didn't think you minded,' he responded, his colour heightened. 'I had no intention of coercing you,' he added rather stiffly.

His austere glare had lost some of its power to intimidate her. It was partly her own fault, she acknowledged honestly. She'd never raised any objections to his habit of making all the decisions that affected her. It was fairly natural he'd assume she didn't have an opinion.

'Jean-Paul will be pleased to hear I'm not quitting.' Her steady stare openly challenged him.

An expression of reluctant admiration entered Ethan's eyes. 'The man seems to think you're his star pupil.'

'Who am I to argue?' It was about time she started standing up for herself. Winning certainly gave a girl a nice glow.

An expression of disgust crossed Ethan's face as he shook his head. 'I've never understood why women are such pushovers for pretty faces. 'He's so *obvious*,' he observed with distaste.

Hannah's mouth dropped open and her lip began to quiver. Had Ethan looked in the mirror recently? she wondered incredulously. He had more raw sex appeal in his little finger than dear Jean-Paul had in his entire body!

'What? What have I said now?'

When Ethan departed in disgust Hannah was curled on the bed in fits of helpless laughter.

*　　*　　*

It had been a week since the evening of their truce. A sort of normality reigned again. Hannah's more obvious scars had faded, with the exception of some multicoloured bruises across her ribcage and faint smudges on her arms. She'd been back to evening class, where there had been a noticeable absence of the dreaded Craig.

So she was in a loveless marriage—people survived worse situations. It was a matter of having a positive attitude. Her new attitude had been firmly in her mind today, when she'd cancelled the shopping trip with Alice. If she had to appear in her role as token wife when Ethan went to some friends' anniversary party, she was going to make the effort not to look like a fashion victim.

'The usual trim, madam?' her hairdresser had asked, disguising his boredom behind a professional smile.

'No, do something different.'

The carte blanche had been seized before she could retract her reckless invitation. Now, the sight of the growing heap of soft brown hair on the floor made Hannah feel a little queasy and she hardly dared look at her reflection. When she did she could hardly believe the transformation.

Cut just above shoulder-length, her cleverly layered mane framed her face in soft, feathery fingers. She could shake her head or rub her fingers through the silky ends and the cut sprang softly back into place.

'I look different.'

'I always knew you had potential.'

'I've got potential, she kept telling herself as she walked around town. The occasional glances she stole in the plate glass windows confirmed this pleasant theory. She'd never be beautiful, but potentially pretty might not be aiming too high.

She was walking in the direction of the expensive

store that Alice always took her to when a dress in a window display caught her eye. After a small internal struggle she decided to go in—the assistants couldn't be worse than the ones in the other store, who always gave her the most terrific inferiority complex with their snooty attitude and heavy make-up.

The middle-aged woman in the shop was neither snooty nor heavily made up. She did, however, shake her head slowly when Hannah mentioned the dress in the window. She ran a shrewd eye up and down Hannah's slim figure.

'Great frock, but you'd need at least another five inches to carry it off. Besides, the style is much too old for you. We do a really good petite range, though. Let's see what we've got.'

Without encouragement Hannah would never have tried the dress on. 'It's so...so red,' she said dubiously as she pirouetted in front of the mirror.

'It's sensational is what it is,' her one-woman fan club assured her. Hannah wondered cynically if she worked on commission. All the same, she thought, glancing into the full-length wall mirror, she hadn't known she was capable of looking—well, sexy!

The simple bodice of deep ruby-red satin was moulded closely but not tightly before it flared slightly into a short skirt. Sleeveless, with a scooped neck, it was the simplest thing she'd tried on. 'I usually wear sleeves—my arms are a bit skinny.'

'Are you mad? I'd kill for your arms, and your collar-bones are so Audrey Hepburn,' the saleswoman sighed enviously. 'I expect you're too young to know who she is.'

Hannah grinned. 'I've seen *Breakfast at Tiffany's* a million times.'

I must have been mad, she thought later as she dithered at her bedroom door. What if Ethan hated it? What
if he thought it looked, horror of horrors, *tarty*? What if
he insisted she changed? What if…?

She shook her head angrily at these fancies. The fact
was he probably wouldn't even notice she looked different. She was making a big fuss about nothing. What
if he didn't like it—so what? *I* like it, she decided firmly.

This firm resolve carried her all the way to the draw-
ing-room door. Getting beyond it was achieved by sheer
will-power.

'Sorry if I'm late.' Her chin went automatically up to
fend off any criticism. She was quite glad that the
strappy sandals gave her an illusion of height.

Ethan was the sort of man whom nobody would ever
mistake for a waiter in his dinner jacket. Whilst Hannah
couldn't be described as a dispassionate observer, she
couldn't believe anyone female could fail to be impressed by his sinfully sexy dark good looks.

He glanced from the file he was flicking through to
his wristwatch. 'Only by five min…' He looked up and
his voice froze as completely as his body. His eyes swept
her from top to toe and back again before he spoke.
'You've cut your hair.'

'An impulse,' she said nervously. He'd noticed, but it
was impossible to tell from his expression whether he
approved of the transformation.

'Did Alice help you choose that?' His eyes touched
the red dress.

'No.'

'It shows.'

Enigmatic could be pretty frustrating at times, she
thought, glaring at his broad back as he moved in front
of her to hold the door open.

Maggie Hilton and her husband, a couple ten years or so older than Ethan, were some of his closest friends. The very first dinner party she'd presided over as Mrs Kemp had been for them. Hannah had wanted everything to be perfect; she'd fussed and worried over the minutest detail for a whole week beforehand.

She'd been desperately anxious to do the right thing, say the right thing, but in the event she'd scarcely said anything. The couple were both solicitors and the conversation had been largely shop talk. Hannah would have liked to say something witty and amusing, but she didn't think they'd be interested in the funny thing that had happened outside the school gates. Occasionally someone would remember she was there and try to include her, but it had all been painfully forced.

She'd been settling Tom, who had woken whilst their guests were leaving. Richard had already got into the car, but Maggie had still been talking to Ethan in the hallway when she'd come quietly back downstairs.

'It's such a permanent solution, Ethan.'

'I know what I'm doing, Maggie.'

'Do you? I wonder? The children won't be small for ever, and then they'll be off to school. Oh, I know you had a horrid time at boarding-school, but you'll change your mind when the time comes, and, I don't care what anyone says, it builds character.'

Looking down from the dark alcove, Hannah could only see Ethan's back but Maggie's expression of pitying affection was highlighted by the light she stood beneath. 'She's very *nice,* but when I think of Catherine…' She shook her head regretfully. 'I know it wasn't all plain sailing, but the best of us have our differences— that's what makes marriage interesting. Catherine was

so alive and spontaneous, and she's so dull. I'm sorry—
I promised Richard I wouldn't say anything.'

'I think you should listen to your husband more often,
Maggie.'

'I know, but I've started now so I might as well be
hung for a sheep as a lamb! You have nothing in common. The poor girl has obviously never had anything to
do with people like us...'

'"People like us."' Ethan repeated the words slowly.
'I never had you pegged as a snob, Maggie.'

This accusation was hotly denied. 'I'm not sure you
did a kind thing, marrying her. She was obviously uncomfortable tonight—I felt quite sorry for her.'

'Your pity wasn't prominent when you brought
Catherine into the conversation at five-minute intervals.'

'Here with you it's only natural to think of Catherine;
you were a pair. She was your social and intellectual
equal, Ethan. I don't know how you can bring yourself
to—'

'Hannah may not have enjoyed our social and intellectual advantages, but she is bright. She's articulate and
thoughtful.'

Maggie Hilton conceded this with a sigh. 'I grant you
that, but she's so *dull*!'

'She's my wife.' It hadn't been a proud assertion, just
a flat statement of fact. He'd sounded like a man who'd
given up on hope.

Over time, when Hannah saw the Hiltons, she remembered that pitch of dull acceptance in his voice. But it
wouldn't be so bad tonight: she'd gained confidence
over the last year, and had learnt a few social tricks. She
was still an outsider as far as they were concerned, and
she accepted the fact.

Ethan didn't say another word to her until they stood

outside the illuminated façade of the Hiltons' home, and even then she had to prompt him.

'Didn't I get it all off?' she asked when his eyes dwelt over-long in the general direction of her mouth. She touched her lips nervously. 'The red lipstick was too much,' she babbled frantically, 'but I thought I'd got it all off.' It had left a crimson stain that made her look as if she'd been eating raspberries, but she thought she'd removed the worst of the 'in your face' gloss.

'Let me see,' Ethan said, placing his forefinger firmly under her chin. 'There's only one sure way to remove lipstick in my experience.'

'What's…?'

The sensuous, slow movement of his warm mouth against her lips sent any lingering concerns about her make-up out of the window. She wasn't the slightest bit bothered when his big hands slid through the silky strands of her hair, obliterating her new hairstyle as his fingers caressed her scalp. The tingling went all the way down to her toes and she was obliged to press her hands against the solidity of his chest to stop herself falling into an inelegant heap.

'Mission accomplished,' he murmured, drawing away. His eyes appeared darker than usual as he examined her quivering lips.

Hannah was dizzily aware that the door was opening. 'Thank you,' she said faintly.

'It was a pleasure.'

'It was?' she asked doubtfully. She pinned her polite social smile on her face as her hostess appeared.

'Definitely.' He flicked a look in her direction which made her stomach dissolve into a warm ache before he surged forward to hug the elegant older woman. 'Maggie, my dear, you look marvellous.'

'Thank you, Ethan, darling, but I know when I've been upstaged,' she said drily, staring at Hannah, who stood a little behind them. 'Poor Richard, I'm afraid his blood pressure is going to be troublesome tonight. You look stunning, my dear.' For a moment Hannah assumed it was Ethan her hostess was talking to; when her error became obvious her eyes widened.

Ethan caught Hannah's hand and urged her gently into the brilliantly lit hallway. 'Doesn't she just?'

Did he actually believe that or was this a sample of his silky society manners? When he chose to wheel out the charm Ethan could leave even Jean-Paul standing, only he didn't normally waste his charisma on his wife. It would be a mistake to read too much into this behaviour, she told herself firmly, and as for the kiss. The kiss…! She couldn't think at all when she thought about that.

She couldn't help but be gratified by the double takes and flattering attention. Alice was very condescending in her helpful criticism of Hannah's outfit, and Hannah couldn't resist pointing out that the lady's own husband had admired her outfit.

'But he's a man, my dear, and men are notoriously drawn to…tacky— Sorry.' She laughed theatrically and covered her mouth with a hand. 'It just slipped out. Don't look so unhappy, Hannah. Its not as if you've got a lot to flaunt, is it?'

'Not as much as you,' Hannah agreed quietly as she turned to go. She regretted immediately that she'd allowed herself to be goaded into the catty response. 'I wish I hadn't said that,' she murmured, closing her eyes.

'If she can't take it, the lady shouldn't dish it up.'

The sound of Ethan's voice at her elbow made Hannah jump. 'Were you eavesdropping?'

'Not intentionally. You've danced with everyone else,' he said, as the soft heavy thud of an evocative melody filled the room. 'I think it's my turn.' He took hold of her upper arm, and his fingers slid experimentally over her skin as if he was somehow impelled to sample the texture of her creamy flesh.

'I didn't think you danced.' The almost imperceptible movement of his fingers had a mesmeric effect on Hannah's nervous system. Why had he kissed her? It was a question that wouldn't go away. Each time her thoughts had returned to the subject her eyes had sought him out. The light food and wine hadn't taken the taste of him from her mouth. Her throat ached with emotion. And no practical good intentions could banish the excitement that heated her blood.

'It was news to me that you do,' he reminded her drily. 'If dancing is what they call those sexy gyrations you've been treating us to tonight.'

Sexy, me? Not for the first time that evening her eyes collided with his, but this time she didn't have the comfort of a room's distance between them. 'I've never learnt to dance properly,' she babbled in panic as his arm went around her waist.

'Then we'll leave the dips and twirls to the people who know what they're doing, shall we?' He took one of her hands and placed it against his shoulder. 'Shuffle step will do just fine. You can't deny you don't have an ear for rhythm after tonight.'

'I can't?' She couldn't attribute the light-headed sensation to the glass of wine she'd nursed throughout the evening. Her proximity to Ethan was a much more powerful drug.

Her legs were pressed against his hard thighs as they moved around the impromptu dance floor. Without doing anything obvious Ethan had unobtrusively drawn her closer. To prevent her hand being squashed between their bodies she had sensibly placed it out of harm's way around his neck. Her fingertips lightly trailed across the area where his dark, thick hair ended in crisp curls.

As the music throbbed Ethan dropped his head until she could feel the warmth of his breath stirring the glossy strands of hair on her head. 'What do you smell of? I don't recognise the perfume.'

'Shampoo, probably. I don't possess any expensive perfumes.' She almost stumbled when his hand slid down from her waist and his fingers splayed over the rounded contour of her behind. 'These heels,' she laughed, recovering her balance but not her equilibrium. Was he doing this on purpose, and, if so, to what end? The heat of his body was absorbed by the thin fabric of her dress and passed directly into her own skin.

'You've got good legs.' Somehow he managed to insinuate one of her legs between his. She grunted softly in shock as she felt the evidence of his arousal graze the crest of her hip before a slight twist of his body moved the pressure to her lower belly.

'If they were six inches longer.' Catherine had been tall, very tall, a Nordic-looking beauty. Hannah wished she hadn't spoilt the moment by thinking of her.

'There's nothing wrong with being petite—small but perfectly formed.'

'If I agreed with you I'd sound conceited,' she said, trying to sound as if his words hadn't raised her excitement levels to a new high. 'If I denied it I'd sound coy.' The effort to be cool took its toll, and she surrendered to the invitation of his broad chest with a small sigh. 'I'm a bit tired,' she murmured in a husky voice, just in case he got the wrong, or rather *right* idea.

'Let's go home.'

'Now?' she faltered, lifting her head as the slow beat was replaced by a livelier tune. 'It's early.'

'I'm sure it's difficult to tear yourself away, but I'm less keen on the spectacle of grown men drooling over my wife.'

'Are you suggesting I was encouraging them?' Her hands slid down his dark-suited forearms and with a small flick of his wrists his fingers closed around hers.

'The transformation from wallflower to belle of the ball must be a pretty intoxicating one—I wouldn't blame you if you enjoyed flirting. I was afraid this would happen,' he mused, watching her broodingly.

'I don't know what you're talking about.'

He looked into the puzzled depths of her clear eyes. 'I know,' he said heavily. 'Come on, we'll make our apologies and leave.'

Richard Hilton insisted on seeing them out himself. He placed an arm around Hannah's shoulders and she could smell the alcohol on his breath. She didn't much mind—he made an amiable, if garrulous drunk.

'I keep telling her she looks gorgeous,' he announced, slapping Ethan heartily on the back. 'You sly dog, you knew what you were about. Like I said to Maggie, nobody knows what goes on behind closed doors.' He tapped the side of his nose and gave a conspiratorial wink. '*I* never said you were a fool.'

'I'm touched,' Ethan said, detaching himself gently but firmly from a maudlin embrace. 'We must go.'

'Yes, that's it, off you go. Would myself in your place.'

Hannah laughed as they walked over to the car. She was determined to show him she wasn't reading anything into his friend's drunken and deeply embarrassing ramblings. 'Richard seems to think we're leaving early to—'

'Do unspeakable things behind closed doors,' Ethan finished smoothly. 'A crazy idea.'

'He's had a lot to drink.' It was hard to sound suitably amused when she had the distinct impression that under the superficially bland expression Ethan wasn't laughing at all; he wasn't even smiling.

'Don't let that bumbling air fool you—I've seen Richard win at poker after imbibing enough to sink a battle cruiser. A very perceptive man,' he mused half to himself. In the darkness she could see the silver flash of his disturbing eyes.

It would be a mistake, she decided, to read anything at all into this cryptic utterance—but of course she did.

CHAPTER FOUR

WHEN the car drew to a halt outside The Manor House Hannah didn't move. She had to know.

'Why did you kiss me, Ethan?'

He clicked open his seat belt and turned slowly in his seat. From what she could make out in the semi-darkness he was less surprised by her question than she was.

'I thought I'd get in first.'

'First?'

'Before someone else did. You look very kissable to-night, Hannah.'

She caught her breath at this husky admission. 'I didn't kiss anyone else tonight.' And she hadn't wanted to, she thought, clasping her hands tightly in her lap to stop herself reaching out for him.

'Only because I brought you home before the wolves closed in.' His jaw tightened as he recalled the increasing rage that had built up inside him as he'd watched men ogling his wife. The last man to say something complimentary about her to him had received a murder-ous glare and retreated looking shaken. Ethan had felt slightly ashamed. In the darkness he paused soberly to examine the violence of his revulsion.

This fanciful description of his very respectable friends brought a gurgle of laughter to Hannah's lips. She felt the silent disapproval of his response to her amusement in the darkness.

'Isn't that a tad dramatic?' she asked.

'You really are determined to make up for lost time,

aren't you?' She could hear him grating his teeth. 'Don't you realise what you could destroy if you insist on experimenting?'

'I only cut my hair and bought a new dress,' she protested. 'It's not my fault if people are so influenced by superficial things.' And he was as bad as any of them, she thought resentfully. Kissing her, dancing with her…inviting her lurid imagination to go into overdrive.

'The change goes a lot deeper than that, Hannah.'

'Well, I'm sorry if you don't like it, Ethan, but I'm a lot happier being myself. Don't worry, I'm not going to jump into bed with the first man who tells me I'm beautiful. That would be taking gratitude to extremes.' It was insulting that he imagined she'd be such a push-over.

'What if that man is your husband?' It wasn't a sudden notion—it just came out that way. He'd been turning the idea over in his head all week. Tonight just made the need for action more urgent.

'What?' she whispered, unable to believe he'd actually said what she thought.

'If you need to discover your sexuality it would be safer for all concerned if you did so with me,' he observed casually. The darkness concealed the fact he was looking far from casual as he tensely awaited her reply.

'I'm touched by your willingness to make such a sacrifice,' she said, her voice shaking. 'Thanks, but no, thanks, Ethan! I'm not that desperate. What's wrong? Didn't you believe me when I said I wouldn't try for an annulment? Did the ultimate sacrifice seem the best way to close off that avenue of escape?' Now she thought about it, it all made awful sense.

She struggled with the handle of the passenger door. Her free hand flailed wildly back at him as he tried to prevent her getting out. As Ethan reached out to stop her escaping his hand came into contact with the spot where her lace-topped stocking ended and her bare thigh began. It had seemed for a split second that his fingers had begun to move experimentally, but he drew back so abruptly she knew she must have been mistaken.

'You imagine I'd be that cold-blooded?' His voice sounded strange and forced in the enclosed space of the car.

'I think you can be ruthlessly practical when it suits you. The facts do speak for themselves. You never looked twice at me before I suggested a divorce.' To her intense relief the door finally opened and she half fell out of the car. Happily this one was stationary.

'You can't think of any other reason why I want you in my bed?' he yelled after her.

Just as well their nearest neighbour was a field away. She could hear his long legs catching up with her shorter stride as she reached the front door. The housekeeper always stayed overnight on the occasions she babysat and she would be long since in bed. Short of waking the entire household, Hannah didn't have much choice but to wait for Ethan.

'I don't have a key.' Her back was pressed against the door as she faced him.

Ethan was breathing hard; his face was shadowed, but she could see he was angry—really angry. She'd never seen him so close to losing control before. A small, objective portion of her mind was amazed that she'd been responsible for this. The rest of her brain wasn't objective—it was a mess of scattered half-formed thoughts.

Her intense visceral reaction to his suggestion wouldn't have been so intense if she hadn't been so hopelessly in love with him. The pragmatic proposal seemed a cruel parody of what she'd longed for and it had cut painfully deep.

He pressed one hand against the wall beside her head as he silently unlocked the door. In the shadow of his body she felt as if she were cocooned in a cave, only the walls weren't cold stone, they were warm, living flesh. As the door swung open she ducked under his arm.

'Not so fast.' He stepped after her and caught her by the shoulder, sending her swirling round a hundred and eighty degrees. The fact that she'd have fallen off her heels didn't really matter, because he literally swept her off her feet as he jerked her towards him.

He wasn't satisfied with a submissive response; he wanted surrender—and he got it. He didn't stop until he'd felt the small, guttural moans of pleasure in her throat, parried the darting forays of her tongue with his own and reduced her body to a trembling, boneless mass of screaming nerve-endings.

Gasping for breath, he pulled away, and Hannah was horrified to see her fingers still twisted in his hair. Shaking, she pulled her nerveless hands free. Taking her by her shoulders, he looked so savage that for a minute she thought he was going to shake her.

'That cold-blooded enough for you?'

Cold-blooded! It had been ruthless—a fact that appeared to be slowly dawning on Ethan too. A spasm of something that might have been regret crossed his features.

'It was most impressive, darling,' a strange voice commented. 'Would you like a cup of tea? Drew has just made a pot.'

'Mother!' Incredulously Ethan focused on the figure casually seated at the head of the long table. 'What are you doing here? And who the hell's Drew?' He looked without enthusiasm at the tall blond young man who was calmly pouring milk into a mug.

'Didn't I say he'd be delighted to see me? It brings tears to my eyes every time I remember him saying to me, "This will always be your home, Mother." So touching.' She dabbed at invisible spots of moisture at the corners of her eyes. 'Drew is a *dear* friend of mine who has travelled all the way from Patagonia with me.' Since she'd been widowed, Faith Kemp had indulged her passion for foreign travel, and usually the odd card from exotic places was the only reminder of her existence.

'Geography never was my best subject, Mother.'

If being caught passionately kissing his wife had embarrassed him, he was hiding it well. Hannah, on the other hand, was wishing she were invisible. Wishing didn't help—she was the focus of her mother-in-law's ill-concealed interest and the silent stranger's blue-eyed sympathy as his sharp gaze noted the faded bruises along her shoulder.

'South America, darling. Some people actually speak Welsh there—extraordinary! My great-grandmother was Welsh; did I ever mention it?'

'Yes.' From his expression it was plain that Ethan was less than fascinated by the lesson.

'Andrew Cummings.' The tall man moved forward, his hand extended. He wore faded jeans and a tee shirt, and a tatty army surplus jacket was hung on the back of a chair. His sun-bleached blond hair was almost long enough to tie back in a ponytail, which would have been in keeping with his unconventional image. For an awful moment Hannah thought Ethan was going to ignore the hand. 'I can see I'm intruding,' Drew's voice was low and cultured—an educated bohemian, Hannah decided.

Hannah rushed in before Ethan could agree. 'Nonsense—there's plenty of room here. Isn't there, Ethan?' she insisted, glaring at him.

'Of course,' Ethan responded. His reluctance was obvious enough to make Hannah blush. She was beginning to feel quite sorry for the stranger.

'I'll show you to a room,' she put in quickly, seizing the opportunity to escape. She thought for a moment that Ethan was going to object, and breathed a sigh of relief when he nodded.

She'd mounted the stairs, their unexpected guest bringing up the rear, when Ethan's deep voice seemed to vibrate off the vaulted ceiling.

'Well, if you think you're sharing a room with your toy boy under my roof, Mother, you're mistaken.'

'My God,' his parent replied clearly, 'you always were an awful prude! I'm curious, Ethan—how exactly are you planning to stop me? Are you planning on patrolling the house all night?'

Hannah risked a look at the blond young man's profile; much to her relief and amazement, he looked amused.

'Sorry.'

'Don't worry about it, I've been called a lot worse.' He unslung his backpack as Hannah paused outside a bedroom door. 'It's me who should be apologising—I had assumed Faith had warned you we were coming. But then she's rather fond of the element of surprise,' he mused with a reminiscent smile.

'I wouldn't know. I haven't seen her since our wedding day.' To her horror Hannah realised that she was close to tears. 'If you want anything, just yell,' she said hurriedly as she opened the door and stepped to one side for him to enter.

'I think I should be saying that,' Drew observed bluntly. He'd have to be made of stone not to pick up the distress this girl was emanating. That, along with her surly husband's attitude and the traces of old bruises, told a story that filled him with anger. The man was obviously a thug.

Hannah flushed as the implication of his words sank in. 'I think you've misread the situation,' she said stiffly.

'It happens,' he agreed with an easy shrug. 'But the offer stands,' he said firmly.

Going back to her room, Hannah reflected ruefully that it was lucky Ethan hadn't heard the conversation. She could imagine he just might take exception to the idea that his wife needed protecting—especially if it was him she needed protecting from!

She'd knocked the bedside light over trying to switch it on. The lamp lay on the floor, its shade at a crazy angle, casting shadows over the deep blue carpet.

Her cream cotton nightshirt was wet with perspiration and she was shaking. It wasn't the first time she'd had the nightmare of being trapped in the car with Craig, but it was the worst.

Her breathing was just calming when the door burst open and their blond-haired guest appeared. His blue eyes swept the room suspiciously before he moved inside.

'What are you doing?' she asked, surprisingly unalarmed by the intrusion.

'You yelled.'

'Sorry about that. I had a nightmare.'

'So I see.' He bent to pick up the lamp from the floor.

'Why the hell did you lock the door, Hannah?' Ethan's eyes narrowed into slits when he saw the well-built and scantily dressed figure of Drew Cummings. 'I'm sure there's a perfectly logical explanation for the fact you're in my wife's bedroom at one a.m.' The soft hostility in his voice was more threatening than any raised voice might have been. 'I suggest you share it— now!'

Broad-shouldered and lean-hipped, Ethan was wearing light silk shorts which did nothing to disguise the athletic power of his tall frame. Hannah felt forbidden stirrings just looking at him. Feelings that had been quite absent when she'd looked at Drew, even though they were similarly attired. Sexual chemistry certainly didn't follow any logical pattern.

To give him his due, Drew didn't recoil from the dark suspicion in Ethan's voice. The edgy atmosphere was heavy with the threat of imminent violence.

'She yelled out. I'm a light sleeper.'

Hannah knew she hadn't imagined the warning held in this statement.

'Are you all right, Hannah?' Ethan's hard glance flicked in her direction.

'Just a nightmare. Thank you, Drew, but I'm fine now.' Please let him go before things get really silly! Considering the fact that until recently the only male who had ventured across her threshold had been a three-year-old child, it occurred to her that she was taking two virile, extremely attractive men circling each other with wary aggression quite calmly.

Drew's blue eyes rested on Ethan with a less than friendly expression. 'If *you* say so.'

'I do.' She gave a sigh of relief as he departed. She whistled softly and sank back against the pillows.

'What was all that about?' Ethan asked, closing the door firmly behind him.

'He appears to think I need protecting.'

'From what?'

'You, I imagine,' she confessed as a bubble of inappropriate laughter rose up in her throat.

'And how did he get that impression?'

'Don't look at me, I didn't say a word. It might have something to do with first impressions,' she mused, throwing him a wry look.

'I don't like being looked at as if I'm a wife-beater,' he growled, in an outraged tone.

'Any more than I like being looked at like a victim. Shall we stop the conversation right there while we're in unexpected harmony?' Her eyes widened in alarm as he sat on the edge of the bed. The light thrown out by the small lamp shadowed the strong curves of his back, highlighting the shift of muscles as he moved. His skin looked so smooth, almost oiled; she wondered what it would be like to rub oil into the hard contours.

'I don't like him.'

'I'd never have guessed.'

'What do you suppose would have happened if I hadn't walked in when I did?'

'You obviously have a theory—do share it,' she urged, propping her chin on her hands. 'I'm all ears.'

'I doubt if it's your ears he's interested in. Prowling around half naked,' he said sourly.

'Like you.' This provocative little jibe earned her a savage glare. She widened her eyes with an innocent confusion that made him grind his teeth audibly. The confusion wasn't entirely faked: she'd let her eyes dwell on the firm contours of his lean, tanned body for longer than was good for her.

'This is *my* house.'

'This is *my* bedroom.'

'You're very territorial all of a sudden.'

'I'm very popular all of a sudden,' she countered drily. It was difficult to be flattered when she knew from experience to what lengths Ethan was willing to go to safeguard his children's happiness.

'I find it bloody perverse that you're willing to give a total stranger the benefit of the doubt, but you attach the basest motives possible to everything I do.'

'You don't have to seduce me, Ethan. I'm not about to run off with Drew or anyone else, even if he is charming and *very* good-looking.'

'My mother certainly thinks so.'

'I don't think your mother is the sort of person who takes kindly to being told how to run her life, especially by her son,' Hannah ventured warily. 'At least, that was the impression I got,' she observed with a shrug. Like her son, Faith didn't seem the type to take advice kindly.

'Forget about my mother,' he said. The thickness in his voice filled her with alarm and excitement. 'Why must I have some ulterior motive in wanting to seduce my wife? Your words not mine,' he added wryly. 'Why can't I just be responding to a basic biological need— the most basic biological need there is?'

'If your biological needs had been a priority in your choice of wife you wouldn't have married me, Ethan.' The honest truth hurt, but she didn't want him to believe she was under any illusions, though sometimes she wished she were! She had to prove to herself as well as to him that she couldn't be beguiled by the smouldering expression in his eyes. 'You're not sexually attracted to me,' she said firmly.

'Is that a fact?'

'I know I'm not beautiful.'

'If men only slept with beautiful women we'd have a serious under-population problem.'

'You mean you're prepared to close your eyes and think of Cindy Crawford! I'm seriously disappointed in you, Ethan. I thought you were much slicker than that!' Her small bosom rose swiftly in outrage.

'Oh, hell, that came out all wrong!' She wasn't even sure he was aware that his hand was massaging the length of her thigh over the down-filled guilt. She wished she weren't so profoundly aware; even through the layers, the contact sent electrical thrills shooting through her body. 'I meant that beauty is a subjective thing. I can admire a beautiful woman without wanting to make love to her.'

Hannah didn't bother to hide her scepticism. This claim didn't tally with the popular conception of the male animal, and, lacking any personal experience to speak about, that was all she had to go on.

'If you think you're unattractive people will treat you that way,' he said in a persuasively positive tone. 'It's all a matter of the aura you project. Tonight you felt sexy and people found you sexy.'

'I...'

'Don't deny it. It was obvious and justified—you did look sexy.'

'A dress and the right accessories are all superficial. Next you'll be telling me I'm beautiful inside.' She tried to sound flippant but it was difficult. Her voice emerged painfully husky. As he developed his theme she found herself wanting more and more to believe all the flattering things he was saying.

'Maybe you are. Kids and animals love you, and they're supposed to know about these things, although personally I've always found them undiscriminating little beasts.' Hannah wasn't sure if he was talking about children or animals. 'As far as I'm concerned,' he continued, fixing her with a very direct stare, 'you've turned into a right royal pain in the proverbial.'

She gasped indignantly at this cool observation. 'Well, *thank you*! I've turned myself inside out trying to make life comfortable for you, and the first time something goes a bit wrong you act like a sulky prima donna! I think you're the most unreasonable, selfish man I've ever met! All take and no give.'

'I'm not big on self-analysis, but just lately I've come to the conclusion I've got a deep-seated masochistic streak,' he confided. 'Apart from the odd steamy dream about that adjoining door. There's something about a closed door,' he mused moodily, 'that invites speculation.'

Hannah choked at this throw-away remark, unable to believe her ears. She felt a tell-tale heat burn her cheeks. Was it possible that he'd been having fantasies that side of the door whilst she…? Had their fantasies had much in common? she wondered.

'I took your contribution to this house pretty much for granted,' Ethan continued, noting her expression with a look of satisfaction. 'The moment you start developing attitude, all I can think about is ripping off your clothes,' he said frankly.

'Attitude?' she said faintly.

'Gallons of the stuff,' he reaffirmed grimly. 'I also happen to like your face. You remind me of one of those Madonna paintings—it's possible the medieval females who posed for those were real pains too.'

'Perhaps you think sex is as good a way as any of keeping me in line. Perhaps you're a control freak!' she accused wildly. He was pushing all the right buttons;

she had to do something! Or any minute now she'd be…
She closed her eyes, unwilling to contemplate what she
might be doing next.

His eyebrows shot up to his hairline and he regarded
her with a virtuous expression. 'It must have something
to do with my careless use of the term ''masochism'',
but I think you've got entirely the wrong idea about the
sort of sex I have in mind, Hannah. I'm not into *that*
sort of thing,' he admitted apologetically.

A gurgling sound escaped the confines of her throat.
'I didn't mean…I…' She swallowed to clear the con-
gestion of scorching embarrassment. 'Oh, you're impossible!'

'Up to this point, nothing short of thumbscrews could
have prised an honest opinion out of you. Now you're
flinging insults. I call that progress.'

'You're weird.' She glared at him with baffled exasperation.

'Insults are intimate,' he explained.

The way his velvet tongue caressed 'intimate' made
the fine hairs on her nape stand on end. 'I thought they
were indicative of incompatibility.' The frost that was
supposed to coat her words thawed the moment she
opened her mouth.

'We've never tried to see if we're compatible.'

'That's the way you wanted it.'

'And you didn't? Come off it, Hannah, you've spent
the last year pretending I wasn't actually here. It was
obvious I was the only part of this deal you found hard
to stomach, and I didn't mind.' Much, he added silently.
There had been times when he'd felt slightly irked that
she showed no interest whatever in the things he did.
But he'd accepted he was nothing but a pay packet to
her. 'The less time I spent here, the more you liked it!'

She wasn't about to say anything that might give a slightly more accurate slant to his interpretation of the past year. 'So what's changed?'

'We both have, I think.'

'No!' She shook her head, refusing to take the next step. He was confusing her with clever words. She couldn't trust him; she couldn't trust herself!

'My mother says she's getting married.' He dropped the bombshell at the most unexpected moment.'

'Not Drew!' she gasped, forgetting for a moment he'd manoeuvred her into a corner. 'Oh, Ethan, you didn't read her a lecture, did you?' she asked anxiously. She knew how tactless he could be when he got protective.

'See what I mean—you've lost your touch with the old cold indifference. You care, and not just about the children,' he said triumphantly.

'You rat!' she cried. 'I hope you're not trying to imply I'm in love with you.' She had been scorching hot seconds before; now shock left her trembling with cold.

'Of course I'm not.'

She could have throttled him when he had the insensitive gall to laugh. 'I suppose you made that up—about your mother?

'I wish I had. No, it looks like Galahad—with a scornful expression, he jerked his head toward the door '—is the lucky man. Whilst she didn't name him, that was the impression I got.'

'Drew? He can't be any older than you.' Faith Kemp was a good-looking woman, but there was no disguising the fact that she was of a different generation from that of her companion. Hannah couldn't help feeling shocked, even though she knew conditioning had a lot to do with her gut response.

'A year younger,' he observed gloomily. 'Thirty-five—she told me so herself. I can't believe that she'd be stupid enough to fall for some itinerant beach bum.'

'He seemed very nice,' Hannah felt impelled to protest. 'You don't know he's a beach bum.'

'I know his type,' Ethan observed with a sneer.

'Nonsense!' she contradicted firmly, and earned herself a scowl. 'And I don't suppose you'd be shocked if it was your *father* marrying a girl twenty—'

'Thirty years younger, and I'd be very shocked, considering he's been six feet under for the past ten years! Anyway,' he said with a frown, 'you're very eager to defend mum's toy boy all of a sudden. Perhaps that's why the door was locked? You didn't want me to interrupt.'

'Sure, I propositioned Drew on the way up the stairs. I'm quite a girl!' she drawled sarcastically.

'The man's a gigolo; he doesn't need an invitation.'

'For goodness' sake, Ethan, anyone would think you're jealous.'

'Wouldn't any man who found that opportunist little creep in his wife's bedroom half naked—' he swallowed hard, having difficulty containing his contempt '—have just cause to be suspicious?'

'But I'm not really your wife.'

'That can soon be fixed.' His eyes flicked to her shocked face. 'I think we'd both like that.' He reached out and touched her cheek; his fingers left a trail of fire against her skin. 'You look as if I've made an improper suggestion. We're married—nothing could be more proper than for us to share a bed.' The lazy amusement was superficial; there was nothing lazy about the expression on his watchful face or the tension in his big body.

'It's a big house—there are plenty of beds.' Inside her breast her heart was beating a wild tattoo.

'Lonely beds. Aren't you lonely in this big bed, Hannah? Why look for someone else to fill it when I'm so handy?'

Looking at him, hearing the soft, inviting purr of his voice, brought a wildlife documentary on predators she'd seen recently irresistibly to mind. So he didn't have sharp claws and a silky pelt—he definitely filled all the other criteria for predator, and she identified totally with the helpless situation of the creature being stalked.

'Sometimes—sometimes I'm lonely,' she admitted breathily. 'But I'm used to it.' The impulse to turn her cheek into the palm of his hand proved too strong to resist. Rubbing her cheek against the slightly callused surface of his hand, she closed her eyes. What's wrong with me? she wondered. A plea of convenience was hardly the most wildly romantic form of seduction, and yet here she was literally panting for his touch.

She recognised that she was fast approaching the point where she wouldn't care what his motivations were. The prospect of reaching a point of mindless acceptance was not entirely an unpleasant one—it was definitely a hotly exciting one.

'This wasn't part of the deal.' She had to put up some sort of defence. It was scary to realise how much she hoped he'd dispose of her last feeble objections with his usual efficiency.

'It wasn't something we excluded. Circumstances change, situations alter… If you're going to fall in love, it might as well be with me.'

'I don't want to fall in love.' He couldn't know the irony of his words, or how much the humorous twist of his lips hurt. 'Has anyone ever told you you're a manipulative bastard?' she asked hoarsely.

'Do you realise that you'd never have said that to me a couple of weeks ago?' He didn't seem to be put out by her forcibly expressed condemnation.

'Probably not, but I might have thought it!'

'I bet you did. Why do you think you're doing it now?'

'Because we…you…we didn't talk then.'

'Or fight, or argue, or kiss,' he added triumphantly.

Meaning that something had altered. Was that something him or her?

'You knew exactly how attracted to you I was when we danced tonight. It wasn't something I could disguise.' He bent closer so the last words were murmured into her ear. 'You were excited,' he told her throatily. He took her face firmly between his hands. 'You liked it.'

'Yes, yes…' she admitted, her eyes glistening with emotional tears as she met the challenge of his stare. His face was so close she could see the fine lines that radiated from the corners of his eyes, see the gold tips on the end of his dark eyelashes, and see the faint silvery line of a scar just below his left eye.

'Our marriage has worked, hasn't it?' His thumb ran softly over the quivering outline of her slightly parted lips. 'Why shouldn't this?' He encountered no opposition when he gently pressed against her breastbone and sent her back against the soft pillows. Supported on his elbow, his long body settled beside her. 'Your hormones are raging, and don't bother denying it. I recognise the symptoms—probably because mine are rioting too,' he added drily.

Ethan with riotous hormones! The idea held a unique fascination for her. 'It makes things complicated.' The idea of placing her hand against the flat-ridged muscles of his belly took root in her mind and swiftly became an obsessive thought.

'We're not losing anything, Hannah,' he soothed her huskily. 'If anything, we're gaining something new—something that will strengthen what we have. Complicated is when we start looking outside this house for fulfilment. And you will,' he said, reading the denial in her eyes.

The convenience factor reared its ugly head again, and it roused her sufficiently to fight against the inevitable. 'You make it sound as if I've no more choice than an animal on heat,' she protested, distressed by the mental parallel she drew.

'We all try and deny it, but primitive instincts are never very far from the surface, no matter how sophisticated we like to think ourselves. Don't underestimate a primal need.'

The rasp of his voice made her shudder. 'I can't imagine you losing control.' The idea sent ripples of delicious excitement through her body. 'You're so disciplined.'

If she leaned forward and pressed her lips against his hair-roughened chest, would that be enough to make him lose control? Or would it take more...' Eyes half closed, she caught her full lower lip between her even white teeth and looked with hungry curiosity at his face. The fantasy in her head intensified until nothing else existed.

'If you carry on looking at me like that you'll soon learn different,' he growled, his chest rising as he exhaled deeply. 'You do want this to happen, don't you?'

'Yes, yes...yes!' Her voice grew muffled as her face burrowed into his chest. An expression of fierce satisfaction flared on his taut face before his arms came automatically around her.

'That's as good a place to start as any.' A strong shudder ran through his body as the tip of her tongue touched the warm skin of his chest.

Feeling his shocked recoil, she stopped. 'Sorry,' she said, immediately raising her head. 'I'd been thinking about it and it just sort of...' She gazed at him guiltily. Her ignorance of the unwritten rules of sexual etiquette was rather frustrating.

Ethan didn't look too offended. In fact, beneath the heat of desire his eyes were filled with warmth and amusement. 'Perhaps we should start with the things you've been thinking about.' His sinfully sexy drawl fed the flames that were making her dizzy with desire.

'I just wondered what you tasted like.'

'And?'

The corners of her mouth lifted as she recalled the salty tang of his skin. 'Nice.'

'I like the taste part too.' Her mind was immediately invaded by a series of steamy, hair-curling pictures to match his provocative words. 'Only I think it might be an idea to start with the kissing stage and progress...'

Kissing was all right—kissing was good, and at least she wasn't a total novice in the kissing stakes. 'I'm in your hands.'

Her wicked little smile knocked him for six yet again. He kissed the smile off her lips. He drove every thought and preconceived idea out of her head with a bewildering alternation between greedy, driving hunger and playful, soft torment.

'Oh, I love your mouth,' she breathed fervently, when she was able to breathe once more. She tensed slightly as she realised his fingers were skilfully slipping the loops that held the bodice of her nightshirt together.

His mouth nuzzled the slender column of her neck

before he reached eye-level. 'What's wrong?'

'I'm not very—I'm too thin.'

'Who said so?' he asked with tolerant amusement.

'You,' she reminded him bluntly.

'What a time to start taking any notice of what I say. I want to see your body. I want to feel it against me. I want to taste it. I want to see if that blush of yours goes all over. I've given the subject a lot of thought just lately.'

'You have?'

He nodded firmly. 'Take it off for me,' he instructed huskily, unable to resist the opportunity to fulfil part of a recurrent dream he'd had—a dream that went back further than the last week.

On her knees now, Hannah pulled the nightshirt over her head and let it slip silently to the floor. Half of her wanted to look away, but the other half knew she'd see his real reaction in that split second. She was right—in that split second his face was naked and strangely defenceless. The intensity of the passion in his eyes had an odd, unfocused blindness. Under her amazed eyes she saw him fight and overcome the strong passions that drove him.

She could now believe and wonder at his hoarse, 'My God, you're so lovely.' And when he said, 'Come here,' she did so willingly. Physically the distance was small, but emotionally it was a leap of faith.

His back was propped up against the bed-head, and she was kneeling, straddling him. His hands glided smoothly over the graceful line of her spine, curving possessively over the firm contours of her bottom. Raising his knee slightly, he touched the sensitive, aching apex between her legs and drew a low moan from her dry throat.

His eyes never strayed from her flushed, aroused face as he changed the angle of the raised leg and sent her sliding downwards until the damp, tangled patch between her thighs was forced against his hip and her breasts were flattened against his chest. The silk boxers he wore were darkened where the dampness of his skin made them cling to his body, and they could barely contain the evidence of his growing desire.

Whilst his lips tugged and sucked at hers, his capable hands slid under her knees, and suddenly she was sitting astride him with her flexed legs pressed up and along either side of his body. He ran his hands down the back of her thighs and used the space between them to manoeuvre himself close enough to claim the twin pleasures of her aching breasts.

All thoughts of inadequacy vanished from her head as he teased the ruched peaks. She felt womanly and irresistible as his teeth and tongue made her breasts tingle and burn.

'When you touch me here,' she said shyly, bringing one finger up to indicate one erect nipple, 'I can feel it here.' She moved her hand to indicate her lower belly, where the muscle spasms clenched her womb in a series of deeply pleasurable contortions. Was this what it was like to be a woman? she wondered with awe. 'I wish I'd known,' she said, turning her sleepily sexy stare on him.

Her actions seemed to stir *him* to action—surging, violent action. Suddenly she was flat on her back and he was over her. She could see the gleam of sweat glistening on the muscle-packed contours of his shoulders and chest.

With one finger he drew a line from the pulse spot in the hollow at the base of her throat, between the valley of her breasts, over her flat belly.

'Here?' he asked hoarsely. 'And here?' He slipped his fingers between her legs and sucked in air noisily as she gasped, her body bucking. The slick heat that greeted his touch made a red haze dance before his eyes. He wanted to plunge into the heat and warmth of her welcoming body. His jaw clenched as he fought for control.

'That's for me?'

'Always,' she agreed fervently, her back arching as he came over her. She tensed her body, half expecting to feel the thrust of him within her. The tantalising brush of his silky hardness against her soft belly made her cry out in exquisite frustration. She couldn't bear this any more; she needed him—she needed all of him!

This had to be special, careful; he had to stay in control. She was so delicate and small, yet the supple strength in her body was a revelation to him. To resist the impatient, erotic undulations of the body beneath him took every ounce of his will-power.

When his lips moved over the silky inner aspect of her parted thighs it was only his hands anchoring her hips that stopped her twisting away from him.

'Ethan, please!' she begged, unable to articulate the elemental needs his erotic caresses were building up. He ignored her soft cries and continued the relentless torment of her senses. The heat pooling in her lower body spread to her limbs, which felt so heavy she didn't think she could move them from the bed.

When he eventually pulled himself up the bed until they lay shoulder to shoulder she was half panting, half sobbing. His own features were taut and strained; his cheekbones seemed to be jutting sharply through the tightly stretched skin and beads of sweat stood out across his brow.

'I needed to taste you.' Apology, confession, challenge, it was all three.

Sensing he needed reassurance, she took his face in her hands and pressed her lips against his. 'I just need you—right now!' she added, her voice low and urgent.

Her back instinctively arched as she rose to meet the thrust of his body. Eyes tight closed, she waited, and when he did move she gave a shuddering sigh of relief as, by slow, sensual inches, he let her absorb all of him.

'Perfect, perfect, perfect,' she said as she pressed her open mouth against the damp skin of his corded neck. Her fingers kneaded the flesh of his shoulders as her body twisted experimentally.

'The rhythm was slow, slick and smooth; it fed the fire inside along with the frustration. Her hoarse, urgent appeals had a rather dramatic affect. One second he was careful, measured co-ordination and the next he was rampant, elemental urgency.

'You waited for me,' she said, some time later.

Ethan stroked her damp hair as she lay curled up, her face nestled on his chest. 'You noticed.'

'It wasn't the sort of thing a person misses,' she said with a sleepy yawn. 'You know, I've never woken up with someone in the morning. I wonder what it's like?' she mused.

'I'd imagine it rather depends on who you went to sleep with the night before,' he responded drily. 'Are you glad about this, Hannah?' His stroking hand hovered above her head as he waited tensely for her reply. The silence stretched, punctuated by the soft sound of her regular breathing. 'Are you asleep, Hannah?' he said sharply.

'I think so,' came the distinct response.

Ethan began to laugh softly.

'What's wrong?' She half raised her head but he pushed her back down.

'Nothing. Go to sleep,' he urged.

CHAPTER FIVE

'Isn't this cosy?' Faith Kemp spooned some more sugar into her tea and looked around the table with warm approval.

Ethan, too experienced in his mother's brand of dry humour to be misled by the artless innocence of her comment, frowned.

'"Cosy" isn't a term I'd have thought appropriate for this room, Mother.'

A small frown pleated Hannah's smooth brow at his words; they carried a definite hint of wry criticism. Mrs Turner, on finding they had guests, had moved breakfast to the formal dining room. It was a charming room, and, with the French windows flung open onto the south-facing lawn, a person would have been hard-pressed to find a more elegant spot in which to dine, but Ethan was right: *cosy* it was not.

'I see your influence hasn't extended this far, Hannah,' Faith agreed. Her eyes went to the vases crammed with wallflowers on either end of the mantel-piece and she regarded her daughter-in-law with a shrewd expression that reminded Hannah uncomfortably of her son.

'You can't improve on perfection,' Hannah said quietly. And I can't compete with it or Catherine.

There was no doubt that Catherine had had perfect taste. Perfect taste, perfect body, perfect husband, and she, Hannah, was a visitor. It was a feeling she couldn't get rid of—she was a visitor in her own home.

'Is that why you haven't changed the decor? I was wondering—it was the first thing Catherine did when she ousted me.' Faith smiled at Drew and patted his hand familiarly. Hannah could see Ethan's knuckles grow white as he lifted his coffee cup. 'Personally I've never seen what's so tasteful about employing someone else to decide how your home should look. I always had a more hands-on approach myself. Could you be an angel, Drew, and pass me some of that honey?'

'You chose to go,' Ethan reminded her stiffly. 'And Hannah knows perfectly well she can do anything she wants to the house.'

'From the expression on her face I'd say she might have felt more comfortable if you had told her that, Ethan.'

Hannah didn't have time to alter her expression before Ethan switched his attention to her. She breathed a sigh of relief when Emma's voice diverted him.

'Will you take me to Louise's party today, Daddy?'

'That might be managed.'

'Louise has a nice house,' she mused, playing with a plastic cartoon figure she'd extracted messily from the bottom of a cereal packet. 'It's not as big as ours. Is that why her mummy and daddy sleep in the same bed?'

'The stunned silence seemed to go on for ever.

Every one's a gem! Hannah swallowed a bubble of pure hysteria. She couldn't look at anyone, least of all Ethan. 'I'll just go and bath Tom,' she babbled, unstrapping the toddler from his high chair.

As she whisked him out of the room she heard Faith say with great panache, 'I'm sure Louise's daddy doesn't snore like yours does, Emma. Tell me, are grannies invited to this party of yours?'

Today, for the first time, Emma's words hadn't been

strictly true. The timing was ironic—the very morning after the night before! If only the childish curiosity had voiced itself when they'd been alone, or at least not in front of what had felt like half the county. Drew already thought they had a very weird relationship. Hannah gave a sudden laugh—they *did* have a very weird relationship!

Hannah sighed and trailed her fingers in the bubbly water of Tom's bath and smiled at his grave expression as he experimented with eating the bubbles.

'I could always have asked you to be my witness, couldn't I, champ?' she said, rubbing a sponge down Tom's back. After all, Tom had been in a perfect position to verify her sleeping arrangements when he'd slipped between their sleeping bodies that morning. He'd been surprised, but not displeased to find his father occupying the bed.

Ethan had glanced at the clock and groaned as he'd awoken with a toddler on his chest. 'Does he do this often?' he enquired, having coaxed his son under the blankets.

'Most mornings.'

'Good God!' Tom, unable to stay still for more than thirty seconds, bouncing on the bottom of the bed. 'We'll have to do something about this young man's body clock. This wasn't the way I'd intended starting the day.'

The quick glance from his eyes didn't speak of two-mile runs or aerobics. It spoke of things much more intimate and leisurely. Her skin began to tingle as heat surged through her body. For once they seemed to be on the same wavelength. Since she'd woken an hour or so earlier her imagination had been running rampant.

Even with her eyes tightly closed she'd been able to

feel the heat from his body, even though he'd shifted to the opposite side of the bed. The muscles of her belly had gone into spasm as she'd breathed in the musky, masculine scent of his skin.

As she'd stretched she was reminded of the previous night. Her body ached from the vigour of his possession. A possession that she could only view with a slightly detached sense of wonder this morning.'

'I should get up and warn Mrs Turner we have guests.'

'How could I forget?' he remarked drily. He didn't turn away as she clumsily struggled to cover her nudity with a thick, shapeless robe.

Hannah was relieved when he didn't comment on her self-consciousness. 'You must be pleased to see your mother.' Didn't he realise how lucky he was to have one? She was constantly amazed at how people took their families for granted.

'Do I detect a hint of disapproval?'

'Well, you weren't very welcoming to her.'

'I didn't feel very welcoming, and under the circumstances I think I was a paragon of restraint. Marriage!' he snorted. 'She must be insane.'

'She didn't want you to marry me either,' she reminded him. 'I overheard something she said,' she added as his brows shot up in surprise.

'But I did, didn't I?' he said softly, an indecipherable expression flickering briefly into his eyes. 'Don't worry, my mother isn't going to lose any sleep over my disapproval—any more than I do over hers, Hannah. She makes her own rules up and changes them when they don't suit her any more,' he said with disgruntled disapproval.

Hannah couldn't help smiling.

'What are you thinking about when you smile so secretively?' he asked, lifting an arm over his head and rubbing his tousled hair. He hardly looked like the same person as the sleekly suited sophisticated animal who left the house every morning. She loved him so much she wanted to yell it out loud; being a cautious girl, she didn't.

'You don't want to know.'

'Try me.'

Oh, I'd like to, she thought, watching the muscles of his shoulders tighten and relax as he moved his head to a more comfortable position. Rather boldly, she let her eyes drop lower to where the sheet skimmed his narrow hips. She was mildly shocked, and much more than mildly aroused by the direction of her thoughts!

'I was thinking genetics have a lot to answer for. You seem to be developing a talent for making rules and then changing them too,' she elaborated.

He got the message and an answering gleam of wry humour shone in his eyes. 'Is that the only talent you think I've got?'

'Everyone says you're an excellent barrister,' she remarked rather primly.

'I wasn't thinking professionally.'

'I don't know how to flirt,' she admitted as frustrated confusion closed in. It was hard to know where jokes ended and the serious stuff began. If she got caught up in this intimate repartee, she might just confess more than she wanted to. More importantly, more than he wanted to hear.

'I'm quite good at repairing gaps in education, if you'll let me.'

He wasn't laughing at her any more. Looking into his

compassionate, warm eyes, she wanted to blurt out the truth.

'I think you're *very* good,' she replied in a breathy, intense voice. 'I'd better go and catch Mrs Turner. Come along, Tom.' She caught the little boy by both hands and swung him off the bed. Sometimes, she reflected, it wasn't just what you said, it was the way you said it. No wonder Ethan was staring at her in that peculiar way!

'I'm sorry about that.'

Hannah started, and twisted around as the deep voice close beside her abruptly broke into her reverie. She inadvertently sent a shower of water over the front of Ethan's pale chinos.

'Sorry.' Flustered, she reached forward and dabbed at the damp spots with her wet hands, making matters worse.

'It doesn't matter,' Ethan choked hoarsely. Seeing her kneeling there had brought a vivid image of her sweet mouth…! He caught his breath as his body automatically responded to the provocative mental picture. He smiled in a strained manner as she looked up. If he answered the puzzled question in her eyes, she'd be shocked. Although she hadn't seemed shocked last night. Recalling the wanton eagerness of her responses wasn't the best way to dampen his arousal, he decided wryly.

'You should change them—not here,' she added hurriedly. Even if I am in a perfect position to assist you… What devilish imp planted that naughty idea in her head? It could have been worse—she might have said it out loud! 'I mean, you could if you wanted to, but I wasn't suggesting…' She took a deep breath. Best stop before she sounded like a total idiot. Who am I kidding? she thought. There's no *before* about it.

Ethan got down on his knees beside her. 'It might be simpler if I got down as you're so interested in the floor.'

'I lost something.'

'What?'

She eyed him rather resentfully; he wasn't being very helpful.

'Dog, Daddy,' Tom said, throwing a large duck at his father. Ethan ably caught it.

'Duck.'

'Dog,' Tom repeated with a grin.

'I get the impression Tom's vocabulary is a bit restricted.'

'He's very intelligent,' Hannah said, automatically defensive at any implied criticism. 'All animals are dogs and all men are Daddy.'

'I noticed he's indiscriminate with his favours when he attached himself like a limpet to Drew this morning,' Ethan observed drily.

'You're determined to dislike him, aren't you?'

Ethan was being so unfair. She could appreciate that the idea of your mother with a younger—a very much younger—man might be hard to take, but he wasn't even trying. 'Why can't a woman fall in love with a younger man? People don't have any control over these things,' she said indignantly.

'Don't mistake your own unrequited passion for Mother's affairs of the heart. She's never settled for unrequited in her life!' Ethan's lips formed into a hard line of disapproval.

'Oh!' she said without thinking. 'I forgot I told you that.'

'Well, I haven't forgotten,' he replied rather grimly. 'I've been thinking—it might be better, considering

Emma's comment, if we stopped having separate rooms.'

Hannah wiped her hands carefully on a towel. 'In the interests of keeping up appearances,' she said carefully.

'That's one reason,' he agreed blandly.

'There's another?'

'I want to make love to you every night and every morning and occasionally in between.'

The towel slipped unnoticed to the floor and Hannah continued to wring her hands, oblivious to the loss. 'Is that being a bit ambitious?' she asked huskily. In her wildest dreams she'd never imagined such an outspoken avowal of desire.

'Worried that I'm not up to it?'

'Well, there is a worrying age gap...'

'You minx!' he said, a hard light glinting in his eyes as he took her by the shoulders. 'There's no comparison and you know it. I'm really sorry if you were embarrassed downstairs, Hannah. Are you happy about last night?'

'I'm glad about last night, Ethan,' she admitted huskily.

'Out, Daddy, now!'

Ethan closed his eyes in exasperated defeat. 'That child has inherited his timing from his grandmother and her domineering disposition. I never seem to see you without the children being around.'

Hannah, who was feeling equally frustrated, tugged the chain on the bath plug with unwanted viciousness. 'What do you expect when you marry the nanny?'

Ethan didn't look too happy at being reminded about this. 'You're not the nanny now—don't you ever have any free time?'

'Nannies have free time, Ethan; I'm the wife. We

don't have a nanny.' She wrapped a fleecy towel around Tom, who, giggling, ran into the nursery.

'*My* wife.' The words emerged with a proprietorial vigour that stopped him short. Dear God, if he went on like this he'd be acting as if he was jealous of his own son. The idea of such pitiable behaviour made his nostrils flare in distaste.

Hannah saw his expression and immediately misinterpreted it.

'A fact that seems to make you ecstatic,' she flashed sarcastically. There was a real danger here that she would forget the simple fact of the situation. Ethan didn't love her.

'Last night…' he began.

'Oh, last night,' she said bitterly. 'I might be flavour of the month right now, but how long is that likely to last?' She voiced the fear that lurked uppermost in her mind.

'I can see you have high expectations.'

'Realistic expectations,' she returned, folding a discarded towel. She began to rise, but Ethan's fingers closed around her upper arm to prevent her.

'You expect boredom to set in?' he suggested, his jaw clenched in a fixed, humourless smile.

Hannah refused to meet his eyes. Of course he was going to get bored with her—it hurt, but she had to face facts and be practical. 'It's possible,' she muttered morosely.

'I think you'll find my imagination is up to the task of holding your attention for the foreseeable future,' he predicted arrogantly.

She let out a tiny startled shriek as she found herself suddenly flat on her back with Ethan kneeling over her. He thinks I'm saying I'm likely to be bored with him!

In a less tense situation this might have made her laugh, but laughter wasn't really appropriate.

As his arms slowly slid further away from her head his body dropped lower—so low that his chest almost touched the upthrust of her breasts, which rose in harmony with her erratic breaths.

'What are you doing, Ethan?' The sensual lethargy that was insidiously robbing her limbs of power had reduced her voice to a throaty whisper.

'Your comments seem to imply you have a low boredom threshold. I'm just trying my humble best to vary my technique.' His features were taut with barely repressed emotion.

'There's no need to take it personally,' she murmured, as he applied his mouth to the extended length of her throat. Her damp flesh where his tongue had touched burned and tingled. A reckless light blazed in the depths of his eyes and, hypnotised by the glow, Hannah couldn't look away. How had she missed the lethal, insolent sensuality in this man she'd married?

'Then I'm sure you won't take this personally, will you?' he drawled, placing a kiss on the tip of her nose. 'Or this?' This time he caught her chin. 'As for this...'

As his teeth nipped her full lips Hannah's mouth opened, and he took immediate advantage of the fact, plunging deeper into the warm, moist sweetness within. All Hannah was conscious of in that moment was the skilful thrust of his tongue and the hard pressure of his lips; nothing else existed. Her fingers sank into the lush thickness of his dark hair and she moaned softly as her body stirred restlessly.

'I can vary it, and I do detached and objective as well as impersonal.'

Hannah blinked, unable quite to bring his face into

focus. 'No, thank you. I think you've proved your point. Will you let me up? I have to go to Tom.'

She felt somewhat ambivalent when he immediately rolled away from her and stretched out beside her on the floor. 'I know, but do you *want* to?'

With trembling fingers, Hannah refastened the two top buttons of her shirt. 'I want...' she said, sitting up and looking down at his prone body. 'I want to...' Tongue caught between her teeth, she placed her palm flat on his chest. 'I want to carry on kissing you.'

What reckless, self-destructive impulse had induced her to say anything so stupid? She didn't wait around to see what Ethan made of this confession—she scrambled hurriedly to her feet and fled into the nursery.

When, a few minutes later, Ethan followed her, he just stood silently watching her dress the squirming youngster.

'Aren't you neglecting your guests?' she asked, when his silent presence had stretched her nerves to breaking-point.

'I didn't invite them,' he reminded her caustically.

'That's no excuse for bad manners,' she snapped, as he dropped in her lap a sock Tom had flung across the room.

'Not trying to get rid of me, are you?'

'Whatever gave you that idea?'

She gave a sigh of relief and buried her head in Tom's hair when Ethan decided quite unexpectedly to leave. What had she started? she wondered with apprehension. And, more importantly, where was it going to lead?

'Where's Emma?' Ethan asked as he walked into his study to find his mother calmly leafing through his address book. 'Anything I can help you with?'

'No, I've got what I want, thank you, Ethan,' she said, untouched by his sarcasm. 'And Drew has taken Emma down to the river to feed the ducks. Now I come to think of it, I think she took him,' she mused. 'A forceful child.'

'It didn't occur to you I might not want my daughter to wander around in the company of a total stranger?'

'Drew is not a total stranger.'

'To me he is. You'll have to pardon me if I don't find your character reference comforting. You can be as irresponsible as you like about your choice of friends, Mother, but when it comes to my children—' He drew a sharp breath of displeasure. 'It's bad enough that I have to stomach the man under my roof. Which way did they go?'

'I wouldn't know, darling. Before you go,' she said, picking up the telephone, 'you didn't have any plans for tonight, did you?'

Ethan paused in the act of leaving, a suspicious frown on his face. 'Why?'

'I thought it might be nice to invite a few old friends round tonight.'

'I was hoping for a quiet night—'

'Don't be such a bore, darling!' she chided briskly. 'You'll be old before your time. I've already spoken to Delia,' she expanded.

'Who is Delia?' he asked in confusion.

'Your housekeeper.' She shook her head at her offspring's obtuseness. 'And she's quite happy with the idea. She's recommended some caterers. Naturally I'll invite some of your friends too.'

'That won't be necessary, Mother.'

'It's no trouble,' she assured him. 'I've already spoken

to that nice secretary of yours and she's ringing round for me.'

'You rang her at home?' He shook his head in disbelief. 'You're impossible!'' he growled. 'Do as you like,' he said, wiping his hands of the whole affair.

'I knew you'd like the idea,' she said imperturbably.

'Just a small party—forty or so.'

Hannah blinked as her mother-in-law placed a friendly arm around her shoulders. '*Tonight?* Isn't that short notice? Perhaps some people won't be able to come,' she suggested hopefully.

'Oh, everyone accepted.'

'I'm not sure Ethan—'

'Oh, Ethan was very enthusiastic about it.'

'He was?' Maybe it was his lack of confidence in her own abilities as a hostess that made Ethan normally veto any large gatherings. 'What shall I do?'

'Don't worry about that; everything is in hand. What are you going to wear? That red dress you had on last night was quite charming. I hope you've got a few more like that in your wardrobe. I want to show you off to my friends.'

'Hannah, whose head was spinning, thought it was time to get a few things straight. This was the same woman who had begged her son not to marry her; Hannah had heard her with her own ears.

'I thought you didn't like me. You didn't want me to marry Ethan.'

'Quite right, but that wasn't because I didn't like you.'

'Then why…?'

'I knew Ethan didn't love you, and in my view marriage with love is hard enough, but without it…' She lifted her shoulders expressively. 'I could also see you loved him.' Her blue eyes grew compassionate as she watched the colour flee dramatically from Hannah's face. 'I didn't want to see you hurt.'

'Did you tell Ethan?' Hannah asked, as her heart continued to hammer sickeningly. She couldn't bear the humiliation if he'd known all along. No, he couldn't have, she reasoned. If he'd even suspected how much her heart had been involved in her decision to accept his proposal, he'd have run a mile.

'What a silly question!' Faith's clear, amazingly youthful laughter rang out. 'I knew he was acting out of concern for the children. Catherine's death was a terrible blow for him; he hadn't recovered. I know he didn't turn to the bottle or neglect his work, but he was hurting more than anyone guessed.'

Not more than I guessed, Hannah thought sombrely. She didn't need anyone to explain to her how unemotional Ethan's motivation for marrying her had been. It was something she was reminded of in a hundred little ways every day.

'I can see now that you've helped him recover.'

'I haven't done anything!' Hannah protested, embarrassed by the warmth of the other woman. Faith was in danger of overestimating Hannah's influence—she'd probably read all sorts of things into that embarrassing but unrepresentative scene she'd witnessed the previous night. Ethan's recovery had more to do with the resilience of his character than anything Hannah had done. Whilst he might be inexplicably sexually attracted to her, she hadn't heard, or expected to hear, a single word of love on his lips.

'You've loved him,' Faith said warmly, 'and as his mother I can only thank you.' She linked her arm with Hannah's and they walked out onto the terrace. 'This view is the one thing I really miss about this house,' she confessed, inhaling the heavy fragrance of the autumn day. 'It's so *English*. It makes me feel quite nostalgic, but then it isn't raining. I find it hard to be nostalgic about rain.'

Hannah, who loved the smell of wet leaves under her feet, just smiled. 'Didn't you mind when your husband left the house to Ethan?' she asked curiously. The idea of leaving this house, even after the short time she'd lived here, was horrifying.

'Not in the slightest. Jordan knew I never felt the same way about this place as he did. We were two very different people,' she reflected, a wistful expression drifting over her face. 'We both made a lot of concessions to make our marriage work. I certainly wouldn't have stayed in one place for thirty years for anyone other than Jordan. I doubt if he'd have gone trekking in the Himalayas for anyone but me.'

'And now you've met someone else,' Hannah said quietly. She was deeply touched by this glimpse of a profound love. It was the sort of love she'd always dreamt of.

'Ethan told you that, did he? Yes, I'm very lucky.'

'But it's not Drew, is it?' Her feminine instincts told her Ethan was wrong.

Faith threw back her head and laughed. 'Of course not.'

'Then why did you tell Ethan that it was? He's really upset about it.'

'I didn't tell Ethan; I just didn't correct him. My son, Hannah, has a tendency towards pomposity, and I feel it my maternal duty to pull him down to size occasionally.'

'Who is Drew?'

'Drew is soon to be Ethan's stepbrother.'

'You're marrying his father!' Hannah cried, unable to repress a chuckle at the joke. She suddenly let out a sharp cry as a red-hot needle of pain bit deep into her shoulder. 'Something stung me,' she explained, rubbing the area, which was already beginning to puff up.

'It looks like the sting is still in. We'd better do something about it immediately.'

Hannah was rather glad she'd weakly allowed herself to be flattered into purchasing several more outfits when she'd bought the red dress. This full-length cream slip dress, which her mother-in-law had heartily approved of, was made of soft, clinging silk. She hadn't expected an opportunity to wear it to present itself so soon.

When Hannah had worried about the puffy, discoloured area around her bee sting Faith had produced some antihistamine tablets, which had taken down the swelling miraculously.

Hannah touched the single string of luminous pearls that hung about her neck as she descended the sweeping staircase. Ethan's mother had dismissed Hannah's reluctance to wear them the way she steamrollered any obstacles.

'Beautiful.'

Pausing on the bottom step of the stairs, Hannah turned around with a smile. 'They're Faith's.'

'I didn't mean the pearls,' Drew said, stepping through the library door. He was pulling at the folds of his tie with a dissatisfied frown. 'I meant the neck. Damn thing—I should have left it the way it was.'

'Can I help?' she offered with an amused smile. Drew looked grateful.

'Help away.'

'Do you always carry a dinner jacket in your ruck-sack?' she teased, adjusting his tie and retreating up one step on the staircase to view her work. 'That's better,' she approved, stepping down the step again and flicking a speck of dust off his lapel.

'Faith arranged for someone to pick one up from my flat.'

'You live in London?'

'Split my time between London and New York.'

'Would I be wrong to assume your work normally involves wearing a tie?'

'I went into the family firm.'

'So what does that make you when you're not being a beach bum?'

'Would you believe a banker?'

His self-conscious grin was contagious, and Hannah found herself laughing back. 'Then why the worn den-ims and rucksack?'

'Would you believe a woman?'

'It must have been serious,' she said sympathetically.

'She got cold feet the night before the wedding.'

'Ouch! Should I ask why?'

'I was too boring. She thought my suit would need to be surgically removed by the time I was forty and I lacked spontaneity. She did go into more detail than that, but I won't bore you.'

'So you turned your back on your suits.'

'I gave most of them to a charity shop, actually,' he recalled with a wry smile. 'That was twelve months ago. I was backpacking across South America when my dad decided enough was enough. We were still discussing the issue, quite loudly as I recall, when Faith appeared. She took on the role of referee as one born to it.'

'And they fell in love. That's so romantic!' she breathed.

'Just how many people have you invited, Mother?'

Unconsciously Hannah's fingers tightened on Drew's jacket lapel as she heard Ethan's voice. 'I've hardly seen Ethan today,' she said, as her stomach began to perform painful contortions. She swallowed hard to relieve the sudden constriction in her throat.

'I suppose it depends on why you're trembling as to whether I'm envious of him or not.' Drew grimaced as she cast a reproachful look at him. 'Sorry,' he murmured pacifically. 'It's probably my fault—he's been shadowing me in case I pocket the silver.'

Hannah winced. 'Sorry,' she said softly. Ethan was going to be mad when he realised how far out his first impressions had been.

'Thirty or so of your *closest* friends! I thought this was going to be a quiet dinner party.'

'Don't fuss, Ethan. We only managed to contact fifteen of yours. Here's Hannah and Drew—what a charming picture they make. Don't you think so?'

Under the ferocity of her husband's regard, Hannah realised she was still clutching at Drew's lapel. Her hand fell away self-consciously.

'Charming,' Ethan drawled. 'Where have you been hiding today?'

Hannah's temper rose at the accusatory note in his voice. 'I could ask you the same question, except I already know. Drew has told me. Do yourself a favour and reduce the surveillance, Ethan, he's not marrying your mother. You may be a great legal mind, but right now you're just in danger of looking rather silly.' Ignoring the shocked look of outrage on his face, she sailed past him, head held high.

The guests, as was often the case, arrived in a deluge,

rather than drips, and Hannah was saved from listening to the scorching response to her reckless words that she was certain Ethan had composed.

He'd deserved it, she decided, flicking a covert glance to the opposite end of the room where he was laughing at something Miranda had said. *She'd* obviously been ready to drop everything at short notice in order to make Ethan laugh. Laugh—I'd like to make him plead for mercy, she thought viciously, draining her glass of wine.

Bringing his mistress into this house, flaunting her under my nose, she silently fumed, ignoring the fact that Ethan was a very reluctant host. How dare he humiliate me?

'Are you feeling all right?' a voice at her elbow enquired.

She turned to find Drew regarding her overbright eyes and flushed cheeks with a doubtful frown. 'You're a man.'

Drew agreed nervously with this accusation. In his experience, conversations that began like this were apt to get uncomfortable.

'Do *you* think she's beautiful?' Hannah demanded. She tossed her head in the direction of the tall redhead. 'Of course she is,' she replied, without waiting to hear his opinion.

'So are you.'

'You're such a *nice* man,' she said, regarding him affectionately. 'You'd never invite your mistress to a party at your wife's home, would you? No, of course not, you're far too consid…conside…thoughtful.'

'I think there's a possibility you're jumping to conclusions here,' he murmured, removing the empty glass from her limp grasp. 'Just how much have you had to drink?'

'Not enough!' she informed him darkly. 'Can you

dance? I can't. You could teach me…' she announced, smiling at this inspired idea. She swayed closer and wound her arms around his neck.

'*I'm* more than capable of teaching my wife anything she needs to know.'

Hannah pulled in the opposite direction as she was pulled from one pair of masculine arms to another. 'I prefer to dance with Drew,' she said haughtily, pushing her hands against Ethan's chest.

'Will you lower your voice?' Ethan said from between clenched teeth as he favoured her with a furious look. 'People are staring.'

As Ethan stepped into the slowly moving throng, Hannah felt the inevitable magic of his touch taking over. She wanted to be angry, she wanted to hate him, but how could she when her whole body was gently throbbing? The strength of his big body, the musky, warm scent of him overlaid by the elusive fragrance he sparingly wore—it all conspired to bewitch her senses.

Throwing her head back, she saw the muscles clench beside his stern mouth as she deliberately plastered herself against the hard length of his body. Well, what did he expect? Was she supposed to stand back calmly and watch him flirt so outrageously with *that* woman? No, it was about time she asserted herself, and if he didn't like it—tough!

'What do you think you're doing?' he asked hoarsely as she reached up and wound her fingers in dark strands of his hair.

She pouted consideringly and regarded him through half-closed eyes. 'I haven't decided yet. Doesn't Miranda dance?'

'You're drunk!' he accused.

'As a matter of fact I've only had two glasses of wine.

I do feel a bit odd, though,' she confessed as she noticed the room beginning to spin faster than she was.

'We should get out of here.'

'You're ashamed of me!' she accused, standing stock-still. She put a hand to her head. 'I feel a bit...' She swallowed as beads of sweat broke out over her upper lip.

'Ethan, dear,' Faith said a little nervously as she appeared at his elbow, 'Drew said Hannah was feeling a little unwell.'

'I'm not drunk, Faith. Tell Ethan I'm not drunk.'

'The thing is, I think this might be my fault.'

'I hardly think so, Mother, unless you've slipped her a Mickey,' Ethan said tersely.

'Not exactly, but I did give her one of my antihistamine tablets for that bee sting she had this afternoon, and I forgot to mention they don't mix too well with alcohol.'

Ethan closed his eyes and swore softly but comprehensively under his breath.

'You can't talk to your mother like that, Ethan,' Hannah protested.

'I think we should get you out of here.'

'Unilateral decisions!' Hannah said, wagging her finger admonishingly in his face. She took him off guard as she pulled free of his supporting arms. 'Oh, dear,' she whispered as her knees began to buckle. Just before Ethan caught her, she asked the question that was uppermost in her mind.

'Is Miranda your Friday night, Ethan?' Call it acoustics or bad luck, but her voice carried clear as a bell from one end of the room to the other.

CHAPTER SIX

'How are you feeling now?'

'If you ignore the headache and the fact a sip of water makes me feel sick, I feel great. Who took my clothes off?' Hannah felt the bed give as Ethan sat down on it.

'Me.'

'I suppose you were there when I was sick too.' Could this humiliation get any worse? she wondered glumly.

'Yes.'

'Oh, God!' she moaned 'I want to die.'

'You mentioned that too. Life will probably look more appealing after you've slept some more.'

Hannah didn't reply, because she knew it wouldn't. Once she was better she'd have to face the full force of his anger and contempt. Selective amnesia would have been nice, but she could recall in horrifying detail every syllable and every sultry pout her lips had formed. There was a strong possibility she could never appear in public again without a brown paper bag over her head. The story of Ethan Kemp's mad, drunken wife would probably become legendary in the rarefied legal circles that Ethan inhabited.

Just thinking about it brought her out in a cold sweat. She'd humiliated and embarrassed him in front of his colleagues and friends. How he must regret the day he'd married her. Tears seeped from under her closed eyelids and ran slowly down the curve of her cheek. She could taste the saltiness as they touched her dry lips...

When she woke again, Hannah did feel a lot better.

Her head felt muzzy and her stomach a little delicate, but other than that things were back to normal. She sat up and gasped. Not quite normal—Ethan didn't normally sleep in her bedroom armchair.

He was sound asleep. His head was thrown back, one of his hands brushed the floor and one knee was hooked over the armrest. The chair was much too small to accommodate his bulk.

Holding her breath, she tiptoed across the carpet. She almost tripped over his crumpled jacket and tie. Through his white shirt she could see the shadow of dark body hair. Sleep softened the lines of his strongly sculpted features; he looked younger—not exactly vulnerable, but softer. She clasped her hands together to resist the impulse to stroke back the hank of dark hair that flopped in his eyes.

He shifted slightly and she held her breath. She became suddenly conscious of the fact she was wearing only a pair of silky pants. If he woke up now and she was caught in all her voyeuristic glory…! With one last covetous look at his sleeping figure, she crept away. Taking great care not to make a sound, she closed the bathroom door silently behind her.

By the time the room was filled by warm steam she was starting to feel more human. She might even be able to take his justified anger. Yelling at a semi-comatose victim couldn't compare with the pleasure of telling a conscious culprit exactly what he thought of her. Not being able to shout at her last night had probably only concentrated his sense of outrage, she concluded gloomily.

If only her lowered inhibitions hadn't brought her submerged jealously so visibly and audibly to the surface. The last thing she could remember before she'd passed out was Ethan's face, white with fury. He didn't flaunt his emotions for the public, and he hadn't needed to spell out the fact that he expected her to emulate his flawless public behaviour. Ethan Kemp's wife did not dance on table-tops and definitely didn't accuse her husband of infidelity!

She still revolved under the warm spray when some sixth sense told her she was no longer alone. It was only a hand across her lips that stopped her screaming. His face wasn't furious this time, more broodingly angry. Anger wasn't the only emotion revealed as the water streamed over his face. She contemplated the hungry, restless look in his eyes with breathless shock.

'I didn't want you to bring Lancelot in here with your screams,' he said, removing his hand from her lips. 'You appear to arouse the chivalrous instinct in my soon to be stepbrother. I suppose you were in on that little secret?'

Obviously I don't have the same effect on you, Hannah thought. She wanted to back away but she was rooted to the spot as firmly as a rabbit caught in the headlights of a car, her fate just as inevitable as that creature's. As Ethan's glance dropped insolently over her slim body, it was almost as if he was daring her to object to his presence.

'I don't think it was meant to be a secret, exactly.'

'I recognise the hallmarks of my mother's twisted sense of humour.'

'Well, at least she has one.' Oops, that had just sort of slipped out. 'You'll get wet if you stand there,' she added shakily. The rolled-up cuffs of his white shirt were already damp, his tanned forearms gleamed with moisture and the steamy heat clung to his hair as tiny, silvery water droplets. 'If you thought I'd scream, why did you creep up on me?' I hope his watch is waterproof, she thought, fretting over this irrelevant detail.

My God, he was impressive enough to take the most objective observer's breath away, and she was a long way from objective! She knew there wasn't an ounce of surplus flesh on his taut, lightly tanned body. Long and lean, with just the right degree of muscle definition, he was the closest thing to male perfection she'd ever seen. If he weren't dressed, what would it feel like to run her hands over his slick skin? She could imagine the sharp contraction of those strong belly muscles and the deep quiver of his thighs. The water ran into her open mouth and she nearly choked.

He observed the minor convulsions with a disturbing smile. 'You want exclusive rights in the surprise department, do you? Isn't that just a bit unreasonable?' He found great difficulty in tearing his eyes from the way the water reached the uptilted peak of her small breasts and then cascaded down the sharply defined valley in between.

Hannah watched in confusion as he closed his eyes and slowly shook his head from side to side. She gasped as, with his eyes still shut, he stepped fully clothed into the cubicle and closed the door behind him. He threw back his head and let the water run over his face. As she watched, the white material of his shirt became transparent, and she could see the clear outline of his muscled torso and the curling shadow of his dark body hair.

'What are you doing?' she asked hoarsely.

'My spine's all tied in knots—a nice hot shower should do it some good.' Now he had his eyes open she had the distinct impression he wasn't missing any detail of her naked body. Unconsciously her chin went up as she met his sensual appraisal head-on.

Those knots couldn't be as complicated as the ones that tightened in her belly. A space that moments before had seemed luxurious was now overwhelmingly claustrophobic.

'Fully clothed?'

She couldn't do anything but stare as he unfolded her fingers one by one from the bar of soap she clutched. Her hands were hardly adequate to cover her growing sense of vulnerability, so she kept them rigidly to her sides. Wondering just what he was going to do next made the blood pound in Hannah's ears.

'Not an insurmountable obstacle. I was hoping my wife might give me a hand. Such a delicate, pretty hand too,' he murmured, turning her hand palm up and pressing it to his lips.

'I suppose you're pretty angry with me?' she said faintly. This was probably part of some elaborate punishment, she thought hazily.

'Why should I be angry?' he enquired, evincing confusion. 'Oh, you mean because everyone knows my wife thinks I have a mistress. And the fact I've had to offer the woman you so publicly slandered a grovelling apology. You've managed to destroy my respectable image with remarkable efficiency.'

She watched as, very slowly, he worked the soap into a lather. Ethan looked at his soapy hand, then into Hannah's wide eyes, and deliberately closed his hand over one taut breast. A deep sigh rippled through his body. 'Like lovely firm tender apples, ripe for the plucking,' he breathed, leaning forward to plant his other hand on the tiled wall behind her head. His thumb moved back and forth over the erect nipple.

'Ethan!' she gasped. Was he trying to say he wasn't having an affair? she wondered, too intensely involved with the movements of his clever, cruel hand to concentrate properly on anything else.

'That's my name,' he agreed grimly, 'and don't you forget it. Not Jean-bloody-Paul, and not Drew what's-his-name. Ethan Kemp, your husband, the man who shares your bed, given the opportunity. Why I let you turn this house into a damn hotel, I don't know.'

'This isn't a bed.'

'Don't be pedantic, Hannah.' He took her chin in his hand and stroked her jawline with his thumb.

'I'm sorry. I...I assumed... I mean, you're a normal man with the usual appetites, and she's attractive, clever...'

'You assumed one hell of a lot. And it didn't bother you when your fertile imagination decided I'd been sharing more than professional courtesies with the nubile Miranda.' He sounded strangely annoyed by his interpretation of her reaction.

'It was none of my business.'

'That's not the way it sounded last night. It sounded like it bothered you a lot.'

'Things are different now...' she said, feeling trapped by his relentless pursuit of her motivation. She could hardly say, I'm jealous as hell because I'm in love with you, could she?

'At least you admit that much,' he grated triumphantly. His kiss was tinged with a driving desperation, and he sucked at her mouth as if he'd drain her. Hannah's hands opened and closed spasmodically as her fingers twisted the fabric of his shirt-front.

She could hardly breathe. His expression was hidden by the mist that filled the small cubicle. 'Your clothes will be ruined,' she reminded him as his hands ran slowly over her from shoulder to flank, turning her body into a quivering mass of burning anticipation.

'To hell with my clothes.'

Considering his lack of concern, it was with a clear conscience that she tugged urgently at the front of his shirt.

'Oh, yes,' he approved throatily as she touched her tongue experimentally to the pebble-hard centre of his male nipple. His fingers pushed roughly into the saturated strands of her hair. Encouraged by his response, she suckled softly. Under his open shirt her arms moved around his waist, drawing her breasts closer to his lean body. She leant into him, revelling in the strength of his muscular thighs which were braced to support her body.

'You like it?' she gloated. Delight and a heady sense of feminine power coursed through her veins as she shook the wet hair from her eyes and gazed up into his face. He liked it—it wasn't hard to interpret that strange mixture of pain and pleasure in his short, irregular gasps and the ripples of muscular contractions that ran beneath the smooth surface of his golden skin.

Drops of water trembled on the tips of her eyelashes and she licked at the moisture that ran into her mouth. Deliciously confident, she reached up to ease the clinging material off his shoulders.

This was a Hannah she hadn't known existed: a sexy, irresistible Hannah. Men were putty in her hands—Ethan was putty in her hands. Maybe not putty—Ethan felt altogether too firm to be classified as malleable, and certain parts of his anatomy were anything but soft. The shirt fell in a sodden heap on the tiled floor and she spread her splayed fingers up over his taut belly and across his chest and shoulders.

'You are so beautiful!' she breathed almost reverently.

'Do it again!' he commanded hoarsely. 'I want to feel your mouth on me.' A harsh cry was wrenched from his throat as she eagerly complied.

Abruptly his hands slipped under her bottom and he lifted her to waist-level. Hannah's legs automatically wrapped themselves around his waist as he walked forward with her until her back was pressed against the tiled wall.

Hannah didn't respond passively to his initiative. She matched the hungry ferocity of his mouth, and the fine, rhythmic rotation of her pelvis drove her closer to him, and drove him beyond reason. Ethan was gasping and groaning as he continued to feed on her lips frantically. He backed out of the shower cubicle and, without lifting his head from the sensual feast, carried them as far as the bed. The metal frame hit the back of his legs and he collapsed backwards with her onto the sheets which still bore the earlier imprint of her body.

Hannah let out a startled cry as she found herself lying on top of him. She sat upright and wiped away some of the wetness from her face.

'The other night was the first time for me in more than three years.'

Hannah stared at him. It wasn't a joke; he meant it! Her instinctive response of smug elation was swiftly followed by the sobering realisation of the reason for his abstinence. The memory of Catherine had been more important to him than the needs of his body. That memory still hung between them, a constant reminder of the contrast between their places in this household and in his heart.

'Would you have been happier if I'd kept a mistress? You don't look very pleased.'

'I'm wondering what's changed. Sex wasn't in the forefront of your mind when you married me.'

Ethan's eyes, dark with passion, moved slowly over the slender, pale curves of her body. 'It is now,' he groaned, reaching for her.

Hannah might not have been satisfied with the absence of an adequate explanation, but in every other way she was totally satisfied!

It began with a cushion lobbed at her from the trio involved in an enthusiastic game on the floor, which involved Drew on all fours, with Tom on his back, being chased around the room by Emma. Hannah's retaliation escalated things to the point where they were all on the floor, panting and laughing as cushions were flung back and forth.

'This will all end in tears,' Hannah predicted as she held her arms across her face to hold off a vicious onslaught from her stepson.

'Being struck repeatedly over the skull by a soft object is the very latest cure for a hangover,' Drew teased softly. 'Surrender?' he suggested in a louder voice.

'Never!' she cried, flinging herself sideways to catch a stray missile. Her retaliatory strike went wildly astray and hit— The room went suddenly silent as they all saw whom it hit.

Miranda Saunders was standing in the doorway beside Ethan. She was casually dressed, but desperately elegant, and Hannah was immediately conscious of her own deficiencies: namely a face pink from exertion and hair which looked neither smooth nor sleek. Dressing for comfort rather than glamour no longer seemed the best decision she'd made today. Brushing down her crumpled clothes, Hannah got to her feet.

'We were...' she began breathlessly.

'It looked like great fun,' the redhead responded with a tentative smile.

'I see your head is quite recovered, darling,' Ethan drawled as she tried to press her tumbled locks back in place. 'Miranda dropped in to see how you are.' He responded to the appeal in Hannah's wide, horrified eyes with a casual and, to her mind, deeply callous smile. 'I'll chase up some coffee for you both. Perhaps we should transfer this rough-house out into the garden. Do you play soccer, Drew?'

Typical—he could make out they were bosom buddies when it suited him! Hannah thought with disgust. She watched the traitors respond eagerly to Ethan's suggestion. He can't do this to me—he *is* doing this to me, she realised bleakly.

'Girls can't play football,' she heard Drew observe with innocence as they left the room.

'Tell him, Daddy!' Emma shrieked, tugging her father's arm. 'Tell him I can.'

'Show him, sweetheart,' she heard Ethan advise as he closed the door firmly behind them.

'I had to come.'

To watch me grovel, Hannah thought weakly. To grind her elegantly shod size six into my face. 'About last night...' she began. There was no point skirting around the issue.

'Are you feeling better?'

'I stayed in bed until midday.' Even in the midst of her present predicament she felt something warm and heavy stir in the pit of her belly as she recalled with whom she'd stayed in bed most of the morning. That memory's not going to help you now, she told herself sternly.

'I owe you an explanation.'

Hannah blinked in bewilderment—either she had missed something or they were talking at cross purposes. Her bewilderment wasn't diminished by the embarrassed expression in the tall young woman's eyes.

'You do?'

'I've no excuse. I knew he was married.'

Hannah froze. What was she saying? Had her first instincts been correct? Ethan had denied it and it hadn't occurred to her to disbelieve him. Had he sent Miranda in here to flaunt their affair as some sort of bizarre punishment? She cursed her willingness to accept everything he said at face value as a tide of bitter humiliation rose in her throat.

'He's so attractive, but I don't need to tell you that.' Miranda's smile was apologetic. 'He was very kind to me, which makes it worse, really. He's such a good teacher.'

Don't I know it? Hannah thought grimly.

'I pulled out all the stops to get him.'

And what man could resist what this woman had to offer? Hannah thought grimly. What man would even try? Not my husband, obviously. The pain solidified in Hannah's chest until she felt as if she couldn't breathe. All that stuff about it being the first time in over three years and she'd swallowed it whole.

'At first he ignored it,' Miranda recalled, her colour heightened. 'Then when I got a lot more obvious he told me straight—he told me he wasn't interested. He was very convincing,' she recalled drily. 'When you go after what you want,' she observed philosophically, 'you have to take the rough with the smooth, but that's part of being a woman today.' She sighed. 'I may be tough, and not as moral as I should be, but I do have a conscience.

So when I realised last night that you thought…' She lifted her slender shoulders and her face twisted in a grimace of self-contempt. 'I couldn't bear it if I was the cause of any conflict. He obviously loves you very much.'

These revelations left Hannah's thoughts in a mad whirl. Ethan had refused this gorgeous creature! Only for a split second did she contemplate that he had done so because of her. In her heart she knew that it was Catherine's image which gave him the strength to resist temptation—that and the fierce sense of protectiveness he felt for his children. She couldn't afford to nurture any illusions on that score; he'd protect this marriage because it gave the children stability.

'You didn't have to tell me this,' she said wonderingly. She didn't think she'd have been brave enough to do so if the circumstances had been reversed.

Miranda nodded slowly. 'I know—maybe I'm not as hard-boiled as I thought,' she mused with a self-conscious laugh. 'I don't usually go after married men. I had heard some gossip that your marriage wasn't all it…' She cleared her throat noisily. 'Not that that's any excuse,' she said hastily. 'And I can see it wasn't true anyway. You must think I'm a total bitch,' she said frankly.

'I don't know what I think of you,' Hannah said honestly. 'I know it must have taken guts to come here and say this.'

'I turned the car around three times on the way over.'

'I appreciate your honesty.' It was hard not to, and she could afford to be generous, she told herself, under the circumstances. 'And I can understand any woman finding Ethan irresistible—I do myself,' she admitted, with the faintest glimmer of a mischievous smile.

Miranda gave a sigh of relief that was half a sob. 'Thank God,' she breathed. 'I thought you might want to…'

'Tear your hair out?' Hannah suggested. 'The thought did occur to me.' It wasn't easy to make a joke out of the violent revulsion of her feelings.

'Miranda gone?'

Hannah turned from her task of preparing vegetables to look at Ethan in a manner as casual as his own. 'I couldn't persuade her to stay,' she quipped waspishly.

'Pity.'

'A real loss,' she drawled. 'Did you enjoy your game of football?'

'Emma has a very pronounced competitive streak,' he mused, rubbing his shin. 'Just like her…'

'Like her mother,' she finished emphatically, even though the reminder hurt.

'I was gong to say like me,' he said, his brows raised a little at her tone.

Her sensitivity had made her jump the gun, and she continued swiftly to extinguish that disturbingly thoughtful expression on his face. 'I'm glad you tell her she can do anything she sets her mind to,' Hannah observed truthfully. 'It's important for any child, not just a girl, to have someone believe in them.' She was unaware of the hint of wistfulness that had entered her voice.

'Did nobody ever believe in you, Hannah?' he asked softly.

She gave him a startled look. 'Are you trying to discover the reason behind my inadequacies?' she asked sharply, instinctively reacting to the pity she thought she read in his voice. 'Just because I can't ride or sail or swim like a fish—swim at all, actually,' she corrected honestly, 'it doesn't mean I don't have self-confidence. When you're on your own you learn a lot about yourself, about your own resources. Don't worry, I won't infect Emma with my lack of self-esteem.'

'Where the hell did that come from?' he asked incredulously when she paused, breathless and flushed. 'Why the hell should I give a damn if you can ride or…? Oh, I see, you think I'm comparing you to Catherine.'

Everyone else did; why should he be different? 'It must be impossible not to,' she observed gruffly.

'You're two very different people.'

'I know that. *She* didn't need a prenuptial agreement,' she snarled, throwing down the knife in her hand. She stopped, appalled at what she'd just said. Why, she wondered with despair, do I keep saying these things?

'The circumstances were very different when I married Catherine. You could say I learnt from experience,' he added obscurely. 'Surely what we have now is more important. I enjoy being with you, Hannah; I *enjoy* you. I think you enjoy me.'

The soft way he emphasised 'enjoy' brought a rash of goosebumps to her warm skin. 'Why? Why do you…enjoy me?' she asked, unable to tear her eyes from the warmth of his regard.

'You…' he began emphatically. He stopped, and she had the impression he was backtracking. 'You make me laugh,' he finished lightly.

Hannah sighed softly. The sense of anticlimax was intense, but she was prepared to accept the pace he set. Slow and steady got there in the end, and she really did feel now that they had a destination to reach together. 'Like a clown?' she suggested.

'Like a warm, funny…lady.'

This time it was Hannah who felt things were running

too fast. The glow in his eyes made her knees tremble. 'You no longer appear to think Drew is a danger to the moral fibre of this family.'

Ethan acknowledged her withdrawal with a wry quirk of one darkly defined brow. 'I must admit it's easier to view him in a kinder light now I know he's not sharing my mother's bed.'

'You're so broad-minded!' she admired with a twinkle.

'Although my good opinion does depend on how often I find him wrestling on the floor with my wife,' came the surprising response.

Glancing up at his face, Hannah couldn't decide whether he was joking or not. 'The children were there,' she reminded him with a scornful laugh.

'That doesn't alter the fact he was enjoying himself far too much.'

She judged this an excellent time to divert the conversation. 'I hear you've been the victim of sexual harassment in the workplace.'

'A sad statistic,' he agreed with sigh. 'Why are you peeling these, anyway?' he asked, biting into a chunk of crisp carrot. 'What's happened to Mrs Turner?'

She sharply tapped the back of his hand as he attempted to filch another. 'This is therapy. Did you know what Miranda was going to say?'

Ethan shrugged. 'Not word for word.'

'I suppose you think I should admire your self-restraint?' she said, running the peeled vegetables under the cold water.

'Not really. I've never been an advocate of mixing business and pleasure. I've seen too many romances between colleagues go sour.'

'I didn't think there were enough women to go

around,' she responded waspishly. The implication that
he might have accepted Miranda's overtures if they'd
met under different circumstances really made her hack-
les rise.

'Did I say all those relationships needed one of each
sex?' His grey eyes sparkled with amusement at her
shocked expression.

'I thought *our* relationship was a business one,' she
challenged, responding to his patronising amusement
with belligerence. She always felt at a disadvantage
when something reminded her of how unsophisticated
she must appear in his eyes. 'We've got the contract to
prove it.'

'Marriage lines—most people have those.'

'I was thinking more of the prenuptial agreement I
signed in triplicate.'

'Does it bother you that much? You didn't have any
objections at the time.'

'I appreciate you have to protect yourself against gold-
diggers.'

His brows drew together at the bitterness in her voice
and his grey eyes raked her face with a shrewd expression. 'You're far too naïve to be a gold-digger.'

'Is that a criticism?' she snapped.

'An observation. I know you a little better now than
then.'

'Carnally, you mean, I suppose?' She literally bit her
tongue—she sometimes forgot that Ethan was an expert
at making people say things they didn't intend to. His
clever mind made thumbscrews obsolete.

'That too,' he agreed. A tiny shiver ran down her
spine as she intercepted the sensual appreciation of his
narrowed glance. 'Did you know you just put the peel

in the pan and the potatoes down the waste disposal?' he enquired with interest.

'It's a new recipe.'

His lips twitched but his expression remained solemn. 'The results should be…interesting.'

'Actually, I'm quite a good cook. I've never been able to afford expensive ingredients but I learnt all the basic techniques.'

'You're very quick at getting the hang of…''basic techniques''. It's something I noticed straight away.'

The innocent expression in his eyes didn't fool her for an instant. 'If you don't believe me, I'll prove it to you. I'll cook you dinner.'

'I do believe you, but I accept the offer,' he responded promptly. 'We'll make a date.'

'Well, that should give me a good couple of months to prepare,' she observed drily.

'Are you suggesting I neglect you?'

'I don't need entertaining.' She bit her lip—the last thing she'd wanted to imply was that she felt like a neglected wife. Their relationship might have changed, but not that much. 'I just think you work too hard.'

'Maybe you're right,' he mused thoughtfully. 'Can you be free for a couple of hours tomorrow morning? I needn't be in chambers until after lunch.'

'Why?'

'Wait and see.' He helped himself to another piece of raw carrot and she could see she'd have to be satisfied with these enigmatic words.

CHAPTER SEVEN

'WHO lives here?' Hannah asked. Ethan had explained that the Palladian mansion they had entered had been divided into four palatial apartments.

'A friend.'

The door opened onto a vast, modern, furnished open-plan living space. 'An unmarried friend,' she observed, looking at the monochromatic decor, leather and chrome. Someone who didn't feel the need to remain faithful to the period feel of the house, obviously.

'How did you know?' Ethan asked curiously.

'It might as well have a notice saying ''Boy's Room'',' she whispered, touching the sharp corner of a head-high metallic sculpture. 'Whatever gave you the idea I'd want to visit your friend, Ethan—especially one with such a questionable taste in art?' Was this his idea of a treat?

'Don't worry, he's not at home.'

'Then why are we here?'

'Come this way and all will be revealed,' he promised enigmatically as he caught hold of her hand.

Trotting to keep up with him, Hannah allowed herself to be led over acres of deep white carpet and down several shallow flights of stairs to wide double doors, which Ethan opened with a flourish.

'Wow!' she said, blinking.

'What do you think?'

'I think it's decadent and splendid,' she breathed. 'I sort of expect to see Roman ladies...' she said softly, looking around the mosaic-tiled pool room with wide-eyed appreciation. With the gentle trickle of the waterfall and the ceiling-height frescoes, it was all incredibly over the top.

'Slipping off their togas—you see that too?'

She laughed at the lascivious grin on his face. 'Why did you bring me here, Ethan?'

'Why does a person usually come to a pool? I'm going to teach you to swim.'

'No!' she said, shaking her head from side to side. 'I can't…'

'Nonsense!' he said bracingly.

Easy for him to say, she thought resentfully. 'It sounds like you're of the ''throw 'em in the deep end'' school of thought. We had a teacher like that at school—I was his Waterloo.'

'Don't be such a defeatist, Hannah. Everybody should learn a basic skill like swimming. You want to set a good example to the children, don't you?'

'That's moral blackmail!' she accused.

'If it works, who cares?'

'Not you, obviously. I can't swim; I don't want to swim.'

'Why?'

'I'm scared,' she burst out. 'There, satisfied? Go ahead and laugh at my athletic incompetence. I'm a physical coward—always have been.'

'Cowards don't throw themselves out of moving vehicles.'

'That was desperation, not bravery.'

'I know you're scared,' he said calmly, placing both his hands flat on her shoulders. He wasn't laughing at all. 'I'm with you; you don't need to be frightened. I won't let anything hurt you.'

It was foolish to read anything deep into his calm words, but she couldn't prevent the warm glow of pleasure that instantly filled her.

'I'll make a fool of myself.'

'You'll have fun.'

Hannah glanced at the glittering depths lit by a very elaborate display of underwater lights. 'I suppose you think I'm a wimp?'

'Don't tell me what I think,' he said firmly, patting the side of her nose.

'I don't suppose Catherine was scared of anything.' She could have screamed with vexation as the words slipped out. It hadn't been her intention to flaunt her insecurities. She could almost hear him wondering how to be tactful without telling huge whoppers. She couldn't imagine he'd be pleased at the implicit invitation to massage her ego.

'We're all scared of something.'

'I know—in this instance, water. Nothing you can do is going to make me brave and fearless.' Or give me long blonde hair and legs that end at my ears, she added silently.

'Do you think I'm trying to turn you into a Catherine clone?' A frown wrinkled the wide sweep of his brow. 'Is that what you imagine this is all about?'

'I think you're too much of a realist for that,' she replied bluntly. Her eyes slid away from the suspicion in his, because his words had exposed some of her very real fears. What did they have in common other than the children? The answer to this question was all too obvious—nothing. Right now he found her a novelty, but today's joke would become tomorrow's embarrassment and he'd start trying to change her.

'Don't say I didn't warn you,' she muttered, when his

regard and her own gloomy thoughts became too uncomfortable. 'I suppose there are swimsuits here somewhere?'

'Afraid not. You have to remember this pool was Adam's ultimate seduction device. Swimsuits would have ruined the ambience, from his point of view,' he added virtuously. 'Myself, I find the idea of peeling away those scraps of clingy Lycra quite…stimulating.'

'You're degenerate,' she said firmly. 'And as for the man who lives here, he must be pathetic.'

'Not pathetic—a professional bachelor, who, alas, is no more.'

'He's dead?' Hannah said, shocked by his callous attitude.

'Married,' Ethan corrected mournfully. He ducked as she aimed a blow at his head. 'For some reason his wife refused to live here,' he observed with wicked laughter in his eyes. 'Strange girl. He's altered beyond recognition these days—she's even weaned him off the Mickey Mouse ties. The flat's in the hands of an agent and we have permission to use it.'

'I suppose you said you wanted somewhere private for your…your…'

'I told him I wanted to teach my wife to swim. Adam's bed does everything short of play the national anthem, and personally I find gadgetry a little distracting. Besides, I've got a perfectly good bed at home.'

'I can't swim without clothes,' she said firmly.

'That's where you've been going wrong—you'll find it much easier without them,' he promised.

'What are you doing?'

'Taking my clothes off.'

'I can see that.'

'I think it must be a gender thing. You wouldn't find a man asking totally irrelevant questions.'

He was completely unselfconscious about his body. Lips slightly parted to draw air into her tight chest, she watched the muscles of his strong back ripple as he bent to kick off his shoes. His clothes were folded into a neat pile and his moleskin trousers slid to his feet. He stepped out of them.

Turning around, he made it clear for the first time that he was well aware of her interested gaze. She gave a small sharp inhalation as he removed his boxers.

'When the shutters are down you have very articulate eyes,' he said by way of explanation, before he turned and dived into the water, his body hardly creating a ripple. He took a couple of lazy strokes before he slid beneath the surface. After a moment's panic she could see him moving.

The condition of his body had made it starkly obvious what he thought her eyes had been saying. The idea that he had been privy to her erotic fantasies as she'd admired him brought hot colour to her cheeks.

As much to divert her thoughts as anything else, she peeled off her clothes swiftly, leaving them in a crumpled heap. Unlike Ethan, she walked around the perimeter to the opposite, shallow end of the pool. She kept on her bra and pants which, she reasoned, covered more than most swimsuits.

She was standing with her toes barely covered by water on the top step when Ethan's dark head emerged from the water several feet away. He waded towards her.

'Coward!'

'I told you I don't like water. I'm cold,' she complained.

'Cold? I have it on the best authority that this place

is kept at a constantly humidified heat of eighty-four degrees. Actually, I was referring to your outfit.' He shrugged as he examined the white cotton broderie anglaise set. 'Maybe it'll make it easier to concentrate on the task in hand,' he conceded.

Hannah shivered again. She wasn't proof against the erotic movement of his hips as he surveyed her through half-closed eyes. 'Nothing will make this easy,' she muttered as she eased her way to the next step.

'Take your time.'

'I've every intention of—' She let out a shrill cry as she lost her footing. 'Ouch!' she gasped as she landed on her bottom. The sudden realisation that water was lapping past her middle made her stroke out in panic.

'Calm down, no damage done.'

Panic receded but Hannah remained tense and suspicious. 'It wasn't your behind that cushioned the fall,' she grumbled feelingly. Ethan's grin was very white and shockingly heartless.

'Come on, take my hands. What's wrong? Don't you trust me?' He looked boyishly injured at the idea.

'Now you come to mention it…' she said slowly, not impressed by his act. Tentatively she reached across to bridge the gap between them. She was genuinely terrified of water. Logic told her she was perfectly safe, but logic didn't prevent the adrenaline being pumped in massive quantities around her body. Her heart was beating so hard she felt physically sick.

'Go on—the first step's the worst.'

He was right, but the second and third weren't much better.

The first time, half an hour later, she put her head under the water she emerged breathless but triumphant.

'I did it!' She flung her arms around Ethan's neck and kissed him firmly on the lips.

'If only all my students showed their gratitude so nicely.'

'How many other women have you taught to swim?' She let her hands rest loosely on his shoulders and very daringly let her feet float gently off the floor. Ethan's wet skin had a gorgeous rich texture.

'I haven't taught you yet.'

'You didn't answer my question.'

'You noticed that, did you?'

'Why do you have to talk like...like a lawyer?' she sniffed.

'I am lawyer.'

'Feeble excuse.'

'Have you had enough for one day?'

'Probably,' she confessed.

'But you enjoyed it. Admit it, Hannah.'

'Sort of, once I relaxed a bit.'

'I'll have a quick swim whilst you get a shower.'

She was rather disappointed; she'd half expected the intimacy of the occasion and the setting would have led inevitably to a less businesslike encounter. But it would seem the only thing he'd had in mind was teaching her to swim. She watched for a moment as Ethan lapped the pool with slow, effortless elegance and then did as he suggested.

Whilst she was still combing her damp hair she heard him turn on the shower. She squeezed the excess moisture out of her wet underwear and took one last glance at her reflection before making her way back to the pool edge, to wait for him there.

'You're looking a bit warm,' Ethan observed, leaning on the back of her lounger.

Hannah opened her eyes and found herself looking up into his face. 'This place must cost a fortune to heat,' she said, dabbing the slight film of moisture over her upper lip with the tip of her tongue.

Ethan caught her elbow as she got to her feet. 'I've been thinking about getting one at home. What do you think?'

'Isn't that a bit extravagant?'

'I think the budget might stretch.' His teasing wasn't of the unkind variety, but Hannah immediately felt gauche and awkward.

'I forget sometimes,' she murmured as they retraced their steps through the flat.

'What did you forget?'

'That you're rich. I expect that sounds stupid to you, but watching the pennies is sort of an ingrained habit with me.'

'How old were you when your parents died?'

'I never knew my father, so I suppose he might still be out there somewhere. Mum died when I was four and I went to live with my gran. I went into care when she had a bad stroke.'

'It must have been tough.'

'I'm tough.' Her frown didn't invite sympathy; it wasn't intended to.

'I'm beginning to realise that.' The quiet reticence had been all he'd seen for a long time, but now he wondered how he had missed the delightful complexity of this young woman. He'd hardly noticed at first that when they disagreed over something to do with the children, although she listened to what he said, somehow he usually ended up agreeing with her without quite knowing how it had happened.

Her recent, more overt rebellions had been impossible to miss, and very taxing on the nerves, but he had to admit they hadn't been boring. Hannah was one book with a very deceptive cover, and, like any good book, once opened almost impossible to put down.

'My survival instincts are pretty well developed.' She was glad of the autumnal chill in the air outside; it cooled her overheated body.

A gardener was working in the communal grounds, collecting the fallen leaves. Ethan called out a greeting to him as he opened the car doors.

'Is that why you married me?'

Hannah blinked in shock as he slid into the car beside her. 'I... I... Why else?' She affected a casual shrug, but the question had really shaken her.

He'd never come right out and asked her before. She'd thought it hadn't mattered to him so long as things were going as he wanted. Was it because he wanted different things now, or did he suspect? The truth had been trembling on the tip of her tongue. She flicked a curious look at his profile. What would he have said if she'd told him the truth?

'Do you mind?' she couldn't stop herself asking.

'Mind the fact you married me for purely practical reasons? Why should I? Under the circumstances it would be a bit hypocritical. If you'd been like Patricia I'd never have suggested it.'

'Who's Patricia?'

'The one in between Sophie and Rebecca,' he said with a frown of concentration as he recalled the roll-call of previous nannies.

'What did Patricia do?'

'Followed me around with big spaniel eyes,' he recalled with a shudder. 'She could always find an excuse to knock on my door in the middle of the night dressed in floaty, transparent things.'

'You mean the poor girl had the bad taste to fall in

love with you.' Thank God she had managed to bite back the truth. The idea of him thinking about her like that left a bitter taste in her mouth.

'Love! I doubt that. Infatuation, possibly.'

'I'd have thought worship would have been a positive attribute in a prospective bride.'

'Under the circumstances, hardly,' he said with a grimace of distaste.

'You mean she'd have expected you to make love to her?' Hannah suggested. Her chin was tilted at a belligerent angle as she turned to glare at him. 'How perfectly horrid for you. Sleeping with the nanny!' she mocked. 'Whatever next?'

The heaving indignation was not wasted on Ethan. 'It's plain ridiculous to compare yourself with what's-her-name, and you know it. So don't get all uppity with me.'

'From where I'm sitting the similarities jump up and hit you in the face.'

'Did *you* expect me to make love to you?'' he shot back.

'No!' Dream, crave and yearn for it, yes. Expect, no!

'Exactly,' he replied triumphantly. 'You didn't marry me thinking I could walk on water either.'

She could say no in all honesty to this. In her case love hadn't been blind, just reckless! 'I didn't hold it against you that you couldn't.'

'You're generous to a fault,' he agreed drily. 'Seriously, it would have been a disaster to enter into a marriage with some starry-eyed female who needed constant reassurance. Perhaps more marriages should be based on friendship.'

'We weren't friends,' she reminded him uncooperatively. What female with blood in her veins would have been co-operative in her place? she thought indignantly. He had some hide, singing the praises of platonic marriage when everyone knew he'd been crazy about Catherine! He'd had it—why should he imagine she didn't want the opportunity to experience the wild impracticability of mutual love? Was she being unreasonable and greedy wanting more?

'But we are now?'

If she'd been standing on the particular rug that question had pulled from under her feet, she'd have been flat on her back. Fortunately she was enclosed by soft, supportive leather upholstery which cushioned the impact considerably.

'I...we...possibly,' she finished lamely. She ought to be glad he thought of her as a friend. Only his words triggered a seething sense of dissatisfaction.

'That's what I like to hear: an unequivocal endorsement. Let's skip over the friends bit. We're lovers, or aren't you sure about that either?'

'I'm not in the witness box,' she retorted. Just as well too, considering!

'There was no compulsion...'

Speak for yourself, she thought, quashing an alarming desire to indulge in hysterical laughter. 'Compulsion' summed up her feelings for this man pretty well.

'Nothing forced,' he continued persuasively. 'It was a natural progression...spontaneous. What,' he enquired icily, 'is so funny about me being spontaneous?'

'It's just not a term I associate with you.'

He gave her a second suspicious sideways glance before returning his attention to the road ahead. 'Neither of us had any expectations and things just progressed naturally. We're not in love, but it doesn't make the

physical aspect any less fulfilling. I think things have
turned out very well.'

Maybe he was right, she reflected. He looked a lot
more relaxed than she'd ever seen him before. Perhaps
sex without the unstable element of love was less
fraught. Who was she fooling? Deep down she knew she
couldn't have slept with him if she hadn't been in love
with him; it was an integral, inseparable part of the equation for her. Men were obviously different.

'Shall I take your silence as agreement, or should I
start to worry?'

My God, I could tear his comfortable appraisal to
shreds with three little words—three little words I'm not
going to use. He'd never know how bitterly ironic his
cutting assessment of the lovelorn nanny was.

'If propinquity and convenience were all that mattered, surely most men would sleep with their secretaries.' She pursed her lips reflectively. 'Maybe most men
do sleep with their secretaries.'

'Obviously I find you attractive.'

'It's not obvious to me.'

He dismissed this statement with a sceptical smile.
'Would you have married me if you'd found me physically repulsive, no matter how attractive the package I
offered you? I don't think so.'

'Correct me if I'm wrong, but the logical progression
of that argument seems to be that if I'd been a real dog
you wouldn't have popped the question. Your frankness
has a unique charm all of its own, Ethan.' Whilst she
didn't expect to be romanced with sweet nothings, this
was stretching her tolerance to breaking-point. 'And it
would be a mistake to assume that, just because you're
a pin-up, all women feel sexually attracted to you.
Women are not as predictable as men.'

'Have I said something to annoy you, Hannah?'

'Whatever gave you *that* idea?'

'I thought you'd appreciate candour. Or are you still miffed because I didn't make love to you back at the pool?'

'My God,' she breathed, her bosom heaving, 'when they handed out ego you got a double dose.'

'You were expecting me to.'

'I was not!' she lied firmly.

'I thought you might think the setting a bit too... obvious.'

'You're so sensitive.'

'I'm glad you appreciate the sacrifice,' he replied with cheerful unrepentance. 'It *was* a sacrifice.' This time there was no humour in his voice. 'When you look at me with those big, hungry eyes I personally couldn't give a damn about the decor.'

'I don't have...' She couldn't bring herself to say 'hungry eyes'.

'Are those sweet little cotton things in your bag?' He moved his hand from the gear lever to flick the handle of her leather bag and she nodded vaguely, her head still spinning. 'So you're wearing what, exactly, under those?' Briefly his glance flicked over the russet cotton sweater and above-the-knee black skirt she was wearing.

She glanced down, just to check the lacy top of her hold-up stocking wasn't showing. Her heart was beating slow and strong and she was conscious of every separate thud.

'Nothing would be my guess,' he said thickly. 'You'd better come clean because I have every intention of finding out for sure when we get home.'

The mental picture that accompanied his words breached her feeble mental defences and robbed her body of strength in one fell swoop. 'Don't I have any say in the matter?'

'The idea excites you as much as it does me.'

'How do you know?' She plucked at the stretchy fabric of her sweater, as it showed an unfortunate tendency to cling to the visible proof that supported his theory.

'I know—the same way I know it's my face you see when you close your eyes when I'm making love to you. My face—not some shadowy figure you still harbour romantic fantasies about.'

'What are you talking about?'

'You told me about your unrequited love. Did you forget?'

Lies had a way of catching up on a person! I really don't have a good enough memory to lie effectively, she thought, trying desperately to recall exactly what she had said.

'I don't want to talk about it.' Did I give this face-saving device a name? she wondered. She racked her brains and still couldn't recall.

'Do you feel guilty because you enjoy it when we have sex? Do you feel you're betraying your love?'

Hannah raised her eyes from her stubborn contemplation of her clasped hands. Was this a classic case of transference? Was that actually how *he* felt when he made love to her?

For some reason he was working himself up into a real temper. One glance at his rigid profile told her that.

'Imaginary lovers are perfect, but bloody unsatisfying. I may not fulfil the criteria of all those mawkish romances you read, but I do assuage your needs,' he assured her with arrogant confidence.

She dismissed the possibility that the idea of her fantasising about another man whilst she was in his arms was fuelling his antagonism. He had no reason to be jealous of her love; he didn't want it himself. He'd spelt that out pretty clearly.

He was also as wrong as he could get about the criteria. He filled all the criteria of dream lover—all except one: he didn't love her to distraction.

'Perhaps the difference is we don't make love, we have sex.'

'I haven't noticed you complaining.'

'I've got lovely manners.'

'I used to think so...' He switched off the engine as they drew up outside the stable block and gave her the benefit to his full attention—something she found hard to bear. 'Will your lovely manners make you feel obliged to agree when I suggest we go indoors and ''have sex''?' There was no missing the irony in his voice.

'No.' She reached out and touched the side of his hard jaw. He turned his head and pressed his lips to her open palm. 'But wanting to touch you will,' she confessed huskily.

Hot satisfaction flared in Ethan's eyes, and without saying a word he got out of the car and tore around to the other side with flattering speed to open her door.

'It's not very practical with a houseful of people,' she said regretfully. Already aroused, she was filled with writhing frustration by the knowledge that this verbal foreplay was going nowhere.

'If you had a spontaneous husband that might be true, but you have me. I've planned meticulously for this eventuality, and we have the place to ourselves for the next two hours at least.'

She gaped at him incredulously, but he was too busy

being distracted by the length of leg she exposed whilst climbing out of the car to notice. 'You planned...?'

'Always be prepared,' he intoned piously. 'The boy scouts had a profound effect on my development.'

'I doubt very much if they had anything like this in mind.'

'And if my house weren't filled to overflowing with strangers,' he responded, sweeping her unexpectedly up into his arms, 'I wouldn't have to go to such elaborate lengths to get my own wife alone.'

'Your mother isn't a stranger, and Dre—'

'Shut up. I don't want to talk about my mother.' He proceeded to tell her what he *did* want to talk about, and Hannah was happy to listen.

Hannah got back home a little after seven. Faith and Drew had left that morning so, after the children had gone to bed, she and Ethan would have the whole evening to themselves. The first time since... Her cheeks flushed with pleasure as she recalled this new and exciting phase in their relationship; this wondrous circumstance was never very far from the forefront of her thoughts.

The passing days hadn't diminished her sense of wonder at the joys of intimacy. Where it would eventually lead them, she didn't know, but for once she was inclined to feel optimistic.

Perhaps it was even the time to admit to him her feelings. She had to tell him before they became too transparent to disguise. Would the gift of her love be something he appreciated? That was the troublesome million-dollar question that made her break off humming the cheery tune under her breath and begin chewing her upper lip.

He had certainly thawed out a lot during the past days, and not just with her. Although he hadn't gone so far as to laugh at his misinterpretation of his mother's matrimonial plans, she had got the impression his wry sense of humour had eventually appreciated the situation. He'd gone along with the proposed family get-together with his prospective stepfather with every appearance of approval, and he and Drew both seemed ready to accept that their mutual first impressions had been wrong. When Ethan capitulated, he did it in style.

Hannah was still on a high, and all things felt possible—even telling her husband she loved him! The afternoon had really boosted her confidence. Jean-Paul had arranged an informal meeting for her with the head of the French department. In retrospect it had been lucky he'd given her such short notice—she hadn't had time to talk herself out of it, or see problems where there weren't any.

It had all been very encouraging, and she'd been bubbling with enthusiasm when she'd stopped off at the pub for a drink with Jean-Paul and his wife, who was on maternity leave from her teaching post in a local secondary school.

The kitchen was empty, so she assumed Ethan was upstairs getting the children ready for bed. She looked at her reflection in a large gilt-framed mirror before going upstairs. The girl with the flushed cheeks, bright, shiny eyes and glossy hair looked unfamiliar to her; it was an image she would like to get used to. She was just straightening the neck of her red chenille jumper when Ethan's voice made her spin round.

'Hello!' she said back, hurrying forward. 'Where are the children?' she asked as she walked into the room and looked around with a puzzled frown.

'Ah, the children,' he drawled. This was Hannah's first inkling that something was amiss—seriously amiss. A sick feeling of dread began to churn in her belly. 'They're in bed.'

'It's early.' Her voice faltered as she met the searing contempt in his grey eyes. 'Is something wrong, Ethan?' Had she been wrong when she'd thought he'd accepted the fact that she wanted to further her education in the future? What else could explain the waves of hostility he was emanating?

'You can ask me that?'

'I don't understand…' His blighting anger seemed totally out of proportion to anything she had done.

'Where have you been?'

Hannah blinked. He must have got her message. It was Mrs Turner's day off, but Alexa had offered to look after Tom and bring Emma home from school. Alexa had been in the room when Jean-Paul had rung, and, much to Hannah's surprise, she had offered to look after the children. Hannah had hoped it meant a slow easing of hostilities.

'Not any local hospital—I tried them.'

'I went to the university and then I stopped for a drink with Jean-Paul. Alexa knew—'

'I'm well aware you dumped Tom with Alexa—it was she who contacted me after the school rang to tell her nobody had picked Emma up. I'm curious,' he said with biting sarcasm. 'Did you genuinely forget, or did you just assume somebody else would shoulder your responsibilities because you couldn't be bothered to spoil your fun? I know you left the university hours ago—I rang.'

Hannah was shaking her head slowly from side to side. He couldn't believe she'd actually desert Emma. The thought of the little girl waiting for someone to collect her, watching all her friends go home, brought a lump of emotion to her throat.

'Was she very upset?' How *could* Alexa use a child to drive a stake between her and Ethan? My God, she must really feel threatened, Hannah thought. She must really hate me!

'And am I to assume from the husky catch that you give a damn?'' he jeered. 'All you had to do, Hannah, was pick up a phone and Alexa would have collected her. But no, you couldn't be bothered even to do that! If the teacher hadn't been alert she might have tried to get home alone. A little girl, lost, alone, a soft target for any sickos out there.'

Her eyes darkened with horror at the picture his words painted. 'Alexa…'

'Alexa was worried sick. I said I'd ring her when you got back.'

Hannah caught his arm. She couldn't believe this was happening. God, what a fool she'd been to take Alexa's overtures of friendship at face value! 'You don't understand, Ethan. Alexa *offered* to look after Tom and pick up Emma.'

His eyes flicked dismissively over her face, icy with contemptuous disbelief. 'What reason would she have for lying? When I asked her to look after the children next week— Oh, yes, I'd planned to take you away,' he said, as she stared at him uncomprehendingly. 'It was meant to be a surprise. New ring, new start!' He extracted a small velvet box from his pocket and pulled out a gold ring. He flung it viciously across the room. 'Not only did you fool the children, you fooled me with your gentle, caring air. You've shown your real colours now, so don't try and shift the responsibility to someone else.'

'I'm not. She hates me!' Hannah cried, willing him to believe her. 'She thinks I've stolen Catherine's children, her home and…' she swallowed the aching constriction in her throat '…and you.'

Ethan laughed; it wasn't a pleasant sound. 'You're not the children's mother and never could be. A mother doesn't walk away from a child who needs her!' His voice shook with outrage, and his hand came down to cover like a vice her pale fingers that curved around his forearm. 'As for this house; you're the hired help here. The only thing that ever made you a possible mate in my eyes was the fact the children adore you and you're a competent nanny. I now discover that you're not even that!'

She recoiled from the undisguised contempt in his voice. He was trying to hurt, and, by God, he was succeeding! 'So now you don't trust me to look after the children?'

'Now I know you'll always put your own pleasure first. Now I'll make damned sure they don't suffer because you're a selfish little bitch. They don't deserve that again!'

As his lips compressed she could see a bloodless white line around his mouth. Hannah had reached the stage where his words hardly mattered. Her pain had reached saturation point; she couldn't hurt any more than she already did.

'If Emma and Tom didn't love you so much you'd be out of that door tonight! I've been inclined to dismiss the things Alexa has told me before as the concerns of an overprotective grandmother. I now see she was right about you all along.'

'What about us?'

'Us? There is no us.' He pulled her hand from his sleeve as if the contact offended him. 'As you pointed out, I'm a healthy man with needs and you were convenient.'

'It was more than that,' she protested. She couldn't let him reduce something that had been so fine and special to a sordid level.

'Believe that if it makes you feel better.' His amused contempt was like a slap in the face.

Ethan turned away abruptly; the sight of her bewildered, distressed face hurt too much. He couldn't let himself be sucked in again. 'Did you enjoy your evening?' he rasped sarcastically. 'Was it business or pleasure, or just a convenient combination of both?'

'Ethan!' She had to try and get through to him one last time. The sight of his broad, uncommunicative back was eloquent enough to tell her that her efforts were wasted. 'You find it incredibly easy to believe badly of me,' she accused.

What he'd find 'incredibly easy' would be taking her in his arms and kissing her. He despised himself for wanting to. 'The facts speak for themselves.'

There speaks the lawyer, she thought with a sudden surge of anger. Why was he doing this? She'd never given him any cause to think she'd neglect the children, and yet he'd tried and sentenced her before she'd even said a word. Anger she could understand, but his reaction seemed out of proportion. When he wouldn't look at her, she moved so that he had to.

'Things aren't always what they seem,' she challenged.

'*You're* not. You want to go to university and you don't give a damn about how it affects anyone else! We've just been a convenient stepping-stone for you.'

She gasped at the sheer injustice of this. She'd spent most of the afternoon trying to work out how and when she could begin a course without disrupting their family life. 'It's all right for you to work all the hours God sends, but if I want to do anything it's selfish. Their mother worked, didn't she?' No woman could run a business and take part in sport at the sort of level Catherine had without a co-operative partner.

'We're not talking about Catherine!' he snarled.

Something in his expression made her wonder for a split second if that were entirely true. Had everything in the garden been as perfect as everyone told her? The notion was banished as quickly as it had come. She was just clinging to comforting straws, like any other soul going under for the final time.

'When my children need me, I'm here. After your behaviour today I'm surprised you can fling around a word like "selfish" without choking on it.'

'Well, I hope *you* choke on the truth when you finally realise what a fool you're being right now!' she cried, running from the room.

She paused on her way back to her own room to look in on the children. They were both asleep. Looking at Emma's sleeping face, she couldn't comprehend how anyone could put a child in danger. Ethan had been right—she might have wandered off. She was only a baby, after all. Hannah was tenderly stroking a lock of golden hair off the childish brow when some sixth sense told her she wasn't alone.

Ethan was standing in the doorway, watching her. Silently their eyes locked. Defiance was the only thing that kept Hannah's tears at bay. As she brushed past him she could smell the alcohol he'd obviously just swallowed, but she was helpless to prevent her response to his closeness, that warm rush that unfurled in the pit of her belly and the light, dizzy sensation in her head.

She closed the door quietly behind her. 'I see now that it was a mistake overstepping the boundaries of my job description. I take it you have no objections if I take the nanny's bedroom in the future. I'll move my things back tomorrow.'

He didn't object, but then she'd known he wouldn't. He'd made it quite clear that as far as he was concerned there was nothing special about what they had together.

CHAPTER EIGHT

EMMA was so excited she hadn't slept the night before. Hannah knew because she had shared the little girl's bedroom in the hotel suite.

'Yes, you look lovely,' Hannah said as she finally secured a blue ribbon in the silk locks. 'Bridesmaids don't bounce.'

'They don't?'

'No, they glide elegantly.' Hannah demonstrated, swaying her hips in a lazy, exaggerated fashion.

'Exactly like a princess.'

'Will we be going soon?'

'I hope so,' said Hannah with feeling. Getting the child to the church before the flowers in her hair curled up and died, or something indelible and probably noxious got spilt down the front of the pink satin, had taken on the aspect of a nightmare.

'The car is here. You look spec-tac-u-lar!' Ethan said, sweeping his daughter high into the air. Ethan didn't comment on his wife's outfit.

Hannah knew she was looking drawn; over the past six weeks she'd lost weight she couldn't afford to. The muted grey and blue striped silk suit didn't totally disguise this fact. 'Shall I get Tom down?'

'No,' Ethan responded curtly. 'You take Emma.'

Hannah wondered how much longer she could take the constant slights before something cracked. Pretending to be part of a happy family was killing her by slow, painful inches. 'Come along, darling. We can't keep Grandma Faith waiting—it's her big day.'

The car was waiting outside the hotel foyer. The doorman ushered them solicitously towards it. A sudden gust of wind lifted her hat and Hannah let go of Emma's hand to catch hold of it.

It all happened so quickly, she never did know what caught the child's eye on the opposite side of the busy road. One minute she was standing beside Hannah, the next Hannah saw the heels of her shiny new shoes and a fluttering pink hem.

With a cry of warning Hannah ran out after her, hardly noticing the sound of horns in her ears. She felt as if her feet were made of lead as she desperately tried to propel herself forward. Panting, she picked the child up from behind as she simultaneously became aware of the fact that she couldn't move fast enough to avoid the metal monster bearing down on them. It was instinct rather than conscious thought that made her throw the child clear just before everything went black.

Those ten minutes before the ambulance arrived were the longest and most nightmarish Ethan could ever remember. The hotel manager had proved to be a pillar of strength and calm. Ethan had been able to leave the children safely in his hands, knowing that his mother would come the instant she got his message.

Why wouldn't anyone tell him anything? They'd shut him out of the emergency room. He ripped the white rose from his buttonhole with an expression of disgust and ground it into the floor with his heel. Nobody came near the tall figure conspicuously dressed in the morning suit; he presented a daunting picture.

Standing in the glass revolving door with Tom in his

arms when it had happened, he'd seen everything. From a position of complete helplessness he'd watched it all. He'd seen the car hit Hannah and heard the sickening thud as her limp, apparently lifeless body struck the metal before sliding to the floor. The image was scorched in his brain.

'Mr Kemp? Would you like to come this way?'

The white-coated figure led Ethan to a small, impersonal office.

'Well?' Ethan didn't bother hiding his impatience. He was wound up tighter than a spring and it showed. His knuckles cracked as he flexed his long fingers.

The doctor didn't take offence at the aggressive tone; he'd seen and heard it all before. All the same, whilst quite a few of his customers might have liked to rip him limb from limb as the bearer of bad tidings, most of them didn't look capable of it. This one did.

'Your wife has been remarkably lucky. There's a hairline fracture of the temporal bone.' He touched his finger to the side of his head to indicate the position. 'That should heal with no ill effects. She is badly concussed but she did regain consciousness for a short time. I was honest with her when she asked me.'

'Asked you what?' Ethan had slumped into a straight-backed chair. The tension had drained from his body so abruptly, he felt as weak as a baby. She was going to live. Whether he had prayer, luck, or modern medicine to thank didn't matter to him—*she was alive*. Things were going to be different, he swore to himself.

'About the baby.'

'Let me get this straight,' Ethan said in a strained voice. 'My wife is pregnant?'

'*Was* pregnant.'

Ethan's head dropped forward onto his chest. 'Oh, my

God!' he said softly. He caught his head between his hands and rocked forward, his elbows clamped together.

'You didn't know? I'm sorry. It was very early, and there's no reason you can't have a healthy baby in the future.'

'Can I see her?' His complexion was tinged with an unhealthy pallor as he raised his head.

Numbed by having been overexposed to too much pain and suffering, the young doctor found his compassion unexpectedly stirred by the bloodshot, red-rimmed eyes of the man opposite him.

'Of course, but it might be quite a while before she wakes.'

The total amnesia only lasted for a few terrifying seconds. 'Mr Kemp?' she whispered in relief as the man seated beside her bed lifted his head. For some reason the man flinched as if she'd struck him.

'So you're back with us, Mrs Kemp?' The nurse hid her surprise at the formal greeting between husband and wife behind a professional smile.

Hannah remembered everything then—it was like walking into a solid wall. 'Ethan.'

'You're awake, Hannah.' Stating the obvious gave him a breathing space. It had been impossible to miss the grief of knowledge that had rushed into her eyes, only to be supplanted by a vague, distant expression.

'My head hurts,' she said dully.

'You fractured your skull.'

'I didn't mean to let go of her hand.'

Ethan looked at her blankly.

'Emma. She really is all right, is she? The doctor said…' Panic was beginning to build up inside her. What if he'd just been humouring her? She tried to raise herself up on one elbow but the intravenous line in her arm got in the way.

'Emma's fine, thanks to you.' The dark colour ran up under his tan. 'It was the most criminally stupid thing I've ever seen!' The words rammed home as he viciously enunciated every syllable. 'And the most brave.'

'I didn't think.' She endangered his daughter; he was bound to be angry. His anger couldn't hurt her. She was numb; she didn't feel anything—even when she made herself remember that her body no longer carried their child. Had anyone told him? The odd expression in his eyes as he'd muttered the taut afterthought did puzzle her.

'Tell me something I don't already know.'

The nurse returned with a doctor and Hannah watched as her husband was bustled from the room.

'I didn't expect to see you, Ethan. Aren't you going to fetch Hannah home this morning?'

Ethan nodded as he kissed his mother's cheek. 'I'm on my way.'

'A very roundabout way. What's wrong?' she enquired shrewdly. Her son wasn't a man who showed strain externally, but right now he looked tense enough to snap.

'Hannah was pregnant when the car hit her. She lost the baby,' he said abruptly.

'Oh, my dear, I'm so sorry.'

'She didn't tell you, then,' Ethan muttered. He'd hoped that she'd confided in his mother; he'd wanted to think she'd had a shoulder to cry on. After what had passed between them it didn't surprise him that she hadn't wanted his shoulder.

It was such a lot of grief for one person to bear alone,

and it tore him up to think of her holding onto all that pain. Seeing the sheen of tears in Faith's blue eyes, he turned away and walked to the window. A long way below the city traffic crawled along.

'No. No, she didn't.' Faith watched the tall figure of her son with a thoughtful expression tinged with concern.

'The thing is…' Ethan turned and faced his mother '…every time I try to discuss it she changes the subject. It's as if it never happened,' he said incredulously.

'People have different ways of coping with these things.'

Ethan glared at her with frustrated anger. 'I know that!' he snapped. Taking a deep breath, he controlled his temper. 'She needs help and I don't know how to help her. I don't think she even wants me to help. It's all very well for the doctors to say I have to be patient and not push things.' He snorted impatiently. 'Oh, she talks—she talks to me as if I'm a stranger. She's polite, the way she used to be.' The way he had thought he wanted her to be. 'She's shutting me out.'

'Perhaps it will help being home.'

'I hope so,' he said heavily. 'She misses Emma and Tom,' he admitted. 'Perhaps you're right.'

'Alexa!' Hannah stiffened as she recognised with shock the figure who walked through the door into her anonymous hospital room. 'I was expecting Ethan. I'm going home today.' Home. What had he said? As for this house, you're the hired help.

'What a lot of lovely flowers,' Alexa observed in a brittle tone.

'Yours were lovely, thank you.' She waited tensely to hear what the other woman was doing here. Then thought, why waste time wondering? 'Why did you come, Alexa?' It was pointless pretending—the enmity Alexa felt towards her was out in the open now.

'I did a terrible thing. It was wrong of me, very wrong...' The young woman opposite Alexa sat with a face of stone. There was no encouragement in the calm hazel eyes; there wasn't much of anything. Alexa fumbled in her handbag for a tissue and cleared her throat. She nearly lost her nerve, but the agony of guilt she'd been experiencing made her plough on. 'You saved Emma's life—my grandchild. I lost Catherine. I couldn't bear to lose Emma too. It made me realise how selfish I've been. I've been feeling so guilty.'

And I'm supposed to assuage that guilt by forgiving you, Hannah thought. It would be the mature, adult thing to do, but she wasn't feeling very adult today. The compassion was still there somewhere, but she couldn't tap into the source.

When Hannah didn't respond, Alexa swallowed hard before continuing in a quavering tone, 'When Ethan told me he was taking you away for a belated honeymoon I knew I had to do something. He was Catherine's. It didn't seem right—he belonged to her. Do you see?'

Hannah saw. He still does, she thought. She knew she should feel something—pity, anger, compassion—but she couldn't get past that great empty space inside.

'I could tell something was going on between you, the way he was looking at you, touching you... I lied to him to make him think you were selfish and irresponsible.' The tears flowed unchecked down her cheeks now. 'Can you ever forgive me?'

'It doesn't matter now,' Hannah said in a tight, unemotional voice. Awkwardly she patted the older woman's hand.

The inarticulate sound that escaped Ethan's throat made her look up. 'Ethan!'

Alexa gasped and twisted around. When she saw Ethan standing in the doorway she went deathly pale. 'I didn't mean any harm.'

Ethan's lips were a bloodless gash; his eyes had narrowed to slits. Hannah could see the inner battle he had to control his turbulent emotions before he eventually spoke. 'Get out of my sight.' He closed his eyes as the woman scuttled past him with a sigh of relief.

'What can I say?' he asked Hannah hoarsely.

She shrugged. 'It doesn't matter now.'

'Of course it matters,' Ethan grated. He reached out to touch her arm and she shied away. He couldn't fail to miss the spasm that contorted her features, as if his touch made her skin crawl. He drew a sharp, ragged breath as he momentarily averted his face. 'I had no idea she…' He paused. Words seemed woefully inadequate to express his regret.

'I told you.' The blankness in her eyes was somehow worse than reproach.

'I haven't forgotten. Are you ever going to forgive me?'

'I suppose a resentful wife would make life uncomfortable. Poor Ethan—you didn't bargain for all this when you gave me the job, did you?'

He shook his head from side to side as she spoke. 'Talk to me, Hannah,' he pleaded urgently. 'If you hate me, just come out and say so. Yell at me if you must!'

Hannah just looked at the upturned palms of his outstretched hands and slowly her gaze shifted to his so familiar face. Did she hate him? Was that what happened to love when it went sour?

'I can't perform to order just for you, Ethan. Besides,

what would the nurse say if I started throwing things?' she asked drily as the figure in white appeared behind him.

The wheelchair seemed excessive, but Hannah was quite happy to fall in with hospital policy. Ethan carried the accumulated clutter of her stay, but even as she got into the car he didn't touch her; she noticed that.

'I asked Mother. I thought you might like to see her,' Ethan said as he opened the big front door at home.

'That's nice,' she observed without any real enthusiasm.

The pain started when she walked into the living room. The part inside her which had been frozen started to thaw. The ice had been so tangible, she looked down half expecting to see a pool of water around her feet. The room was full. They all seemed so happy to see her. Faith's new husband was beside her, and Drew. Even Mrs Turner had forgotten her usual reserve. There were flowers everywhere.

'Grandma fetched them for you,' Emma said excitedly when Hannah admired them. 'I baked biscuits for you. Alison helped me.'

Hannah looked incuriously at the tall, strapping figure of the young girl standing in the corner of the room. The girl smiled back shyly. Emma was obviously reluctant to let go of Hannah's hand, but when Ethan motioned her to fetch the plate of home-made biscuits for Hannah she did so.

Hannah was surprised the crumbs would go past the immense, aching constriction in her throat. 'You're all so kind, but it's a bit…'

'Overwhelming,' Faith said, immediately noting the tell-tale signs of disintegration on the drawn face of her daughter-in-law. 'Come on, children, let's go for a walk before tea. Come along, Robert.' She tugged at the arm of the tall, distinguished-looking figure of her new husband. 'Alison, will you get the children's coats on?'

Hannah could hardly see them through the mist of unshed tears that welled hotly in her eyes. Ethan was still there—he was the last person in the world she wanted to display her weakness in front of.

'Who is Alison?' She willed back the tears and even managed a stiff smile.

'A girl from the village. You needed help.'

'You mean Mrs Turner needs help. What's happened to Grace?' Grace was the student who supplemented her grant helping Mrs Turner with some of the domestic chores.

'Not with the house; with the children.'

Hannah's eyes followed him as he walked over to the baby grand piano that sat in the corner of the room. He lifted the lid and played a single chord.

Suddenly her heart was racing with panic and anger. 'Whilst I was in hospital, possibly. I'm home now.' She'd already realised her place here was tenuous. Was he trying to wean the children away from their dependence on her? She loved them as if they were her own and she couldn't even contemplate the idea of losing them. She'd fight Ethan over that.

'You'll still need help.'

'No, I don't,' she insisted belligerently.

Ethan viewed her dogmatic denial with thinly concealed frustration. 'She's well qualified,' he said, as if she hadn't spoken. 'She hopes to get a job in a kindergarten eventually—she was quite honest about that—but as a short-term measure—'

'You're employing her as a nanny?' Hannah asked,

breathing hard. Was this Ethan's brutally efficient way of showing her how dispensable she was?

'She's only doing a few hours a day, but she's quite flexible. I said we didn't want her living in or anything, and I made it quite clear that it was a trial period. If you don't like her—'

'Oh, I still come into it, then!' Breath coming hard and fast, she glared at him with dislike.

'Naturally you still come into it.'

His calm was beginning to infuriate her. 'Why? You've just replaced me the moment my back was turned.'

'That's nonsense and you know it.'

'Don't patronise me, Ethan. Why do we suddenly need a nanny? *I'm* the nanny, in case you've forgotten.'

'You're my wife.'

'I've been your wife for the past year; we didn't need a nanny then. Have you decided I'm not up to the job?'

'I should have done something about it earlier—you need some time for yourself.'

'Oh, I see,' she drawled, 'it's a shift system you have in mind. Are Alison's duties going to take her as far as the bedroom too?'

She had managed to ruffle his tranquillity good and proper this time. The tightening of his mouth had been accompanied by an intimidating flare of fury in his grey eyes. She observed the changes dispassionately.

'I married you. You're my wife,' he snapped, as dark colour seeped up from the collar of his open-necked shirt until his olive-toned skin looked several shades deeper.

'It's not what you did, Ethan,' she said. 'It's *why* you did it. You married me because you wanted someone to care for your children. Someone who expected nothing from you.' Her voice rose until it sounded hysterically shrill in her own ears, but she couldn't stop. It was as if the floodgates had been opened and nothing could prevent the backlog of repressed emotions escaping. 'Everyone must have realised. Faith did,' she babbled wildly. 'That's why she begged you not to marry me. The people you work with talk about us. Did you know that? Do you know how it makes me feel when I think of all those people speculating about us? I feel degraded!'

'I'm sorry if you find being my wife degrading.'

'Being the focus of smutty speculation and pity is degrading!' she yelled back. With the back of her hand she mopped the tears that had begun silently to slide down her cheeks.

'Who pities you?'

'All those smart women that know you, that knew Catherine. They know...'

'Know what?' he asked, taking a step closer.

'What a sham this marriage is. If the baby had lived they'd probably have put it down to immaculate conception.' She stopped abruptly, confusion creeping into her eyes.

Ethan almost sighed with relief. At last. It was the first time she'd actually referred to the lost child. Don't hurry things, he'd told himself. Let her decide when she wants to talk about it. He'd felt impotent listening to the doctor's explanations of denial and the grieving process.

He'd never felt so clumsy and inept in his life. Words were his trade but they came awkwardly now. 'I know it hurts,' he said softly. 'I wish I'd known about the baby.' What was the *right* thing to say? They hadn't told him that, had they?

Anger and resentment moved inside her She'd wanted to tell him. It should have been a time of shared joy but it wouldn't have been like that. She'd been robbed of that too—Ethan's distrust had robbed her.

It was the scent of his cologne which made her realise he was standing close to her. The evocative scent of his male body made her uneasy; it stirred memories she'd carefully blanked out.

'It was very early on. It was only a collection of cells, so tiny,' she said. The pragmatic words didn't help at all; the baby in her mind was whole and perfect. Her lips quivered. 'Why?' she wailed in a small, bereft voice. 'It isn't fair!'

'I know, honey, I know,' he crooned softly as she laid her head against his chest. He could feel the tremors that racked her body as he wrapped his arms around her. 'It's bloody unfair.'

She sobbed out her grief against his chest. When she pulled away Ethan's arms dropped to his sides, letting her go. His heart sank as he saw her expression. It was set and hard. The words she uttered were like a knife-thrust.

'You're probably glad.' In her pain she needed some-one to blame. Part of her registered the intense pain on his face as he flinched. Part of her wanted to reach out for him and deny her words, but the impulse of a wounded animal to strike out was stronger at that mo-ment. 'You don't think I'm responsible enough to look after Emma and Tom. You can take them away from me, but the baby was mine, the only thing in my entire life that's been *mine*. You couldn't have taken him off me.'

'I'd trust you with my life, Hannah.'

She frowned and stared at him in confusion. It was hard not to believe that calm certainty in his voice.

'I trust you with the lives of my children.'

Her resolve hardened as she recalled the awful things he'd accused her of. She couldn't forgive him for being so quick to condemn her. 'You didn't. You believed I put my own pleasure before Emma's safety,' she reminded him stonily. 'You treated me like a leper.' He could have no inkling of how much that had hurt. It had been like being cast out of paradise. At the first hurdle he'd failed the test; he didn't trust her. She'd thought something special had grown between them, but his attitude had shown her what an idiot she'd been to believe that.

'I was a fool!' he said urgently, trying to break past her icy disdain.

'*I'd* be a fool if I believed anything you said to me now. It's easy to be generous when you know the truth, Ethan. Now you know I'm not the selfish slut you accused me of being, what do you want to do? Does this mean a promotion back into your bed?' she suggested with blighting scorn. 'What makes you think I'd want that sort of professional advancement?'

'I know you're hurting, Hannah, but stop this before you say things you'll regret.' His eyes were dark with pain, but she made herself blind to the fact. In the tunnel of her restricted vision all she wanted to see was her own pain and his lack of trust.

'I don't suppose Catherine would have been as crude and...vulgar...' Her eyes went automatically to the walnut bureau where a whole cluster of smiling portraits of her predecessor sat. Her voice died away as she saw, much to her amazement, they had vanished. An antique pewter bowl held a casual arrangement of late, over-blown faded roses.

'On the contrary, Hannah, Catherine would have approved of your disgust at the thought of sharing my bed.

We conceived Tom on the only occasion during a six-month period when we slept together. So you see I wasn't exaggerating when I said it had been more than three years. You look shocked.'

'I don't understand.' His words made no sense to her. They'd been the perfect couple—a shining example that she could never aspire to.

'What don't you understand?'

'Everyone says…' The ironic gleam in his eyes made her voice fade uncertainly. 'The pictures… Alexa said…'

'"Alexa said"—oh, then it must be true,' he drawled. 'The pictures were for the children. I didn't want them to forget who their mother was. I owed her that much. Guilt made me go overboard.'

'Guilt?' The bitterness in his voice cut through her miasma of self-pity and aching loss.

'If I'd let our marriage die a natural death, instead of being so bloody-minded and stubborn, Catherine would still be alive.'

Hannah's chaotic thoughts couldn't make sense of the things he was saying. The habit of thinking of his first marriage as perfect was too ingrained to drop immediately.

'I'm not going to force you back into my bed, Hannah. I'm not even going to beg you.'

Of course he wasn't. Ethan didn't have to beg—he was too clever for that. She was awake to the danger she was in. A self-destructive part of her *wanted* to believe in him. Loving Ethan hurt, and she couldn't bear to hurt any more.

'I know you hate me, but don't let your grief twist things.'

'I'm not twisting things; you are.'

'When you're grieving for the baby, Hannah, try and remember that he was my child too. Do you think I don't feel the loss? You don't have a monopoly on grief! I learnt I had a child and I'd lost him in twenty seconds. I nearly lost you.' His voice cracked with emotion. 'I couldn't have borne that, Hannah.'

She took a step away from the message that blazed in his eyes. Why hadn't he said he cared before? she thought angrily. When there was still time. Couldn't he see it was too late now? Everything was spoilt.

'I love you, Hannah.'

'No!' she said, pressing her hands to her ears. 'Don't say that. You bought me, that's all. I'm like any other investment. You can't love me, Ethan. If you did you couldn't have thought all those wicked things about me! You didn't give me a chance.'

'Let me explain,' he begged.

'Nothing you can say could make me feel any different. You set out to make me love you, didn't you?' she accused. His silence spelt out his guilt in her eyes. 'I know you had no use for my love—it was just a way you saw of controlling me. You must have been pleased when your plan worked so well. The irony is you needn't have bothered—you didn't have to lift a finger. I didn't marry you for financial security—I married you because I loved you. I loved you from the first moment I set eyes on you.' She broke off, her bosom heaving with emotion.

The colour drained dramatically from his face as she watched. 'Is that true?' he asked, in a voice she scarcely recognized. He closed his eyes. 'I didn't know. I didn't know…'

Hannah still didn't know what had possessed her to blurt out the truth, but it was too late to deny it now.

'Of course you didn't know—you wouldn't have married me if you had. But don't worry, mistrust and suspicion did what complete neglect couldn't.' Even as she spoke she was suddenly unsure whether her words were actually true. Part of her knew they should be comforting each other through this hard time, not hurting each other.

Ethan turned on his heel and walked towards the window. He missed the quiver of uncertainty that made her lips tremble and filled her eyes with sudden doubt.

'I hear what you're saying.' She saw his broad shoulders lift and then straighten. 'I won't give you any more pain by inflicting my feelings on you, but if you change your mind...I'll be here.'

This was the point where she was meant to say scornfully, I won't. Her mouth opened but she couldn't bring herself to say the words. She stood for a long time staring out of the window after he'd gone. Ethan had said he loved her and she'd sent him away. Hadn't punishing him been meant to make her feel better? She felt wretched, and too confused by the amazing things he'd said to make sense of anything. She started crying and didn't stop for a long time.

CHAPTER NINE

'It's Hannah, isn't it?'

Hannah looked blankly at the smart young woman in the fashionable, businesslike trouser suit for a moment. Then recognition dawned.

'*Helen?*' She didn't bother to disguise the incredulity in her voice.

It was hard to reconcile the image of this smart, confident young woman with the girl she had known. Helen hadn't had an easy time after she'd left the children's home.

'You look marvellous, Helen. The last time…'

The young woman grimaced. 'I know. I must have looked pretty desperate, but then turning up on your doorstep out of the blue was an act of desperation. When I saw the announcement of your marriage in the newspaper I didn't have anywhere else to go.'

It was the only time Hannah had gone to Ethan for help. She'd half expected him to be angry, or refuse, but he'd agreed to listen to the girl's story of how she'd been forced out of her bedsit by a landlord who'd been about to sell the building for redevelopment.

All Hannah had been able to think about was that it could so easily have been her standing there with no place to go but the street. 'I hope the place Ethan found you wasn't too awful. I meant to keep in touch, but things have been…' How exactly did you explain the strain of being in love with your husband?

Helen laughed. 'Are you kidding?' she said. 'The trust

167

has changed my life. They don't just provide a roof and food; they encourage you to gain skills to go out and help yourself. Listen, have you got time for a coffee? I'd love to tell you about it.'

Hannah shrugged. She was escaping; she had nowhere to go. Originally she'd thought it might be easier to think away from the house, away from everybody. It hadn't worked out that way—she'd been wandering around for the past hour, unable to string two thoughts together.

In the small coffee bar Hannah listened to her friend's description of the charitable trust that was there to help young people who would otherwise have ended up on the streets.

'I'm probably preaching to the converted,' Helen laughed as she sipped her neglected drink. 'This is stone-cold. I do go on once I get on my hobby-horse. I'm sure Ethan has told you all about it.'

'Ethan?' Hannah said blankly. There appeared to be some sort of conspiracy which prevented her hearing his name. Not that her memory needed jogging—he was constantly in her troubled thoughts. She still hadn't come to terms with his astonishing announcement.

'You're probably cursing me—apparently he's been giving them a hell of a lot of freebie legal advice at the moment, with the big legal wrangle. It's a test case, so it means a lot.' A frown gathered on her face as she looked at Hannah. 'You don't know what I'm talking about, do you?' She looked astonished and a little embarrassed. 'I just assumed that you'd know... I didn't mean to speak out of turn,' she said uncomfortably.

'Ethan's involved with this charity, professionally?'

'He did some research about them when he was looking for somewhere for me to go, and he must have liked what he found out. He's been giving them free legal

advice since, and that's not something to sneeze at. Have
you any idea how much a top barrister like him costs?
Are you all right, Hannah?' she asked anxiously.

'I'm stupid.'

'The way I remember it, you were always the bright
one at school—the teachers all wanted you to go to college.' The smile died from her lips as she saw the distress on Hannah's face. She planted her elbows squarely
on the table and regarded her friend with frowning concern. 'Can I do anything? Do you want to talk about it?'

Hannah's distracted glance was darting and Helen
gained the impression that she wasn't actually hearing
what she was saying.

'I've been so terrible to him.'

'To who? Ethan?'

'It's probably too late.' Hannah pressed her hand to
her quivering lips. What have I done? I love him and I
hurt him. I rejected what he was offering. I threw it back
in his face. The strong clasp of Helen's hand concentrated her scattered thoughts.

'You could always say you're sorry,' Helen suggested
softly.

A tentative smile curved Hannah's lips and a determined light entered her eyes. 'I could, couldn't I?' she
said, her mouth setting in a firm line. Sorry wasn't
enough, but it was all she had. 'Thank you, thank you
so much, Helen.' She pulled a note from her purse and,
without even looking at the denomination, flung it on
the table. She left the startled young woman staring after
her in astonishment.

All she had to do was convince him that she hadn't
meant the things she'd said. *All!* Ethan had been an innocent scapegoat for her grief and anger. Since the accident she'd felt as if they'd been slipping further and

further apart. The distance that had already developed beforehand had expanded in the emotional, hothouse atmosphere of the accident's aftermath until all she could see was a stranger. Not the man who'd fathered her child, the man she loved.

It was as if seeing Ethan from Helen's perspective had reminded her of all the things that had been *right* between them. She'd spent so long morbidly examining the negative aspects that she'd forgotten what a warm, strong, loving man he was. Ethan wasn't perfect but he came as a package, good points and bad. I'm no bargain myself, she thought wryly.

Did he really say he loved me? she wondered. A sense of wondering disbelief made her almost fall beneath the wheels of a bus. She smilingly brushed away the concern of a passer-by and took several deep breaths. That had been close! Once might be careless, but twice! She'd better be more careful. It would be the ultimate in bad timing to get killed before she'd told him she loved him—especially considering how long she'd been sitting on this particular piece of information.

She'd been walking for ten minutes before it occurred to her that she was on the opposite side of the city to Ethan's chambers. She flagged down a taxi and gave him the address.

'Can I help you?' she was asked on her arrival.

Hannah wasn't in the mood to be intimidated by a superior attitude.

'Yes.'

'Do you have an appointment?' The guardian of the inner sanctum fingered the leather-bound appointment book as if it were sacred.

'No.'

'I'm afraid—'

'I'd like to see my husband.'

'Who exactly is your husband, madam?'

'Ethan Kemp.'

The shift from patronising to deferential was achieved in the space of a single breath. 'I'm afraid Mr Kemp doesn't want to be disturbed today. No exceptions. He refused to see—'

'He'll want to see me.' Hannah picked up the internal phone and held it out. 'Tell him I'm here.' Sometimes pushy worked where nothing else would.

Will he? she wondered. Will he *want* to see me? She maintained her confident stance with great difficulty whilst she strained to catch one side of a low-toned conversation. What will I do if he won't see me?

She wasn't left in suspense for long; the conversation was brief.

'I'll show you the way.'

Hannah wasn't sure why she was feeling relieved— the hard part was yet to come.

Rich oak panelling, one wall covered with books from floor to ceiling, the affluent antiquity of the furnishings sat cheek by jowl with a top-of-the-range computer and fax which was spilling its information unheeded onto the floor as the door closed behind her. The soft sound made her jump.

'I didn't know you were planning a visit.'

'Neither did I,' she confessed.

Ethan was sitting on the edge of the enormous antique desk. He twirled a pen between his fingers and she found the controlled mechanical movement distracting.

'Is there a problem at home?'

'No, not now.' Her reply quelled the brief flare of concern in his eyes. They didn't give anything away now as she screwed up her courage and her nose and thrust her hands deep into the pockets of her jacket.

'You must be wondering why I'm here.'

Her colour was fluctuating from one extreme of the spectrum to the other, and her fingers were spasmodically clenching and unclenching. 'If you don't tell me soon I'd say there's a strong possibility you'll explode,' he observed quietly.

The breath she'd hoarded up escaped her lungs in one audible gasp. 'I came to say sorry and I love you!' She couldn't look at him, but she had to—one eye closed, but the other remaining fixed with anticipation on his face.

Ethan didn't move, but the expensive pen slipped from his fingers. 'You're sorry that you love me?'

'The sorry was for being cruel and mean and despicable to you.' The mingled bronze and green in her eyes misted over emotionally as she opened her eyes earnestly wide in an effort to convince him of her sincerity.

He closed his eyes and let his head fall back. She saw his chest lift as a deep sigh vibrated through his big body. When he lifted his head again some of the tension seemed to have dissolved.

'Family are there so you can be despicable when you're in pain.'

'Am I your family, Ethan?' she whispered huskily, hardly daring to believe what his warm, firm voice was telling her.

'Do you want me to be?'

'I want you to be my heart and soul and…' she began, her voice throbbing passionately. She gave up. Some things words just couldn't express, and, with a sob, she walked into his arms, which opened wide and closed firmly around her. 'I'm so, so sorry…' she murmured as he stroked her hair. 'I've always loved you. I never stopped, even when I was hurting you. I could feel your pain as well as my own, but I couldn't stop all those awful things coming out of my mouth.'

'I've said my share of awful things,' he said, pressing his mouth against the glossy top of her head. 'It's like conkers,' he mused, breathing in the fragrance of the slippery, clean tresses. 'I should have been able to stop your pain and I couldn't. He took her face between his hands and looked into her eyes. 'I did an unkind, selfish thing when I married you, Hannah. It's probably the thing I'm most ashamed of in my life, but, my God, I can't regret it because it's led me here to you.'

His warm lips were strong and tender as they pressed firmly against her own. 'I can't tell you the exact instant I knew I loved you, or the first time I knew how bleak my life would be without you in it. I've lived through an earthquake, but it was nothing compared with the impact of realising I loved you. I've been sitting here...' He gestured towards the leather swivel chair and then shook his head. 'Actually I couldn't sit still. I've been pacing back and forth, trying to compose a winning argument that would convince you to give me a chance. I couldn't do it!' he confessed. 'All I could see was the pain and reproach in your eyes and I knew I was responsible for putting it there.'

Hannah pressed her hands to either side of his head. 'Don't say that!' she said urgently. She couldn't bear to see the dark shadow slip back into his eyes.

She'd been blind to the toll the past days had taken on him up until now, but seeing the dark circles around his eyes, and the deep scoring of the lines between his mouth and nose, made her appreciate that she hadn't been hurting alone. Normally he was the epitome of the sleek, sophisticated professional, but today the designer suit was creased, and a cut which looked suspiciously like a razor cut marred the olive clarity of his cheek.

'It was an accident, Ethan. I shouldn't have blamed you. I know that now. I wanted your baby so badly, but I thought you would be angry after the way you regretted making love to me in the first place.'

With a groan Ethan gathered her close; she could feel the thud of his heartbeat. 'I never regretted making love to you—how could I?' he asked hoarsely. 'I thought *you* regretted it—after all, I did coax, cajole and bully you into my bed. I was mad to believe Alexa and I was blind not to see how jealous her grief over Catherine had made her.' Ethan felt her body stiffen defensively. He stepped back and held her at arm's length.

'It might make you understand better if I tell you a few things about Catherine and myself. No,' he said gently, placing a finger over her lips to stifle her instinctive objections, 'I think you should know. Catherine was beautiful and talented, and at first our marriage was exactly what it appeared. The cracks started appearing when she was pregnant with Emma—she accused me of rushing her into things before she was ready. Her business was flourishing and so was her riding. We got a nanny as soon as Emma was born and things calmed down, but they were never the way they had been. You see, Catherine never really wanted a family, and she resented the fact that I did. Then she discovered she was pregnant with Tom. It wasn't planned and I found out by accident. She'd already booked herself into a clinic,' he recalled, taking a deep, painful breath.

'An abortion?' Hannah tried to compose her features to disguise her shock. Knowing how Ethan felt about his children, she could imagine how devastating that discovery must have been.

Ethan nodded, his eyes desolate as he relived the memory. 'She accused me of engineering the pregnancy deliberately, which, considering she was taking the pill, was an impossibility. I begged her to reconsider, give herself time to think about the consequences of what she was doing. Whatever else it might have been, it wasn't going to be the quick-fix solution she wanted. I knew Catherine, and I honestly didn't think she could have lived with the guilt. She only got as far as the clinic door; she never went inside. Maybe what I said swung it, or maybe she would never have gone through with it anyway.'

'And after Tom was born?'

'She didn't even hold him. She refused to accept professional counselling, and we continued to present the façade of one big happy family!' The bitterness in his voice made Hannah long to comfort him, but she knew he hadn't finished yet, and she instinctively knew he needed to expose what he saw as his shortcomings.

'If Catherine had married someone else she'd probably still be alive now. Someone who hadn't coaxed away her doubts about starting a family. When she kept putting it off I said there was never a perfect time to start.'

It felt strange, feeling pity for someone she'd envied for so long, but Hannah did. 'Lots of women fit families into successful careers, Ethan.'

'Because they *want* to. I convinced myself that deep down she wanted all the things that I did, but she didn't. With Emma, I think it was just a matter of getting it over with as far as she was concerned. Oh, she loved her, but she was never demonstrative. I suppose I resented all the times Emma got pushed into the background. That's why I overreacted when I thought you'd forgotten about Emma—Catherine forgot about Emma all the time.' The bleak way he said it brought tears to Hannah's eyes. 'I tried to compensate, and then Catherine would accuse me of spoiling the child. It was an impossible situation.'

'I think it's likely Catherine was conforming with society's expectations rather than yours when she decided to have a child, Ethan. Women are expected to want children.'

'Are you trying to make me feel better about myself, my love?'

'Am I your love, Ethan?' she asked softly, winding her arms about his neck.

'Do you still want me? I'm a bit of a flawed hero, and you haven't heard the worst yet.'

'You can't get rid of me so easily.' She'd banish the torment from his voice and heart if it took her for ever. She and Ethan had for ever now; the knowledge made her heart soar. 'You'll *never* get rid of me.' Her body vibrated with the deep sincerity of her words. He could save the worst for later—right now the priority was to show him exactly how much she loved him.

'You have no idea how much I've missed holding you, touching you,' he breathed as his lips slid down the side of her neck.

'When I agreed to marry you I never thought you'd love me. I thought I could be satisfied with just being close.'

'And were you?'

'Not once you'd kissed me. Could you kiss me again, Ethan?' she whispered.

'Whilst he willingly obliged, Hannah's fingers were busy flicking open the buttons on his shirt. 'What are

you doing?' he gasped throatily when her busy fingers
didn't stop there.

Hannah gave a voluptuous sigh and buried her face in
the soft hair that was sprinkled over his chest. 'I've not
worked out the details yet,' she admitted frankly as she
pushed his shirt firmly out of the way, 'but it sort of
goes like this…'

Ethan watched through half-closed eyes as she slid to
her knees. A harsh, guttural groan was wrenched from
the depths of his chest as her mouth touched him.

'Hannah!'

'I thought I'd work out the details as I go along.' It
was a liberating feeling, being shameless.

His fingers brushed the top of her glossy head before
tangling deep into the soft waves as she became more
engrossed in her self-appointed task to drive him insane.
'What are you trying to do to me?'

Her head fell back against his circling hands and she
gazed up at him with hot-eyed, sultry provocation. 'I'd
have thought that was obvious,' she challenged huskily.

His thumbs were locked at the back of her head. She
turned to one side and took one of his fingers inside her
mouth, suckling slowly and luxuriously. She felt the
muscles in his thighs bunch and tighten as if the relatively innocent action was just as stimulating as the intimacy of seconds before.

'Don't!' she protested weakly as he drew her to her
feet. Her legs could hardly bear her weight. Under the
light covering of sweat, her body burnt. The burning
continued inside too, in the aching hunger that writhed
deep in her belly. 'I thought you liked…' Her voice
trailed off under the impact of his molten gaze. The pu-
pils had expanded to obliterate almost all of the light
grey of his eyes. The driving, almost mindless need she

saw there killed off any sudden nagging doubts she'd
begun to nourish about offending him. 'Why?'

'I don't want to be the only one who is satisfied.' He'd
been tempted by her obvious willingness to set aside her
own needs; what man wouldn't have been? 'I want to
feel your pleasure too.' He ran a hand that wasn't quite
steady down the curve of her cheek. His fingers trailed
across her chin before touching the pink outline of her
lips. His chest expanded rapidly as her tongue darted out
and the sound that emerged from his throat was one of
pain.

Hannah could empathise—the pleasure did bring pain,
the wrenching pain of anticipation and need. 'It was
pleasure,' she assured him throatily. 'You're pleasure,
touching you…tasting you. I didn't know just seeing you
aroused and knowing I can make you…' She shook her
head, still stunned by the discovery that to give pleasure
could be just as erotic as receiving it. 'I've fantasised
about…' Bands of hot colour flared across her cheekbones but she didn't remove her luminous eyes from his.
'I didn't know it would feel like—that *I* would feel like
that.' A voluptuous shiver ran through her body and,
despite the heat she was generating, goosebumps broke
out over the slick surface of her skin.

'Dear God, Hannah!' His mouth devoured the ripe
fullness of her soft lips. The raw hunger in him nearly
suffocated her with pleasure as his tongue drove with
frenzied fervour into the warm moistness of her mouth,
and his teeth nipped and bit at the swollen outline of her
parted lips. 'Shall I tell you what I've fantasised about?'
She wouldn't like it—it might make her hate him—but
he had to unburden his guilt.

Hannah's reply was lost in Ethan's hot mouth as he
lifted her up and carried her over to the leather chaise

longue. The material of her sweater peeled away under the rough eagerness of his hands. Very deliberately he untied the three ribbons that held the thin camisole she wore beneath. There was a taut stillness in him as he looked down at the pale outline of her slender body.

'You're so beautiful,' he breathed thickly.

Hannah was inclined to let this gross misinterpretation of the truth pass—besides, Ethan made her feel beautiful. He made her feel desirable and womanly.

With great care, he parted her thighs. The touch of his hands on her skin made an imprint that went soul-deep. She belonged to this man; she *needed* to belong to him.

'I was going to say it was outside my control, but that's not true.' Like a man being torn in more than one direction, his tortured eyes continued to roam over her body.

'What isn't, darling?' If he didn't touch her soon she'd die. Her desire had pooled into the lower half of her body, making it almost impossible for her brain to function beyond the single imperative message it was screaming. But, despite this, the strangeness in his voice penetrated her passion-fogged mind.

'I knew you could have got pregnant. Like now, I wanted to implant my seed in you, fill you to overflowing.' The words emerged in a strange, disjointed staccato. 'It was selfish, but it overrode every logic circuit in my head. It honestly wasn't like that with Tom—we did take precautions.' He shook his head as if to chase away old, painful memories. 'I don't think you can trust me, Hannah.'

'Why can't I trust you?' she asked gently. It was his deep distress that touched her rather than his words; she was too engrossed by the primal message that sang in her head. 'Make love to me,' she pleaded, reaching out for him.

'Don't you understand what I'm saying?' he asked, staring at her hands. 'Part of me *wanted* you to be pregnant. I *wanted* to see your body grow big with my child. I've never felt like this before in my life, Hannah. I took advantage of your inexperience.'

This catalogue of imagined injuries had gone on long enough. 'Nobody of my age is *that* inexperienced. I knew what could happen, Ethan. You can't really knock a primitive urge which has served the human race pretty well so far. Don't confuse primal with barbarous.'

'I didn't consider how you felt, what you needed!' he continued angrily. 'Even now...I was going to...to ravish you! I can't explain how basic...raw—'

'I didn't know you felt like that too!'

Her husky amazement cut off his soul-searching confessions. 'What did you say?'

'Do you think I have ever imagined doing the things I do with you with anyone else? I'm totally shameless with you and I like it that way. And I'd love to have your baby. The doctors told me there's no reason why we can't...soon.' There was no conflict in the desire that shone out of her eyes. Ethan let out a hoarse cry.

At last! Deprived of his touch for several minutes, she let out a cry of delight as he was upon her. He was within her too, sliding so deeply between her flexed legs that it felt as if they were one.

Ethan retrieved his jacket from the floor and draped it over her shoulders as their sweat-slicked bodies cooled. Hannah gave a sigh of pure contentment as she snuggled against his body. She giggled as he drew the fine grey wool up over her nose.

'Hey, are you trying to suffocate me?' she asked, poking her nose over the top. The teasing smile was replaced by a serious look. He ought to look mellow and relaxed, but she could still see the tension in his lean body. 'I hope the door was locked.'

'Nobody's going to risk disturbing me today.'

'Been a mite tetchy, have you?' she teased lightly.

'I've scandalised the whole building by telling a High Court Judge that I'm too busy to talk to him. I suppose you could call that tetchy.'

'It's more impressive than yelling at the cat.'

'Did you do that?' he asked fondly.

'I would have if we had a cat.' She knew he had something else he wanted to tell her and she was trying to work out how to give him the opening. 'I've been jealous as hell of Catherine ever since I knew she existed.' You could drive a double-decker bus through that particular opening.

'And now?'

'Not jealous.' She felt pity for a confused, unhappy woman. She believed that from Ethan's compulsive need to account for all the crisis points in his tragic marriage would come a lightening of the burden he'd been carrying.

'Catherine always wanted to be the best at everything she did—she was ambitious. I admired it, but it went deeper than simple ambition: she *needed* to be the best. She always enjoyed having her talent publicly recognised; the medals meant a lot to her. Please believe I accepted her wishes, even if I was revolted by the very notion.' His nostrils flared and she could see a pulse throbbing in his temple.

'Of course I believe you.'

'When it came down to it, it was her body not mine.'

He closed his eyes and she saw the muscles in his throat work hard. 'Perhaps I should have kept my mouth shut?'

'You weren't a disinterested party, Ethan.'

'When she accused me of using the baby to cement our relationship perhaps she was right, although I denied it at the time. We'd been drifting apart for some time. She hated being pregnant.'

'Lots of women do, Ethan, but it's worth it in the end.'

'It wasn't the easiest pregnancy,' he admitted, 'and Catherine hated to make concessions to her condition. I tried to coax her to do as the doctors said and that caused quite a lot of conflict. I told you when Tom was born she wouldn't touch him,' he said heavily. 'She wouldn't even look at him. She said I'd wanted him, so I could look after him. The doctor's label was post-natal depression, and it would pass. She didn't live long enough to prove them right or wrong, and I didn't provide the support she needed. But I always knew that the depression was only half the story. There was more to it than that.'

'It must have been terrible—for you both,' Hannah said, tears of compassion glittering in her eyes.

'She said I'd ruined her life—a fairly accurate conclusion given subsequent events.'

'You can't blame yourself for her death, Ethan. It was an accident.'

'She was determined to act as if she'd never been pregnant, not had a baby. That's why she climbed straight back into the saddle; that's why she was racing three weeks after Tom's birth. If I hadn't forbidden her to take that injured rider's mount when Moonlight went lame, she wouldn't have. She knew the brute's reputation; it was too strong for her. She just had to prove to me that I had no control over her life. I can hear her

now. ''You made me carry him for nine months, Ethan,''
she said, ''but that's the last thing you make me do.'''

'She was confused and in pain, Ethan. People hit out
when they're in pain. I did.'

'Promise me you'll never shut me out again, Hannah,'
he said imperatively.

'Never,' she agreed instantly.

'Have you really been lusting after me since the very
beginning?'

Hannah was delighted to see the wide, rather smug
grin chase the last remnants of melancholy from his face.

'Lust had nothing to do with it,' she responded firmly.

'Nothing?' he repeated with a pathetic spaniel expression.

'Well, maybe this much,' she relented, holding her
thumb and finger a hair's breadth apart. 'The rest was a
pure, elevated emotion.'

'That's a bit of a blow.'

'It's easy for you to joke about it, but unrequited love
is no laughing matter,' she observed, as someone who'd
done it and had the tee shirt.

'It seems to me we wasted a lot of time.' He pulled
her thigh over his and stroked the sensitive hollow behind her knee. 'I think we were meant to be together.'

'Why, you closet romantic, you,' she cried with
delight. The faint colour that drew attention to the sharp
angle of his cheekbones made her smile.

'I was just examining the facts.'

'Of course you were.'

'Top of my list when I interviewed for the post...'

'Was that the one of nanny or wife?' she enquired
innocently.

'Less cheek or I'll...'

'You'll what?' she asked huskily, tracing the outline

of her lips with the tip of her tongue. She gave a contented sigh as he swiftly responded to her provocation
with a sizzling and very satisfying kiss.

'I'm being deep and profound. Can't you behave for
five minutes?'

Hannah turned his wrist and glanced at his watch.
'Right, five minutes it is.'

'I wanted a female past the age of being troubled by
romantic entanglements.'

Hannah chuckled. 'I wouldn't repeat this to your
mother if I were you.'

'It wasn't my plan,' he acknowledged. 'There were
several candidates of a…certain age.'

'You do like treading on thin ice, don't you, my love?
I fully intend to be a romantically active granny. So start
taking the vitamins now.'

He grinned. 'I passed them over and gave the job to
you.'

'Then it must have been fate because it wasn't my
startling good looks. I can remember exactly what I was
wearing.'

'For some reason the words "grey and shapeless"
spring to mind,' he observed slyly.

How unkind! 'Do you mind? That's my best interview
suit you're talking about.'

'When I realised you were dating that drippy…'

'I was not dating, and he was very nice!' she exclaimed indignantly.

'I got pretty disturbed at the thought of you walking
out. I told myself it was just because the children would
miss you, but it was more than that.'

'You're just saying what you think I want to hear!'
she accused, lapping up every word.

'Show some respect, woman, I'm baring my soul here.'

'I thought you weren't into all this self-analysis.'

'Do you really think I'm the sort of man who'd marry the nanny just to stop her handing in her notice? I rationalised it every step of the way until I was almost convinced I was acting in everyone's best interests. I didn't want to think there might be anything else behind my desire to keep you around. Something kept telling me that I shouldn't let you go.'

'I'm awful glad you didn't,' she sighed, gazing at him lovingly. It didn't matter to her when he'd fallen in love with her. He loved her now—that was the important thing. 'What are you doing?' she asked as he suddenly leapt up.

He stepped into his trousers as he walked across the room and turned the dial on the wall safe. 'I'm going to have a bonfire,' he said, pulling a document out of the safe. She watched in astonishment as he picked up the heavy lighter from his desk and lit the corner of the thick paper. 'There,' he said with satisfaction as the corner caught alight. He pressed the flaming material into a metal waste-paper basket as the flame took hold.

'Was that…?' She looked to him for confirmation.

'Yes, the pre-nuptial agreement, all three copies. I know the symbolism is a bit clumsy, but…'

Slipping her arms into his jacket, she walked over to him. 'You didn't have to do that, you know.'

'I wanted to. If I trust you with my life, which I do, it follows that I trust you with everything else. It's a bit late to endow you with all my worldly goods, but I do.'

'I'm not interested in your goods, Ethan. It's your heart I have designs on.'

'It's yours, my love,' he said instantly. His arms went

around her and Hannah put her heart and soul into the tender kiss that went on and on until...

'Is it my imagination or is it raining in here?' she asked vaguely, as his lips lifted from her own. She held out her hand and felt the definite touch of water.

'It's real.'

'And what's that noise?' she asked, suddenly conscious of a strident ringing.

'The fire alarm—the one that connects with the fire station. We had the system put in last year at great expense.'

'Does that mean the building's on fire? Shouldn't we be doing something?' She was slowly getting saturated. She lifted a hand to her wet hair. Calm in the face of a crisis was impressive, but wasn't Ethan taking it a bit far?

'The fire, my love, is there.' He nodded in the direction of the smouldering waste-paper basket.

'Oh, my goodness!' she exclaimed, horror-struck. 'You mean you...'

'Triggered the sprinkler and alarm system with my impromptu bonfire? Yes, I'd say you have the situation in a nutshell.'

Hannah clasped her hands in agitation. 'We should do something.' Getting dressed wouldn't be a bad start, she thought, seeing in her imagination the door being smashed down at any minute by axe-wielding firemen. 'Don't just stand there—put a shirt on.' She stopped, her sweater half over her head. 'Are you *laughing*?' He was; he was actually laughing. 'Well, I'm glad you're happy. Can you imagine what people will think when they find out you—?' She broke off. The expression on his face was jubilant.

'I don't care,' he said simply. 'I don't care what peo-

ple think, and you know what? It's liberating. You're
my liberation, Hannah Kemp, and I'm laughing because
I'm happy. I'm happy because you're mine!'

'What are you going to do when the fire service walks
through that door?' She tried to sound severe but his
frivolity was contagious.

'Tell them to go away. This party is strictly by invitation only.'

'Am I invited?' For some reason she couldn't stop
grinning like an idiot.

'To share my life,' he said huskily.

Hannah stopped grinning and began to sob.

'My love, what's wr—?' Gulping back her tears,
Hannah pressed her fingertips to his lips. 'Nothing's
wrong. You just keep saying such beautiful things,' she
wailed. 'And I'm so happy. It's a well-known fact...'
she sniffed '...that a person can't cry while being kissed.

Hannah was delighted to discover that her husband,
clever man, had caught the drift of her subtle hint immediately.

Liz Fielding started writing at the age of twelve, when she won a writing competition at school. After that early success there was quite a gap – during which she was busy working in Africa and the Middle East, getting married and having children – before her first book was published in 1992. Now readers worldwide fall in love with her irresistible heroes and adore her independent heroines.

Visit Liz's website for news and extracts of upcoming books at www.lizfielding.com

Liz Fielding is one of Tender Romance's best
loved, award winning authors.
*Don't miss the chance to read the latest book
in her new exciting trilogy…*

BOARDROOM BRIDEGROOMS!

It's a marriage takeover!

**Read all three books in this exciting trilogy
by Liz Fielding!**

**May 2002: The Corporate Bridegroom
June 2002: The Marriage Merger
July 2002: The Tycoon's Takeover**

In Tender Romance™

THE TYCOON'S TAKEOVER

India Claibourne is the boss of an exclusive
department store. Jordan Farraday is a devastatingly
handsome tycoon – and his aim is to take over the
store! There is only supposed to be one winner – but
perhaps this time there will be two…

ELOPING WITH EMMY

by

Liz Fielding

CHAPTER ONE

TOM BRODIE regarded the man sitting behind the ornate desk. It was the first time he had met Gerald Carlisle; clients of such importance were usually dealt with by partners with pedigrees as long as his own.

Brodie was the first to admit that he didn't have a pedigree of any kind. What he'd achieved in his thirty-one years had nothing to do with family background or the school he'd been to, it had been in spite of them.

It was the source of infinite satisfaction for him to know that one of the City's oldest law firms, the august legal partnership of Broadbent, Hollingworth & Maunsell, had been driven to offer him a partnership because of their desperate need for sharp new brains to drag them out of their Dickensian ways, bring their systems up to date and put them on track for the twenty-first century.

They'd tried offering him a consultancy. They'd tried a lump sum fee. He'd watched them wriggle with a certain detached amusement as they'd tried to buy his brains without having to take him and his working class background into their august establishment, well aware that they needed him far more than he needed them. Which was why he'd refused to consider anything but a full partnership.

One day, quite soon, he would insist that they add his name to the discreet brass plaque beside the shiny black front door of their offices. They wouldn't like that either. But they'd do it. The thought made listening to Gerald Carlisle's worries about his tiresome daughter almost bearable.

Gerald Carlisle was not his client. Brodie was too egalitarian in his principles, too forthright in his views to be let loose around a client who had a family tree with a tap root that reached down to the robber barons of the Middle Ages, with land and money as old. This didn't worry him. He had his own clients, companies run by men like himself who used their wits and their brains to create wealth instead of living off the past. Companies that brought in new money and big fees. It was the reason for his confidence about the brass plaque.

But today was the twelfth of August. When Carlisle's call for help had come through to the BHM offices, Tom had been the only partner at his desk. Everyone else had already packed their Purdeys and headed north for the grouse moors of their titled clients. It was tradition, apparently, and BHM, as Tom was constantly reminded, was a traditional firm with old-fashioned values which apparently included shooting birds in vast numbers in the middle of August.

Tradition also required that when a client of Gerald Carlisle's importance telephoned, he should speak to nothing less than a full partner, and so he had been put through to Tom Brodie.

Gerald Carlisle, however, did not wish to discuss business over the telephone, and so Tom had regretfully cancelled his dinner engagement with a delectable silver-blonde barrister with whom he had been playing kiss-chase for some weeks and driven to Lower Honeybourne.

Now, with the dusk gathering softly beyond the tall windows, he was sitting in the panelled study of Honeybourne Park, an impressive stone manor house set in countless acres of rolling Cotswold parkland, while Carlisle explained the urgency of his problem.

'Emerald has always been something of a handful,' he was saying. For 'handful', Brodie thought, read 'spoilt'. 'Losing her mother so young…'

Anyone would think, from Carlisle's hushed tones, that his wife had expired from some tragic illness rather than running away with a muscular polo player and leaving her young daughter to the tender ministrations of a series of nannies. She had been a bit of a 'handful' too—still was if the gossip columns were to be believed. Like mother, like daughter, apparently.

'I can see your problem, Mr Carlisle,' Tom said, his face blank of expression. He was well used to keeping his feelings to himself. 'I just don't understand what you want me to do about it.'

Upon hearing the man's proposed solution and the part he was expected to play in this, Brodie sincerely wished that he, too, had had some pressing engagement at the other end of the country that had taken him out of the office today.

'Won't your daughter object?' he asked.

'You don't have to concern yourself with my daughter, Brodie. I'll deal with her. All I want you to do is talk to this…gigolo…and find out how much it will take to buy him off.'

Buy him off. Beneath that smooth aristocratic exterior,

Brodie decided, Gerald Carlisle was a bully. He didn't like bullies and for just a moment felt a surge of sympathy for Carlisle's daughter and for the young man she had declared it was her intention to marry. But only for a moment because he didn't doubt that she was a spoilt brat who was always having to be bailed out of trouble. Maybe for once she should be left to get on with it, stew in a broth of her own making...

For one giddy moment he was tempted to suggest such a strategy, just to see the look on Carlisle's face. But it wouldn't do. Emerald Carlisle was an old-fashioned heiress on the grand scale. He knew that because BHM managed her trust. Or rather Hollingworth did. Personally. It was that big. And even a man of Tom's egalitarian principles understood that a gigolo— he almost gagged on the word—could not be allowed to prosper at the expense of one of BHM's most valuable clients. At least not while he was responsible for her.

Carlisle pushed a file across the desk. 'You'll find everything you need to know about Fairfax in there.'

Tom opened the folder and glanced at the top sheet—a report on Kit Fairfax from an investigation company which, from the thickness of the file, had been extremely thorough. He wouldn't have expected anything else. It was a perfectly reputable company that his own firm used when necessary, and Hollingworth had undoubtedly recommended them to Carlisle.

He flicked through the papers, glanced at the black and white photographs of a man in his early twenties, his hair long and curling over his shoulders. He had a slightly distant expression, as if unaware of the extraordinarily pretty girl at his side, her arm looped through his, her head resting on his shoulder, although such an idea seemed extremely unlikely.

As unlikely as the idea of a man setting an investigation agency to watch his own daughter simply because he didn't much care for her boyfriend.

The whole business left Tom Brodie with a bad taste in his mouth, but as he closed the folder he made a determined effort to bury his own personal prejudices. Gerald Carlisle was simply concerned about his daughter, probably with good cause. Doubtless she was the target of all kinds of fortune hunters. 'And if Fairfax won't be bought off?' he asked.

'Everyone has a price, Brodie. Try a hundred thousand. It's a nice, round sum.' Roundish, Brodie thought. In the way that peanuts were roundish. The guy must surely know that Emerald Carlisle was worth millions? But maybe he wasn't that ambitious; maybe a 'roundish' payoff was all that Fairfax was after. But somehow that dreamy face didn't quite fit such a cynical scenario. Carlisle must have seen the doubt in Brodie's face. 'It's a pity Hollingworth is away; he knows what he's doing.'

Tom's glance flickered to the other man. 'Is this a regular occurrence?'

Carlisle stiffened. 'Emerald is rather gullible. She needs protecting from unscrupulous people who would take advantage of her.'

'I see.' Obviously it was.

'I doubt it, Brodie. I very much doubt it.' He made it sound as if having Emerald for a daughter was like bearing the world on his shoulders. Maybe it was time he let the girl make a few mistakes. The longer he protected her, the harder it would eventually become. But Carlisle did not want to hear that, and Tom wasn't there to offer 'agony aunt' advice. 'I'm relying on you to deal with this situation quickly and without any fuss. Do whatever you have to. Hollingworth—'

'I'm sure Mr Hollingworth would be more than happy to come back from Scotland if you prefer that he handle such a delicate matter,' Brodie interjected quickly. His own speciality was corporate law. Buying off an unsuitable husband was new territory for him, territory he was not anxious to explore.

But there was no escape. 'That would take too long. I want this settled and I want it settled quickly, before Emerald does something she'll regret. You're Hollingworth's partner and I'm relying on you to do whatever you have to to stop my daughter marrying this man.'

Emerald Carlisle was fuming. She was nearly twenty-three years old, for heaven's sake. Quite capable of making a rational decision about the rest of her life.

But not quite so capable of anticipating her father's ruthlessness when it came to getting his own way.

She grasped the doorknob in both hands and shook it furiously. It didn't budge. It was locked, and cursory examination of the keyhole revealed that the key had been removed. He had obviously foreseen the possibility that she might try poking it out of the lock onto a piece of paper. Assuming she had a piece of paper. She gave the door a kick, but it made no impression. It was still locked.

How dared her father lock her up in the nursery like

some Victorian papa? Did he think she'd just sit quietly and take it?

Easily, was the answer to her first question. And, no. He knew she wouldn't take such treatment quietly, which was why he had tricked her into the second-floor nursery, conveniently equipped with safety bars across the window.

She abandoned the door and rushed across to the open window as she heard a car crunching over the gravel carriage drive that swept in front of the house, pulling herself up on the bars to get a better view.

It was a dark BMW, not a car she recognised, and it was parked too close to the house to get a good look at the driver as he climbed out. Just a glimpse of thick dark hair, a pair of wide shoulders as he shrugged into his jacket, a feeling that he was above average height, although with her foreshortened view from the second floor it was impossible to say for sure. From the expensive cut of his charcoal-grey suit it was obvious that he was some business connection of her father's, in which case he was definitely not the kind of person to whom she could appeal for help. She gave a little sigh.

It would have been so perfect if it had been Kit come to rescue her, driving up in his battered white van like some latter-day Galahad and hammering on the front door. But Kit was no Galahad. Kit had no idea what had happened. She hadn't dared tell him her plan or he would have been thoroughly shocked.

He was such a hopeless *dreamer.* Despite all his problems he'd packed his paints and taken off for France for the summer. At the time she'd been furious, but at least her father didn't know where to find him. Yet. But she had to get out of here before he did or her neat little plan would simply fall apart.

She had underestimated her father. She'd known he'd been having her followed, that was what had given her the idea in the first place. He was so *protective*. Which was why she'd known exactly what his response would be to her announcement that she planned to marry Kit…

Well, she mentally conceded, she hadn't known *exactly*. She certainly hadn't anticipated that he would lock her up like the heroine of some ridiculous melodrama or she would never have walked into his trap. He must have planned the whole thing after she'd telephoned to say she had to see him about something important. Her biggest mistake had been to put him on his guard, but it had been the only way of ensuring her father's attention. She twisted the small diamond engagement ring around her finger.

'Ooh!' she growled, venting her frustration on one of the bars fixed to the window frame to prevent small children from falling out by just the kind of careful Victorian papa she had been castigating, striking at it with a tight little fist. It shifted beneath the blow and she immediately forgot the pain caused by her temper. Instead she stared at the bar for a moment, then, slowly uncurling her fingers, she reached out and grasped it, giving it a sharp tug. She had not been mistaken; there was a small but quite positive movement.

Her spirits immediately began to rise and she looked about her for something to lever the horrid thing out of the frame. But the room was furnished with only a bed, a dresser, and a small hard-backed chair. And the built-in cupboard was bare, as she had already discovered to her disgust.

There was nothing in the least bit useful to be found, but she refused to be put off by this set-back. Instead, she returned to the window and gave the bar another, rather more vigorous shake. It was definitely loose, and, seized by the same enterprising spirit that had got her into this scrape in the first place, Emerald put her foot against the wall for leverage, took the bar in both hands and gave it a sharp tug. There was the promising sound of wood splintering against the screws, and, cheered by this success, she did it again, yanking on the bar with all her might until the window frame split with a satisfactory crack, disintegrating beneath the pressure and sending Emerald sprawling back on the floor, the bar still grasped tightly in her hands.

She stared at it for a moment in amazement, then she laughed out loud. The frame was rotten. It had rotted beneath the paintwork and no one had noticed. It was hardly surprising. The dreary old nursery hadn't been used since her grandfather was a baby, when children and servants had been expected to keep their proper place. Her mother had insisted on a bright, modern suite of rooms on the first floor for her baby girl, not that she'd hung around very long to enjoy them.

But Emerald didn't waste time congratulating herself on her luck, which was just as well, since even though the rest of the bars were dispensed with easily enough her problems were far from over. The nursery was on the second floor and there was the better part of fifty feet between her and the freedom of the gravel driveway.

It was a pity, she thought, that she had taken so much

trouble dressing to create the right impression. Jeans and a pair of Doc Martens would have been far more practical for climbing down the ornate drainpipe than the elegant linen dress and high-heeled shoes she had decided would convince her father that she was serious. Her father, she knew, would never have taken her seriously in jeans, and it had been desperately important that he be convinced that she was in earnest. Unfortunately she had achieved her objective rather too well.

She considered the problem for a moment, then took off her shoes and dropped them out of the window onto the rose border below. She peeled off her stockings and, lacking a pocket in which to stow them, she stuffed them into her bra, because her high-heeled shoes would rub against her feet in five minutes without them and the last thing she needed right now was blisters.

She didn't have a handbag; she'd left it in the study when her father, brushing aside her declaration that she intended to marry a penniless artist, with or without his blessing, had asked her to give her opinion on some old toys that had been found in the attics during recent roof repairs.

After completing her fine arts degree, she had taken a job in an auction house where she had become fascinated with old toys. Her father had been furious that she had chosen to take a job at all, even one that any well-brought-up young heiress might covet. He had wanted her to stay at home, where he could keep an eye on her until he found her a suitable husband. Although she'd recognised the device was in the 'if we don't talk about it, it will go away' category, she had been sufficiently touched that he should have brought himself to acknowledge her expertise to fall for it.

She wasn't usually so gullible where her father was concerned, but with the lure of a lost hoard of Victorian toys discovered in a cupboard she had walked into the nursery without a suspicious thought in her head. That was when he had slammed the door and locked it behind her.

Pride, Emerald thought ruefully, always came before a fall. And of course there weren't any toys. If there had been, he would have summoned a *real* expert; he would certainly never have consulted his tiresome daughter.

Emerald gave the door a look that should have incinerated it. It wasn't even scorched, but in an attempt to slow down discovery of her flight she jammed the solitary chair beneath the doorknob. Then she hitched up her skirt and swung one leg over the window sill.

'I'll expect to hear from you within twenty-four hours that this matter has been settled, Brodie,' Carlisle was saying as he walked with him down the steps. 'I want no delay.'

'That should be all that it takes.' Brodie considered whether to mention the possibility that the lovebirds might already have flown, probably to one of those romantic destinations where weddings could be arranged in a matter of days, in which case it was already too late. But as they reached the bottom of the steps he decided against it. What clinched it was the sight of Emerald Carlisle, her dress hitched up about her waist, clinging just above head height to an ornate lead drainpipe about twenty feet behind Gerald Carlisle's back.

Brodie knew that he should draw his client's attention to what was happening behind him. Something stopped him. It might have been a pair of large, pleading eyes. Or the deliciously long legs wrapped about the drainpipe. Or even, heaven forbid, the glimpse of something white and lacy that he was certain was a pair of French knickers peeping from beneath her tucked-up dress.

Or maybe it was just simple distaste that any father could conceive of locking up a fully grown woman simply because her idea of what made a good husband did not coincide with his own. Whatever it was, he decided to take Carlisle at his word. Emerald Carlisle, he had been told, was no concern of his. And when the girl let go of the pipe with one hand and urged him to get her father inside the house, with an unmistakable gesture that left her swinging in the most perilous fashion above a well-tended rose border, he didn't hesitate. Patting absently at his jacket pocket, he turned and headed back up the steps. 'I think I left my car keys on your desk, sir.' The 'sir' almost choked him.

Carlisle glared after him. 'Oh, for goodness' sake,' he said, irritably, but followed Brodie back into the house.

Emerald's heart, already beating an adrenalin-charged tattoo as she eased herself down the drainpipe, had gone into overdrive at the sudden appearance of her father. But the moment her gaze had collided with the dark-eyed stranger standing with him she had known instinctively that she had an ally. He hadn't batted an eyelid at the sight she must have made, had not given her away by so much as a twitch of an eyebrow. Instead he had quite coolly considered his options.

He could have informed her father that he appeared to have an incompetent cat burglar clinging to his drain-pipe.

Or he could have ignored the situation, pretended he hadn't seen her and hoped she didn't fall into the roses.

Only a man without a scrap of imagination would have considered either of them. What the dark-eyed stranger had done was offer her the opportunity to escape by creating a diversion.

That kind of swift thinking was so *rare*, she thought. Poor Kit would have dithered and blushed and quite given the game away. He was sweet and wonderfully talented, but not in the least bit decisive, which was why she had to get to him before her father's henchman.

As she searched amongst the lavender and roses for her shoes she felt a moment of regret that she wouldn't be able to stay and thank Dark-eyes for his chivalry. Were they grey? she wondered. Or brown? Distance and the dusky light had made it impossible to tell.

Unfortunately she didn't have time for politeness, but she was sure he would understand her need to put the maximum distance between herself and her father before he discovered her escape. If only she could find her other shoe!

She spotted it at last, half-buried behind the tall lavender that edged the border, filling the air with sweet scent as she brushed against it. The roses were not so kind, snagging at her bare arms as she reached for her shoe, catching and tangling her hair with their thorns. She didn't have time to worry about it, or take time to extricate herself carefully, and tugged herself free. The rose retaliated by whipping back and catching at her neck with its thorns. She scarcely noticed. All she knew was that she was taking far too long to get away.

But there was no way she could make her escape barefooted. Her feet would be cut to ribbons on the gravel by the time she had sprinted around to the old coachhouse where her car had undoubtedly been stowed after her incarceration. She could just hear her father speaking to the chauffeur. 'Miss Emerald has decided to stay for a few days. Put her car away, will you, Saunders?' All perfectly natural. She made a rude noise as she tipped the dirt out of her shoes and slipped her feet into them.

'Maybe you left your keys in the car, Brodie.' Her father's impatient voice carried through the open front door, pinning her back against the wall.

'I might have dropped them in the hall.'

Brodie. The name had a nice, solid ring to it and Brodie, bless the man, was giving her all the time he could, delaying her father, apparently quite unconcerned at the tetchiness in his voice. Not many men were that brave. Unfortunately his valour would be to little avail. There was no cover within a hundred feet of her exposed position, and any second now she was going to be discovered and dragged ignominiously back to the nursery, where she would probably be put on a diet of bread and water. Not that she cared about that. But poor Kit...

Of course, she could always throw herself on Brodie's mercy. In fact the thought of flinging herself into his arms had a definite appeal. She hadn't been mistaken about the shoulders, or his height. And his character spoke for itself.

But, no. He had already done more than enough. To

demand he choose between her and her father was more than could be expected of any knight errant. But she was hanged if she was going to give in without a fight. She had mere seconds in which to act before the two men appeared on the steps and she was discovered. She didn't waste it, flinging herself at the BMW, praying that it wasn't locked. Her guardian angel must have been listening because the rear door opened at her touch and she dived in, pulling it shut behind her with heartfelt thanks for the superb German engineering that ensured it closed with scarcely a sound.

She didn't know where her knight errant was going, but at least he was going somewhere. Away from her father, away from Lower Honeybourne. She would throw herself on his mercy, and once they reached civilisation it would only take a telephone call to bring any number of gallants racing to her aid. Meanwhile, she tucked herself down behind the front seats and congratulated herself on her luck.

This might not be the most comfortable way to travel but, on reflection, escape this way was far more likely than in her own car. Any attempt to retrieve that would undoubtedly have attracted the attention of her father's chauffeur, who had a flat above the garages, and by the time she'd reached the electronic security gates they would have been firmly closed.

She would, of course, have climbed over them, but she was well aware that walking along a deserted country road as night fell and without a penny to her name was not an entirely sensible course of action.

Brodie, on the other hand, would drive straight through unchallenged, and since he had already connived with her escape he could scarcely turn around and take her back when she popped up. In fact she rather hoped he might be persuaded to take her home. By morning she would be in France with Kit, and then Hollingworth could do his worst.

There was the added bonus that once they were clear of the park she would be able to sit up and thank Brodie for helping her. The thought brought a smile to her lips. She was absolutely sure that she and Brodie were going to be friends.

There was a crunch of shoes, the driver's door was opened and through the gap between the front seats she saw Brodie palm the keys from his pocket before turning to her father.

'It seems they were on the seat all the time,' Emerald heard him say, almost certainly without a trace of a blush. No one who acted with such swift decisiveness would be fazed by such a tiny white lie. 'I must have dropped them.'

Gerald Carlisle snorted, impatient with such incompetence. 'I thought you were supposed to be Hollingworth's bright new man.' His voice betrayed what he thought of bright new men in general and Brodie in particular. And Emerald froze as he added, 'I just hope you're capable of dealing with this situation efficiently. I don't want it bungled. I particularly don't want it all over the newspapers,' he said, with feeling.

'I'll speak to Kit Fairfax,' Brodie promised. 'If it's money he's after it'll just be a question of haggling.'

'Haggle all you want. Whatever it costs will be cheap if it keeps my daughter out of the hands of some idle layabout who's only after her money.'

'And if he's actually in love with the girl?'

Gerald Carlisle made the kind of explosive, disparaging noise Brodie had always assumed to be the colourful invention of nineteenth century novelists. Apparently not.

'Just use whatever methods you have to ensure they don't get married, Brodie. I'm holding you personally responsible.'

Emerald, tucked behind the passenger seat of Tom's car, froze. *Brodie was being sent to deal with Kit?* Where was Hollingworth? She could deal with that pompous old fool with one hand tied behind her back, but suddenly Brodie's treasured decisiveness was not so welcome, and she gave a little shudder of apprehension.

The beauty of her plan had been in its simplicity. She had been convinced that nothing could possibly go wrong. Which just showed how foolish one person could be.

Brodie tossed the folder he was carrying onto the passenger seat and climbed behind the wheel while Emerald made herself as small as she could. Suddenly popping up the moment they were clear of the estate and introducing herself no longer seemed so appealing.

Brodie might be terribly kind to girls who flashed their knickers when they climbed down drainpipes, but she was very much afraid that he wouldn't be anything like as soft-hearted when it came to dealing with fortune-hunters. Or as easy to mislead as the unimaginative Hollingworth.

Which made it imperative she get to darling Kit before Brodie could talk to him, or she had a feeling the poor sweetheart wouldn't know what had hit him.

CHAPTER TWO

BRODIE leaned forward, started the car, then lowered the window. He paused for a moment, taking in the great, sweeping parkland of Carlisle's estate, curling his lip at the privilege it represented, at the man's absolute certainty that money was the solution to every problem. The truth, he had discovered in the course of his legal career, was that money was the cause of most of them. It was certainly the cause of the problem that confronted him now. If Emerald Carlisle had been a penniless working girl she could have married whom she pleased and no one would have given a damn, except to wish them happy.

He dwelt momentarily on the image of the long-limbed girl who, ten minutes ago, had been clinging to the drainpipe, and wondered if Kit Fairfax loved her enough to resist the bribe. He discovered that his feelings were oddly mixed.

Then, as he pulled away from the golden stone frontage of Honeybourne Park, he put the distasteful task ahead of him firmly out of his mind and began to think about a more pressing concern. He hadn't eaten since his secretary had brought him a sandwich at his desk at lunchtime and he was hungry. He had noticed a promising-looking inn in the village, but on reflection decided it might be advisable to put some distance between himself and Carlisle before he stopped. It had been made quite plain that he was expected to get back to London and deal with Fairfax without delay. Somehow he didn't think hunger would be considered an adequate excuse for putting off the evil moment.

Brodie pulled a face. Even if he drove straight back to town it would be too late to do anything useful. The situation was unpleasant enough without the additional farce of hammering on Fairfax's door in the middle of the night to remind him of his lowly status and demand he forget all about marrying Emerald Carlisle.

Remembering the girl's expressive eyes, her warm mouth that had formed a natural smile, he knew that if the situation were reversed he would tell any legal busybody who came interfering in their relationship to get lost. Forcefully. Somehow, though, he couldn't see Kit Fairfax hitting him. The man had a slightly distracted look, a gentleness about his face, and Tom Brodie knew that whatever happened he was going to feel like a heel. Which was ridiculous. Kit Fairfax had been cast in that role. Maybe he was. The one thing Tom had learned over the years was to keep an open mind.

He shrugged. Whatever. Food was his first priority. Well, perhaps not quite his first priority. He was suddenly aware that he had another and rather more pressing problem. Spotting a lay-by ahead, he slowed and pulled into it.

It hadn't taken Emerald long to realise that travelling undetected all the way to London on the floor of the car was not going to be as easy as she had thought. Within minutes her legs had begun to cramp from the awkwardness of her position, and she was losing the feeling in one of her shoulders. She eased herself slightly and for a moment there was some relief. Then the pain was back, settling itself in her lumbar region like a cat making itself at home in a favoured chair. Nothing was going to shift it while she remained crouched in this awkward position. She pulled a face; she could stand a little pain in the cause of freedom. All she had to do was hold on for a little and hope that Brodie would have to stop for petrol, or even, she thought as her stomach began to remind her just how hungry she was, something to eat. Then she would be able to make her escape.

Even as she shifted the weight back to her shoulder the car began to slow. She held her breath, trying to make out where they were but not daring to raise her head. A pub car park maybe. There certainly weren't enough lights to suggest a garage forecourt. She crossed her fingers and eased her head slowly around to check the other window. Brodie, half-turned in his seat, his face unreadable in the gathering darkness, was watching her cautious manoeuvring. She froze, suddenly knowing exactly how a mouse felt when cornered by a cat. If she closed her eyes and kept very still perhaps he would lose interest, think he had imagined the whole thing. Except that Brodie had a lot more imagination than your average moggie. Far better to brazen it out.

So she gave a little shrug. 'Don't mind me,' she said, with a dismissive little gesture. 'I won't cause you any bother.' Her grin, she knew, was disarming. 'Honest.'

He was not, apparently, disarmed. Maybe he couldn't see it. Whatever, he didn't smile back. 'You'll forgive me if I reserve judgement on that for the moment. In the meantime, since you're not wearing a seatbelt—' his

voice didn't give much away either '—I'm going to have
to insist you join me up here. For your own safety.'

There was something about Brodie that suggested she
was safer where she was. Nothing overtly threatening.
Just an uneasy feeling that she might have done better
taking her chances with the unlit country road. Well, not
even the most gallant of knights errant appreciated being
taken for a ride. Or vice versa.

'I could sit in the back,' she offered. 'You could pretend I wasn't here. If that would help.' He didn't answer,
simply waited for her to obey him. There was something
unnerving about that. Her father would have blustered,
bullied. Hollingworth would have spoken to her in that
maddeningly patronising way of his, treating her like a
little girl who had to be cajoled into taking a spoonful
of nasty medicine. Brodie was different. A few minutes
earlier she had been congratulating herself on that.
Maybe she had been too quick in her judgement.

Emerald shrugged. At least he hadn't turned around
and taken her straight back to her father. Yet.

She took a certain comfort from the awkwardness of
his position in regard to her father. After all, it was because of him that she had managed to escape in the first
place. Which didn't answer the question uppermost in
her mind. What *did* he propose to do with her? Since
Brodie had been engaged to deal with Kit, buy him off,
she couldn't expect him to actively aid and abet her runaway marriage.

It took Emerald a few moments to extricate herself
from her cramped quarters. She didn't hurry about it,
giving herself as much time as possible to decide on a
plan of action, slowly stretching each of her cramped

limbs in turn even while her mind was whirring into action. By the time she was perched on the rear seat, her elbows propped on the seat in front of her, her chin resting in the palms of her hands, she had decided that there was only one way to handle Brodie. She would have to make him fall just a little bit in love with her. It was something she had always found extremely easy to do and, while she knew she would feel incredibly guilty afterwards, she didn't have time to worry about that right now.

'Hello, Brodie,' she said, with the kind of smile that made the street lighting redundant. 'I'm Emmy Carlisle. But you already know that.' She extended her hand. He took it, held it for just a moment.

'I'm Tom Brodie. How d'you do?' he replied, with just the barest trace of amusement at such formality.

She'd known he'd have a sense of humour. A promising start. 'How d'you do, Tom Brodie? Are you by any chance going to London?'

Her smile was infectious. It was the kind of smile to tempt the unwary, to captivate and charm the jaded sensibilities of a man who had ground his way to the top of his profession with never a moment for simple fun. Innocent of guile and yet oddly seductive, it was the kind of smile that would get a man into all sorts of trouble. It already had, Brodie acknowledged wryly, as with difficulty he resisted the urge to smile right back.

'And if I'm not?'

Emmy Carlisle wasn't in the least put out by this unpromising answer. 'Then I'm afraid you're on the wrong road,' she told him, poised as a duchess at a garden party and apparently not in the least embarrassed at being caught stowing away in his car. 'And it would be just the tiddliest bit of a nuisance. But if you could drop me at the nearest hotel I'm sure someone could be persuaded to come and fetch me.' Her smile never wavered. 'If you could loan me the money for the telephone.'

It was becoming increasingly difficult to keep a straight face. 'Shall we start with the hotel and take it from there?' Brodie replied dryly. 'Maybe you can suggest somewhere. I'm not familiar with this road, and I was looking for somewhere to eat.'

'Oh, what a good idea. I am absolutely starving.' Confident now that he wasn't going to take her back, she wriggled through the gap between the seats, settled herself beside him and fastened her seatbelt. 'My father locked me in the nursery, you see, so I went on hunger strike.'

'Since four o'clock?' It was a guess. Carlisle had summoned him to Lower Honeybourne just after four. Apparently he was near the mark because she pouted. He normally loathed women who pouted. But it was impossible to loathe Emmy Carlisle, especially since she was laughing at herself and inviting him to join her. 'How fortunate I happened along; you might have expired by morning.'

'It's quite possible,' she told him, her earnest tone belied by a flash of mischief in her eyes. 'I've already missed afternoon tea and dinner. In fact I haven't eaten a thing since lunchtime.'

'I seem to have missed out on the cucumber sandwiches, too. And my own dinner engagement had to be cancelled at the last moment.'

'Oh, I'm sorry,' she said, with feeling. Then, 'Was she very cross?'

He recalled the icy politeness with which his telephone call had been received by the silver-blonde. The lady was not used to being stood up. 'It doesn't matter,' he said. He discovered, rather to his surprise, that it didn't.

'I'm sorry.'

'You should be.'

She gave him a thoughtful look. 'I don't think we should leave it too long before we find somewhere to eat,' she said, 'or our blood-sugar levels will be dangerously depleted. That could be why you're so irritable.'

'Quite possibly.'

She gave him a long look, as if not quite sure how to take that remark. 'You're angry with me for stowing away in your car.'

'No. With myself. I should have locked it.'

'Yes,' she agreed, 'I suppose you should. But I'm very glad you didn't. How did you know I was there?' she asked as they pulled away from the lay-by. 'What gave me away?' He glanced at her. 'I wouldn't want to make the same mistake again,' she pointed out.

'Your scent.' Chanel. He'd saved every penny he had earned on his paper round to buy his mother a bottle for her birthday. He still remembered her face as she had opened the wrapping, seen the tiny white box with its black edging. He'd never been quite sure whether the tear she had blinked back had betrayed pleasure or simply frustration that he had spent so much money on something utterly frivolous. Perhaps it had been a little of both. But she had unstoppered the bottle and dabbed a little of the precious liquid behind her ears so that the room had been filled with that distilled essence of femininity. And then she had smiled and he had known it was all right.

Emerald's scent had been masked initially by the sun-warmed roses of Honeybourne Park, the leather interior of the car, but when he had finally caught a breath of it it had been unmistakable, the aroma of it imprinted on his memory.

'My scent? Oh, Lord, I didn't think of that. I wouldn't be any use as a spy, would I?' She didn't wait for him to answer, but, casually retrieving her stockings from her bra, kicked off her shoes and, stretching out one long leg, began to slowly draw the fine nylon up to her thigh, apparently oblivious of the effect this performance was having on Brodie. Or perhaps she wasn't. He glanced briefly across at her, then kept his eyes firmly fixed on the road ahead.

Emmy, smoothing the stockings into place, continued, 'Actually, I am rather pleased you noticed me, Brodie. I wasn't going to embarrass you by declaring my presence, but I did want to thank you for not saying anything back there.' She looked up and gave him another of those incandescent smiles. 'When I was hanging from the drainpipe,' she added, in case he wasn't sure what she was talking about.

'I should have,' he said, rather hoarsely.

'Oh, no. You were an absolute brick. It's so rare one meets a real knight errant these days.'

'I'm no knight errant,' he warned.

'Don't underestimate yourself. But it's a pity my father asked you to sort out Kit. I was sure he'd get Hollingworth to do the dirty deed.'

'I wasn't his first choice,' he assured her. 'Unfortunately Hollingworth is in Scotland decimating the grouse population, along with choices two, three and four.'

'Bother.'

'I said much the same thing,' he said dryly.

'I'd forgotten the Glorious Twelfth.'

He glanced at her. 'It won't work, you know.'

'Work?'

Innocence personified. 'I may have turned my back when you shinned down the drainpipe, Miss Carlisle, and you've managed to hijack a lift to London, but first thing in the morning I shall carry out your father's instructions.'

'Not first thing in the morning.'

'I can assure you, I'm an early riser.' And this was one job he wanted over and done with.

'If you want to talk to Kit first thing in the morning you're going to have to drive all night. He's in France.'

He threw her a startled glance. 'France?'

'He went last week.'

'Where in France?' Brodie demanded.

'Why don't we pull in here and we can talk about it over dinner?'

He glanced at the cheerful, twenty-four-hour café, scarcely crediting that she was serious. 'You're kidding?'

'No. This place serves breakfast all day and that's my favourite meal.' Then she grinned at him. 'We're not in London, Brodie. It's rather late for the more conventional restaurants in this part of the world. Anyone who arrives much after nine is likely to get seriously scowled at.'

Brodie doubted that anyone had scowled at Emerald Carlisle in a very long time, if ever. Except perhaps her father. He was beginning to have a guilty twinge of sympathy for the man. If he had locked her up it was quite possible that he had good cause. The girl was clearly quite capable of behaving in an entirely irresponsible manner, and, if he was not exactly conspiring with her, there was no doubt he was an accessory to her bolt for freedom. Determined to put a stop to any impression that he was prepared to help her any further, he forced his face into its sternest expression and turned to her.

He was confronted by Emmy Carlisle, her eyes pleading beneath the most fetchingly arched brows, her mouth suddenly uncertain, her curls tousled about her cheeks… What colour was her hair? When he had seen her hanging from that wretched drainpipe the twilight had leached away the colour. Suddenly he had to know. He reached up and switched on the light. Red. Not auburn. Not chestnut. Nothing muted or understated, but brilliant coppery curls that glowed around her head like a halo against her shadowy face. What else?

For a moment neither of them spoke. They simply stared at one another. Then they both spoke at once.

'Red. Of course—'

'Grey,' Emmy said. 'I knew they would be.'

There was another moment of silence. Then Brodie said, 'You've scratched your neck.'

'It must have been the rose. When I was looking for my shoes,' she said, lifting her fingers to feel for the damage as Brodie released his seatbelt to reach for the glove compartment and his first-aid kit. There was a moment of confusion as they became entangled and the smooth skin of her arm, ripened to a delicate apricot by the long, hot summer, momentarily entwined with his, a bewitching contrast to the dark grey of his jacket. And as he turned to extricate himself her face was just below his, her eyes shaded by long silky lashes, her lips softly parted over small, very white teeth. There was a split second, an immeasurable moment, when every cell in his body urged him to kiss her. When he knew she was waiting for him to kiss her. And he knew it would have been special.

Too special. To kiss her would be wrong, and somehow he resisted. He hadn't come this far, travelling light-years from his working class roots in the Midlands, to throw everything away on a moment of madness. Besides, the idea that she wanted him to kiss her was ridiculous. She was on the way to her wedding. It might be his job to stop it, but not like that.

'What's grey?' he asked, his voice catching slightly.

'Your eyes.' She opened hers wide. They were hazel, bewitchingly green-flecked, with tiny strands of gold. 'I wondered.'

He turned away quickly, retrieved the first-aid kit from the glove compartment with fingers that were not quite as steady as they might have been and flipped it open. 'Here,' he said, tearing open a small pouch containing an antiseptic wipe and handing it to her. 'You'd better clean that scratch.'

Emmy let her head fall back, exposing her neck. 'Will you do it for me? Please, Brodie? I won't be able to see what I'm doing.'

Idiot. He should have given her the pouch and pointed her in the direction of the café's cloakroom. Instead he turned her chin slightly, aware of the soft warmth of her skin beneath his fingers as he dabbed at the scratch that jagged vividly across her long neck, grateful for the sharp tang of antiseptic blotting out her scent, clearing his head. Roses smelt sweet and their petals were like velvet, but they had thorns, too, he reminded himself. She might be an English rose, but Emerald Carlisle was trouble. With a capital T.

As Brodie dabbed at her neck Emmy drew in a sharp breath, flinched slightly. 'Did that hurt?' he asked.

She had the fleeting impression that he hoped it was hurting like hell. Well, it was, but she wasn't about to admit it. Besides, it proved that he wasn't quite as immune to her charms as his straight face would have her believe.

'It was cold, took my breath away for a moment, that's all.' If she was honest with herself, she had been feeling decidedly breathless ever since Brodie had turned on the light and looked at her with those slatey dark eyes. And a moment ago, when she had been sure that he was going to kiss her, her entire heart had momentarily stopped in its tracks. Now it was trying to make up for lost time.

She wondered what had stopped him. Then she blinked. Was she quite mad? Had she quite forgotten about Kit? Having Brodie fall in love with her was one thing. Encouraging him to make love to her was something else entirely.

'That's fine now,' she said, with determined briskness,

raking her fingers through her hair in an attempt to make it look tidy.

Brodie considered offering her his comb, but decided he rather liked her hair the way it was. But he couldn't resist the smallest dig. 'Don't you have a comb secreted somewhere about your person?' he asked, his gaze lingering momentarily on the point where the scooped neck of her dress dipped down over her breasts. 'How disappointing.'

This veiled reference to the way she had stored her stockings, the display she had made of herself putting them on—a suggestion that he knew exactly what she had been up to—brought colour flooding to Emmy's cheeks. She could hardly believe it. A blush. It was impossible. She hadn't blushed since she was six years old. 'I have,' she fibbed. 'But I'm too modest to retrieve it.'

'Liar.'

'Are you suggesting that I'm not modest, or that I haven't got a comb, Brodie?'

'Both.'

Emmy regarded Tom Brodie thoughtfully. A minute earlier he had been eating out of her hand and she had been sure that everything was going to be all right. Suddenly she wasn't so sure. It would be a mistake to underestimate him. She opened the car door. 'Come on. I'm starving.'

The cheerful comfort food was quickly produced by a motherly waitress wearing a badge that invited them to call her Betty and promised that she would do everything she could to make their day a happy one.

Emmy tucked into a pile of bacon and scrambled eggs. Brodie, feeling overdressed in the informal atmos-

phere of the café took off his jacket and hung it over
the back of his chair, loosened his tie, then attacked his
own more conventional lamb cutlet with equal enthusiasm.

'I'm sorry if I've caused you a lot of bother, Brodie,'
Emmy said when she had finished. She propped her elbows on the table and rested her chin on her hands so
that her long, slender fingers formed a frame for her face;
her nose, he decided, had just the right number of tiny
pale freckles. As if it had been lightly dusted with gold.
'But I really couldn't allow Fa to get away with locking
me up in the nursery like a naughty child, could I?'

Freckles? Gold dust? Brodie made a serious effort to
pull himself together. 'He does appear to have left it
rather late. Maybe if he had put you over his knee when
you were little you wouldn't be such a pain in the backside now.'

She pulled a face. 'I'm twenty-three next month.
That's old enough to make decisions for myself.
Wouldn't you say?' she persisted, when he was slow to
reply.

'Under normal circumstances,' he said, carefully. 'Unfortunately your money makes things anything but normal.'

'My money,' she said, with disgust. 'Everything
comes back to that. It's positively indecent that any one
person should have so much. I wanted to give it away
the minute I reached twenty-one, but Hollingworth
wouldn't hear of it.'

Brodie might agree with the sentiment but he knew
better than to say so. Gerald Carlisle's anxiety about his
daughter appeared to be well founded. 'Maybe Mr

Hollingworth thinks you'd regret it. Later,' he offered, noncommittally.

'Hollingworth.' She said the name with disgust. 'He treats me like a two-year-old. He actually lectures me if I spend more than my allowance.'

'Does he?'

'It's *my* money,' she declared. 'You'd think I could do what I wanted with it.'

That rather depended on what she wanted to do with it. Brodie poured a second cup of coffee. Anything rather than meet those eyes—all flashing indignation, he had no doubt. Anything rather than dwell on the thought of James Hollingworth reading Emmy Carlisle the riot act over a spending spree. He was having enough trouble keeping his face straight as it was.

'He's just doing his job.'

'Will you do yours with the same dedication?'

He finally gathered himself sufficiently to meet her gaze. 'If you mean will I try and persuade Kit Fairfax that marrying you is not in his best interests, I'm afraid the answer is yes.'

'There isn't anything I can do to dissuade you?'

'Why would you want to? If he loves you nothing I say will have the power to change his mind.' Emmy didn't bother to answer. Why on earth had Hollingworth had to go away *this* week? The man might be an old stick-in-the-mud, but he was two-dimensional in his thinking and absolutely predictable. It would never occur to him to doubt her sincerity, but after only a few minutes in Brodie's company she sensed that he was quite different. She simply had to get to Kit before he did. 'Tell me about Fairfax,' Brodie invited.

Emmy regarded him suspiciously. 'What do you want to know?'

'How did you meet him?'

'He came into Aston's for a valuation.'

'The auction house?'

'Mmm. I work there.'

It hadn't occurred to Brodie that Emerald Carlisle might actually have a job. 'Was he buying, or selling?'

'The lease on his studio runs out soon.' Too late she saw the trap. 'It's not easy getting a loan when you're an artist,' she said, defensively.

'That depends on how successful you are.'

'He's very talented. He will be successful. But at the moment...' She shrugged.

'I can see that it might be difficult.' He could also see why he might be keen to latch onto a gullible heiress. 'And was it love at first sight?'

There was the merest hesitation before she said, 'What else?'

Brodie glanced at the modest engagement ring she was wearing. It was oddly touching. 'And now he's in France waiting for you to join him. Are you going to tell me where?'

She gave a little sigh. 'I've already told you far too much.'

He wasn't convinced by the sigh, but he didn't press her for an answer. Instead he finished his coffee and excused himself. He had noticed a pay-phone in the lobby on the way in. There was a telephone in the car, but he would prefer that Emmy didn't know he was making a call.

He punched in the number. 'Mark Reed Investigations.' The response was laconic.

'Mark, it's Tom Brodie. I understand you've been investigating Kit Fairfax for Gerald Carlisle.'

'What if I have?'

'I've been told he's in France. Would you have any idea where?'

'Not a clue. I was just asked to find out anything I could about his background when Miss Carlisle started to take an interest in him.'

'You didn't turn up any French connection? Has he got friends there for instance? Someone he might be staying with for a while? Somewhere he might be waiting for her to join him?'

'Not that I know of. He certainly hasn't got the money to keep a place of his own.' There was a momentary pause. 'You could try looking at it from the opposite direction. I imagine Miss Carlisle has any number of friends with converted farmhouses in the Dordogne or Provence where they might get together.'

Brodie stifled a groan. 'Just see what you can dig up, will you? Maybe he left a number with a neighbour in case of emergencies.'

'Maybe, although I wouldn't have put him down as the kind of man to worry much about emergencies. He's a bit laid back.'

'Do what you can.' He momentarily considered calling Gerald Carlisle. It didn't take much imagination to guess the state the man was in. He decided against it. Emerald Carlisle, he had been told, was not his problem. Well, once he had dropped her off at her apartment, she wouldn't be.

When he returned to their table, Emmy had gone to powder her nose. He settled the bill and glanced at his watch, calculating the length of time it would take them to get to London, mentally rescheduling his appointments for the next couple of days while he tracked down Kit Fairfax.

'Everything all right, sir?' Betty was clearing their table.

'Yes, fine, thank you. At least...' He glanced at his watch again. Emmy was taking an awfully long time to powder her nose...considering she didn't have any powder to start with. He felt a sudden lurch of alarm. 'Would you mind checking the ladies' cloakroom for me, Betty? I'm just a little concerned about my companion.'

'No problem.' She was back in thirty seconds, her calm exterior seriously ruffled. 'The young lady isn't in the cloakroom, sir. But she left you a message. You'd better come and see for yourself.'

Emmy had written on the long mirror, using green liquid soap. 'Thanks, Galahad. I'll send you an invitation to the wedding.' She'd signed her name with a flourish and added a cross for good measure.

The window was open, swinging slightly in the warm breeze and he didn't need to look out into the car park to know that his car was missing; he knew exactly what she'd done. A quick check of his jacket confirmed that while he was on the telephone she'd helped herself to his car keys, then legged it through the toilet window.

And, if she drove with the same dash that she did everything else, she was probably miles away by now. His only hope was that she would be stopped for speeding. He considered calling the local police to report his car had been stolen. A night in jail would certainly slow Miss Carlisle down, he thought grimly.

A nice thought, but he discarded it immediately. It was his responsibility to keep Emerald out of the papers, not hand them a story. Gerald Carlisle would, quite rightly, have a fit if his daughter was hauled before the local magistrate for stealing his solicitor's car, and the press would have a field day. And when Carlisle had finished having a fit about that, he'd want to know exactly what his daughter was doing in Brodie's car in the first place.

He couldn't believe he had been so careless. No, he corrected himself, not careless. Far worse than careless. Just plain stupid. He'd already seen irrefutable evidence of Emerald's determination to get her own way. Good grief, she'd already shinned down a fifty-foot drainpipe without turning so much as a hair—a small ground-floor window wasn't going to cause her any problem.

He wanted to swear, loudly and at length, but he didn't. He'd already over-indulged on idiocy for one day. Emerald Carlisle had batted her long silky eyelashes at him from that drainpipe and he had been putty in her hands ever since.

Nor was there time to waste in berating himself for getting himself into such a jam, telling himself that he should have ignored those pleading eyes and ratted on her the moment he'd spotted her behind Gerald Carlisle's back. What he had to do, without delay, was to get the genie back in the bottle. But first he had to catch the genie.

'Betty,' he said, turning to the waitress, 'I need a car.

Right now. So tell me, is that badge you're wearing just so much window dressing? Or are you about to make my day a happy one?'

CHAPTER THREE

EMERALD could not believe her luck. Talk about out of
the frying pan and into the fire.

She'd noticed the telephone in the entrance lobby
when they'd arrived and had decided to put out a re-
verse-charge call for help the moment the opportunity
presented itself. Just in case Brodie decided that it was
in his best interests to return her to her father.

She waited until he went to the washroom, and the
minute he was out of sight she made for the phone.
Except he didn't go to the washroom. He was using the
telephone himself. Fortunately he had his back to her
and didn't notice her abrupt about-turn.

She had to admit that she was disappointed in him.
For a moment there she had hoped he might just be
something *really* special. A Galahad with just enough of
Lancelot to add a little excitement. He had come so close
to kissing her. She felt a tiny clench of disappointment
in her midriff as she wondered what had stopped him.
The thought of her father at their heels? No, she decided,
with a certain satisfaction, at that moment the last thing
on his mind had been her father. She should have made
it impossible for him to resist...

She swallowed the thought down, hard. That wouldn't
help right now; this wasn't the moment for self-
indulgence.

She had escaped once; she could do it again. Her gaze

alighted on the jacket slung across the back of Brodie's recently vacated seat and she wondered—but not for long. She didn't have time to waste wondering. It was time for action and she acted, dipping her hand into the pocket. Her fingers tightened around the keys to the BMW. *Yes!* She glanced towards the lobby. Did she dare take them? Brodie would be livid. Off-the-scale angry.

The thought sent a little frisson of alarm tingling up her backbone. If he caught up with her…*when* he caught up with her… She quelled it. This was not the moment for faint heart. Or an attack of conscience.

Right now he was telephoning her father, she reminded herself severely. Telling him where she was.

Yet even as she eased herself through the tiny washroom window she was prepared to give him the benefit of the doubt. She was sure that he didn't *mean* to rat on her; he just wanted to reassure her father that she was safe. It was what any knight errant would do, after all. But she knew her father a whole lot better than Brodie did. And she wasn't sure that a father who treated his grown-up daughter like a five-year-old deserved to have peace of mind. At least, not one who locked her in the rotten nursery.

The real problem was that Brodie was working for her father. He might sympathise, but he'd done just about as much as she could expect. More than anyone could expect. She giggled. He hadn't invited her along for the ride after all, although she had to admit she had enjoyed it while it had lasted.

And she hadn't finished with Brodie. Not by a long chalk. But he was going to need careful handling if he wasn't going to mess up her plans.

Emmy reached the motorway and regretfully put all thoughts regarding the handling of Brodie on hold as she moved out into the fast lane to overtake a truck. She'd gained herself a little time, but it wouldn't take Brodie long to smell the proverbial rodent. She very much doubted that he was still sitting patiently in the café, waiting for her to emerge from the ladies' loo. It might take him some time to organise alternative transport. But not that much time. He wasn't the kind of man to sit on his backside and wait for fate to lend a helping hand; he was a man of action. And, with that thought to lend urgency to her mission, she put her foot down and concentrated on getting to London as quickly as she could.

Betty's badge had been anything but an idle boast.

'Is it,' she had asked, putting a sympathetic hand on Brodie's arm, 'an affair of the heart?'

'Yes. It's an affair of the heart,' Brodie assured her with considerable feeling.

'You're in love with her?'

That was trickier, and he couldn't bring himself to actually lie to the woman. 'She's going to marry someone else, unless I can stop her,' he said, obliquely.

'Oh, no. That will never do. Your auras were quite definitely linked.'

Brodie wasn't sure that was something to be entirely happy about, but Betty clearly expected some response. 'Linked?' he repeated, trying to sound happy.

'There was no mistaking it. You were made for each other.' He stifled his impatience. He needed transport—what he'd got was a mystic with a romantic streak a mile wide. 'Now, you just wait here, dear.' She patted his arm absently. 'I'll be right back.' For one awful moment he had thought she was going to fetch a pack of tarot cards, but Betty had something far more practical in mind, and when she returned it was to press her car keys into his hand. 'Go after her. You can let me have the car back when you like.'

Brodie gave her the money for a taxi home at the end of her shift, but he still felt guilty about taking advantage of her good nature. The poor woman was probably chewing her fingernails down to the quick right now as the romantic auras evaporated and cold reality asserted itself. She'd be wondering if she'd ever see her precious little car again, wondering what her insurance company's reaction would be when she tried to explain what she'd done in the event that it disappeared for good. Worst of all, she would have to face her husband's ridicule for allowing herself to be taken in by a perfect stranger.

He'd just have to make sure he made her day a really happy one when the car was returned. He'd leave instructions for his secretary to have it valeted first, and make sure the tank was filled with petrol, with a cheque in the glove compartment to cover the inconvenience. And a hand-tied bouquet of roses delivered to the café along with a bottle of something warming for her husband. Sorting out Betty was a piece of cake compared to Emerald Carlisle. The smile abruptly left his face. That young woman was another matter entirely.

He was making good time, but he knew he didn't have a hope of catching her. He had called Mark Reed again before he'd left the café to ensure that there would be someone to keep an eye on her when she arrived home. And, more embarrassingly, to get her address. The file her father had given him was still in the car. He'd thrown it on the back seat when she had come up to sit beside him, and he hoped she didn't notice it, or, if she did, would have the good manners not to look at it. And he was praying that she didn't drive straight down to Dover and onto the first ferry that happened to be sailing.

It seemed unlikely. He could easily have reported the car stolen. She must know that he would be angry enough, but she was also bright enough to know that was the last thing he would want to do. Would she risk it?

Or would she go home for a change of clothes? All she had with her were the clothes on her back, and there wasn't a woman in the world—not even Emerald Carlisle—who would run away to get married without so much as a lipstick to her name.

And then certainty brought a grim little smile to the hard line of his mouth. Just the clothes on her back. A dress, to be more precise. An elegant, sleeveless creation in French blue linen that skimmed her figure and flared gently over her hips. A dress for a lady, with nothing as practical as pockets to spoil the line. She had no money, no passport, no driving licence. She had to go home; she had no choice. And he'd be right behind her.

She had, he judged, about twenty minutes' start on him, but while she had a much faster car it wouldn't give her that much of an edge since, under the circumstances, she wouldn't risk getting stopped by the police for speeding. Maybe. He hoped she was seriously worried by the prospect, but somehow he doubted it. He didn't think that worrying was something Emerald Carlisle had had a lot of practice in.

Still, twenty minutes was a lot of time to make up, and she wouldn't waste too much time packing because she had to assume her father had missed her by now and was moving heaven and earth to find her. He just hoped the man hadn't worked out how his daughter had managed to disappear so completely.

Emerald pulled into her parking space outside her apartment block. 'New car, Miss Carlisle?' the porter asked as he opened the door for her.

She pulled a face. Nothing would induce her to change her bright red MG, not even Brodie's whisper-smooth monster. 'It's not quite my style, Gary,' she said, handing him the keys. 'It belongs to a friend. Keep an eye on it, will you? His name's Brodie, and he'll be along to collect it later.' And he wouldn't be in a good mood. 'Will you give him the keys and tell him thank you for me?'

'Of course, Miss Carlisle.'

'And I need a taxi in about fifteen minutes.' Everything was packed, ready. Passport, traveller's cheques. She just needed time to shower and change. 'I'll be away for a week or so. Will you cancel the papers and milk for me?'

'I'll see to it, Miss Carlisle. Are you going somewhere nice?'

'France,' she said, after a moment's consideration, then, because she didn't want to give Brodie more trouble than absolutely necessary, she added, 'The South of France.' Then she smiled. 'I'll send you a postcard.'

'I'll look forward to it. Give me a buzz when you want me to collect your bag.'

She did. But when she opened the door it wasn't the porter standing in the hall, it was Brodie.

'Carry your bag, lady?' he asked. He was smiling, but it wasn't a smile that suggested good humour.

She opened her mouth to ask how on earth he'd caught up with her so quickly. Then, realising that it didn't matter, she closed it again, backing into her apartment as Brodie picked up her bag and advanced on her, shutting the door behind him with a finality that made the tiny hairs on the back of her neck stand on end.

'I didn't expect to see you again quite so soon,' she said.

'No,' he said, dryly. 'But you must have expected I'd turn up eventually. Or did you hope I wouldn't make it until the wedding?'

'How on earth did you do it? Did you steal a car?'

'Like you, Emmy? No. A kind lady lent me hers because your aura was linked with mine. She didn't want to see you make a mistake.'

'What?' He didn't enlighten her. 'I didn't steal your car, Brodie. I had no intention of depriving you of it permanently.'

'Is that right? Maybe I should call the police now and leave you to argue the point of law with a magistrate.'

'You wouldn't.' Her challenge had the confidence of experience. 'My father would…would…'

'Would what? Get Hollingworth to fire me? I'm a partner, Emmy. Hollingworth couldn't afford it. Or the publicity. But you know your father better than I do. Would you like to try?'

Emerald hated to be bested by anyone, but it occurred to her that a display of temper would not be in her best interests right now. So she smiled. 'Come on, Brodie. You've won. Don't be sore. Have a drink. You could probably do with one.'

'I probably could,' he agreed. 'But not right now.'

'Coffee, then?' She headed towards the kitchen.

She wanted him to relax, Brodie thought. She hadn't given up. Everything she really needed was in the bag slung over her shoulder. Clothes could be bought anywhere.

The minute he sat down in one of her comfortable armchairs, she'd abandon her luggage and tiptoe out of the front door. While he found himself in sympathy with her determination, he really couldn't allow her to get away with it again. 'Kit Fairfax's address will do just fine to be going on with,' Brodie replied.

She stopped, turned in the doorway, that pleading look back in her eyes. It touched something in him, tugging at some almost forgotten sweetness from that time before he had become utterly single-minded, focused on success to the exclusion of everything else, and for a moment he wavered. But only for a moment. That was the look which had got him into this situation in the first place, while he'd been still irritated by Gerald Carlisle's 'other ranks' attitude. He told himself that it was a look she practised in front of the mirror, like the one that had nearly made him lose his head completely and kiss her.

'I'm sorry to spoil your plans, but I don't have time to wait for the formal invitation. I have to talk to Fairfax now, Emmy.'

'Talk him out of marrying me, you mean. It won't work.'

'Won't it?' For a moment, for her sake, he wanted to

believe her. Then common sense kicked in. 'If you believed that, Emmy, you wouldn't care whether I talked
to him or not. If he loves you nothing I can offer him
will change his mind.'

'My father believes that everyone has a price.'

'And you agree with him? Well, maybe Fairfax will
prove him wrong.' There was a part of Brodie that would
like Fairfax to prove Gerald Carlisle wrong. But there
was another, more insistent part of him that was determined she wouldn't marry the man. As he glanced
around at the exquisitely furnished sitting room, the delicate water-colours on the wall, the tiny antique treasures
in a glass-topped display cabinet, he thought that Fairfax
would be mad to settle for as little as a hundred thousand
pounds.

He turned back to face her. 'You know, Emmy, if
you'd wanted a speedy wedding you'd have done a
whole lot better to get a licence from a registrar here in
London. You could have been married in three days before anyone knew a thing about it.'

'I wanted a proper wedding,' she said, defiantly. 'In
the village church with everyone there. Including my
father.'

'Really?' Why didn't he believe that? Because
Emerald Carlisle hadn't done anything to date to suggest
she was that conventional? Even unconventional girls
wanted a white wedding. 'Why didn't you take Kit with
you to meet your father?'

She shifted her shoulders awkwardly. 'I thought it
would be better if I paved the way first. And Kit wanted
to paint,' she said. He noted the slightly defensive tone
in her voice, stored it away for consideration at leisure.

'And that was more important than making a good impression on his future father-in-law?' This time she didn't answer. 'You'll have to live in France for a month before you can marry, you know.'

'A whole month? I didn't know that.'

'And provide a stack of documents, all translated into French.'

'Don't go all lawyerish on me, Brodie. We'll sort it out.'

'Eventually. I'll find him before then, so you might as well tell me where he is.'

'And if I don't?'

'If you don't I'll have to take you back to Honeybourne Park, where I'm confident your father will keep a very close eye on you until I've run him to earth. Of course, your father might very well turn up here any minute and save me the bother.'

'I'll tell him you helped me escape.'

'I'll tell him you stowed away in my car and stole it when I stopped for petrol.'

'You wouldn't! That's a downright lie.'

Brodie's grin was slow and tormenting. 'I know. But who do you think he'd believe?' She glared at him. 'You must see that I couldn't possibly take the responsibility of leaving you to run loose…' He waited a moment, then raised his hand in a gesture of resignation when she didn't volunteer her lover's whereabouts. 'No? Well, as you said, France is a very big place. It might take some time, but I'm sure you'll be comfortable at home, locked in the nursery.'

Emmy made a very rude noise. Brodie's arrival had thrown her momentarily, but it needn't, after all, be that much of a problem. She wanted him to find Kit, but not until after she had talked to him first. 'I've had an idea,' she said. 'I won't tell you where Kit is. But I'll take you to him.' Brodie's laugh had a hollow ring to it. 'No, honestly—' she began.

'Honestly? As in "I won't cause you any bother, honest" honestly?'

She had the grace to blush. That was twice in one day; Brodie was becoming a serious problem. 'I'm sorry about taking your car, truly. But you can't blame me. When I saw you on the telephone I knew you were telling my father where I was—'

'It's just as well I wasn't, or we'd both be in trouble.'

'Oh.' He waited. 'You weren't calling my father?'

'It didn't seem such a good idea at the time. I can assure you I won't be so soft again.'

'Who were you ringing, then?' She was curious.

'Someone I hoped might have a line on where Fairfax has gone to earth.'

'You mean that odious little man that my father employs to investigate any man who looks at me twice?' He didn't confirm or deny it. But she thought she saw a touch of compassion in those dark eyes. And he hadn't told. The man might have a disconcerting ability to make her blush but he was still a treasure, Emmy decided. One well worth collecting. 'And did he?' she asked. 'Have a line on Kit?'

'No, but fortunately your hall porter was not aware that your destination was a secret. The South of France narrows it down just a little.'

Emerald had to admit she had been careless. She had intended the porter to pass on the information—that was why she had given it to him—but she'd thought she would be well on her way to join Kit when he did. 'You didn't intend to search the *whole* of France, then?' she said.

'I'll have my work cut out, but I'm sure you'll be comfortable at Honeybourne Park while I'm making my enquiries. Can I use your telephone?' Brodie's face broadened into an engaging, slightly lopsided grin that made Emmy's heart give a strange little lurch. What was it about the man? The fact that he refused to be twisted around her little finger? That alone was a challenge. She had never been able to resist a challenge, and she promised herself that she'd bring Brodie to heel in her own good time. But not yet. It was more important to convince him that she was genuine.

'I'll behave, Brodie. I know you've got to do your job, no matter how distasteful it is. I'll take you to Kit and you can put your offer to him. All I ask in return is your promise that if he turns you down that will be an end of it.' That sounded reasonable, didn't it?

'I'd rather you just gave me his address,' Brodie said, unwilling to make any promise he might not be able to keep. 'Or perhaps you think he won't be able to resist your father's money without you there to put a bit of backbone in him?'

Emerald crossed her fingers behind her back. 'I have total confidence in Kit. I just want to be there to see fair play.' She gave a little shrug. 'It will take for ever to find him without my help,' she assured him, her smile seraphic. 'Just how much time can a busy man like you spare?'

Not long, Brodie thought irritably. It had been a

straightforward enough matter to deal with Kit Fairfax in London, no matter how distasteful he found it. A few hours at the most. Finding the man in France was something else.

While he didn't trust Emmy further than he could throw her, he knew that he had little choice but to go along with her suggestion. 'All right,' he said. 'You take me to him. I'll talk to him.' And if Fairfax was unexpectedly staunch to his love they still wouldn't be able to marry for a month. Plenty of time for Gerald Carlisle to think of something else. Or maybe even get used to the idea.

Emerald, knowing she had scored the winning point, held out the softly draped slub-silk of her trousers and sketched a little curtsey. 'I'm glad that's settled.' She picked up her bag and handed it to him. 'Shall we go?'

'Go?'

'I'm going to rent a car and drive down to Dover.' She grinned. 'Although now you're here I suppose we could take your car.'

'I've been working since seven this morning, Emmy. Driving all night is not an option.'

'I can drive,' she pointed out. 'You can sleep.'

He would certainly give her ten out of ten for effort. She never gave up. 'Forgive me if I decline the opportunity to be abandoned in the nearest lay-by.'

'I wouldn't—'

'Of course you would.' He didn't add that he wouldn't blame her. She didn't need any encouragement. 'And I don't have two days to spare to drive south.' Or another two to drive back. 'We'll fly to Marseilles in the morning and I'll hire a left-hand-drive car at the airport.'

'You're a whole lot more than a pair of broad shoulders, Brodie,' she said, with reluctant admiration. He should have been surprised she'd even noticed what he looked like. After all, she was supposed to be head over heels in love with Fairfax. So why wasn't he? He filed the thought away, along with all the other oddities about this business, at the back of his mind. This wasn't the moment to be sidetracked by blatant flattery. 'But there's a problem.'

He stared at her for a moment. 'Go on, surprise me,' he prompted.

'I don't fly.'

'I wasn't expecting you to sprout wings,' he remarked. 'We'll use a regular aircraft, with engines and everything.'

'No, Brodie, I don't fly, even with the aid of engines.'

'Don't or won't?' he asked, suspiciously.

'Both. It's a phobia. The minute they close the aircraft door I have hysterics.'

'I don't believe you.'

Emmy smiled at him. 'Would you like to risk it?'

Brodie regarded her with something close to loathing. He might not believe her, but he didn't underestimate her. He suspected that Emerald Carlisle was perfectly capable of throwing a fit of hysterics that could bring Heathrow to a standstill if she put her mind to it. 'It isn't a problem. We'll take the train.'

'Oh.'

'You're not frightened of trains too, are you?' he asked.

She was tempted. There was, after all, that great big tunnel... And it would have been so much easier to get away from Brodie in a car. But she knew when to give in gracefully. 'No,' she said, demurely. 'I love trains.' Trains made stops.

'Good. That only leaves one thing to be decided.' Emmy raised one of those beautifully arched brows of hers. Something else she practised; he'd bank on it. 'Are we going to spend the night here, or at my place?' And, before she could object, 'I'm not taking my eyes off you until we're safely on the train.'

As Emmy opened her mouth to tell him what he could do with his cheek, the telephone began to ring. She threw it a startled glance. 'Oh, Lord that'll be my father,' she said, making no move to answer it.

'Perhaps you should answer it and put his mind at rest. He must be worried about you.'

Emmy pushed her hair back from her face. 'He's worried, you can count on it. But only about money.'

She saw Brodie's brows dip in surprise. 'That's a little harsh, surely? He's just got your best interests at heart.'

'Has he?' The telephone abruptly ceased ringing, and for a moment they both stared at it. 'I wonder if that's the first time he's rung,' Emmy said uneasily.

'Probably not,' Brodie ventured. 'I worked out that you'd have to come here to collect your passport and money, and at least a change of clothes. He's quite capable of making the same calculation. Does it matter?'

'Yes.' Brodie raised a querying brow. 'The answering machine was on,' she explained. 'I checked my messages when I came in and there were a couple of hang-ups that might have been him. I must have forgotten to reset it, so now he'll know I'm home.'

'You're not having a terribly good day.'

She glanced at him, remembering the moment their eyes had met above her father's head. Remembering that moment in the car when he had come so close to kissing her. 'It hasn't all been bad.'

'No?' He clearly wasn't convinced. 'Whatever. It's time to choose the lesser of two evils, Emmy. We can wait here until your father arrives. Or you can come with me.'

For a moment she stared at him. 'No contest. Let's go.' And there was still the taxi waiting downstairs.

She picked up her bag and headed for the door. He hooked his fingers in her belt and brought her to an outraged halt. 'I think I'd be happier if you handed over your passport,' he said.

She pulled a face. 'You're no fun, Brodie. You think of everything.'

'Amusing you was not part of the brief. And if I thought of everything you wouldn't have run off with my car.'

'For all the good it did me. You're just too smart for me.'

He wasn't taken in by her flattery. 'I thought you were going to behave.'

'I am,' she declared.

'Then you won't need your passport, will you?' He wasn't to be distracted, she realised as he stood there, one hand grasping her waistband, the other outstretched, demanding obedience. 'Maybe it would help if I told you that I sent your taxi away?' Emerald capitulated with a shrug of resignation, retrieving her passport from her shoulder bag and handing it over with a grudging smile.

Let him think he'd won some major victory. Once

they were in France she wouldn't need her passport. And he couldn't keep his eyes on her *all* the time, could he?

Brodie smiled right back. He had her for the moment, but he was under no illusions. Once they were in France he would have to keep a very close eye on Emmy Carlisle. Fortunately, that wouldn't be a hardship.

Brodie's flat was not in the same class as Emmy's. He lived in a converted warehouse loft, on the wrong bank of the Thames to be fashionable, that he'd bought at the bottom of the slump when the developer had been glad to be rid of it at any price.

It didn't have a hall porter to take messages and run errands, or a carpeted lift panelled in some rare tropical hardwood. In fact it was served by a vast goods lift that would have taken Brodie's BMW without flinching.

In its favour it had huge open spaces with high ceilings and acres of polished wood floors that gleamed with a dull richness, the perfect setting for the tribal rugs, radiating with almost barbaric colour, that broke up the huge floor area. The furniture, what there was of it, was old and comfortable.

But the white-painted brick walls provided the perfect backdrop for a stunning collection of paintings, the work of talented students, bought before they became unaffordable for a man who worked for his living.

Emmy stood in the centre of the living area and turned slowly around, absorbing every detail. 'I love this,' she said, at last. 'You've got a good eye for a picture. Can I look around?'

'Help yourself. But, I warn you, I've deadlocked the

front door and I'm taking the key into the shower with me.'

She swivelled round. 'Really?' Her gaze travelled swiftly over his body. 'I'd be interested to know where you plan to keep it.'

'In the soap dish?' he offered.

'Don't be boring, Brodie. I'm not going to run for it. I promised.'

'So you did.' And butter wouldn't melt in her mouth, he thought. 'While you're looking around the kitchen do feel free to make some tea.'

'Do you really want tea? Or is that just your way of keeping me out of mischief?'

'I have more confidence in your ability to make mischief than that,' he said cynically. He didn't wait for her retort. He was sure she had one, but he wasn't in the mood to hear it. He was tired and suddenly rather irritable. He was certainly in no mood to play nursemaid to a wilful young woman who was set on getting her own way, even if she lived to rue the day. On top of which he was going to have to surrender his bed. He glanced at the low, wide bed. It was plenty big enough for two. The thought rose unbidden in his head, tormenting him with images of a pair of long, elegant legs, bright, laughing eyes and a mouth that would tempt a saint. He quashed it mercilessly.

He stepped out of his suit and hung it carefully in a walk-in wardrobe full of expensive clothes. There had been a time when one suit had been all he could afford. Old habits died hard.

Perhaps he should have made the effort to find himself an heiress with a father who would rather pay out a fortune than see his daughter married to the son of a miner. With his luck, he chided himself, the father would have called his bluff. And there were very few heiresses who looked like Emerald Carlisle.

He stripped off the rest of his clothes, flicked on the shower and stood for a few moments beneath the hot, reviving needles of water, and while he soaped himself he considered what other tricks Miss Carlisle might have up her sleeve.

She could protest that she was going to 'behave', flash those big innocent eyes and say 'honestly' until the cows came home, but he didn't believe it. Her father had said she was a handful, and Brodie had to admit that the man knew what he was talking about. But going along with Emmy's plan was still the quickest way of getting to Fairfax. Provided she didn't manage to give him the slip.

He wasn't stupid. He knew that it wouldn't be difficult for her to get away from him once they were in France. She had already demonstrated a reckless daring, a facility for thinking on her feet, the kind of spirit that you would cheer from the sidelines if you weren't the poor sucker being made to look a fool.

He might have learned his lesson regarding car keys, but he knew he wouldn't be able to keep her in sight twenty-four hours a day. However, since the only alternative would be to take her back to her father and own up, he would certainly have to try. A small crease appeared in one corner of his mouth at the thought.

He considered her mop of tousled red hair and a pair of the most bewitching green-gold eyes that he had ever encountered and vowed to make it a priority. About one thing he was in total agreement with Gerald Carlisle.

There was no way he was about to let her marry some layabout who called himself an artist and had his eye on her money.

He reached for a towel and wrapped it about him, but as he walked into the bedroom the telephone at the side of the bed gave the faintest ting. It hadn't taken Emerald long to make herself at home. She was calling someone from the kitchen phone.

He reached for the receiver, lifted it carefully from the cradle and held it to his ear. He was rewarded with the low purr of the dialling tone. Correction. She *had* been calling someone. Fairfax? Or someone else? Only the telephone in the kitchen could give him the answer to that one.

CHAPTER FOUR

EMMY was excessively pleased with herself. To have found Kit in the local café was too much to hope. But the *patron* had taken a message for him, promised to pass it along as soon as he saw him. At least she hoped that was what he'd said. She wished she had paid more attention to French at school.

But in a day that had alternated between exhilarating ups and frustrating downs, the ups had, in the end, come out marginally ahead. And this time Brodie hadn't caught her. That alone was almost enough to put the smile on her face. The kettle boiled, she poured the water on the tea and, picking up the teapot, turned to put it on the tray.

Brodie was standing in the doorway watching her. There was nothing in his expression to indicate how long he had been there. It took every ounce of self-control not to cast a guilty look in the direction of the telephone. Every ounce of self-control to stop her wrist from shaking. And it wasn't just a nervous reaction to coming so close to getting caught once again. Brodie, stripped of the civilising uniform of his business clothes, was a thoroughly dangerous-looking male.

He had discarded his formal suit, the crisp white shirt, regulation dark silk tie and polished shoes for a track-suit bottom worn thin with use and an equally worn T-shirt that hung loosely about his torso. The tendons on his upper arms stood out in relief, as did the veins on his forearms. Deeply tanned forearms. It wasn't sunbed colour, and his outfit was only thin from being put vigorously to the purpose for which it was intended. His feet—long and beautifully shaped feet—were bare. Which was why she hadn't heard him coming.

It occurred to Emmy that Brodie was wearing this rather unlikely outfit for her benefit. Not the kind of man to wear pyjamas—she suspected any overnight guest wouldn't usually be worried about such niceties—this had been the best he had been able to come up with on short notice. 'Milk, sugar?' she asked as her wrist finally succumbed to the shakes and she put the pot down rather suddenly.

Brodie raked his hand through hair still wet from the shower. He hadn't expected her to do what he'd asked. It wasn't in character. Maybe Emmy thought if she was obviously busy he wouldn't wonder what else she might have been up to while he'd been in the shower. 'Just milk. Thanks. Aren't you having a cup?'

'Not before going to bed.'

'Oh, well, the bedroom is all yours,' he said. 'Come on, I'll show you.'

'Bedroom?' she enquired, looking in at the austere white room, the enormous bed covered by a plain black quilt. 'Singular? Haven't you got a spare room?'

'Not with a bed in it. The need hasn't arisen in the past.'

That she could believe. 'But where will you sleep?'

He shrugged. 'I'll be fine on the sofa.'

'Really?' She looked doubtful. 'It's an awfully big bed, Brodie. If you had a pillow-bolster we could share

it,' she offered, unable to resist a down payment on re-
venge for his making her blush.

Emmy realised, but far too late, that she should have
resisted, taking a step back as Brodie's eyes flared with
anger, and with something else, something far more dangerous. She had done something very foolish. That was
nothing new; she was famous for it. But this time she
didn't quite know how to handle the outcome of her
foolishness as Brodie slowly advanced on her.

'Share it?'

She took another step back, and another, before she
finally came to a halt. Retreating was not in her nature.
But it was a real effort to stand her ground when Brodie
was up close with a six-inch height advantage and an
edge to his voice that would have cut glass. But stand
her ground she did, and launched a counter-offensive.
'Like they did in the Middle Ages?' she offered. 'A
sword dividing the bed?'

'A sword? Wasn't that terribly dangerous?'

'You're missing the point, Brodie. It was symbolic. A
true knight errant wouldn't cross the dividing line, even
if the sword was sheathed. For safety,' she added, in case
he should think she meant something else.

'I've already told you, Emmy. I'm no knight errant.'
He took another step towards her. 'But it's an interesting
idea. Perhaps a couple of pillows would do the trick.'

'No, Brodie,' she said quickly, putting out her hand
to stop him coming any nearer. 'I was joking…'

Her palm collided with the tight muscle of his chest
but it did nothing to impede his progress, and as the
warmth of his body seeped into her through her hand,
along her arm, until her entire body seemed to be heating

up from within, her fingers closed over his T-shirt, bunching it in her fist, holding it tight.

'Joking?' he enquired softly.

For a moment she thought she had a chance, and opened her mouth to reinforce her contention. But he stroked the backs of his long, slender fingers slowly and gently from her throat to her chin, mesmerising her with his touch, and a delicious languor stole through her body as he captured her chin. Then he began to trace a slow, sensuous line across her bottom lip with the tip of his thumb. It was like that moment in the car when he had so nearly kissed her. When she had, for one crazy moment, wanted him to kiss her more than anything else in the world. She still did, and when she saw the reflection of her own heart in his eyes Emerald Carlisle trembled.

'What is there to joke about, Emmy?' he finally asked her, his voice no longer diamond bright, but soft, like cobwebs tearing.

Brodie knew she had been teasing him with her invitation and he had planned to tease her right back, nothing more. If he had given the matter any thought he might have expected a slap for his impertinence, outraged virtue from a woman who had declared her determination to marry the man she loved, no matter what. But the tiny shiver as he touched her lip felt like an earthquake beneath his thumb. The shock waves of it ran up his arm and through his body and nothing mattered beyond the moment.

That was when Tom Brodie stopped thinking and did what he quite suddenly realised he had been wanting to do from the instant he had set eyes on Emerald Carlisle clinging to that damned drainpipe.

Emmy realised too late that it had been a mistake to stand her ground. She should have kept retreating. At least with her back to the wall she could have said she had done everything she could to avoid the results of her own stupidity. Custer had made a stand, and look what had happened to him. Oh, yes, indeed, there was no doubt about it, stopping had been a serious mistake, and now there was nowhere to run, and even if there had been she was transfixed, held prisoner in the magnetic force field Brodie seemed to be generating while he slowly lowered his head until his lips were level with hers.

And as he held her gaze with his hot grey eyes, her entire body captive to the crook of one finger beneath her chin, she slammed her eyes shut and expelled an involuntary groan through lips that she knew were too soft, too inviting. By the time she had decided she ought to do something about that, it was too late.

The kiss began with a touch as light as his thumb trace, the petal-soft brush of his mouth as his lips discovered hers in a slow, seductive tango that stole away any lingering thoughts of resistance. Her lips parted as his tongue dipped against her teeth, and instinctively her free arm wound about his neck.

For a moment Brodie revelled in the sweetness of her mouth, her softness, the scent of her skin and her hair brushing against his cheek as she clung to him. The hand at her chin slipped behind her head, his fingers sliding through her hair to cup her nape. His other hand was at her waist, drawing her closer into his body as it tightened with desire. He wanted Emerald Carlisle, and in that lost moment, when the air stood still about them, he knew that she was his for the taking.

Then his masculine back-up system, the one that knew all the pitfalls, all the traps for the unwary male, kicked in, cruelly reminding him that he was older and supposedly a whole lot wiser than this girl in his arms, this girl whose interests it was his duty to protect.

When Gerald Carlisle had instructed him to do anything required to stop his daughter from marrying Kit Fairfax, taking her to his bed, Brodie felt certain, was not what the man had had in mind.

As he stiffened and pulled back Emmy gave a faint mewl of protest, and for a moment he considered consigning Gerald Carlisle to the devil, along with his conscience and quite possibly his career. Only the certain knowledge that she had been teasing him, had never intended things to go this far, stopped him. So why did he feel as he let her go that she had won? That it was giddy girl, one, wiser and older lawyer, nil?

Because this was a game he could never win?

Perhaps it was time he remembered that lawyers weren't supposed to play games. And that Emerald Carlisle would dare anything to get her own way.

He raised his head and looked down his long, straight nose at her. 'That's quite a sense of humour you've got, Emmy. And you've a nice line in distraction, but since your passport is locked away in my safe your sacrifice would be pointless. That is if you're still planning to go ahead with the wedding?'

He had finally persuaded his reluctant fingers to release her and he took a step back, just to be on the safe side. 'You *had* remembered that you're desperate to

marry Kit Fairfax?' he said, to punish himself as much
as her. Then, more harshly, as he suddenly realised what
she had been doing, just how far she would go to get
her own way, 'Or is the wedding just this month's attempt at winding up your father? I'd rather you told me
now, because I've got better things to do than—'

'Desperate,' Emerald flung at him, with just the
slightest crack in her voice. His expression suggested
doubt, and who could blame him for that? she asked
herself. Damn Hollingworth for going to Scotland. She
wouldn't have had all this trouble with Hollingworth.
She certainly wouldn't have made the terrible mistake
of kissing him. But then, he wouldn't have let her escape
down the drainpipe in the first place. 'I'm going to marry
Kit as soon as possible,' she declared, sounding rather
more than desperate in her need to convince Brodie of
her sincerity. 'And there's nothing you can do to stop
me.'

'No?' He reached out and pressed the tips of his fingers against her lips. Cool fingers that smelt of good
soap and in some indefinable way of *him*. 'I'm certainly
going to try,' he said. 'Whatever it takes.' Then he
crossed to the night table and bent to unplug the telephone. As he straightened he caught the smallest smile
of satisfaction cross her lips. She assumed he was removing the telephone to prevent her from making calls,
assumed that she had got away with her call from the
kitchen phone. Well, that was good.

But, while it was true that he didn't want her making
any more unauthorised telephone calls, his intention in
removing the bedroom phone was actually to prevent her
from listening to his own call. He wrapped the wire

slowly around the receiver and then crossed to the bedroom door.

'Goodnight, Emmy. Sleep well,' he said, before he pulled the door shut behind him with a decisive click.

Emmy closed her eyes, gritted her teeth and clenched her hands into tight little fists as a deep, shuddering breath racked her. Then very deliberately she forced herself to relax, and let go of the desperate urge to erupt in temper; after all she had nobody but herself to blame for what had happened.

Under the circumstances, flirting with Brodie had been quite unforgivable. And totally stupid. If he even suspected what she was up to the game would be over before it had begun.

But flirting with Brodie had an edge to it, an excitement that was dangerously addictive. For a moment there she'd had only one thought in her mind, and she suspected Brodie had been light-years ahead of her. She glanced at his enormous bed as she undressed, pulled on an old rugby jersey that she wore as a nightshirt.

Light-years. But she had been catching up with him fast.

Then, smiling a touch ruefully as she threw back the quilt, she decided that they could have managed without a pillow-bolster to make a barrier between them and still have been perfectly chaste. It was, after all, an awfully big bed. But then Brodie was an awfully good-looking man, so presumably he wouldn't ever need to be lonely in it.

But that was a horribly disturbing thought, and as she slipped beneath the freshly laundered cover, Emmy discovered that she absolutely hated the idea.

*   *   *

Brodie returned to the kitchen and, crossing to the wall-mounted telephone, lifted the receiver and pressed 'redial'. After a moment or two the call was answered.

'Directory enquiries, which town?'

He stared at the receiver. *Directory enquiries?* 'I'm sorry, I misdialled,' he said, and hung up. Of all the devious women... She'd obviously dialled Directory Enquiries after her call so that he wouldn't be able to check who she had rung. No wonder she had looked so damned pleased with herself.

More fool him for thinking that anything involving Miss Emerald Carlisle could be that easy. It seemed that if he wanted to find Kit Fairfax he had no choice but to go with her to France.

He rang his secretary. 'Jenny? I'm sorry to call so late, but I'm going to be out of the office for the rest of the week, running an errand for Gerald Carlisle. I'll leave you to rearrange my appointments, but there are some things I need you to do as a matter of urgency. First, there's a car I borrowed...'

'Emmy?' She opened her eyes at the tap on the door, the sound of her name. Then she closed them again, quickly. Sun was streaming in through the high-arched windows and it was far too bright after what had been a decidedly restless night. She rolled onto her stomach and buried her face in the pillow. The tap on the door was repeated, louder this time, imperative in its demand.

'Go away, Brodie,' she mumbled. But the pillow apparently muffled her words because behind her the door opened. 'I said, go away. I haven't finished sleeping.'

'I've brought you a cup of tea. You can wake up while I'm in the shower.'

'I don't want to wake up.'

'You don't have any choice. I've managed to get a couple of seats on the eight-twenty-seven train from Waterloo.'

Eight-twenty-seven? For a moment she lay perfectly still and ignored him. With trains leaving for all points south during the entire day, he had to choose the early-morning one? How efficient. How really, wonderfully, bloody efficient.

'Great,' she mumbled.

'It was that or the six-fifty-three. I didn't think you'd appreciate being woken at five.'

He was right about that. Even so. 'I thought they went every hour,' she grumbled into the pillow.

'They do to Paris, but we're changing at Lille. I've booked through to Marseilles, and we can hire a car when we arrive.'

'Marseilles? Why Marseilles?'

'You said the South of France,' he pointed out gently. 'If you'd like to be more specific…?' he invited.

'I suppose Marseilles will do as well as anywhere.' Brodie was obviously still one step ahead of her, but not that far ahead.

'I just knew you'd be pleased.'

And because Emmy realised that under the circumstances she *should* be pleased—and because she knew he wasn't about to let her go back to sleep—she finally turned over, sat up and pushed the hair back from her face.

She was rather glad she'd made the effort. If you had

to have an early-morning wake-up call, Brodie—hair tousled from sleep, his jaw so dark with the overnight growth of his beard that she wanted to reach out and rub her palm over it—was a whole lot more appealing than an alarm clock. She eased herself up the pillow and reached for the mug he was holding out to her, turning on a smile of lambent brightness. Marseilles was a big city. Anything might happen in Marseilles.

She glanced at the gold Cartier Panther on her wrist. It was just a little after six-thirty. Instead of groaning, she sipped her tea and said, 'Hadn't you better get a move on if we're going to catch that train? You've got fifteen minutes, Brodie, then the bathroom's mine.'

'If we shared it would save time.'

The casual way he said it jolted Emmy. She had known all along it would be crazy to underestimate the man. He had said he would stop the wedding whatever it took. If he'd decided that seduction was the easiest way, she was in big trouble.

She lowered her lashes, demure as a nun. 'I make it a rule never to share a bathroom with a man I've only just met,' she said.

'Just a bed?'

By the time she had absorbed the insult, opened her mouth to protest her innocence, Brodie had removed himself to the bathroom and shut the door fast behind him. She thought she might throw her mug, tea and all, at it, but since he would undoubtedly insist on her clearing up the mess she changed her mind and drank it instead. But she wouldn't forget.

She swung her legs over the edge of the bed and opened her bag, considering what she would wear for the long train journey south, with the weather getting hotter every mile of the way. After a moment she shook out a short dark green bias-cut dress with tiny sleeves and a sprinkling of tiny ivory spots. It was fresh, neat and cool, and today she'd need to be all of those.

She gathered her underwear, sandals and matching handbag, into which she transferred everything she would need from the shoulder bag she had been using the night before. It was a pity about her passport, she thought as she flipped through her wallet, checking the francs she had collected from the bank a couple of days earlier.

Emmy glanced at the bathroom door. The shower had stopped a while ago and there was no time to dither. She took five one-hundred franc notes from her wallet and wrapped them up in the froth of ivory silk underwear that she had piled on the bed beside her dress.

She would have to get up very early in the morning to outsmart Brodie, she decided. Fortunately, he had been a most efficient alarm clock.

The train was comfortable and Brodie had booked first-class seats. Well, why wouldn't he when her father would pick up the bill? Even so, Emmy was beginning to regret faking her fear of flying. It hadn't got her what she'd wanted and now she would have to sit next to Brodie for the best part of seven hours. Under normal circumstances that would not have been a hardship; normally she would have regarded the opportunity to flirt at length with a man like Brodie as the most delightful prospect.

These, however, were not normal circumstances,

which was why, on arrival at Waterloo International, she had headed straight for the book stall and picked up three paperbacks. She wasn't about to risk taking just one book that she might hate after three pages. She'd turned to Brodie. 'I'll need some money to pay for these,' she had said, abruptly.

It was the first time she had deigned to speak to him since he had confiscated her credit cards and all her money except small change. She had anticipated the move, but sustained indignation had been the only possible response. If she had been too meek he would have smelt a rat, and, since he had already had a demonstration of her most likely hiding place, it wouldn't have taken him long to find the five hundred francs hidden in her bra. She wished she had dared to take more, but that would have left too little money in her wallet.

It was a small victory, but she was pleased with it. And she was determined to take the first opportunity to put it to good use.

'I was beginning to think we were going to spend our entire journey in silence,' he'd said, taking the books from her and paying for them.

'We are,' she'd replied. 'You'd better get something for yourself.'

Brodie had shrugged. 'I've got plenty of work to keep me occupied. All done here?' he'd asked, handing her the books, but keeping the receipt. 'No mints, chocolates, barley sugar?' She'd glared at him. 'Then we might as well board the train.'

Breakfast was served, and was passed in deliberate silence on Emmy's part, in apparent oblivion on Brodie's. He ate absent-mindedly, more interested in the document he was reading than her apparent bout of the sulks.

'It's incredibly rude to read at the table,' Emmy declared, finally driven to protest at this lack of attention.

He turned, surprised. 'Oh, I'm sorry. I didn't think you wanted to talk. At least, not to me.' He closed the file he had been reading and waited.

She felt foolish. Having protested that she was being ignored, she now had to say something, but under that cool, slightly distant gaze all she could think of was last night, when his eyes had been anything but cool and he had kissed her. Desperate, she made a gesture towards the papers he had been reading and sent her orange juice flying. She watched in horror as the thick, pithy liquid spread over the file and began to seep towards the legal documents it contained.

The steward, spotting this minor catastrophe, immediately mopped up the worst of the spill and whisked away the cloth. Brodie took the papers from the folder, wiped them on his napkin and handed the folder to the steward. 'Perhaps you could dispose of this?'

'Of course, sir. And I'll bring the young lady another glass of orange juice.'

'No,' Emmy said, quickly. 'There's no need. Thank you.' The man departed and she turned to Brodie. 'I'm sorry. Are your papers ruined?'

'No. They're fine.' He reached for his document case and slipped them inside, but not before she'd seen the name on the top sheet.

'Good grief, is he your client?' she asked. He flickered a glance at her and she realised he was just a touch amused that she was impressed. 'Since when have multimillionaire pop stars been clients of a stuffy old firm like Broadbent, Hollingworth & Maunsell?' she demanded.

'Since I've been a partner.'

'Oh, I see.'

'I doubt it.'

It wasn't in Emmy's nature to sustain a feud, or remain silent for long no matter what the provocation, and this was her opportunity to break the ice. 'Then tell me.'

Brodie regarded her for a moment, the wide, innocent gold-flecked eyes set beneath dark, delicately winged brows. Despite her red hair, Emmy's lashes and brows were dark and lustrous against a creamy complexion. She was very beautiful. And all the more dangerous because of it. Despite that, or maybe because he enjoyed dicing with danger, he accepted this tentative olive branch.

'I've known Chas since primary school,' he said.

'Chas?'

'That's his name. Charles Potter.'

'I can understand why he changed it.'

'When he was offered his first contract, he couldn't afford a proper solicitor so his mother suggested he ask my advice—since I was going to study law.'

'You're kidding?'

'We don't all have the benefit of being born with a whole canteen of silver spoons in our mouths, Emmy.'

'Oh.' For a moment she looked crestfallen. Then, 'Tell me about the contract.'

'It looked impressive—the numbers were big, and it was the sort of contract no eighteen-year-old musician would have turned down. A lot of them didn't and have lived to regret it.'

'You advised him not to sign?'

'The contract was for the number of albums recorded. It didn't have a time scale. It seemed to me that if he was still recording in twenty years' time it might just be on the same contract. I suggested he went back to the company and asked for a contract for five albums. They wanted him, and, let's be honest, how many pop stars last that long? They agreed. He was impressed. And I was relieved,' he admitted. 'As a result I'm still checking out his contracts, only these days I rely on more than a hunch to make sure they're watertight.'

'Which is just as well since he's a multi-million-pound corporation with his own recording company. It's a nice story, Brodie. Do you still hand out advice for free?'

'I get my best clients that way and some of my worst ones.' She raised one of those glossy brows. 'I run a legal clinic at an advice centre in one of the less salubrious parts of London.'

'A regular Mr Nice Guy.'

'One who'll give you some advice for free right now.' His face was grave, his eyes serious. 'Catch the next train home, Emmy. Rushing into marriage is always a mistake, and if Fairfax is genuine he'll wait for your father to come round.'

Emmy reached for a book, but before she opened it she gave him an enigmatic little smile. 'You think it's going to be easy to talk Kit into taking my father's money, don't you?'

'Do I?'

For a moment she held his gaze. 'You're wrong about him, you know.'

Brodie was startled by the glowing sincerity with which she spoke, but she was right. He had been assuming, like Carlisle, that it would simply be a matter of numbers...how many pound notes it would take to buy the man off. As Emmy settled back to read, however, he put himself in Kit Fairfax's shoes. If Emmy loved *him* just how much would it take to make him change his mind?

It was then that he realised he'd better give some serious thought about his next move if the man refused to take the bribe.

It was early evening by the time the train pulled into Marseilles. Another half an hour before they were sitting in the comfortable Renault that Brodie had hired.

He turned to her. 'Well, Emmy, we're in the South of France. Where now?'

'Head north,' she said. 'Then east.'

'North and then east?' He regarded her with a degree of amusement. 'You'll forgive me, but that isn't very precise. Where exactly are we going?'

'I'll give you directions as we go,' she hedged.

'Not directions like that, you won't. It'll be dark in a couple of hours and I have no intention of ending up lost on some remote track miles from anywhere.' Which was what she undoubtedly had in mind.

'Just head north, Brodie. I'll tell you when to turn off. I'm really good with directions.'

He hadn't expected her to tell him where they were

going; in fact he had rather been banking on her obsti-
nacy. 'In the dark?' he pressed. 'Honest?'

'Of course,' she said, not quite meeting his eyes. He
gave her a thoughtful look before he started the engine
and, pulling out of the garage, headed for the nearest
intersection. It was then that Emmy abandoned her careless pose. 'You've taken the wrong turning, Brodie!' she
declared as he headed towards the old port area of the
city. 'I said *north.*'

CHAPTER FIVE

BRODIE was unmoved. '"North" is not good enough, Emmy. I've been sitting in a train since first thing this morning and I'm not about to be driven all over France on some wild-goose chase of yours. We'll spend the night in Marseilles and set off first thing in the morning. Once you've told me exactly where we're headed.'

She stared at him, clearly not believing her own ears. 'I thought you were desperate to get this finished with.'

'I am.' Then he shrugged. 'But not so desperate that I'm prepared to drive off into the night without any idea of where I'm going. Besides, it does seem a shame to come so close to the home of bouillabaisse and not treat ourselves to a dish.'

He'd been in an odd mood ever since they'd left this morning, Emmy thought. As if he knew something that she didn't, and it bothered her. But she knew why he was doing this. She had refused to tell him exactly where they were going, afraid that he would find some way to leave her behind and take off into the interior to deal with Kit without any interference from her. After all he thought she was penniless and entirely in his hands.

Well, she would let him think it. It would probably be a lot easier getting away from him in a busy city like Marseilles than out in the country. But it wouldn't do to let him see she didn't mind that much.

'I hate bouillabaisse,' she said, sitting back in her seat, folding her arms and staring out of the opposite window.

'It's not obligatory. I know a restaurant down by the old port where I'm sure you'll find something to your taste. The view, if nothing else. Perhaps we should take a boat ride out to the Château D'If in the morning? I'll show you the cell in which the Count of Monte Cristo was incarcerated if you like.'

'Don't be ridiculous, Brodie, *The Count of Monte Cristo* is a novel. Fiction. Dante wasn't *real*.'

'I know,' he replied, teasing her gently. 'Neither was Sherlock Holmes, but people still write to him at his Baker Street lodgings.'

'Anyone would think *you* were on holiday,' she declared, crossly. 'My future is at stake here. Aren't you taking it seriously?'

'I am finding it rather difficult,' he confessed. 'Hollingworth might be able to justify a jaunt like this as business but then he's more used to this sort of thing than I am.' He paused, waited; she didn't reply. 'You have done this before?' he prompted.

She blushed. 'I'm sure my father gave you all the details.'

'Some,' he agreed. Gerald Carlisle had told him that Emmy had fallen for a smooth-talking fortune-hunter who had eloped with her from a villa where they had been staying with friends. Brodie suspected that it had been more a case of a summer romance that had got out of control; a real fortune-hunter would have taken a great deal more money to dislodge.

'I was barely eighteen, Brodie,' she said defensively

as the silence continued. 'A child.' She set her lips in a firm line. 'This time I know exactly what I'm doing.'

'Maybe you do, Emmy.' And when *he'd* worked out what exactly she was doing it would be soon enough to confront Fairfax. 'But, since I had planned to take a few days off this month, I've decided to combine business with pleasure.'

'Oh, really? And do you always bring work with you when you're on holiday?'

'I brought you.'

She glared at him. 'What did you do, Brodie? Ring your secretary in the middle of the night and get her to rearrange your schedule? Just like that?' She snapped her fingers.

'I wasn't given much choice. Apart from a diary full of appointments that needed to be changed, I had to organise the return of the car I borrowed after you—' Emmy glared at him, daring him to say the word 'stole'. 'After you helped yourself to mine.' He grinned. 'I think you owe Jenny a bunch of flowers at the very least for getting her out of bed. Make it a big one and I won't say another word about it.'

She wasn't proud of taking his car and didn't like being continually reminded of it. 'Is that a promise?'

'Cross my heart.' He took one hand off the wheel and sketched a cross above his heart.

'Then it's a deal.' Emmy remained silent while Brodie wove through the evening traffic and pulled into the space in front of a small hotel. 'You're serious, aren't you?' she said as he flipped the release on his seatbelt. 'Why don't you just forget about me and take your holiday?'

'Because I'm very conscientious. However, I'm quite prepared to relax tonight and forget why we're here. Why don't you try and do the same?' Emmy regarded Brodie with suspicion. She didn't think he was on holiday; she thought that he was being horribly devious about something. But Brodie smiled and offered her his hand. 'Come on. You might as well accept that the only travelling we're doing tonight is going to be a gentle promenade below the fort to admire the sunset over Vieux Port. I promise you, it won't hurt a bit. You might even enjoy it.'

Emmy thought that he was probably right, but as she took his hand and allowed him to help her from the car she reminded herself not to let it show too much.

Brodie, Emmy realised as they entered the small but charming hotel, had never intended to drive into the interior that night. The proprietor, Monsieur Girard, was clearly an old friend, greeting him with warmth and enthusiasm but certainly no surprise.

She strained to follow Brodie's excellent French as he signed the registration card, but the two men were speaking too quickly for her own inept schoolgirl version of the language.

'Your secretary is remarkably efficient,' Emmy said, just a little sourly, as it became obvious that his decision to stay overnight in Marseilles had nothing to do with her reluctance to tell him exactly where they were headed.

Brodie caught her look, gave the slightest of shrugs. 'I knew we wouldn't arrive until late afternoon so I asked her to ring ahead and reserve a room for me.' He pushed the card he had filled in across the reception desk. 'You should learn to overcome your fear of flying, Emmy. We could have been here several hours ago and you would by now have been in the arms of your own true love.' He said that with a certain cynicism. Presumably her enthusiastic reponse when he kissed her had reinforced his view that she was simply winding up her father. That had been a mistake, she acknowledged, but an understandable one, surely? The assured manner of that kiss had suggested that he was used to enthusiasm. 'Have you tried hypnosis?' he asked.

'Hypnosis?'

'I believe it can be quite effective in dealing with irrational fears. If, of course, your fear is genuine.' He clearly wasn't convinced about that either. He took the key the proprietor handed him and, picking up both their bags in one hand, headed for the antiquated lift with its wrought-iron gates.

'One key?' she demanded.

Brodie's jaw tightened. 'One key. And you'd better hope there's a bolster, Emmy. This is an old-fashioned hotel; they don't go in for twin beds.'

'Really?' She stepped into the lift. 'Then I hope, for your sake, Brodie, that the floor is comfortable.'

'It wouldn't be the first time I'd slept on a floor. I just hope there isn't a draught under the door.'

Emmy smiled so much that it felt as if her face was cracking in half. 'You think I'd make a bolt for it? In Marseilles, in the middle of the night?'

'It sounds unlikely when you put it like that. However, your track record to date suggests I would be foolish to ignore the possibility. And just in case there's a handy drainpipe I'm warning you now that I'll have all our documents and money locked in the hotel safe overnight.' And, apparently able to read her mind, he continued, 'You may not need your passport to travel now, Emmy. You'll certainly need it to get married.' He paused. 'Along with your birth certificate, an affidavit of residence in France, a prenuptial medical certificate, a solicitor's certificate regarding a marriage contract, a Certificate of Law from the British Embassy in Paris—that is if you haven't already applied for one from the Foreign and Commonwealth Office—the declaration of forenames—'

'You've been doing your homework,' she said, interrupting what was obviously going to be a lengthy list.

'It's my legal training. You only have one chance to get it right. And the French do take marriage very seriously—as you'd have discovered if you'd done your homework before starting out on this madcap scheme. It would have saved us both a lot of trouble,' he told her as the lift finally jolted to a stop.

'Trouble is my middle name,' she retorted. 'Didn't my father tell you that?'

'We didn't discuss names, but according to the file he gave me you were registered at birth simply as Emerald Louise Victoria. Was Trouble a baptismal addition?' He opened the gate for her and, apparently not expecting an answer to his question, said, 'After you, Miss Carlisle.'

He was confident that he had her, she thought as she stepped from the lift. Well, that was good. He would relax. He would be less cautious. And for now she would be very, very good.

But there was no need for pretence as she looked

around the delightful suite of rooms they had been allocated on the first floor, overlooking Vieux Port. Old-fashioned provincial French, with heavy ornate furniture, the sitting room and bedroom were charming.

And, since the sitting room was furnished with a large and comfortable-looking sofa, he had obviously been just teasing about sharing the huge, inviting bed that dominated the inner room.

'Didn't your secretary query just one suite of rooms, Brodie?' she asked, glancing into the bathroom.

'My secretary isn't supposed to know that you are with me,' he pointed out. Which didn't quite answer her question, she noticed. But then, he *was* a lawyer.

'Then who did she think the other seat on the train was for?'

'In the interests of discretion, I decided to book the seats on the train myself.'

'You're hoping to keep the whole thing quiet?' she enquired as she turned back to him.

'If you want to make a spectacle of yourself in the tabloids, Emmy, I really couldn't care less. I am simply acting as your father's agent—'

'You mean you're just obeying orders?' Brodie's slate eyes hardened to granite, his face darkening ominously. And he was right to be angry. She knew that it had been an unforgivable, hateful thing to say. Emmy, immediately repentant, took half a step towards him. 'Brodie…' she began, but he cut off her apology.

'In a situation that is totally repellent to me. However, since I wholeheartedly agree with his sentiments when it comes to avaricious men who take advantage of young women cursed with an abundance of wealth, I will do everything I possibly can to carry out his wishes. Not for him, but for you.' And, picking up his briefcase, he crossed to the door. 'I'll leave you to use the bathroom first, Emmy. I suggest you take the opportunity to wash your mouth out while you're in there.'

She couldn't let him go like that, and she rushed across the room, grasping the sleeve of his jacket to detain him. 'I'm sorry, Brodie,' she blurted out. 'Truly.'

'So am I.' He glanced down pointedly at her fingers and she instantly removed them. 'Take your time in the bathroom. I'm going to have a drink.'

Emmy flinched as the door closed with a firmness that would have equalled a slam from anyone less controlled, and she leaned back against it with a little shudder. 'Damn,' she said. 'Damn.' Her father had no doubt told him that she was a spoilt brat and now, with one stupid remark, she had apparently confirmed it.

She realised that she couldn't bear to have Brodie believe that. She didn't want him to think she was a thoughtless girl who was simply going out of her way to give her father the maximum amount of grief. But short of telling him the truth what on earth could she do?

Nothing. She'd already learned that people believed what they wanted to believe, and most people chose to believe that she was just like her mother—wild, irresponsible and selfish. But she wasn't. Oh, she'd had her moments, but nothing worse than most girls of her age. But her wealth, and a mother with a string of lovers, had put her under the spotlight so that every minor indiscretion was magnified out of all proportion.

What was so unfair, so bloody unfair, was that her

mother would never have got herself into this kind of situation. Or, if she had, would have quit at the first sign of difficulty.

But Brodie would discover that Emerald Carlisle was not a quitter; unlike her mother she would never run out on a friend, or her family, or a lover just because the going got tough. She'd see this through to the end, and she refused to allow either her father or Brodie to stop her. Only Kit could do that, which was why she simply had to get to him before Brodie. It would be hard enough even then...

Why was it that life threw you these horrible little trials to test your determination? Just when you were sailing happily along without a care in the world, when plans had been made, when putting them into practice had seemed to be a piece of cake?

Why on earth had Kit decided he simply had to go to France at that very moment, for instance? Nothing she could say or do had been able to dissuade him. He'd just dropped one of those absent-minded kisses on her forehead, told her not to worry about him, that everything would sort itself out. But she knew that Kit's optimism was misplaced. Everything would not sort itself out, it never did unless someone did something to give it a helping hand.

Still, that had been a minor inconvenience; it had only become a disaster when her father had demonstrated an unsuspected ability to think on his feet. Or maybe not. Once she had decided what she would do, she had flaunted Kit quite shamelessly...even staying overnight at his studio once she had realised he was being checked out by her father's pet investigator. And because of that her father had been ready for her. She wondered idly what he would have done if, as Brodie had suggested, she'd revealed a three-day licence for a register office wedding... Have Mark Reed snatch her off the pavement and bundle her down to Honeybourne in the boot of his Bentley?

Then, as if she hadn't enough to cope with, Hollingworth, a man with a severe imagination bypass, a man she could rely on to do exactly what her father said without question, had departed for Scotland and the grouse moors, leaving her to the tender mercy of Tom Brodie, whose imagination was in full working order and who didn't respond predictably when someone pulled his strings. In fact she was willing to wager that he hadn't responded to string-pulling since the midwife had cut the umbilical cord.

She brushed a stupid tear from her cheek and stood up. Tomorrow she would have to escape her clever watchdog in order to get to Kit before him. Tonight she and Brodie were in Marseilles, with an evening stroll on the agenda followed by a candlelit supper and a chance to redeem herself just a little in his eyes. And finally a smile softened the determined line of her mouth. Tonight she would be good.

But not for another few minutes. She'd use the time Brodie had given her to check the layout of the hotel. It would undoubtedly be the only chance she'd get.

Brodie had discarded his jacket and was stretched out on a pavement chair soaking up the lingering heat of the sun. He stared at the glass of *pastis* he was holding, its cloudy depths as obscure as the problems raised by

Emerald Carlisle. He shifted uncomfortably. What on earth was he doing, chasing around the South of France with a runaway heiress, for heaven's sake? The whole thing was like some 1940s romantic comedy with Cary Grant. Except there was nothing funny about the situation, at least not from his point of view.

He specialised in Corporate Law. It was serious stuff. He took his work seriously. This nonsense…and Emerald Carlisle…who could possibly take her seriously? But he already knew.

He closed his eyes. What on earth was the matter with him? He wasn't in the habit of losing his head over a pretty face. Yet that he had was demonstrable by the fact that they were here together in Marseilles, sharing a hotel suite, when common sense suggested that he should have phoned her father the moment he'd caught up with her in her flat. Or before that—called him from the café where they had stopped. Or simply turned around and taken her back to Honeybourne the moment he'd realised she had stowed away in his car. So why hadn't he? Why had he connived with her escape in the first place?

Above the mingled smells of the traffic and the harbour her scent lingered in his memory, the way she had felt in his arms, the taste of her mouth as she had melted against him, and he knew why.

His hand tightened around the glass. She hadn't meant it, he reminded himself. She had been desperate to distract him, bewitch him…and for a moment she had succeeded. The way she had looked up at him just now with those huge green-gold eyes as she had tried to apologise; it had taken every ounce of will-power not to take her into his arms, to just walk away.

Damn it, he should have driven her straight to Fairfax and sorted the whole thing out tonight. He'd brought her here to delay her, not for her own good, but for his. Because he wanted to get to know her. Understand what was driving her. There *was* something. And he could swear it wasn't undying love for Kit Fairfax. Or maybe he just wanted to believe that...

The glass disintegrated in his hands, showering him with *pastis* and shards of glass.

He was immediately descended upon by Madame Girard, who rushed out to cluck and coo over him, checking his hand for cuts while the waiter swept the glass from the pavement. But there was no damage except for a damp patch on his trousers, and he refused a replacement for his drink; there were no answers to his problems to be found at the bottom of a glass.

He would be much better occupied calling his office to see what messages Mark Reed had left for him, if any.

But Mark Reed had no news for him. Gerald Carlisle, however, had left several messages. 'He's desperate to know if you've managed to speak to a man called Fairfax,' Jenny told him. 'I take it you know what he's talking about?'

'Yes, unfortunately. And the answer is no. I've discovered he's in the South of France and I hope to find him tomorrow. That's all. Anything else?'

'Mmm. He asked if you'd said anything about seeing his daughter, given her a lift into London last night, perhaps? I said you hadn't mentioned anything to me.' She paused. 'It *was* just one suite of rooms you asked me to book for you?'

'There is nothing wrong with your hearing, Jenny.'

'No. I thought not. Only I wondered. What with all that business about your car. You never did explain why you'd had to borrow that little purple VW.'

'No, Jenny, I didn't. And if you continue to interrogate me like some overpaid QC I'll never tell you what happened. I promise you, you'll be sorry.'

'No, I won't. I'll ring Betty and ask her.'

'Betty?'

'What a sweet lady. She rang to thank you for the prompt return of her car and for all the lovely presents.' Jenny paused. 'She also gave me a message to pass on. She asked me to tell you…no, hold on, I wrote it down because I didn't want to get this wrong…she said ''The cards are warning against taking affairs of the heart at face value''. She said to tell you that ''Nothing is what it seems''. Does that make sense to you?'

'As much sense as anything else that's happened this week,' he replied caustically. 'If she calls again ask her if the cards can locate Kit Fairfax.'

'I won't wait for her to ring, Tom. I'm going to call her right now. Do you want me to tell Mr Carlisle that his daughter is with you? Or would you rather he didn't know?'

'I can get another secretary any time, Jenny,' he warned. 'I'll ask the agency to replace you with one of those leggy blondes—'

'And here was me thinking leggy redheads were the flavour of the month. I'll give your love to Betty, shall I?'

Returning to their suite, Brodie discovered that Emerald had taken him at his word when he'd told her not to hurry in the bathroom. She was wrapped in a bathrobe, her curly hair still damp from the shower, when he tapped at the bedroom door and was answered with a cheery, 'Come in.'

He stopped abruptly in the doorway. 'I'm sorry, I thought you would have been dressed by now.'

'Did you?' She paused in the careful application of mascara to look up at him, and immediately noticed the damp patch above his knee. 'Did you enjoy your drink?'

'Not particularly.' He headed for the bathroom. 'If I pass my trousers out to you, will you give them to Madame Girard? She's waiting outside, desperate to give them a sponge and press.'

She put down her mascara wand and followed him to the bathroom door, leaning with her back to the architrave while she waited for him to remove them and pass them out to her. 'This is all delightfully intimate, Brodie,' she called back through the door. 'But do you think it was what my father had in mind when he instructed you to stop at nothing to prevent my marriage to Kit?'

'Stop at nothing?' Brodie didn't recall Gerald Carlisle couching his instructions in quite those terms. 'That seems rather desperate.'

'Desperate situations need desperate measures. Kit, you know, is not his idea of a suitable son-in-law.'

'I had already gathered that.' Brodie, wrapped in a bathrobe, began emptying his pockets onto a small table just inside the bathroom door. 'What exactly is wrong with the man?'

'Haven't you read that great big file he gave you?'

'Not all of it.'

'Just enough to know all my horrible names.'

'I haven't had a lot of time.' He certainly hadn't been able to bring himself to take it out and read it while she'd been sitting next to him on the train. In fact he didn't want to read it at all. He'd much rather hear Emerald's story from her own lips. Over dinner.

'Oh, well, let me enlighten you,' she said obligingly. 'Kit is an artist, which, on its own, is sufficient reason to rule him out of the son-in-law stakes, you understand. Then there's the problem of money. He doesn't have any—'

'Which is why he's about to lose his studio.'

'He's not going to lose his studio—'

'Not if he marries you.'

She glared at him. 'Finally, and probably worst of all…' Brodie waited and she gave a wicked little shrug. 'Well, his hair comes down below his collar. Or would do, if he ever wore one.'

'Beyond the pale, without a doubt,' Brodie said dryly.

'You don't think that combination makes him a totally unsuitable husband?'

'Not necessarily—'

'Hollingworth would be very disappointed to hear you say that, Brodie, and so would my father. Are you sure you're the man for the job? It's not too late. You could still summon Hollingworth from his ritual Highland slaughter—'

'Just a totally unsuitable husband for you. While you, Miss Carlisle, would appear to be all Fairfax's dreams come true.' All *most men*'s dreams come true, if it came to that. *Without* the multi-million-pound inheritance from her grandmother.

'That's very cynical of you, Brodie. Don't you believe in true love?'

'Not when the advantages are so loaded in one direction.'

'Only on paper. You haven't met Kit, yet,' she said, pushing herself away from the doorframe and turning to take the trousers from him. 'So you're in no position to judge. He's going to be a great artist one day.'

'With you as his muse? You don't strike me as the kind of woman to live a second-hand life in someone else's shadow.'

She threw him a startled glance. 'I'd better hand these over to *Madame* if we're going to eat tonight.'

'A good idea. And just in case it occurred to you to do something drastic to them, Emmy, I should advise you that I do have another pair.'

She laid one hand against her breast, looking thoroughly shocked. 'Nothing so dreadful had crossed my mind, Brodie.' Then she rather spoilt the effect by adding, 'But I'd seriously advise you not to put ideas into my head.'

He grinned. 'You don't need anyone to put ideas into your head, Emmy. You've quite enough of your own.'

Emmy's answering smile was seraphic. 'A compliment, how sweet. But I promise I'll be good tonight. I'm hungry, and I have this strong suspicion that if I chop up your trousers with my nail scissors I won't be getting room service. I'll just be sent to bed without any supper.'

'You could be right. And I would consider it my duty to make sure you stayed there.' His own smile could scarcely be described as angelic. More like the devil in a good mood. 'You choose,' he said.

And suddenly she wasn't looking at him, challenging him. Instead her glance flickered self-consciously towards the big, cushion-heaped bed that dominated the room, and he saw a slow flush of colour steal into her cheeks before she once more turned her huge hazel eyes upon him. For the space of a heartbeat it seemed that the world stood still, a heartbeat in which nothing mattered but two people alone in a room...somewhere... Then a sharp rap on the sitting room door shattered the spell, and Emmy spun around and walked from the room without another word.

And Brodie turned and closed the bathroom door, leaning against it as he let out a long, slow breath. It was a long time since he'd felt an urgent need for a cold shower, but right now seemed like a good time. For a solicitor acting *in loco parentis*, he was spending altogether too much time in bedrooms with Emerald Carlisle.

Which, if she was as in love with Fairfax as she proclaimed, shouldn't have been a problem. So why was it? For both of them?

CHAPTER SIX

EMERALD was shaking as she opened the door and handed Brodie's trousers to Madame Girard. She returned cautiously to the bedroom. But there was no sign of Brodie, just the sound of water running from beyond the bathroom door.

She wasted no more time, but slipped out of the bathrobe and stepped into the simplest pale peach silk jersey dress that skimmed over her figure, stopping well short of her knees. Far too short, and the neck scooped in a way that suddenly seemed recklessly flirtatious. And, dear God, how she wanted to flirt!

Oh, no. Not just flirt. Whenever Brodie was near her all she could think of was reaching out to touch him, feeling his skin beneath her fingers, against her body. And he felt the same way—she knew it, had seen it in his eyes just now. Whatever that flash of recognition between them as she had hung from the drainpipe had been, it was like an irresistible force drawing them together. And the more time they spent together, the stronger it became. There was only one place it could end, and her eyes were drawn once more to the bed.

Why now? Why now when it was all just so impossible?

She was shaking with the sheer force of her feelings; her hands were trembling. She couldn't possibly wait until tomorrow morning to make a dash for it. The way things were going, tomorrow might well be too late. It would have to be now. She cast around her for the car keys, then remembered that Brodie had emptied his pockets in the bathroom.

The shower was still running—inside the frosted-glass cubicle he wouldn't see her—but her heart was beating in her mouth as she slowly eased the door open a crack. His wallet, some loose change and the keys were lying on the small table just inside the door. She carefully lifted the keys and began to back out, then she stopped and helped herself to the wallet as well, taking a thousand francs. After all, she reasoned, he wouldn't be short of money—he had hers in safe keeping.

Then she grabbed her low-heeled sandals and tiny shoulder bag into which her precious five hundred francs had already been transferred. Yet still she hesitated, glancing at the bathroom door, hating to leave like this, knowing what he would think of her.

Then the water stopped and she caught her breath. Why on earth was she dithering? She had seconds, not hours, and Brodie would come after her, she had proof enough that he wouldn't hang about wringing his hands. He was a man of action. She hung onto that thought as she beat a hasty retreat down the stairs, ignoring a startled cry from Monsieur Girard as she passed him in the lobby.

Her fingers were shaking so much as she tried to fit the key to the lock of the car that she was afraid she would set off the alarm, but finally it slid home without incident and she flung herself into the driving seat, dropping her shoes and bag on the seat beside her.

'Deep breaths, Emmy,' she said. 'Deep breaths. He

doesn't even know you've gone yet. And this time he won't know where you're going.' She glanced over the controls. They were all on the wrong side. Still, she'd been driving about her father's estate since she'd been able to reach the pedals with the help of a cushion. She would manage. She started the engine. It purred as gently as a contented kitten, and she carefully selected reverse. This was not the moment to demolish the front of the hotel.

She glanced behind her. Left or right? It was so confusing. Right…it was right… She looked…the road was miraculously clear, and she eased her foot down on the accelerator and began to move backwards.

'Emerald!' Brodie's voice thundered from the first-floor window in a manner that echoed a number of unpleasant incidences earlier in her life. The time she'd run away from school. The occasion on which she'd borrowed her father's Bentley to run down to the village shop for some hairspray. She'd been fifteen at the time. Or was it fourteen? The last time had been when she'd run away with Oliver Hayward…

She didn't hang around to discover if Brodie in a temper resembled her father in any other way. She jammed her foot down hard on the accelerator and swung out of the parking space. Behind her there was a screech of brakes and a crunch of rending metal that sent her flying forward. In her hurry she'd forgotten her seatbelt, but the airbag erupted with admirable efficiency, saving her from the worst effects of her own stupidity.

It did not, however, save her from a torrent of Gallic abuse that she was fortunately largely unable to understand.

Besides, an angry Frenchman was nothing compared to what she could expect from Brodie. She looked up as, white with rage and shaking with fury, he wrenched the car door open.

'Are you hurt?' His voice was shaking too, she noticed. He had a smear of shaving cream beneath his right ear and he was standing in the street barefoot, wearing nothing but a bathrobe. And they were being rapidly surrounded by a crowd of onlookers, each of whom had an opinion about what had happened and was determined that someone should listen.

It was very loud and rather frightening, and all she wanted was for Brodie to hold her and tell her that it would be all right. But he wasn't about to do that. He was going to shout at her for being a stupid, irresponsible *girl*, and that was worse, because he was right. So she put her hands over her ears and closed her eyes.

But he took her hands away from her ears. 'Emmy?' Brodie's voice almost cracked, and she turned as she realised that he wasn't angry, that he couldn't care less about the car, or the crowd, or the fact that she had behaved like an absolute idiot and had no doubt brought down a whole barrel-load of trouble on their heads.

He was only concerned about her.

At that moment she could have thrown her arms about him and kissed him. Instead she just shook her head. 'No. I'm not hurt,' she said as a tiny shiver seemed to sweep over her from head to toe.

He noticed. 'You're sure?'

'I'm sure,' she snapped irritably. Much as she longed for him to hold her, kissing him was not an option.

But he must have put her irritation down to shock

because, rather than responding in kind, he eased his arm gently beneath hers to help her out of the car, as if she were made of something very precious, very fragile. And she discovered that she needed the help as her legs buckled and she sagged against him. He put his other arm about her and held her against him.

'Emmy?' he repeated, more urgently.

Oh, God. He was so gentle, so concerned that she wanted to weep at the unfairness of it all, but as the tears squeezed from beneath her eyelids she laid her head against his chest so that he shouldn't see.

'I'm sorry, Brodie,' she muttered into the fluffy white towelling. 'I'm so sorry.'

He said something soothing, and she was almost sure he kissed the top of her head. That just made things ten times worse. Especially as the driver of the other car had come closer in order to abuse her more directly, and was perfectly happy to include Brodie in his insults.

But as she flinched Brodie began talking quietly to the man, and although she didn't understand everything he said she understood enough to know that he was taking the blame, telling him that she had not been looking because she had been upset, because they had quarrelled.

The onlookers began murmuring amongst themselves, uttering wonderfully Gallic exclamations of understanding, warmly reminiscent of French wine commercials, and she caught phrases such as *'affaire de coeur'* spoken in a knowing manner. And then she was aware of a sudden and expectant hush.

'Emmy?' She glanced up. 'I'm afraid everyone is waiting for us to kiss and make up,' he murmured.

'Oh?'

He pushed the tumbled curls back from her cheek, gently brushing the tears from her lashes with the pad of his thumb. 'This is France, you see,' he said, as if that explained everything.

'I see. And if I kiss you it will help…?'

In answer, he cradled her cheek in his hand. '*Je suis désolé, chérie…*' he murmured softly, for the benefit of the onlookers. They clucked encouragingly but she didn't rush the moment.

'Don't be *désolé*, Brodie,' she said. 'I'm the one who should be apologising. I did promise to be good…'

'You did…but I assumed you had your fingers crossed.' His eyes were cloaked beneath heavy lids as he looked down at her.

'A girl has to take every opportunity that presents itself,' she said, by way of justification. 'You should have locked the bathroom door.'

'I thought I had. Apparently the lock doesn't work.'

'No, I'd already discovered that for myself.'

'Of course. Well, here comes the payoff and you'd better make this look convincing, sweetheart, because you weren't insured to drive that car, and if this fellow turns nasty no amount of your father's money will save you from a trip to the magistrates' court.'

'Not even with my own personal lawyer in tow?'

Her own personal lawyer did not look particularly happy about that. 'Your own personal lawyer can only offer advice. It's up to you whether you take it.'

'And he advises a passionate reconciliation?'

'Please, Emmy.' *Please, Emmy.* How blissful that sounded. 'Now,' he urged, 'they're getting impatient.'

But she needed no urging. Rocking up onto tiptoe,

reaching up to put her arms around his neck, she looked straight into eyes as dark as rain-washed slate and then she closed her own and touched her lips to his. Around them the crowd drew in a single, audible breath. But Emmy didn't hear. All her senses were concentrated on Brodie. On the warmth of his skin beneath her fingers, the scent of his body, the taste of his mouth against hers.

His lips were cool and he made no move to deepen the kiss. He had just brushed his teeth and she could taste his toothpaste, clean, sharp and stimulating, against her lips, but she wanted more than this chaste salute, and so, she suspected, did the onlookers. Make it look convincing, he had said. Take your lawyer's advice…please. And for once it would be her pleasure to obey him.

Her lips parted softly, inviting his participation, and her tongue teased gently inside his lip. For a moment he remained quite still, as if transfixed by her touch. Then, without warning, Brodie took control, his mouth coming down hard on hers, meeting her invitation head-on until the desire she had been desperately trying to suppress since their eyes had met over her father's unsuspecting head pooled in her body and she melted against him.

It was madness, but it was blissful madness. But this had been Brodie's idea, and for a brief moment she could let herself go, forget any concern about betraying her feelings. This was one kiss she could enjoy without ever having to pretend and she was going to make the most of it.

After a few moments she became aware at some basic level of consciousness that the crowd were beginning to clap in time as the kiss was drawn out, then there was a long, juddering mass sigh as Brodie seemed to gather himself, easing back from the kiss.

Her eyes flickered open; she was suddenly afraid of what she might see in his eyes. Would he be angry with her? Disgusted, even, that she could declare love for one man and kiss another as if one of them were going to war? But he was simply staring down at her, his face a mask, betraying nothing.

Then he turned away to murmur something to Monsieur Girard, before bending to catch her behind the knees, lifting her into his arms and carrying her back towards the hotel, pausing briefly in the entrance, turning with a slight bow to acknowledge a chorus of cheers.

Once inside, however, Brodie dropped her to her feet, looking at her as if he didn't know quite what do with her.

Emmy, suddenly rather afraid that his tender concern was about to evaporate, hurriedly said, 'What about the car?' It was still slewed halfway out into the road, presumably with a sizeable dent in its rear.

'Girard is dealing with it. And he'll settle things with the other driver, too.' He regarded her with exasperation. 'You're running up quite a bill, Emmy. I hope you think your artist is worth it.' He didn't wait for her reply but turned and headed for the stairs. She began to follow him but he turned and blocked her way. 'Stay here, Emmy.'

'Why? What are you going to do?'

'Nothing.' There was a muscle working overtime at his jaw, she noticed. He was a man holding himself very firmly in check. 'Absolutely nothing if you stay here and behave yourself while I get dressed. I'll be ten minutes, no more, and then we'll go and find somewhere to eat.'

'But—'

'Don't argue with me. Just do as you're told for once, because next time you try a stunt like that I promise you won't get off so lightly.' She was right. The concern had burned out in the heat of that kiss. Well, it had been worth it. But she wasn't about to let him see that, so she glared up at him.

'What will you do, Brodie?' she challenged, arms akimbo, as beneath his scorn she forgot all about being sorry for causing so much bother. 'Put me over your knee?'

'Something like that,' he said tightly. Then repeated the words. 'Something like that.'

Like? *Like?* What the heck did that mean? And then with a little shiver she realised exactly what he meant. When he had referred to her 'stunt' he hadn't been talking about her bid for escape, or the car accident. He had been referring to the way she had kissed him.

And, remembering exactly what had driven her to make a run for it, her poor cheeks heated up in a blush that would have jump-started the national grid.

Brodie had not been idly boasting about the extent of his wardrobe. When, rather less than ten minutes later, he returned to the hotel lobby he was dressed in a pair of lightweight chinos and a polo shirt in an uncommon shade of petrol-blue that did something curious to the shade of his eyes. In a more self-conscious man Emmy would have suspected that it was deliberate. In Brodie's case she had the depressing suspicion that it had been the choice of some woman, some incredibly glamorous, sophisticated woman who never gave him a moment of trouble and whose kisses were responded to with rather more enthusiasm. Although, come to think of it, his response had been extremely enthusiastic at the time…it was only on reflection that he had decided she had followed his instructions with rather too much enthusiasm. The thought served to cheer her slightly.

'You're still here, then,' he said, looking up from fastening his watch.

'I didn't have much choice.' She wiggled her bare toes. 'I left my shoes and bag in the car, and your tame hotelier has them tucked away somewhere.'

'And you let a little thing like that stop you?' He regarded her with a certain wry amusement. 'You really mustn't let these minor set-backs dampen your determination, Emmy.'

'I won't,' she promised. 'But all the determination in the world won't get me beyond the end of the street without shoes.'

He retrieved her possessions from the girl behind the reception desk and handed them to her. 'All you had to do was ask.'

She made no attempt to disguise her disbelief. 'You really expect me to believe that?'

He shrugged. 'It was worth a try. Now you'll never know whether you'd have got away with it.'

'There's about as much chance of pigs flying,' she retorted irritably. 'Besides, I'm hungry.'

He smiled at that. 'If you want to eat I'm afraid you'll have to return the thousand francs you took from my wallet.'

She opened her bag and handed the money to him. 'It was only a loan. You would have been quite welcome to reimburse yourself from the money you took from me,' she informed him.

'I'll remember that, should the need ever arise.' He made it sound extremely unlikely. He waited while she slipped into her sandals. 'Ready?' She nodded, rising to her feet. He frowned. 'Sure? You still look a bit pale.'

Only because she spent so much time in his company blushing. 'I'm absolutely fine. Don't fuss.'

'I'm not fussing. If you hit your head in that shunt, just tell me. I don't want you passing out with concussion.' He *did* care, she thought happily, before he spoilt the effect by adding, 'I'd never be able to explain it to your father.'

For a moment she was tempted to consign her father, and Brodie with him, to the devil. But she couldn't stay cross with Brodie for more than two minutes together, and instead she giggled. 'It would almost be worth it to see you try,' she said. Then she slipped her hand through his arm. 'Come on, Brodie. Let's have a look at this sunset you've been promising me. I warn you, it had better be good.'

The sunset was brief but spectacular, colouring the sky in a kaleidoscope of reds and pinks and purples that provided a brilliant backdrop to the city and the harbour with its forest of bobbing masts belonging to all kinds of crafts, from huge luxury yachts to the more workaday fishing boats.

'Well,' Brodie asked as he settled her at a restaurant table on a terrace overlooking the harbour. 'Did it live up to its billing?'

'Not bad,' she said. 'A bit flashy for my taste. I prefer the silver and pink ones with the little bubbly clouds.'

'I'm afraid there is a cloud shortage in this part of the world right now, and frankly I hope it stays that way. Storms in this area tend to be rather like the sunsets.' Emmy lifted a querying brow. 'Spectacular with a definite leaning towards flashy,' he said.

'You seem to know your way about around here.'

'Yes, well, I worked as a deckhand on a yacht based here for a couple of summers. While I was at university.'

'Lucky you. After the unfortunate affair with Oliver Hayward I was condemned to spend all my long vacations trailing around museums in the company of an aunt.'

'Poor lady,' he said, with feeling. 'She has my sympathy.'

'No, I was good.' She flickered a glance in his direction. 'Honestly, Brodie. She would have been so distressed if I'd done anything scandalous... Besides, the Victoria and Albert Museum has a very sobering effect on me,' she added seriously.

'I wish you'd told me that before we left London; I'd willingly have sacrificed half a day in the interests of dampening your sudden urges to bolt. But I'm sure I could work up a fairly convincing degree of distress if it would encourage you to behave,' he offered.

'Could you?' She smiled absently. 'No, Aunt Louise felt so utterly responsible, I just couldn't upset her. She's a perfect love.'

'And I am not?' He grinned. 'Don't worry, you can say it. You won't hurt my feelings.'

'You are not in the least bit like my aunt Louise,' she said, carefully.

'And, besides, you had the whole of term-time in Oxford in which to get up to all the mischief in the world.'

'That's true.' She regarded him evenly. 'I also managed to cram in a first-class honours degree. It was a busy three years.'

He stared at her for a moment and then he shook his head. 'I'm sorry, Emmy. I was being extremely rude—'

'Yes, you were.' Then she reached across and laid her hand on his. 'But there's no need to apologise. I've given you a rotten time and you've been wonderful. I don't know what I would have done about that man who ran into me if you hadn't been there.'

'Yes, you do.' He ignored the fact that if he hadn't been there she wouldn't have felt the need to make a dash for it. But, no matter how sweetly her hand lay on his, he wasn't about to let her think she was kidding him. 'You'd have batted your eyelashes at him and had him at your feet in ten seconds flat.'

'That's a perfectly horrible thing to say!' she protested, jerking back her hand.

'Is it? You forget I've had first-hand experience of the technique—when you were swinging from that drain-pipe. And then you have a very interesting technique with stockings—'

'I did not bat my eyelashes! I was far too desperate to think of it at the time, and I had to put on my stockings or my shoes would have rubbed. Anyway, it's perfectly obvious that you're not at my feet, Brodie.'

He wasn't so sure about that, but it would undoubtedly be a mistake to tell her so. The slightest sign of weakness and she'd be twisting him around her little finger.

'No, well, I seem to spend all my time chasing after you. Even when you've promised to be good. I can't do that if I'm on my knees.' The waiter was hovering and, glad of the distraction, Brodie asked Emmy what she would like to drink.

'St Raphael, white, please,' she replied.

'And a Ricard for me,' he added, taking the menu. 'So, if it's not to be bouillabaisse, Emmy, what would you like to eat?'

'Grilled *rougets*, and a *mesclun*, please.'

'Wouldn't you prefer to look at the menu before you decide?'

'No.' She smiled, propping her elbows on the table and her chin in the palms of her hands. 'I know what I want.' He turned and asked the waiter if it was possible to have simple grilled *rougets* with a leaf salad. The waiter, eyes fixed on Emmy, assured him that it could be done.

'Do you always get what you want that easily?' he asked, once he had given the man his order.

'Not always. I didn't get Oliver Hayward. And if you and my father get your way I won't get Kit.'

'Oliver Hayward? He's the guy your father bought off when you were eighteen? Are you still mad at him about that?'

'No, I have to admit that Oliver was a mistake,' she told him. She gave a little shrug, embellished it with a tiny smile. 'I met him on that really long holiday you get between A-levels and university. I was staying with friends in Italy for the summer and so was he. Long, golden days with nothing to do except eat, drink, swim and fall in love. And Oliver was terribly easy to fall in love with. He was as pretty as a picture, a charmer of the first water, the kind of man that mothers warn their daughters about.'

She pulled a face. 'Unfortunately my mother was always so busy having affairs with men exactly like him that she never got around to it. I suppose I should be grateful that he took my father's money. It showed him up for what he was.' She leaned back and linked her hands behind her head. 'He was very apologetic about it. Assured me that he was heartbroken, but he could see my father was serious about stopping the wedding whatever it took. He said he didn't want to make life difficult for me.'

'For *you?*'

'Hmm. Thoughtful, huh?' She grinned, broadly, dispelling any thoughts that she might be harbouring a lingering passion. 'And he managed to console himself with a new car.'

'Were you really in love with him, Emmy?'

'Or just winding up my beloved papa? Not guilty, Brodie. I've never had to work at it that hard. All I was guilty of was being eighteen years old and madly impressionable.' She shrugged. 'Then I was just mad. At Dad *and* Oliver. Dear God, the man could at least have held out for more...to have taken Hollingworth's first offer suggested a certain lack of...'

'Commitment?' Brodie offered, when she hesitated.

'The word I had in mind was guts.'

'Maybe he just had a particularly firm grasp of reality.

Maybe, once someone had offered him the choice, he weighed the advantages of a hundred thousand pounds in the bank against the responsibilities of marriage and realised that he needed a new car more than he needed a wife. Particularly one who was likely to cause him a whole lot of bother.' He paused. 'What is Kit Fairfax driving, by the way?'

She lowered her lashes. 'That was below the belt, Brodie.'

'Just a thought.'

'Well, think about something else. As far as this conversation goes, Kit is off-limits.'

'Whatever you say.' He leaned back and, taking a swallow of his drink, regarded the harbour. 'It's odd, though. In my experience women usually find it impossible to stop talking about the man they are in love with.'

'I am not most women.'

He glanced briefly at her. 'That has not escaped my notice.' Then he gestured to the scene in front of them. 'Which of those boats do you wish you were on right now?' She regarded him distrustfully. 'I'm changing the subject, as requested, Emmy,' he said, quite gently.

'Oh.' She glanced at the harbour, then pulled a face. 'I sail in nothing smaller than the QE2. I get seasick.'

'You do have a bad time travelling, don't you? Frightened of planes, sick in boats... Now, me, I'd like to be aboard that big job over there, setting out for the Aegean, cruising around all those lovely islands, poking about the ruins, picnicking on the beach, sunbathing.'

'Is that what you used to do? When you were a deckhand?'

He gave her an old-fashioned look. 'No, Emmy.

That's what the people who chartered the boats did. I fetched and carried and cleaned up after them.'

'Did you enjoy it?'

'Not all of it. But I had the sun and the chance to swim whenever I had an hour to spare. And some of the people who chartered the boats were really kind.'

'The women, you mean,' she said, cynically.

He laughed, revealing a full set of white, even teeth. 'Maybe I do. I can assure you that it beat the hell out of stacking shelves in a supermarket. And I didn't have to pay rent.'

She looked at him for a moment, then said, 'You must think I'm very stupid.' She stared down into her glass. 'Over-privileged and thoughtless and very stupid.'

'No, I don't think that. We come from different worlds, that's all. I've had to work for everything I've ever had. But that's okay. The harder you work for something, the more you appreciate it.'

She thought about his amazing apartment, the pictures he had collected. Everything by the sweat of his brow, unlike her own flat, filled with hand-me-down antiques. Even the flat was a hand-me-down, inherited, along with her wealth, from her grandmother.

'Where do you come from, Brodie? What kind of people?' He didn't answer straight away, and once more she reached across the table as if to touch his arm, then apparently thought better of it and withdrew. 'I'd really like to know.'

He shrugged. 'My father was a miner. He was a big man, full of life. He loved to play cricket—he was good too. And he liked to walk—anything, really, to be out of doors breathing good, fresh air.'

'What happened to him?'

'He was killed in an accident underground when I was twelve. A machine...' He caught himself. What the machine had done to his father was not a fit subject for polite conversation. 'I'd just been picked for the school cricket team. The youngest boy ever. He'd spent hours coaching me and he was so proud...'

'He never saw you play?' He shook his head. 'Life's a bitch, isn't it?' she said, and it suddenly occurred to Brodie that being abandoned by your mother as an infant couldn't have been a great start in life, no matter how many silver spoons Nanny had to feed you with. 'Did your mother never remarry?' she asked.

'No, she always said that Dad was too big an act to follow. But once I was off her hands she went to live near her sister in Canada.'

'She must miss you terribly.'

'She doesn't have time. Meg, her sister, had half a dozen children and they're well into the second generation now. I'd have to start competing in the baby stakes to persuade her to come back.'

'Why don't you?'

'It requires two, Emmy.' He glanced at her. 'The right two.'

'You're a "till death us do part" man, are you?'

'If you don't at least start with "till death us do part" as your goal there doesn't seem to be a lot of point. Marriage is enough of a lottery without being handicapped by a lack of commitment.'

'I suppose so. I guess I had a lucky escape when Oliver chose the money.' Emmy glanced at Brodie and discovered that she, too, was the object of thoughtful contemplation. 'Oh, look, here comes our supper.' She smiled brilliantly at the young waiter and he blushed, and when she caught Brodie's eye again he was no longer regarding her thoughtfully, but with exasperation.

'Do you have to do that?' he demanded.

'What?'

He just shook his head. 'It's not kind, Emmy.' She continued to stare at him, eyes wide. 'Nor is that,' he said, suddenly angry.

CHAPTER SEVEN

BRODIE sat back while the man served their food, taking the chance to regain mastery of a libido racketing out of control. What on earth was the girl playing at? Was it unconscious? Had she no idea of the effect she had on him? Or was she doing it deliberately to distract him, knowing damn well that he was in no position to respond to the signals she was flashing at him?

The way she had kissed him outside the hotel had been a no holds barred, one hundred per cent effort, and for a few giddy moments he had forgotten everything but the way she felt in his arms, the way they seemed to fit together like two halves of the same piece, how desperately easy she would be to love. Well, he had urged her to be convincing, so perhaps he'd deserved everything she'd thrown at him.

But any more convincing and he'd have found it hard to remember the reason they were in France, to have left her downstairs in the hotel lobby when the only thing on his mind had been a bed that seemed to be taking on vast proportions, filling their suite, filling his head with thoughts of Emerald Carlisle that had nothing to do with business and everything to do with pleasure.

His desire for her, fired the moment he had set eyes on her, had now settled into a permanent dull ache that made him feel too small for his skin, made him long to be able to tear off his clothes and jump into the harbour to cool off.

The situation was intolerable, and a sane man would be wishing himself anywhere but here. But he wasn't. He couldn't think of anywhere he would rather be. Which made the thought of what would happen tomorrow unbearable. Either way. Because, whilst he was determined to carry out Gerald Carlisle's instructions to the letter, he couldn't bear the thought of Emerald being hurt. Again. No matter how lightly she had brushed it off, rationalising it as a lucky escape, he knew that Oliver Hayward's faithlessness had hurt.

And he hated Gerald Carlisle for the kind of heavy-handedness that had made it inevitable. It had obviously been a holiday romance, the kind that flares and dies as quickly, leaving precious, bittersweet memories, a few old photographs to be smiled over years later when the kids found them stuffed away in a box in the attic. Her father had destroyed all that.

'Tell me about your job, Emmy,' he said abruptly as the waiter reluctantly moved away. When she didn't say anything he looked up. She was regarding him with a slightly puzzled expression, rather like a puppy who has been yelled at but has no idea why. He wanted to wrap her in his arms, kiss her, reassure her that everything would be fine. But he couldn't do that. There were no guarantees, even if he knew exactly what she wanted. All he really knew was that she was determined to get to Kit Fairfax before him.

'Please,' he added, aware that he had been curt, that as his throat had tightened with longing his words had come out like an order rather than a conversational gambit.

She continued to look at him for another thirty seconds before she finally lowered her eyes and picked up her fork. 'I told you, I'm a trainee at Aston's, the auctioneers. I'm doing the rounds at the moment—you know, three months in each department.' She toyed with her fish. 'But I want to specialise in toys and automata. Mechanical toys,' she explained uncertainly.

'Little singing birds in cages, that sort of thing?'

She laughed, breaking the tension. 'That sort of thing,' she agreed. 'And a whole lot more. Some are wonderfully elaborate groups of figures—beautifully dressed musicians, clowns, beggars even. They were always rare and prized.' She pulled a tiny moue. 'Rich men's toys, Brodie. They cost a fortune even when they were first made. The very finest ones were made here in France.'

'Really? I didn't know that. Do you collect them?'

She gave him an odd look. 'Do you really think that Hollingworth would let me loose with that kind of money?'

'I couldn't say. He doesn't discuss his clients' business with me unless he wants a legal opinion. Your petty cash hardly comes into that category, Miss Carlisle.'

'Hardly petty cash, Brodie. But it's academic anyway. I believe the best pieces should be in public collections where they can be properly cared for and everyone can enjoy them. Too much wonderful stuff is locked away, never looked at until it has appreciated in value sufficiently to be auctioned on to someone else who'll probably do exactly the same with it.' She was positively glowing with fervour, her red curls shining like a halo under the lights. 'It's such a waste.'

'You could buy one and donate it to the V and A,' he suggested. 'Maybe it would make the place less sobering...'

'The Victoria and Albert Museum, Brodie, is sobering in the right kind of way. It makes you stop and think. All that work, the skill, the dedication of centuries of craftsmen, some of them working for just pennies to make useful things as beautiful as the heart could aspire to, things that the people who made them could never afford to have themselves...' She trailed off, slightly embarrassed. 'Actually I did buy a little automaton a few months ago. It's just a moth-eaten little monkey with some cymbals, with a very simple movement. It needs some work but a craftsman I know is going to help me to restore it.'

This was safer ground, for both of them. 'How do you go about that?' Brodie prompted. But she needed little encouragement as her enthusiasm for her subject carried her away. Describing the mechanical figures she had seen, amazing finds unearthed in barns, the fabulous prices some had made at auction, carried them easily on through fish and a melt-on-the-tongue apple tarte, to coffee and cognac.

'I'm sorry; I just get carried away once I start,' she said eventually. 'I've bored you rigid.'

Recalling the animated manner in which she had described her job, her enthusiasm, her obvious love for her work, he shook his head. 'You don't know how to be boring, Emmy.'

'Was that a compliment?' she enquired, so doubtfully that Brodie laughed out loud.

'Now you're just fishing. Come on, I think it's time we went back to the hotel. You've a big day ahead of you tomorrow, and I'd like to make an early start.'

'You're a glutton for punishment, Brodie. Don't you ever just turn over and lie in for half an hour?'

Yesterday his response would have been to offer to lie in all morning if she was prepared to join him. But flirting with her was no longer an option for him. He wanted her too much.

'You've clearly never slept on a sofa,' he said, taking care to keep his voice expressionless.

She had, but not in circumstances she was willing to discuss. 'I'd offer to swop, but you'd undoubtedly think I was planning to tiptoe out and make a run for it the moment you were asleep,' she said.

'Now, why on earth would I think a thing like that?' he enquired gently.

'But then again,' she continued, ignoring his question, 'you did make the reservations, so presumably you knew what to expect.'

'I wish. Come on, let's go and look at the boats.' She looked doubtful. 'Don't worry, I'm not planning to shanghai you.'

'Shanghai me?'

'Slip you a Mickey and whisk you aboard while you are senseless.' She still looked puzzled. 'Don't you ever watch old movies?' he asked. She shook her head. 'You don't know what you're missing. A Mickey Finn,' he explained, 'is something slipped into a drink to knock you out. Once you're unconscious you get smuggled aboard some boat that's just leaving harbour, and by the time you wake up you're miles out to sea.'

'But why?'

'In your case to whisk you out of harm's way.'

'Kit would never harm me,' she said, her eyes pure gold in the reflected light. 'Unlike your friend Mickey,' she added solemnly. Then a dimple appeared at the corner of her mouth. He wanted to kiss it so badly that it was like an ache.

He probed at it, like a man worrying a bad tooth, taking her hand in his to cross the road. Her fingers were long and slender, the bones seeming impossibly fragile beneath his broad palm, stirring in him a desperate longing to protect her. What was it about this girl? She made him feel like a boy, awkward, foolish with his spiralling need for her.

She wasn't the first woman who'd turned his head. No man could reach thirty-one without making a fool of himself more than once. But she was the first woman he'd ached to love and yet whose desires and needs he knew he would always put above his own.

Tomorrow he was very afraid that he would lose her. But if Kit Fairfax was strong, if he was the man she wanted, he knew he would do everything in his power to help them. Was that the difference between lust and love?

But for the moment he retained his grasp on her hand as they wandered back towards their hotel along the edge of the harbour, and she seemed perfectly content to leave her fingers curled about his.

It was one of those perfect, bittersweet moments to store up against an empty future, he thought as his hand pressed against the small, hard circle of gold that she wore on the third finger of her left hand, the tiny diamond that Kit Fairfax had given her as a token of his love. She'd been fiddling with it unconsciously all evening, as if clinging to what it represented. Brodie punished himself with that thought. But he didn't let go of her hand.

'Is that the boat you would like to be on?' Emerald asked, stopping to point to one of the larger yachts.

He dragged his mind back to the harbour and less dangerous thoughts. 'Yes, that's her. Not exactly the QE2,' he observed, turning to lean on the rail, tucking her hand beneath his arm. 'But she's quite a beauty.'

'Yes, she's lovely. Perhaps in the right company I wouldn't notice the motion.' She turned to look up at him. 'Tell me, Brodie, if you could sail away right now where would you go?'

He thought for a moment, staring out across the harbour, listening to the rattle of the rigging as the yachts rose and fell on the water, remembering sun-filled days when he'd still had everything to prove. He'd proved it. Worked his way out of a pit village until he was standing in the South of France with an heiress on his arm. But he was suddenly faced with the realisation that unless she was his none of it meant anything. She was still looking at him, waiting for an answer. Where would he go?

> 'The isles of Greece, the isles of Greece!
> Where burning Sappho loved and sung,
> Where grew the arts of war and peace,
> Where Delos rose, and Phoebus sprung!

Eternal summer gilds them yet,
But all, except their sun, is set.'

Brodie quoted the words softly, yet with such an intensity of feeling that Emmy suspected his real reason for working as a deckhand had owed more to some romantic schoolboy notion to visit the magical isles of Greece than any disinclination to stack supermarket shelves. Beneath that lawyer's stern exterior there beat the heart of a poet, an adventurer.

But then she had known that the moment she'd set eyes on him. And he had confirmed it by not betraying her. Lord, how she hated what she was doing to him! One more day. Just one more day…

It took every ounce of determination to instil a teasing note into her voice. 'I ask for an itinerary and I get Byron,' she said, with forced lightness. *'Don Juan*, no less. You're not exactly boring yourself, Brodie.' Then a yawn caught her by surprise.

'Not boring, huh?'

Her face, illuminated softly by the lights of the boats and the reflections off the water, filled with sudden laughter. 'No, Brodie,' she said. 'Whatever else you could say about today, it was certainly not boring.' She stretched up on her toes and kissed his cheek. 'Thank you for being so kind about the car.'

Kind? She left him bereft of words. What had she expected him to do? Shout at her? Shake her? He loved her, for heaven's sake. Loved her. In twenty-four hours she had swept into his life and turned it upside down. And he knew without the slightest doubt that he would gladly die for her.

Yet tomorrow he had to do everything in his power

to persuade a man she thought she was in love with not to marry her. If he succeeded would she think him kind then?

Or was she simply trying to disarm him?

He resisted the temptation to turn his head, shift the kiss to her mouth. Instead, he lifted her hand to his lips and kissed the tips of her fingers.

'Just don't do it again,' he said thickly, turning her towards the hotel.

'No. No, I won't.' They walked on for a moment. 'Brodie?'

'Mmm.'

'Tomorrow, will you let me talk to Kit first? Just for a few minutes?'

He glanced down at her, but she was looking straight ahead, avoiding his eyes. He guessed that answered his question. 'No, Emmy,' he said, his heart like lead in his chest. 'If he loves you, you've got nothing to worry about.'

Emerald, lying tucked up in the huge bed all by herself, lay awake and worried. She simply had to speak to Kit before Brodie started on him or all her plans would just come crashing down around her ears.

She fiddled with the ring she was wearing. The wretched thing didn't fit properly and she had to keep bending her finger to stop it from slipping off. Well, one more day and she could take it off, and good riddance, but first she had to get to Kit, explain the situation to him before Brodie turned on the pressure. And this time there must be no mistakes. She needed a proper plan rather than making a grab for freedom when a chance presented itself. She'd tried that three times and it hadn't got her anywhere.

Well, actually, taking her chances had got her as far as France. If she hadn't taken the chances when they had been offered she would still be mouldering at Honeybourne.

And taking her chances had got her Brodie. Emmy's smooth brow puckered momentarily into a frown. Brodie was very special, a strong man who didn't use his strength to bully her like her father.

She could hear him moving about the other room, as wakeful as she was. What was he doing? Just pacing about, unable to sleep on that wretched sofa? It was the second night he'd been forced to surrender his bed to her. She was six inches shorter than him and fifty pounds lighter. The least she could do was offer, sincerely this time, to change places with him.

She eased herself out of bed, padded across the darkened room and opened the door a few inches. Brodie had come to rest in a large armchair on the far side of the room. He was wearing the thin track-suit bottoms but hadn't bothered with a T-shirt, and the golden light from a lamp on the table behind him pooled on the silken skin of his shoulders, throwing the sculptured lines of his chest into sharp relief, hinting at the darker cruciform shadow of body hair.

He was so beautiful that her heart clenched with longing to throw open the door and run to him, fling her arms about his knees, beg him to sail away with her to his wonderful islands. If he would just look up so that she could see his eyes, see them unguarded as he suddenly noticed her. Then she saw the open file on his knees. He wasn't about to look up; he was too absorbed in Mark Reed's file to be aware of her presence, too busy trying to work out what kind of man Kit Fairfax was and just how likely he was to take the money and run.

A mixture of emotions boiled up in her. Resentment, mostly, but with an undertow of something raw and painful. Brodie was supposed to be her knight in shining armour. He was. Or rather he had been. But tomorrow would be different.

And if tomorrow was going to produce the results she wanted she had better start thinking instead of dreaming.

She closed the door and climbed back into bed.

So far she had relied on chance, taken her opportunities as they had presented themselves. But now she would have to make things happen. She needed a plan.

It didn't take a lot of devising; she didn't have a lot of choices open to her, or much time. She abandoned any thought of trying to creep past him while he was asleep. The risk was too great, and if she failed, he would make certain she didn't have another chance.

No, she would wait until Brodie was taking a shower in the morning. He was sure to let her use the bathroom first. Then, once he was at his own ablutions, she would have a few moments in which to escape. She'd only take her handbag, leaving her overnight case, her make-up on the dressing table, so that he wouldn't be immediately suspicious.

Maybe she should leave her handbag, too? All she

really needed was the five hundred francs she had hidden from him. And a handkerchief. And a lipstick. Her little diary with directions to the farmhouse. Nothing that wouldn't slip into the pockets of her jeans.

If only she could have been sure she had enough money for a taxi, but she didn't know how far the village was from Aix. How far the farmhouse was from the village. Kit had been terribly vague about distances; extracting the directions from him had been difficult enough when he'd been absorbed in his work.

She wished she had taken a closer look at that street map of Marseilles downstairs in the hotel reception, taken more notice of the buses and where they stopped. But the truth of the matter was that she hadn't been taking notice of anything except Brodie.

'Où est l'arrêt d'autobus pour Aix, s'il vous plaît?' she murmured half a dozen times or so, until the phrase rolled off her tongue without difficulty.

Satisfied, she slipped down beneath the cover and closed her eyes. The question was no problem. All she had to worry about now was whether she would understand the answer.

'Emmy? Are you awake?' She groaned. To anyone with half a brain it was perfectly obvious that she was fast asleep. The man was obsessed with getting up at the crack of dawn, and not even the smell of fresh coffee could redeem him this time. 'It's nearly eight-thirty,' he added.

Her lids flickered open. *Eight-thirty?* Could she have possibly heard that right? She eased herself into a sitting position, pushing her hair back from her eyes, and blinked sleepily. It had been a long time before she had slept last night. 'It can't be,' she said.

'I'm sorry. I left you as long as I could, but I do want to get this over with. I'm sure you do too.'

She groaned again. Kit. Her neat little escape plan all blown out of the window because she had overslept. Brodie, showered, shaved, dressed and ready to go, sat on the edge of the bed and handed her a cup of coffee.

'Here, this will help,' he said.

He was wrong, nothing would help, but she took it and sipped it anyway. 'Thank you.'

'Any time. There are some fresh croissants in the other room whenever you're ready.'

Coffee, croissants—room service? 'I thought we were supposed to eat those out on the pavement in the sun, watching the world go by?'

'Maybe tomorrow,' he said vaguely.

'Tomorrow?'

'You with Kit, perhaps. Me on some pavement café somewhere. Wherever the mood takes me.'

She gave him an old-fashioned look. 'Not if you can help it.'

'It's not what I'd prefer,' he agreed. 'But we have a deal. If your artist is the kind of man that money can't buy, I'll leave the field.' Then, 'Honestly,' he said, with the faintest of smiles. And it was then she noticed a slight greyness around his mouth, a heaviness to his lids. She was not the only one who had had difficulty sleeping last night.

'I believe you,' she said, putting out an impetuous hand, but he moved before she could touch him, stood up, and, remembering his accusation that she was not kind, she thought she understood why. *Oh, Brodie!* she thought, wistfully. *Hold on. Just hold on.*

'I cannot, however, guarantee your father's reaction,' he continued. 'If you stay in France he'll have a month in which to regroup. I've no doubt he'll summon Hollingworth from Scotland. Maybe he'll even call on your aunt Louise.'

'Maybe he'll ask you to shanghai me,' she offered. Not that she'd need a Mickey Finn to persuade her to sail away with Brodie into the sunset. Well, maybe just to get aboard. Once at sea she was sure he would distract her from any inclination towards *mal de mer*.

Her attempt at levity, however, was not appreciated.

'He could ask,' Brodie said, stiffly, 'but as his lawyer I'd have to inform him that it would be a criminal offence.' Then, slightly exasperated with her, 'You're an adult, Emmy, you can marry any number of fortune-hunters if you want to.'

'Always provided I remember to keep to one fortune-hunter at a time,' she said, dryly.

'Maybe you should try telling your father that.' He paused, but only to gather breath. 'And, while you're telling him maybe you should ask him whether your happiness is less important than preserving a bank full of money that your family has been handing down since time immemorial, each succeeding generation increasingly nervous that someone might cheat them out of it.'

His concern cloaked her in warmth. But it was more than just concern. There was real feeling in his eyes, in his voice. And something more. Something she suspected he would not wish her to see. She wanted so much to reach up, put her arms about him and pull him down beside her, forget about the outside world. She only hoped that when this was all over he would be able to forgive her deception. That his eyes would still burn when he looked at her.

'My father isn't bad, Brodie. He just worries about me. Probably with good reason,' she admitted. 'He's afraid I might turn out like my mother.'

'Then he's a bigger fool than I thought.'

He took the empty cup from her. He would have liked to add that it was his sincere wish that Fairfax would send Gerald Carlisle a message that would leave the man in no doubt as to what he should do with his money. But he couldn't bring himself to frame a sentiment that wasn't true. He wanted Kit Fairfax to be a snivelling, miserable reprobate who'd snatch his hand off. Unfortunately, he didn't think that likely. He didn't think Emmy was the kind of girl to make the same mistake twice.

'Quick as you can, Emmy,' he urged, although why he should have to urge her to hurry to her own wedding he wasn't quite certain. It wasn't something he wanted to think about.

Emmy waited until the door closed behind him. Then she rocketed out of bed, already adjusting her plan to meet the unexpected changes thrust on her by Brodie's thoughtfulness in letting her sleep on.

She rushed into the bathroom, turning on the shower full blast, leaving it to run while she retrieved her few basic essentials from her handbag and stuffed them into her jeans pocket while she had the chance. Then she took her time about showering and dressing in jeans and a white T-shirt, the kind of clothes everyone was wearing and would not be immediately noticeable, or memorable. And she took ages putting on the minimum of make-up. Brodie was impatient to be off. The more impatient he got, the more chance she had of succeeding.

She was zipping up her bag when Brodie finally knocked. 'How're you doing in there, Emmy?'

'I'm all ready.' She opened the door and handed him her overnight bag. 'But starving.' She tossed her handbag onto an armchair and headed for the croissants. 'Is there any more coffee?' she asked, settling herself on the sofa. Brodie poured her a cup, then picked up her bag. 'Oh, aren't you going to have one with me?'

'No. I'll go and pay the bill and put the bags in the car. It'll save time,' he said pointedly.

She smiled serenely, apparently oblivious to his urgency. 'Oh, right. Good idea.' She bit into the warm, buttery pastry. 'Mmm. These just don't taste the same when you buy them in London, do they?' she said, capturing a crumb with the tip of her finger and redirecting it towards her mouth. She was being quite deliberately provocative, sensing that it would drive him away more quickly than anything.

'I wouldn't know. I require rather more than a piece of pastry to see me through a working day.'

The minute the door closed behind him, she abandoned the croissant and crossed to the bathroom. She turned on the tap at the sink then carefully shut the bathroom door. She left the bedroom door open so that he would hear the water running and think she was in the bathroom. And she left her handbag on the chair where she had thrown it. Because every man knew that there wasn't a woman born who could manage without her handbag.

And then she let herself out of the bedroom and hurried towards the back stairs, startling a chambermaid with a pile of towels as she rounded a corner.

'Non, non, madame,' the girl said, pointing to the main staircase as she rattled out a rapid stream of French. But Emmy, an imploring look in her eyes, put her finger to her lips and gestured towards the staff stairs. The girl's eyes widened, then Emmy saw understanding dawn. She pointed again to the back entrance of the hotel, and once more the girl launched into incomprehensible French.

The French might have been beyond her, but it was obvious to Emmy that she had an ally—an ally, moreover, who would know the way to the bus stop. She repeated her carefully rehearsed question, but as she had feared the directions were too rapid, too complicated, and time was running out.

Emmy, the star of countless school plays, pointed dramatically to her watch and threw an anguished look in the direction of the main stairs. The girl, thrilled to be part of some romantic conspiracy, abandoned the towels on the hall table and led her by the back way from the hotel, dodging the kitchen staff, taking care that she was not seen.

She took her first down a narrow lane and then around a corner, where she stopped and pointed across the road to the bus stop. Emmy pressed one of her precious hundred-franc notes into the girl's hand. Her help had been worth every centime.

Ten minutes later she was on a bus headed towards Aix-en-Provence. It was, she knew, about twenty miles, half an hour by car, give or take a few minutes for traffic. By bus it would take longer, and she sincerely regretted telling Brodie which direction to take.

CHAPTER EIGHT

BRODIE was feeling absolutely bloody. He hadn't slept; he hadn't even tried. Instead he'd spent the night going through the file Carlisle had given him, trying to put his finger on what it was that was bothering him about this whole business. Trying, he knew, to find some damning piece of information about Kit Fairfax, some lever to use to make him back off without having to offer him money, because if he took it Emmy would never trust another man. And Brodie wouldn't blame her.

But Mark Reed had found nothing about Kit Fairfax that he could use as an arm twister. No drugs, no wife in the attic, no horde of illegitimate children. He was just one more struggling artist.

He would have liked to see some of his pictures, get a feel for the man through his work, but there was nothing like that in the file to help him.

Emmy had visited him at his studio a couple of times a week. A couple of weeks ago she had stayed overnight. He forced himself to ignore the hot rush of jealousy that engulfed him. Jealousy would not help; emotion would simply cloud his judgement. He uncurled fingers that had tightened around the folder, and after a few moments he continued to scan Mark Reed's notes. Not that there was much to learn.

Emmy had always gone to Fairfax's studio; he had never been observed going to her flat. She'd stayed an hour or so on each occasion…his fingers tightened again…then sometimes they'd gone to the local pub for a drink and a sandwich then she had gone home or on to somewhere else with friends. Fairfax had gone back to his studio. That was all. He'd never called her at work, or sent her flowers or behaved in any way like a besotted lover. Scarcely the whirlwind romance that Emmy had presented her father with. Or maybe that was what Brodie wanted to believe.

Yet Gerald Carlisle must have had some reason to put Reed onto Fairfax. He bent to pick up a piece of paper that had slipped onto the floor. It was a cutting from one of those glossy country magazines. There was a picture of Emmy looking wonderfully glamorous at some charity auction. And the man she was looking at with every appearance of stars in her eyes was Kit Fairfax.

If he'd been asked to make a judgement, he would have said that Emmy had simply thrown herself at the man. And if the affair was so one-sided it was possible that Fairfax would be a push-over.

He stared up at the hotel window. One girl, two days, and his life would never be the same. Whatever happened.

But delaying things was not helping. He'd stowed the bags in the car, paid the bill and still Emmy hadn't appeared. He continued to stare up at the window, unwilling to return to their suite, wishing he had told her to come down when she was ready. But there was no point in putting the moment off any longer. He went back inside, mounting the stairs two at a time.

'Emmy, are you ready?' he called as he opened the

door. 'Let's go,' he added, without waiting for an answer.

She wasn't in the sitting room. The bedroom door was open and as he approached it he heard the water running and shrugged. He returned to the sitting room, glancing around to make sure that nothing had been left behind.

There was nothing. Just her handbag on the chair. A croissant with one bite missing. The cup of coffee he'd poured her gone cold. He glanced back at the bedroom, anxiety clutching suddenly at his stomach. Was she sick? The change of water, different food…

'Emmy?' he called. 'Are you all right?' When she didn't reply he tapped at the bathroom door. 'Emmy?' He turned the handle, half opened the door.

And then in a flash he knew. He didn't need to see the water trickling from the tap into the sink, or to fling back the door on the empty bathroom to know what she had done.

He didn't stop to turn the water off. He didn't waste his breath on calling himself every kind of fool he could lay his tongue to. It might have made him feel marginally better for about ten seconds, but it wouldn't help him find Emerald Carlisle.

Hurtling through the door, Brodie practically bowled over the chambermaid. He grabbed her to steady her, full of apologies. Then as, blushing, she ducked away from him he turned back. She might have seen Emmy leave the hotel by the back way; it was certainly worth asking.

'Excusez-moi, mademoiselle,' he began. 'Avez-vous…?' But she backed nervously away before he could even complete his question, jabbering nervously about how busy she was, how late it was, diving into the nearest bedroom in her anxiety to avoid him.

Such obvious panic at the thought of being asked the simplest of questions made him pause. He could have been about to ask if she had seen his car keys, or if she had some soap, or something as mundane as the time. But from her reaction it would appear she knew exactly what he had been about to ask her and that she had something to hide.

He followed her to the doorway. 'Which way did she go?' he asked in French, without further preliminaries. Then, 'Did you lend her money?' He took out his wallet, intending to repay her.

'*Non, non, monsieur!*' She shook her hands at him, holding him at a distance as he advanced upon her.

She was young and very nervous. Realising that he would get nowhere by scaring the girl, he explained patiently that he only wished to repay her. Dumbly now she shook her head, and took out a hundred-franc note to show him.

So, Emmy had had money all the time. He wondered how much. The one thing he didn't need to ask himself was where she'd kept it hidden. Clearly babysitting Emmy Carlisle was no job for a gentleman.

'Where was she going?' he asked, firmly but quietly. 'Tell me now, or I'll have to fetch Madame Girard.' The prospect of interrogation by that indomitable lady was too much for the girl and she began to weep.

Brodie raised his eyes to the ceiling. Heaven alone knew what Emmy had told her. Not much. Her French was not up to some elaborate tale of wife-beating or worse. Even supposing she'd had the time. But with a sigh, a gesture… He'd experienced the technique first-hand and she'd reduced him to slavery with little more than a look. He handed the girl his handkerchief and waited, curtailing his impatience with difficulty, until her sobs had subsided. Then he set about convincing her that he intended Emerald no harm.

Placing his hands gently on her shoulders, he looked down at her. *'Mademoiselle,* she is in the gravest danger,' he said, with quiet urgency, disregarding the truth. The truth was that he hadn't the slightest idea what kind of danger Emmy had got herself into, if any, but until he did he wasn't going to let her off the hook. The girl's eyes widened. 'I have to find her before she does something foolish.' The girl continued to stare at him. 'I love her,' he declared in desperation, his hands tightening on the girl's shoulders. 'I love her.' He repeated the words in the manner of a man who had just discovered some hitherto unsuspected truth. 'I swear that I would never do anything to hurt her.'

Thirty seconds later he was reversing the car out of the parking bay and heading for Aix, while the young chambermaid was sitting on the bed she was supposed to be stripping, clutching a hundred-franc note in each hand, a big grin on her face, congratulating herself on having swopped shifts with her sister.

'Aix' wasn't much of a clue. But it was a start. Once there she would undoubtedly be heading out into the country for some cottage or converted farmhouse belonging to friends. She would only have to make a quick phone call once she'd reached the town and Fairfax would come and meet her. Then it would be like searching for a needle in a haystack. If he didn't find her first.

Halted at a junction blocked solid with traffic, he punched Mark Reed's number into his mobile phone. 'Mark? Tom Brodie. What have you got for me?'

'Not a lot. None of Miss Carlisle's friends seem to know where she was going, or if they do they're not telling. The only lead I've got is a postcard sent by Fairfax to his next-door neighbour, telling him that things were taking longer than he anticipated and asking him to continue feeding the cat until he comes home—'

'Things?'

'Your guess is as good as mine. The postmark is un-readable, but the picture is of a painting by Cézanne of a mountain—'

'La Montagne Sainte Victoire?'

'That's it. He said on the card that it was the view from his farmhouse window.'

'I know it. Unfortunately it's the view from half the region. But at least we're in the right area. All right, Mark, that's some help.'

'Given you the slip again, has she?' he said, not with-out sympathy. 'She's quite a girl for that. Ducking you in Harvey Nic's and then giving you a little wave when she gets home with her shopping. Just to let you know she knows you're there.'

'I'm considering handcuffs,' Brodie said, tight-lipped.

'Poor kid's been in handcuffs, metaphorically speak-ing, ever since she was old enough to have a mind of her own. Carlisle should try trusting her for once; she's his daughter, not his wife.' He seemed to hesitate. 'She's a nice girl, Tom.'

'Yes.' The traffic began to edge forward. 'Tell me,

you've seen them together, would you say she's in love with Fairfax?'

'I couldn't say. She always seemed flirtatious around him, but, as I said, she knew she was being watched. It could all have been a bit of a game to tease her father, if you know what I mean.'

'Yes, I know exactly what you mean,' he said, with considerable feeling. She liked to tease.

'She's done it before, you see. Once she cottoned on to the fact that he checked up on her boyfriends. She moved into a flat with one of them once and the Honourable Gerald was fit to be tied. In fact the bloke had gone away and she was just looking after his plants. At least that's what she said, when he went charging around there, as if butter wouldn't melt in her mouth.'

'Is that right? Well, if her friends are being cagey, why don't you try the diary editors? They can't resist showing off just how much they know about what's going on. It's getting urgent, Mark.' Another couple of hours and she would have won.

The traffic began to move and gradually he edged free of the town centre traffic and headed for Aix. He caught up with the bus after half a dozen miles or so.

A bus, he reminded himself; it might not be the right bus. And the possibility that the chambermaid might have been lying to protect Emmy had not escaped him, although she had been in such a state of confusion that it seemed unlikely. But Emmy must have anticipated he would question the staff, and she was quite capable of laying a false trail. He was beginning to think she was capable of anything.

Hadn't she escaped from a second-floor room at

Honeybourne, stowed away in his car, then stolen it the moment the opportunity had presented itself? She had never ceased trying to evade him, trying to get to Kit Fairfax before he could talk to him.

Why? What did she have to tell the man that would make such a difference to the outcome? Whatever it was, she clearly wasn't convinced that love would be enough to hold him steadfast.

It was that belief that drove him on. There was, after all, no imminent danger of the marriage taking place. But there was *something*...and he refused to be beaten by a leggy girl, even if he was crazy about her.

He tucked in a few cars behind the bus and mentally crossed his fingers, hoping that Miss Emerald Carlisle hadn't had time for anything as complicated as laying false trails.

No. There was Kit's postcard. He frowned, picked up the mobile lying on the seat beside him and pressed redial. 'Mark? Tom Brodie, again. Did Fairfax say *his* farmhouse on that postcard?'

'I think so. Hold on a minute, I wrote it down.' There was a pause while he consulted his notebook. 'Yes, that's what he said; "my farmhouse". Ah, I think I see what you're getting at. I'll ring you back.'

Emmy had chosen to sit in the centre of the bus on an aisle seat. The last thing she needed was Brodie cruising past in his car and spotting her carrot-coloured mop of hair. It stood out like a beacon amongst the dark-haired locals. She should have worn a hat, or a scarf. Except she hadn't packed one. There was no way she could have anticipated that she would be hiding out on a bus...

She leaned forward to see past the plump matron who occupied the window seat. Cars sped by, but there was no sign of Brodie. She tried to recall exactly what she had said to him. North and then east. Would he be able to work it out? In time?

She turned the other way and glanced behind. There was a stream of traffic, any number of dark-coloured Renaults. But this was France; what did she expect? As she straightened a young man in the seat opposite smiled at her. She smiled back automatically.

They were coming into a village, and the bus pulled over. The woman beside her made a move to get out and Emmy stood up to let her by. It was at that moment, as the cars behind swooshed past, that she found herself looking straight down out of the back of the bus into Brodie's face. For a moment she froze, unable to decide whether to stay put, run for it, or simply surrender.

The bus moving forward, throwing her sideways, made up her mind for her. She lowered herself onto her seat and tried to think. Tried not to look behind her. He had been so quick! Whatever had he done to that poor chambermaid to get her to tell? She grinned. Smiled at her. That was all it would have taken. But even so. To get so quickly on her trail…

But then, what had she expected? It was his quick wits that had so delighted her when he'd allowed her to escape from Honeybourne in the first place. But since then he had matched her every step of the way, countering every move she made with a persistence that was driving her to the point of desperation.

The bus had seemed for the briefest space of time to be her salvation. Now she was trapped on it. The moment she stepped off it he would be there, and this time there was the distinct possibility that he wouldn't be as kind as he had been when she had reversed into that car.

She would thank him for that, properly, when all this was over. The briefest of smiles crossed her lips as she paused momentarily to dwell on the pleasures to come. But for now the most important thing was to get away from him. An hour, that was all she needed...

In the front of the bus the driver was using a radio, or telephone, to talk to his control centre, and Emerald gave a little gasp as an idea came to her.

She immediately rejected it. No. No, she couldn't do that. It would be too dreadful... Brodie would never forgive her... But there was Kit to think of...

She got up, made her way to the front of the bus. *'Pardon,'* she began, hesitantly. The bus driver glanced at her. *'Parlez-vous anglais?'* The driver shook his head. Aware that all the other passengers were straining to hear, she turned to appeal to them. 'Please,' she said. 'I'm being followed by a strange man. He stole that car.' She pointed to the rear of the bus. Two dozen pairs of eyes glanced behind and then turned to regard her expectantly. *'Un stalker!'* she tried, a little desperately. They were getting close to Aix. *'Un stalker anglais!'* She picked up the driver's telephone. *'Appelez les gendarmes!'* she declared dramatically.

As the driver, urged on by his excited passengers, summoned assistance on her behalf, Emmy collapsed back into her seat, vowing that she would enrol for French lessons the moment she got home.

Brodie wasn't sure what Emmy thought she could accomplish by staying on the bus. She would have been more comfortable getting off and joining him in the car. Yet at each stop she seemed to make a point of showing him that she was not getting off, turning to look at him with those luminous eyes as he waited patiently for the passengers to alight and the journey to continue. It made him uneasy. But what could she do on a bus?

On the outskirts of Aix he discovered exactly what Emerald Carlisle was capable of as two police cars, lights flashing, moved in on him, one swerving in front of him forcing him to a halt, the second closing up behind him.

Brodie switched off the engine of the Renault and climbed out of the car, holding his hands clearly in sight as the *Gendarmes* descended upon him, but he wasn't looking at them. He was watching the bus pull away from him. And Emmy looking back at him. She mouthed something. Could it have been 'Sorry'? He rather thought it had been.

But he was in no hurry to forgive her for this. In fact at that moment he sincerely regretted not having called the police when Emerald Carlisle had stolen his car. He could so easily have told her father that he hadn't known he had Emmy on board. She wouldn't have betrayed him.

A few hours in a police cell might have made her think again about the advisability of runaway weddings. And she would have been handed straight back to her father. He was beginning to sympathise with the man.

No. Sympathising with Gerald Carlisle was going too far.

But as his hands were fastened none too gently in

handcuffs and he was bundled into a police car he wondered just what she had been finally driven to. What had she accused him of to bring the police down on his head at breakneck speed? Nothing trivial, he could be certain of that. And unlike an angry driver with a dent in his front wing, the French *gendarmerie* would not be soothed by a few thousand francs.

Emmy stared out of the bus window as the police cut Brodie out of the traffic and brought him dramatically to a halt. Everyone on the bus cheered and smiled at her approvingly.

She felt truly terrible. Terrible for what she had done to Brodie. Terrible for deceiving these kind people. She shouldn't have done it. She should stop it now, but as she rose to her feet the bus accelerated away from the scene. She stood, clutching the back of her seat, her heart doing ridiculous, impossible things, one moment in her throat, the next in her boots as she saw the *Gendarmes* advance on Brodie, saw him climb from the car, saw him staring after her. She mouthed a desperate 'sorry', but it was too late.

The moment she arrived in Aix she would go straight to the local police, explain to them what she had done. Then they would have to let him go. She subsided into her seat, oblivious to the excited chatter around her.

But suppose they let him go and kept her in custody for wasting police time? He would still be angry with her, maybe so angry that he would leave her there in the police station until he had found Kit and discovered exactly what she had been planning. Maybe he wouldn't even do that. Maybe he would just go straight back to

England and leave her locked up until Hollingworth was despatched to extricate her from yet another mess. She wouldn't blame him. She wouldn't blame him one bit. But she couldn't take that risk.

No. What was done was done. She would wait until she got to the village near Kit's farmhouse and *then* she would telephone the police, or it would all have been a waste and Brodie would have been arrested to no avail.

At least this way his suffering would have some point. She knew he would come after her, if only to tell her what he thought of her. She was counting on that; she had every confidence in her ability to make him see reason. She smiled a little in anticipation. Once it was all over he would have to admit that she had done everything from the best of motives. And he would understand. He would forgive her.

She would make him forgive her. She had to, because although it had been her intention to make him fall in love with her, just a little, she knew without doubt that she had fallen head over heels in love with him. It had been impossible not to. He was her match. Her equal. The man she had been waiting for ever since Oliver Hayward had taken her father's money and run.

And they struck sparks off one another, sparks that were all the more potent because although they had both felt the same urgent attraction, they had both been constrained by the situation. Emmy because she had to keep up the pretence until everything was settled…and Brodie, well, Brodie had a job to do.

Even so, she thought, they had had a couple of close calls. But it was impossible to do anything, say anything until the decks were cleared, until Kit—

Damn, damn, damn. She banged little clenched fists against her knees. Why on earth had it all been so complicated? If that wretched woman…what was her name? Betty. If Betty hadn't loaned Brodie her car none of this would have been necessary. She would have been away, free.

But Brodie, it seemed, could charm an apple right off a tree. It was just as well he hadn't realised how easily he could have charmed her…how easily he could have driven everything from her mind…

Or maybe he had. Maybe he was waiting for her to make the first move, admit that she wasn't being entirely honest about Kit.

Or maybe she was just kidding herself.

She absently twisted the ring on her left hand, then, realising what she was doing, she held out her hand to look at it. It was a pretty little thing. She'd seen it in the window of one of those shops that sold second-hand wedding rings and old silver forks and she'd bought it on an impulse. She'd never said it was an engagement ring, or that Kit had bought it for her, but had simply slipped it onto her ring finger and left her father to draw his own conclusions. It had served its purpose well enough, but now she eased it off her finger. The time for deception had passed.

The youth on the other side of the aisle was watching her, apparently fascinated by the flash that even the tiniest diamonds could produce when combined with sunlight. And there was plenty of sunlight. She pushed the ring into her jeans pocket and lifted her hair from her neck, letting the air to her skin.

The bus slowed as it reached the station and she rose

quickly, eager to be away, to get everything organised before Brodie showed up—and he would certainly do that, one way or another, before the day was out. She might have set the police on him, but her story had been so outrageous that it would soon be seen for what it was and he would be released.

Then he would be able to conclude his business with all the speed at his command and get on with his holiday. Or maybe not. He could hardly leave her with Kit once he'd bought him off. Could he?

As she swung down from the bus she looked about her, uncertain which way to go. The young man who had been sitting opposite her stumbled as he followed her down the steps, and she put out a hand to help him as he fell against her.

He muttered embarrassed thanks and hurried away. Several other passengers stopped to wish her *"bonne chance"*.

It was her turn to suffer embarrassment, and she too moved quickly away from the bus stop, looking around for a taxi rank, anxious to get to the village as quickly as possible.

Once inside the police station Brodie was deprived of all means of harming himself and was left to cool his heels in a cell, presumably while they checked his identity against his passport and his business card. He made no protest at his treatment, remaining polite, calm and co-operative as he answered the officers' questions, aware that bluster and bad temper would only delay things.

Once the police realised that they had been made fools

of, they would be only too happy to help him find Miss Emerald Carlisle.

Her story had better be a good one, or he might be tempted to leave her locked up until her father came to bail her out. It was certainly what she deserved, he thought grimly.

Emmy was hungry. She didn't dare waste time going into a café but, spotting a patisserie she decided to buy something to eat in the taxi. She chose a couple of savoury pastries and asked for a can of soda.

It came to twenty-seven francs. She didn't have enough change from the bus fare, and put her hand into her other pocket for a hundred-franc note. The woman waited patiently while she searched. Two jeans pockets, no matter how deep, did not take a lot of searching. The notes had gone. And so had the little engagement ring. She remembered the youth stumbling against her at the bus stop and realised, with a sinking heart, that her pocket had been picked as cleanly as a ripe plum.

He had seen her put the ring in her pocket. The money had just been a bonus.

'*Pardon, madame,*' she said, backing away from the counter. '*J'ai perdu ma monnaie…*' Her French, at least, was coming on in leaps and bounds. She hadn't even had to think about that.

There was some sympathetic clucking, but Emmy knew she did not deserve sympathy. She had behaved badly and this setback was no more than her just deserts.

As she turned and walked from the shop someone called after her, advising her to go to the police station and report her loss. She raised a hand in acknowledge-

ment, but it was hardly an option under the circumstances. Brodie might be locked safely away. On the
other hand, he might just be telling the local police all
about Emerald Carlisle and what she had done. They
would not be amused. Neither would he.

She counted the change in her pocket again.
Twenty-two francs, a few centimes. That wouldn't take
her very far. All that was left was to telephone the bar
in the village and hope Kit was there. Or that someone
would go and find him if she could summon up sufficient
French to explain how urgent it was, that she was
stranded… She glanced around, looking for a telephone
kiosk, and spotted the post office. There was bound to
be one there.

The phone did not take money, only *jetons*. She parted
with a few more of her precious francs to buy the tokens
and went back to the box. It was only then that she
realised the pickpocket had taken her diary too, undoubtedly assuming that it was a wallet. How on earth could
he have got away with so much in that quick stumble
against her?

She sighed. She'd been told once that a skilled pickpocket could empty a buttoned-down shirt pocket while
he looked you right in the eye and smiled. Besides, it
didn't really matter how it had been done, what mattered
was that she now had no idea of the telephone number
of the café.

The dial at the centre of the telephone tantalisingly
offered Renseignements. Unfortunately Enquiries would
not be able to help since she didn't know the name of
the café or the proprietor.

Kit had simply telephoned with the number as a contact point. And she'd only managed to persuade him to do that on the pretext that someone she knew had seen one of his landscapes and wanted to commission him to paint the view from her house.

And there was worse. The directions to the farmhouse were written in her diary. Without it she would never be able to find the wretched place.

Emmy wandered back out into the late-morning sunshine. It was blisteringly hot, but the air was heavy, threatening, full of electricity. She bought a cold soda from a kiosk, sat on a bench and drank it slowly, trying to decide what to do next. Phone her father? Tell him where she was and that she was stranded without enough money to buy herself a sandwich? Or should she walk across to the police station and throw herself on Brodie's mercy?

She took a franc from her pocket and twisted it round and round in her fingers. Heads or tails?

She didn't need to toss a coin. Her choice had been made the moment he had kissed her. No, before that. The moment he had nearly kissed her. The moment she had known that being kissed by him would be a definitive experience and that ever afterwards anyone else would be an anticlimax. But she didn't intend there should be anyone else.

Across the square a musician was playing a violin exquisitely. He was playing a piece she loved, 'Romance' from *The Gadfly*. On an impulse she got up and crossed the square, dropping every last centime that she had into the hat. Everything that she had. A libation to the gods.

Then she turned towards the police station.

CHAPTER NINE

BRODIE was offered sincere apologies for any inconvenience he might have suffered, coffee and any possible assistance—in that order. He accepted the apologies gracefully, assuring the officers that they had nothing to reproach themselves for.

He declined the coffee; he had already had two cups while he was waiting for his bona fides to be confirmed. As for assistance, he wondered if it would be possible for the police to help him trace an Englishman residing somewhere in the region.

It took no time at all for them to locate the whereabouts of Mr Christopher Fairfax, and furnish Brodie with his address. He was offered an escort to show him the way. He declined. He'd managed to convince the police that this was a lovers' quarrel, that Emmy had taken a step too far. They had been amused, sympathetic and a donation to the police welfare fund had ensured that they would not pursue the matter. He didn't want them present when he finally caught up with Emmy and Kit, or they might have cause to doubt his word. Besides, he'd had quite enough of policemen for one day.

Then as he turned away from the desk he was confronted by the most unexpected sight. Emerald Carlisle, her red curls glowing like a copper halo in the sunlight, walking through the door of the police station.

Some angel.

Yet it was all he could do to prevent himself from going to her, wrapping her in his arms and telling her that it was all right. That he understood. Because he did understand. Not why she had done it, perhaps, but that she had been driven to it by desperation.

'I thought you would be miles away by now,' he said, keeping his distance.

Emmy stopped uncertainly at the sound of his voice, blinking as her eyes adjusted themselves to the dimmer light after the glare outside. Then she saw him, his face utterly without expression as he faced her. Relief flooded through her that he was free. She made a move towards him, wanting to fling her arms about him and beg him to forgive her. The rigidity of his posture stopped her. No. It would take more than a kiss this time to put things right.

So she lifted her shoulders a touch awkwardly, attempted a wry smile. 'Me too,' she said. It would have been so easy to lie at that moment. To tell him that she had been so full of remorse about what she had done that she had turned back, unable to leave him to the terrible fate she had inflicted upon him. 'I would have been, but I had my pocket picked as I got off the bus.'

'Really?' He was cool. She could hardly blame him. 'And have you come to report this heinous crime to the police? They are incredibly efficient. Believe me, I have first-hand experience.'

'Brodie—' she began, then stopped. She would not plead with him to understand. 'No.' She pushed a damp curl back from her forehead. 'No. I came to confess what I had done to the police and throw myself on your

mercy, but obviously you've managed to extricate yourself without my help—'

'I have, with a little help from my friends. But I
should warn you that I'm feeling a little short in the
mercy department at the moment, Emerald.' He regarded
her with ill-disguised irritation. 'Why didn't you just
phone Fairfax and ask him to come and fetch you?'

'The only number I have for him was in my diary.
All that my youthful thief left me was my handkerchief.'

'Perhaps he suspected that you would need it when I
caught up with you.'

'I'm sorry, Brodie. Truly. I shouldn't have done it.'
He made no move to meet her halfway. 'Was it dreadful?'

'I've had better mornings,' he said, moving towards
the door, leaving her to choose whether to follow him
or not. For a moment rebellion threatened, then Emmy
turned and followed him. She had no choice. He glanced
at her. 'At least you had the sense to tell them the car
was stolen. It took the police all of five minutes to call
the rental agency and establish that was a lie. After that
they were more inclined to believe me—'

'What did you tell them?'

He stopped, turned and looked down at her. 'That I
am simply a hard-working solicitor trying my level best
to keep a tiresome young woman out of trouble.'

'Oh.' And succeeding rather well, she thought. 'Did
they phone my father? To confirm your story,' she
added.

'It wasn't necessary. My office was able to reassure
them that I wasn't a kidnapper, or a stalker, or whatever
story it was that you told them.' Although how long it

would take him to live it down when he got back did not bear thinking about. Jenny would have a field day. 'And then, of course, Monsieur Girard was happy to confirm that he'd known me for at least ten years.'

'I am sorry, Brodie. I just couldn't think of any other way.'

'Don't keeping saying you're sorry, Emerald. You'd do it again without a moment's hesitation if you thought you could get away with the car.'

She remembered the awful sick feeling as the police had closed in on him, as the bus had pulled away from the scene, when all she'd wanted to do was go to him. 'No, Brodie, I wouldn't—'

'I realise that you're getting desperate, Emerald. Perhaps it's time you did me the courtesy of explaining what exactly you're so desperate about. Over lunch?' he offered. 'Since you skipped breakfast.'

His formality was chilling. The way he had started calling her 'Emerald'. Well, what else had she expected? It could have been worse; it could have been 'Miss Carlisle'. One thing was certain: he wasn't about to hug her and tell her how glad he was to see her. Right now he was probably wishing he had never set eyes on her, and she could hardly blame him.

'Thank you,' she said. 'But actually I'm not feeling very hungry.'

'There's no need to be pathetic, Emerald. I'm not going to beat you.'

'I'm not being pathetic,' she said, with a flash of fire. 'I'm not hungry.' And it was true. Her stomach was in knots of anguish. She climbed into the car and quickly wound down the window to let out the suffocatingly hot air. The musician on the other side of the square had stopped playing. He had packed away his violin and was picking the coins out of his hat. So much for her libation. Perhaps the gods had taken offence at the *jetons,* although surely even violinists must need to make phone calls. She turned to Brodie as he climbed in beside her. 'And I never for a moment thought you would beat me.' And then some tiny devil inside her prompted her to add, 'Just put me over your knee. Or something like that. Wasn't that what you said?'

His eyes darkened, dangerously. 'My God, Emmy—' Then, clearly regretting the outburst, he said simply, 'You would try the patience of a saint.'

Satisfied that she had at least broken through the ice, she smiled at him. 'You're no saint, Brodie, although I realise that you've been trying very hard to give that impression.' Her reward was to see his fingers shaking, just a little, as he fitted the key to the ignition and started the engine. 'Where are we going?'

'The police, in an effort to recompense me for the discomfort of the past hour or so, have gone out of their way to be helpful. Fortunately for both of us they have managed to discover the whereabouts of Mr Fairfax. I think the sooner we go and talk to him, get this nonsense over with, the better. Don't you?'

'I've been trying to get to him ever since I climbed out of the nursery window, Brodie. But I promise you, it isn't nonsense. If you'd only agreed to let me have a few minutes alone with him before you put my father's proposition to him, I wouldn't have run away this morning.'

'Why?' He turned briefly to look at her. 'What are

you going to promise him? Double whatever your father is prepared to pay to get rid of him?'

Her face flamed. 'Do you really think I'd do that?' she exploded, angrily. 'After Oliver?'

'I don't know what you'd do, Emmy. Whatever would most upset your father, I suspect.'

'This isn't anything to do with my father.'

'Isn't it? Aren't you determined to marry a man you know your father will disapprove of simply to spite him for the way he broke up your romance with Hayward?'

'No!' She was shocked that he could think such a thing. 'It isn't like that. Honestly.'

'Honestly? Then why don't you tell me what it *is* like?' he suggested, rather more gently. 'Maybe I can help.'

'I can't. And if I did explain you wouldn't be able to help. You couldn't. Don't you see, Brodie? I'm just trying to do my best for everybody.'

'Then God help us all if you ever decide to do your worst.'

She turned to face the road. 'I really don't want to talk about it any more.'

He shrugged, swallowed a yawn. 'Whatever you say.' As they reached a crossroads he fished a piece of paper out of his shirt pocket and consulted it before turning left. 'Are you any good at navigating?' he asked, handing it to her.

'You'd trust me?'

'I'm simply assuming that you're as tired of these games as I am.' Another yawn crept up on him.

'Are you all right, Brodie?' Emmy asked, finally noticing the dark hollows beneath his eyes. 'Do you want me to drive?'

'No, I don't want you to drive,' he snapped. 'I want you to navigate.'

'Your halo is slipping,' she said, then when he refused to respond she shrugged and consulted the sheet of paper. 'This is written in French.'

'That's because it was written by a Frenchman. Didn't they teach the language at your school?'

'They must have done. I just don't seem to recall going to any of the lessons. I think we turn left just up here.'

'You think?'

'Left, definitely.'

'So long as you're sure,' he said, with heavy irony.

'There should be a signpost.' There was. Vindicated, she made a little bow.

'Don't get carried away, Emmy. We've miles to go yet.'

'Kilometres,' she corrected. 'How many?'

'You've got the directions; work it out for yourself.' He glanced at her. 'Are you beginning to wish you'd taken me up on my offer of lunch?'

'Mmm. Still we could stop in the village,' she said hopefully. 'I know there's a café there. It's where I leave messages for Kit.'

'Did you leave one the night we stayed at my flat?'

'Only to say that I was on my way. He might not have got it, if he hasn't been into the village. Perhaps we should stop there anyway and check whether he's left a message for me.'

'He seems a somewhat tepid lover.' She didn't reply.

'Don't worry, Emmy, I won't let you starve. I didn't have much breakfast myself. And I could do with something long and cold.' He wiped his sleeve across his forehead and peered up at the sky. It had lost that clear, deep blue, become murky and threatening.

They drove on for a while through rugged hills, woods, and mellow, rolling farmland splashed with russets and sharp greens. And always in the distance, first ahead of them, then shifting to the right as the road veered away, was the evocative marbled ridge of Montagne Ste Victoire.

It was early afternoon by the time they pulled up in front of a small café in the village square. It had to be the one. There was only one. They went inside to get away from the relentless heat and Brodie asked for two citron pressés and a large bottle of mineral water.

Emmy left the talking to him. She was just too hot, too exhausted to even think about Kit.

'The *patron* is asking his wife to make us a couple of omelettes,' he said, joining her at a table.

'Fine.'

'Fairfax hasn't been here for days.'

'Great.' She put her head down on her arms. 'Is it always this hot?'

'I think it's probably building up to a storm.' She groaned. 'Don't tell me, you're scared of thunder.'

She managed a grin from beneath her curls. 'I had a series of perfectly bloody nannies, Brodie, each of whom made a point of passing on her own particular neurosis. But actually it's not thunder that bothers me. At least, not much. It's lightning. Nanny number six hundred and thirty-two knew someone who had been struck by it.'

She sat up and drew a finger dramatically across her throat. 'Fried to a crisp.'

Brodie regarded her doubtfully. 'That's quite a line in bedtime stories.'

'It certainly makes Beatrix Potter appear rather tame,' she agreed. 'Although I seem to remember something about a fierce, bad rabbit. He got blasted by a hunter with a shotgun so that only his tail and whiskers were left.'

'You're kidding me?'

'No, I swear it. Her stories weren't all sweet and innocent, you know. Just look what happened to Peter Rabbit's father.'

Brodie, who had been spared these bloodthirsty tales as an infant, was curious. 'What happened to him?'

'He was put into a pie. Oh, look, here comes our food.' Omelettes, salad, bread and a bowl of local olives were spread on the table. 'It looks wonderful.'

Brodie spoke to the *patron*. Emmy, her ears becoming attuned to the language, picked up a little of what was said. 'Is there going to be a storm?' she asked.

'There's one forecast for late tonight, but apparently the forecasters have been promising it for a week so he's not holding his breath.'

'What do you think?'

'I'm a lawyer, Emmy; forecasting the weather is as much a mystery to me as it seems to be to the meteorologists. But I don't think we'll linger over this.' He picked up a fork and broke his omelette.

'That's reassuring,' Emmy said, following suit.

'If you've got a better plan I'm perfectly happy to listen to it.'

'No. We've come this far; we might as well get it over with.' She reached for the pepper grinder.

Brodie beat her to it, catching her hand. 'What happened to your engagement ring, Emmy?'

'It was picked, along with my money and my diary,' she said, flippantly.

'From your finger?' he asked, concerned, and was surprised to see the faint flush of colour rise to her cheeks.

'No, it was a bit loose. I put it in my pocket.'

'You must have been distraught when you realised it was gone,' he said evenly. 'You really should have reported it to the police or your insurance company might be difficult about covering the loss.'

'I hadn't got around to insuring it,' she mumbled.

It was doubtful if her insurance company would have believed her if she had, he thought. Women like Emerald Carlisle wore diamonds worth thousands of pounds. Or in Miss Carlisle's case surely an emerald would have been the stone of choice? An emerald flanked with diamonds. She certainly didn't seem to be desperately upset at the loss of the ring Kit Fairfax had given her. And he was quite certain that, no matter how tiny it was, she would have been distraught to lose a ring given her as a promise of love.

'Finished? Can I get you anything else?'

'No. I just need to go and freshen up; I won't be a moment.'

'Take as long as you like, Emmy. But if you decide to do a disappearing trick I'll turn around and drive straight back to Marseilles. And the car is locked, if you were thinking you might get away with your bags.'

'I wasn't. There wouldn't be any point. You know

where Kit is now, Brodie, and you'd get there before me. I know when I'm beaten.'

He watched her as she turned and walked away. Did she? Really? Somehow he doubted that. Half a chance, less, was all she'd need and he'd be the one left to find his own way home.

He took out his mobile and dialled Mark Reed. 'There's no need to spend any more time on this case, Mark; I've found out where Kit Fairfax is staying.'

'Staying is right. Apparently his father, a Frenchman by the name of Savarin, died recently, and young Mr Fairfax has inherited his farmhouse in Provence, a vineyard, an olive grove and considerable acres of very pretty countryside, along with some very nice property on the coast. According to the diary correspondent I spoke to, he has no intention of returning to England in the immediate future. All in the nick of time, because the lease on that studio of his was about to run out.'

Something prickled at the back of Brodie's mind. 'Why didn't he ask his father for help with that?'

'I understand they hadn't spoken for years. The father walked out on the mother—a common enough story— and when his mother reverted to her own name—Fairfax—the boy did too.'

'The son refused to acknowledge the father, but under French law the father couldn't disinherit his son.'

'So I understand. Maybe the Honourable Gerald won't be quite so disappointed with his daughter's choice after all. I wonder why she didn't tell him?'

'Who knows? Maybe she just wanted her father to accept the man she loved, no matter how unsuitable he seemed. Thanks for your help, Mark. I won't forget it.'

'Neither will the Honourable Gerald. My bill for services rendered promises to be memorable.'

Brodie stared out through the café door, seeing nothing. Something Mark Reed had said was important. He pressed his fingers against his eyes, rubbing them hard. If only he wasn't so damned tired.

'I'm ready, Brodie.'

He looked up to see Emmy standing in front of him. 'Oh, right. Let's go, then.' He paid the *patron* and led the way out of the café.

They turned off the narrow paved road that led from the village and had been climbing steadily for about twenty minutes along a country track carved into the hillside, its sandstone slabs worn away by cartwheels, when the first fat raindrop splashed on the windscreen, stirring the dust.

'How much further?' Emmy asked nervously, peering up through the windscreen at a sky that seemed to have darkened in seconds. A few sheep grazing on the hillside above them began to shift nervously, moving into a huddle around a little stone shelter.

'You've got the instructions,' he reminded her. 'But once we're on the other side of the hill we should be able to see the farm.' He hoped.

He used the washers on the windscreen and for a moment or two nothing happened. Then without warning the rain began to fall in a sudden torrent, cutting visibility by half as the weather closed in and the wipers struggled to keep up with the downpour.

Within minutes thick gouts of red muddy water were spilling off the hillside onto the road, churning up the loose dust on the surface and washing it away as the flood continued on down the hill.

Brodie's hands tightened on the wheel as potholes that had been filled with loose earth were washed out and the car began to bounce and shift on the uneven surface. Emmy clutched at her seat and fervently prayed that there would be no lightning. Neither of them mentioned turning back. There was nowhere to turn on the narrow track.

'Maybe we should stop,' Emmy suggested nervously. 'Just until it eases.'

'This could last for hours.'

She groaned. 'It's all my fault. We could have been here hours ago. Yesterday, even, if I hadn't lied about flying—' She broke off with a little scream as lightning flashed behind the hill swiftly followed by a low rumble of thunder. Brodie stopped the car and turned to her.

'Emmy, sweetheart—' he began, but another, more vivid flash had her diving into his arms, hiding her face in his shoulder.

'Hold me, Brodie. I can't bear it.'

She was trembling against him. She might have lied about her fear of flying, but this was real enough. He unfastened his seatbelt and then hers, pulling her into his lap to hold her, cradling her against him, covering her with his body as he murmured softly against her hair, against her neck. Words of comfort, words of love that he knew she could not hear.

The noise was unbelievable. A fierce tattoo of rain, gusts of wind that rocked the car so that she made tiny, mindless sounds against his chest. And then there was the thunder, moving closer with each succeeding flash of lightning, each time a little louder, until a crack directly above them seemed to match the lightning and split the sky. And the rain continued like an impenetrable wall of water.

Emmy was whimpering against him, clawing at him with her hands so that he was forced to capture them, tuck them against his chest so that he could hold her tightly. She was beyond reason and he couldn't blame her. Faced with the uncontrollable forces of nature, anyone who said they were not scared would be lying.

Something heavy hit the top of the car, denting it so that the roof caved in behind them, but, worse, shifting the back end round where the ground had been washed from beneath the wheels.

'What was that?' Emmy cried out, her nails digging through his shirt.

A sheep. It must have lost its footing on the slope above them. He'd seen the poor creature as it had rolled on down the hillside. 'Nothing. The branch of a tree,' he told her. If anything the rain was coming down harder, and as the car shifted again, sliding towards the downward slope, he knew they would have to make a move, one way or another. He glanced at the girl cowering in his arms. He would have to make the choice. Start the car and try and drive on, or get out before they joined the sheep in the bottom of the gully.

Not much of a choice. Driving was near to impossible with visibility not more than a yard in front of him. If the road had been washed out ahead of them he would never see it. And Emmy was close to hysteria.

'Emmy.' He gave her a little shake. 'We've got to get out of here,' he shouted above the noise of the storm.

She didn't appear to hear him. 'Darling, please…' It was no use. The daring girl who had shimmied two floors down a drainpipe without turning a hair was now quite unable to help herself.

He released the door catch and the door was immediately whipped away from him by the wind, banging hard against the bank. He didn't bother to shout any more. He half leaned, half fell out of the car with Emmy, dragging her clear, holding onto her as the back slewed round with a rending of metal as the underside dragged against the lip of the road and slipped over the edge.

It remained there, poised, rocking for a moment. Emmy screamed as it slipped another foot or so, but then it stuck, caught on a tree stump, or a rock perhaps. Whatever, it wouldn't stay there for long.

Emmy, shivering with terror and now with cold, was already soaked to the skin, her jeans and T-shirt, already mud-splattered, clinging to her. 'Wait here,' he shouted, pushing her back against the bank. 'Don't move.'

She stared at him as if unable to comprehend what he was saying, wide-eyed, terrified, the rain pouring down her face, her red hair plastered against her head, the white skin almost transparent at her temple. He knew then that he loved her, would die for her if need be, but this was not the moment for crazy declarations of love. Instead he bent down and kissed her, hard, on the mouth.

Emmy momentarily forgot the storm, her terror; all she felt was the heat that surged through her as Brodie kissed her. But even as she made to grab him, hold him by the shirt-front and kiss him back, he turned away and dived across the road towards the car.

'Brodie!' Her voice was dashed away by the wind and

he didn't hear it. 'I love you, Brodie,' she shouted. He half turned, as if her words had finally penetrated the noise of the storm, but without warning the ground beneath him gave way and he disappeared from sight.

CHAPTER TEN

EMMY flung herself to the ground and crawled across the road to the edge. 'Brodie,' she called, her voice hoarse, her breath blown away by the wind. 'Please come back. Oh, darling, please don't be hurt. I love you so much. I should have told you.'

His face suddenly appeared just below her. There was a smear of mud across his cheek and the rain was dripping over his dark brows, down his nose and running off his chin. He dashed it away with his shirtsleeve, but the torrent was so strong that it made little impression. 'I thought I told you to stay over there,' he said, gasping a little as he fought for breath. But down at ground level, protected by the bulk of the car, the wind wasn't so strong.

'I thought you'd fallen. I thought—' She hesitated, aware that she had exposed raw feelings that she needed to examine, think about. Had he heard her? There was nothing in his expression to suggest that he had.

'What did you think, Emmy?' She shook her head and after a moment he shrugged. 'I was just rescuing your bag before the car fell down there into the river.' He held out his hand to help her down. 'Come on, there's a hut—'

She slapped away his hand, scrambling to her feet.

'My bag? You risked your life for a few clothes?' She couldn't believe a man could be so stupid. She loved him! How dared he risk his life when she loved him? 'You stupid, idiotic…' she struggled for a suitably scathing insult '…*man!*' she yelled at him as anger obliterated all fear of the thunder still crashing around the hills, the distant flashes of lightning. 'How could you?'

He pulled himself up onto the road. 'A simple thank you would have done,' he said, when he was certain she was finished.

But she wasn't finished with him. She was far from finished. 'Thank you?' She glared down at him. 'You expect me to thank you? What would I have told your mother if the car had come down on top of you, Brodie? That you died because I couldn't survive without a change of clothes?' She swung angrily, flinging her fist at his shoulder. 'What kind of a mindless bimbo do you think I am?' She swung again, but evidently he had had enough because he moved and she missed.

She let out a yell as her feet went from beneath her and she found herself sliding on her bottom down a mudslide. Then she had no breath to waste on anything so trivial as yelling for help. Every time she managed to grab a mouthful of air it was knocked right out of her again.

But Brodie came after her anyway, grabbing at her T-shirt to slow her, pulling her over onto him as they bumped and bounced over the uneven ground so that he took the worst of the pounding. Eventually the ground levelled out and they slithered to a halt in a tangle of arms and legs.

For a moment they stared at one another, breathless, grinning a little at the crazy roller-coaster ride they had just taken and survived. 'Let's go back and do that again, Brodie,' Emmy said finally as her heart began to return to something like normal.

Brodie's smile faded. 'I've got a much better idea.' She was poised above him, her hips pressed against his. She didn't need a phrasebook to interpret his meaning, and suddenly her heart rate was back in the stratosphere.

The rain hammering down on them washed away the worst of the mud and as he carefully lifted the strands of hair away from her mouth, her cheeks, his touch sent fingers of heat racing through her, a new, rare heat that sent her spirits soaring, her pulse hammering in her ears. There were moments, perfect moments in life, that were a special gift and she knew without a doubt that this was one of them.

And because of everything that had happened, because of Kit and her father and because she recognised that Brodie was in a situation that made it impossible for him to make the first move, she would have to take the lead.

His eyes never left hers as she pushed the black strands of hair back from his forehead, as she lightly touched a graze where a stone had caught his cheek, as she ran her hands down his throat. But they grew darker, luminous with desire.

But he made no move as she slowly unbuttoned his

shirt, pushing it back so that the rain poured over his naked chest, lowering her head to touch his slick golden skin with her lips. No move, but she felt the sudden catch in his breath, the vibration of a low growl deep in his throat as her teeth teased momentarily at his small male nipples, a growl that intensified as the tip of her tongue swirled in the hollows of his neck.

Suddenly desperate to feel the rain on her own naked skin, she sat up, raised her arms and pulled her ruined T-shirt over her head. Then she reached behind to unfasten her bra, and when it swung free held the tiny scrap of lace at arm's length and let it fall.

She felt him shudder with suppressed desire as she swayed forward until the taut peaks of her breasts touched him. But still he held her only with his eyes as, slowly, she lowered her mouth to his.

She made no immediate move to kiss him, but touched the sensuous curve of his lower lip with her tongue.

It was running with rainwater and she took it between her own lips, sipping from it like a hummingbird taking nectar from a flower. Then she dipped her tongue into his mouth, and after that the question of who was taking the lead was no longer a question that either of them was interested in.

There was just an urgency to be free of clinging denim, wet, muddy cotton chinos, to feel skin against skin, and for long moments they hungrily explored each other with hands and lips until Brodie, ignoring Emmy's cries of protest as he stopped kissing her for a moment, picked her up and carried her towards the dry stone shepherd's hut.

It was dark inside the *borie,* but dry, and much warmer out of the wind. And the ground was thickly covered in a bed of dried heather and herbs that smelt sweet as they lay down together.

'Brodie,' Emmy began, her voice sounding unnaturally loud in the sudden silence away from the wind. But he covered her lips, first with his fingers and then with his lips, and after that there was no need for words. The moment was perfect, the man was perfect and she loved him. That was all that mattered. Explanations would wait. Everything would sort itself out. Later.

Emmy woke to a golden light edging around the door of the *borie.* She eased herself from Brodie's arms and knelt up to look out. The storm had passed and the sun was making everything steam. She eased her head out of the door, the brilliant light making her very conscious of her nakedness, but there was no one about, and spotting her bag lying a few yards away, she made a dash for it.

Brodie hadn't stirred, didn't move as she pulled on not quite dry pants and a crumpled dress.

She knelt down beside him, put out a finger to touch his cheek and then hesitated, remembering the tired hollows beneath his eyes, in his cheeks. Two nights' sleeping on a sofa had taken its toll. She wouldn't disturb him. Instead she pulled the baggy rugby shirt she wore at night out of her bag and tucked it round him.

She sat for a while, smiling, as she watched the even rise and fall of his breathing. His hair had dried in rumpled curls and she was unable to resist the temptation to tease one out, see it spring back. 'Oh, Brodie, darling Brodie,' she murmured. 'I do love you so much.'

He didn't stir. She glanced at her watch, tilting it towards the slightly open door so that she could see the time. It was just after five. They should be moving soon or it would get dark, and she had no idea how far they would have to walk.

She wondered what had happened to the directions to the farmhouse. She had been reading them when the storm had started. Had she dropped them? Or pushed them into her jeans pocket? She rose quietly and let herself out of the hut. Their clothes were scattered where they had torn them off, and, blushing just a little at the memory of her wanton behaviour, she gathered them up. The paper was not in her pocket.

She dropped the clothes inside the hut door and climbed up to the road where the car remained, wedged against a large rock at a crazy angle to the sky. The floor of the car by the front seats was on a level with her head, and, peering through the open door on the driver's side, she saw the piece of paper he had given her where it had fallen as he had pulled her into his arms. She reached across and caught it between outstretched fingers, jumping back quickly as the car seemed to rock a little.

She looked at the directions and realised the farmhouse wasn't very far. Less than a kilometre, according to the directions the police had given him. She looked along the road; it was steaming as it dried out in the sun. She looked back at the hut.

She could be at the farmhouse in ten minutes. She would be back with Kit and a truck to pull the car back onto the road before Brodie had woken up. It would be something to make up for what she had done this morning. She blew a kiss back towards the *borie* and then turned and hurried towards the farmhouse.

Brodie stirred. His body felt as if it had been in a concrete mixer but he didn't care. He felt warm and fulfilled and quite unbelievably happy. He turned to Emmy, planning to wake her with a kiss, pull her into his arms and tell her just how much he loved her. But Emmy wasn't there.

For a moment it didn't sink in.

He shrugged off the rugby shirt and then pulled it over his head. He saw her bag, open where she had rifled through it for something to wear. He saw the pile of wet clothes by the door, fished out damp boxer shorts, soggy shoes and stepped into them before going outside.

'Emmy,' he called. The ground was steaming and it was like looking through a golden mist. 'Emmy?' But there was no answer. She had gone. And his blood ran cold as he realised where she had gone. And Tom Brodie let out a loud, animal bellow as pain and anger washed over him.

Selfish, spoilt, determined to get her own way, she had tried everything to shake free of him. Each time he had found it so easy to forgive her, to understand. Even this morning, locked up in the police station, he hadn't believed it was personal, had been so sure that once he saw her with Kit it would all fall into place and he would know exactly what she was up to.

But now she had used him and betrayed him. Now it felt very personal, and whatever happened in the next few hours he was determined that Miss Emerald Carlisle would not get her own way. And once he had dealt with Kit Fairfax he would make it his business to see that she suffered for what she had done.

He looked down at himself. First he would change into dry clothes. He wasn't about to confront either of them looking like a refugee from some disaster.

His own bag was still in the car, and he climbed back up to the road. Then he stripped off, rubbed himself clean with the rugby shirt and dressed in a fresh shirt, the lightweight suit he had worn on the train—trousers neatly sponged and pressed by Madame Girard—and a pair of clean, dry shoes. He knotted a tie about his neck and combed his hair.

Not quite his usual standard of grooming for a business meeting, but it would have to do. Then he took his briefcase from the rear seat and slammed the door irritably behind him before setting off down the road towards the farm.

Behind him there was a rending of metal, a crash as the rock propping the Renault in place finally succumbed to the undermining effects of the rain, the weight of the car and gravity.

Brodie did not even turn around.

He wasn't sure how far he would have to walk, but reasoned, if Emerald had decided it was worth taking the risk of running for it, it couldn't be that far. It wasn't. After about half a mile the track curved round the hill and he saw the farmhouse below him. It was grey stone, the roof that wonderful mottled mixture of faded pink and brown rounded tiles that looked like knitting, the ridge like some crooked seam.

Behind it a cypress tree provided a dark exclamation point, in front there was a neat courtyard that suggested careful husbandry. And away to the right neat rows of olive trees, leaves silvering as the remnants of the storm's wind lifted them gently.

Fairfax had inherited a well-cared-for and prosperous estate. It would take more than a hundred thousand pounds to buy him. But perhaps Mark Reed was right. Maybe money, property would be all that was needed to change Gerald Carlisle's mind, Brodie thought coldly, when love had been unable to move him.

How on earth had he come to believe that the daughter was so different from the father? They were cut from the same cloth—wilful, selfish people who cared for nothing or no one, only getting their own way.

He crossed the courtyard, rapped at the open door and walked in without waiting for an invitation. Emerald Carlisle and Kit Fairfax turned, startled, wine glasses in their hands. There was a suitcase by the door.

'I've obviously arrived in the very nick of time,' he

said. 'You shouldn't have wasted time toasting your great escape.'

'Brodie!' Emmy exclaimed, putting down her glass and rushing across to him. 'We were just coming to fetch you in the Jeep. Kit is going to pull the car back onto the road—'

'The car is down at the bottom of the gully. It will take more than a Jeep to get it up.'

'Would you like a glass of wine, Mr Brodie?' Kit offered.

'It's a little soon to celebrate, surely?' he said, his voice like chipped ice. 'Let's get the formalities over with first.' He walked across to the huge scrubbed table that dominated the kitchen and placed his briefcase on it, taking out the file that Carlisle had given him. 'Would you care to sit down, Mr Fairfax? This shouldn't take long.'

'Brodie…' Emmy began uncertainly. She took a step towards him. 'Tom?' She put her hand out to touch his arm. 'What's wrong?' She glanced at the suitcase by the door. 'Surely you don't think…? I was coming straight back…'

He was used to hiding his feelings, but it took all his will-power to keep his face from betraying all the pain, all the hurt. 'I'm sure you were. Once you had got what you wanted—your five minutes with Fairfax to make sure he understood exactly what he had to do.'

'No…darling…'

Darling? What more did she want from him, for heaven's sake? She had his heart, his mind and finally his body. Did she want his soul, too? He stared down at her, then pointedly at the hand on his arm. She snatched it back as if her fingers had suddenly been burnt.

'Fairfax?' he said, turning to the fair-haired young man watching this interchange with a perplexed expression. 'I'd like to get on with this.' Kit, his boyish face crumpled in consternation at his visitor's tone, glanced at Emmy. But she was no help, staring at Brodie as if she couldn't believe her ears. Brodie shrugged. He was perfectly willing to conduct business on his feet if necessary. 'I have no doubt that Emerald has already explained the purpose of this visit.' He didn't wait for confirmation. 'Gerald Carlisle is of the opinion that you are not a suitable husband for his daughter—'

'But Emmy said—'

Brodie was in no mood to listen to what Emmy had said. 'And he has authorised me to offer you a sum of one hundred thousand pounds,' he continued as if Fairfax had not spoken, 'on the understanding that you will withdraw from the scene and never see her again.' He produced a sheet of paper that Carlisle had provided for the man's signature. 'Sign this and the cheque will be immediately drawn in whatever currency you prefer.'

Fairfax had the kind of skin that flushed crimson when he was angry or embarrassed. It was crimson now. 'I don't believe I'm hearing this,' he said.

It was anger, Brodie noted.

'Does that mean you were expecting more? I dare say he would go a little higher. A hundred and twenty?' he suggested. 'It's a very generous offer—'

'You bastard!' Fairfax took a step forward and swung. The move was so unexpected that although he saw it coming Brodie didn't react. Instead he watched the man's arm swing up and round as if in slow motion.

Then the fist at the end of the arm connected with his chin, knocking him clean off his feet, hurtling him back against the sink, jarring his back. Dazed, unable to prevent himself from falling, he slid down onto the floor and for a moment lay there as he tried to come to terms with what had happened.

Was that a refusal? Suppose he told the man about the way he and Emmy had made love, tearing at each other's clothes as the rain had poured over them, lost to everything but desire…

No. Oh, God, no. He couldn't do that to her. Even now. He closed his eyes.

'Tom! Tom, darling…' Emmy darted forward, flinging herself to her knees, cradling his head in her lap. She smelt of Chanel and rainwater and the love they had shared, and all he wanted to do was hold her, tell her how much he loved her. Because he couldn't hate her. He would never hate her, no matter what she did.

'Get me some water, Kit, quickly.' He felt her lips press against his brow. 'Tom, dear Tom, please wake up.' She took the water from Kit, dipped her fingers in the glass and rubbed them over his forehead. 'I'm not going to marry Kit. I was never going to marry him—'

He opened his eyes. 'Never?'

She stared down at him. 'You weren't unconscious,' she said, accusingly.

'Just resting my eyes. Tell me about Kit.' Then suddenly it all fell into place and he knew. 'No, there's no need. It was the money, wasn't it? You just wanted him to have the money so he could buy the lease of his studio.' He struggled to sit up. 'But why was it so important that you talked to him before I did?'

'Because he didn't know anything about it. If Hollingworth didn't treat me like a three-year-old, refusing to let me have more than pocket money—but I'm just a stupid, feeble girl who can't be trusted—I wouldn't have had to do this—'

'So you remembered what happened when you ran away with Oliver Hayward and decided to try it again. If you couldn't use your own money, you'd get your father to bail the man out?' He laughed. 'Betty was right.'

'Betty?'

'She told me that nothing was what it seemed.'

'Oh.'

'Emmy! Is that true?' Kit demanded. 'You pretended...? I can't believe you could do something so dreadful.'

'Dreadful? What was so dreadful about it?' she demanded. 'If my father hadn't had me followed after he saw our picture in *Tatler* at that charity thing it would never have occurred to me.'

'That's why you asked me to paint your portrait, isn't it?'

Emmy grinned. 'How else was I going to spend all those afternoons at your studio?'

'And why you insisted on sleeping on my sofa, going on about having too much to drink at lunchtime when you scarcely touch a drop?'

'Sorry,' she said.

'So you should be.'

'I know. But my father is a rich man, and he doesn't do nearly enough to support the arts...'

Brodie began to laugh. 'All that plotting and planning, for nothing.'

'No,' Emmy said. 'It doesn't have to be for nothing. He can still have the money. You won't say anything, will you, darling? Please, Tom. My father expects you to settle with Kit. He'll be pleased with you...'

'But I don't need it, Emmy,' Kit explained. 'I have this farmhouse and some property down at the coast. That's where I was going when you turned up. I've got a meeting with a lawyer about selling a villa.'

'A *what*?'

'A villa. One of three my father left me. In fact if it hadn't been for the storm you'd have missed me.' He glanced at his watch. 'Look, why don't you two make yourselves at home here? I'll be back tomorrow.' He glanced at Emmy and Brodie. 'No, not tomorrow,' he said hurriedly. 'It'll be the weekend at least. I'll stop at the village, Brodie, and sort out something about the car on my way. Just leave the key under the flowerpot when you leave.'

Brodie raised a hand to acknowledge that he'd heard. His mouth was too busy kissing Emmy.

*   *   *

'Brodie!' Emmy's urgent whisper brought Brodie drifting up from sleep and he half opened his eyes, smiling into her morning face. Her curls were tumbled about her cheeks, her green-gold slumberous eyes were full of love.

'Hi, sweetheart,' he said softly, then, suddenly and urgently wide awake, he pulled her down to him and kissed her. For a moment she protested, mumbling something beneath his mouth, but, laughing, he turned her onto her back. 'Oh, no. When you wake up a man, my darling, you have to pay a forfeit,' he said. 'Now, then, what will it be?'

'Brodie—'

'I thought, last night, that we'd agreed you'd call me Tom,' he said, kissing her shoulder. 'Now that we're better acquainted.'

'Tom—'

'That's better. Now this forfeit… A kiss, here, perhaps?' He grazed her throat with his mouth. 'Or here? Or here?' He eased down her body, liberally planting kisses over her shoulders, her breasts, her stomach, and for a moment she relaxed, giggling as the night stubble of his chin tickled and tormented her delicate skin.

Then her body stiffened beneath him. 'Tom!' she said, and there was something about the urgency with which she said the name that made him stop, look up.

But Emerald wasn't looking at him, she was looking towards the door. He turned, and in the entrance were framed the shocked faces of Gerald Carlisle and James Hollingworth.

'I was going to tell you,' Emmy said faintly, 'that I thought I heard someone downstairs. It was why I woke you up. But I forgot.'

Gerald Carlisle looked as if he was about to have a stroke.

'Would you mind telling me what the devil you think you're doing, Brodie?' he demanded.

For one delicious moment Tom Brodie considered the obvious, then discarded it. 'I'm carrying out your instructions,' he said. 'You did say that I was to use whatever means were necessary to prevent Emerald from marrying Kit Fairfax?'

Gerald Carlisle stared at him. Then at his daughter. 'I give up,' he said. 'Do what you want. You've made your bed once too often, my girl. Well, now you can lie on it.'

Brodie raised one darkly defined brow at Emmy, who was clutching the sheet to her neck. 'You heard the man, sweetheart. Lie down. I'll be right with you.'

Emmy gasped, catching her lower lip between her teeth to stop herself from laughing out loud at her father's outraged expression. Then she slid back down against the pillows. Brodie, his face expressionless, turned to Carlisle and Hollingworth.

'As you can see, gentlemen, the lady has made her choice. Please shut the door on your way out.'

Tom Brodie regarded the man sitting behind the ornate desk and waited. He could afford to be patient. He held all the cards—a fact he was sure that Gerald Carlisle was quite aware of.

'What exactly do you want from me, Brodie?' he asked finally. 'I mean, a hundred thousand pounds isn't going to shift you, is it?'

'No, but if you've got that kind of money looking for a good home I can suggest a couple of worthy causes that would be grateful for the help.'

'How much?' he replied bluntly.

Brodie didn't lose his temper. He was being tested. He'd expected that. 'I only want your daughter. And your blessing.'

'So you came to ask for her hand in marriage like some old-fashioned suitor?' Gerald Carlisle didn't sound convinced.

'I thought that was how gentlemen did it. I would have given you chapter and verse of my family history and my prospects, too, but I imagine you've already had James Hollingworth down here to lay it out in words of one syllable.' Hollingworth had already told him as much. 'In your shoes, that's what I would do.'

'Oh, you would, would you?' He paused. 'Well, I have. And the man had the nerve to tell me Emmy was lucky to find you.'

Brodie buried his grin. James Hollingworth hadn't told him that. 'We found each other. And I think I'm the lucky one.'

'I'm sure you do.' He glared at Tom. 'If you do get married, where will you live? Emerald's flat isn't big enough—'

'Mine is.'

'A converted warehouse on the wrong side of the river?' He was dismissive. 'No. You'll need a house. I suppose it had better be my wedding present. I'll get my agent—'

'All in good time.'

'But—'

'We can find our own house. When we're ready to move. And I'll pay for it.'

Gerald Carlisle, already reaching for the telephone, paused. Then, quite suddenly, his face softened and he began to laugh. 'By God, Brodie, Emmy met her match when she crossed your path. Whatever else it is, your married life won't be dull.'

Suddenly recognising in Gerald Carlisle a father who cared desperately about his daughter, wanting nothing bad to happen to her, ever, Brodie found himself responding with an unexpected warmth to the man. 'No, I don't suppose it will be. But love should never be dull. And I do love her. I'll do everything I can to make her happy.'

'Will you?' Carlisle rose. 'Then I suppose all that's left is to set the date and have a drink.'

As Tom stood up to take the hand extended to him Emmy burst into the room. 'Darlings, it's all fixed. The vicar is reading the banns on Sunday and the wedding will be on the last Saturday in September—'

'*This* September?' Gerald Carlisle was stunned.

'Well, we could have waited until October...' She slipped her arm through her father's and looked up at him. 'But your diary is solid with shooting parties all through October *and* November. Then it's Christmas, and I absolutely refuse to get married in the middle of winter...' She gave a little shiver. 'The photographs would be all mud and gooseflesh.' She turned wide gold-green eyes on Tom and linked her other arm with his. 'Of course, if you think it's too much trouble I suppose we could forget all the formalities and just elope—'

'September's just fine with me, Emmy,' her father intervened hurriedly. 'Tom?'

But Tom was smiling at Emmy. 'If that's the earliest we can manage...'

'Do you think Betty will come?' Emmy asked.

'We'll stop by on the way home and ask her.'

Gerald Carlisle considered asking who Betty might be, but decided against it. Instead he crossed to the phone. 'I suppose I'd better ask Mrs Johnson to bring up a bottle of champagne,' he said, trying very hard not to smile too much. Then he paused as Emmy wound her arms around Tom Brodie's neck, raising herself on tiptoe to kiss him. 'Perhaps, on second thoughts, *I'd* better go and get it...' he murmured. But he was talking to himself.

Modern Romance™
...seduction and
passion guaranteed

Tender Romance™
...love affairs that
last a lifetime

Sensual Romance™
...sassy, sexy and
seductive

Blaze
...sultry days and
steamy nights

Medical Romance™
...medical drama on
the pulse

Historical Romance™
...rich, vivid and
passionate

27 new titles every month.

*With all kinds of Romance for
every kind of mood...*

MILLS & BOON®

MB1

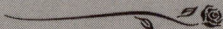

MILLS & BOON®

0502/05

Don't Miss
Passionate
Playboys
next month

On sale 5th July

*Available at most branches of WH Smith, Tesco, Martins,
Borders, Eason, Sainsbury's and most good paperback bookshops.*

0702/73/MB38a

Coming next month…

BETTY NEELS

THE ULTIMATE COLLECTION

A stunning 12 book collection beautifully
packaged for you to collect each month
from bestselling author Betty Neels.

On sale 5th July

*Available at most branches of WH Smith,
Tesco, Martins, Borders, Eason, Sainsbury's
and most good paperback bookshops.*

Emma Darcy

"Emma Darcy delivers a spicy love story...a fiery conflict and a hot sensuality"
— *Romantic Times*

This award-winning Australian author has sold nearly 60 million books worldwide. Watch out for Emma Darcy's exciting new trilogy:

KINGS OF AUSTRALIA

The King brothers must marry – can they claim the brides of their choice?

THE ARRANGED MARRIAGE
7th June 2002

THE BRIDAL BARGAIN
5th July 2002

THE HONEYMOON CONTRACT
2nd August 2002

Available at most branches of WH Smith, Tesco, Martins, Borders, Eason, Sainsbury's and most good paperback bookshops.

0602/01/LC03

MILLS & BOON
FOREIGN
AFFAIRS
A captivating 12 book collection of sun-kissed seductions.
Enjoy romance around the world.
DON'T MISS BOOK 10
caribbean caress–
Indulgence in the sun...
Available from 5th July
Available at most branches of WH Smith, Tesco, Martins, Borders, Eason, Sainsbury's and most good paperback bookshops.
FA/RTL/10

From the award winning Tender Romance™ author

LIZ FIELDING

is an exciting new trilogy

BOARDROOM BRIDEGROOMS.
It's a marriage takeover!

*Claibourne & Farraday is an exclusive
London department store run by the beautiful
Claibourne sisters, Romana, Flora and India.
But their positions are in jeopardy – the seriously
attractive Farraday men want the store back!*

The Corporate Bridegroom
May 2002

The Marriage Merger
June 2002

The Tycoon's Takeover
July 2002

*Available at most branches of WH Smith,
Tesco, Martins, Borders, Eason, Sainsbury's
and most good paperback bookshops.*

0502/02/LC04

MILLS & BOON®

Modern Romance™

THE BRIDAL BARGAIN *by Emma Darcy*

The Kings of Australia trilogy continues with a second grandson claiming his bride. This time a pretend engagement turns into the perfect marriage! As soon as Hannah meets her new boss, the dynamic Antonio King, she is thrown into turmoil by the fiery attraction that flares between them. And Tony is on hot coals, trying not to mix business with pleasure...

THE TYCOON'S VIRGIN *by Penny Jordan*

An enchanting tale of accidental seduction! When high-powered Leo Jefferson falls into bed after a string of meetings, he finds a surprise waiting for him: a gorgeous semi-clad siren! But the next morning his fantasy woman confesses to being the strait-laced local schoolteacher who fell asleep in the wrong room!

TO MARRY McCLOUD *by Carole Mortimer*

Look out for the second sexy hero in the Bachelor Cousins trilogy! Fergus McCloud couldn't remember how he'd first met Chloe Fox, but circumstances indicated that they'd slept together soon afterwards! Actually, they hadn't – but Chloe let Fergus believe it. Her mission was to prevent him publishing a book that would ruin her family – what better way than pretending to be his lover...?

MISTRESS OF LA RIOJA *by Sharon Kendrick*

An emotionally intense story with a hot-blooded Spanish hero... There had been a searing attraction between Sophie and Don Luis de la Camara, but she'd had to return to England. Now Luis had come to ask her to return to Spain – as his son's nanny – and *his* mistress!

On sale 5th July 2002

Available at most branches of WH Smith, Tesco, Martins, Borders, Eason, Sainsbury's and most good paperback bookshops.

0602/01a

MILLS & BOON®

Modern Romance™

THE BLACKMAILED BRIDE *by Kim Lawrence*
A classic romantic fantasy with a colourful, upbeat mood! Kate was determined to protect her sister from scandal – and Javier Montero was the only man who could help. But Javier wanted something in return. As head of his family's business empire, he needed a wife. Kate was about to become a blackmailed bride!

THE SICILIAN'S WIFE *by Kate Walker*
Enjoy the sizzling sexual tension and a proud Sicilian hero! Marriage to Cesare Santorino is all Megan has ever wanted – but not like this! She's in deep trouble and has no choice but to agree to a mutually beneficial, convenient union. Cesare makes no secret of his passion for her, but Megan hopes that he'll come to see her as more than just the body that he desires...

THE DOCTOR'S SECRET CHILD *by Catherine Spencer*
Experience deep emotion in this tale of young lovers reunited... When Molly Paget fell pregnant, her father made her leave town. Nobody knew about the baby – including Molly's ex-lover Dan Cordell. Now a family crisis sees Molly's return as a successful businesswoman with a young daughter. But what happens when doctor Dan learns about their child?

THE MARRIAGE DEBT *by Daphne Clair*
An intensely passionate read! Shannon's new project offers international success. But she needs millions of dollars in funding and the only person she knows with that kind of money is her estranged husband, Devin Keynes. Devin agrees to help on one condition: she gives their marriage another chance...

On sale 5th July 2002

Available at most branches of WH Smith, Tesco, Martins, Borders, Eason, Sainsbury's and most good paperback bookshops.

0602/01b

MILLS & BOON®

Blaze™

EROTIC INVITATION *by Carly Phillips*

Her sexy colleague has no idea what she's really like,
and if Jack Latham wants to provoke cool lawyer
Mallory Sinclair into showing how passionate she can
be, he'll end up with a whole lot more than he
bargained for! But even as she seduces and savours the
man she has secretly desired for so long, she can feel
herself falling in love. There's no going back – so what
will happen when the game comes to an end?

ACTING ON IMPULSE *by Vicki Lewis Thompson*
HOT CITY NIGHTS

Trudy Baxter is the new girl in the city, and she's
determined to take the male population of New York
by a sexual storm. But her enthusiasm and naivety
means Linc Faulkner has been drafted in to watch out
for her. Neither is interested in commitment and thinks
they are safe from each other – despite the instant
chemistry. However, Linc and Trudy have not counted
on the power of attraction, and soon they are deliciously
tangled in an erotic web of fantasy and seduction…

On sale 5th July 2002

*Available at most branches of WH Smith,
Tesco, Martins, Borders, Eason, Sainsbury's
and most good paperback bookshops.*

0602/14